CASPERSEN

BEACH

D1547740

CASPERSEN
BEACH

A Wrongful Conviction Mystery

JANET HEIJENS

Canterbury House
an Imprint of Dudley Court Press

Published in the USA by
Canterbury House
An imprint of Dudley Court Press
www.CanterburyHousePublishing.com
www.DudleyCourtPress.com

Author's Note:

This is a work of fiction. Names characters, places and incidents are either the product of the author's imagination or are used fictitiously, and any resemblance to actual persons living or dead, business establishments, events, or locales is entirely coincidental.

Publisher's Note:

For information about permission to reproduce selections from this book:
Email: publisher@dudleycourtpress.com
Please put Permissions in the subject line.

Cover Design by Dunn+Associates

Names: Heijens, Janet, author.
Title: Caspersen Beach : a wrongful conviction mystery / Janet Heijens.
Description: [Sonoita, Arizona] : Canterbury House Publishing, [2021] |
    Series: Heijens, Janet. Wrongful conviction mystery ; 2.
Identifiers: ISBN: 978-1-940013-84-8 (paper) | 978-1-940013-85-5 (ebook) |
    LCCN: 2020944115
Subjects: LCSH: Judicial error--Fiction. | Cold cases (Criminal investiga-
    tion)--Fiction. | Murder-- Investigation--Fiction. | Kidnapping--Flor-
    ida--Fiction. | Legal stories. | GSAFD: Mystery fiction. | LCGFT:
    Detective and mystery fiction. | Legal fiction (Literature) | BISAC: FIC-
    TION / Mystery & Detective / Women Sleuths. | FICTION / Mystery
    & Detective / Private Investigators. | FICTION / Small Town & Rural.
Classification: LCC: PS3608.E3655 C37 2021 | DDC: 813/.6--dc23

For Vincent

Chapter 1

Gator stopped checking his hairy legs for ticks and turned his attention to the two children playing under the fishing pier. "Which one is it this time, Mags?"

"The baby."

The little one, her arms crusted in sand, sat in her soggy diapers shoveling globs of wet sand into a plastic bucket. The older child stood knee-deep in the Gulf of Mexico, shrieking with laughter every time a wave lifted her to her toes. A deep crease formed on Maggie's brow. Cutting through the indistinct chatter in her head, she turned back to Gator.

"What did you say?"

"I said she don't look nothing like that photo you showed me."

Maggie stared at the child. She was about the same age as her own little girl when they took her away. And her hair, yellow as corn silk, was exactly like Poppy's. A chorus of voices sang in her head.

Perfect, perfect, perfect.

Maggie mumbled a reply.

Gator went to work inspecting his dirty feet. "Are you talkin' to me or are you havin' one of them conversations with your imaginary friends?"

As Maggie watched, the children ran from the water's

1

edge and plopped down on a large beach blanket covered with Disney princesses. Their mother, her rings flashing in the sun, gestured toward the restaurant at the end of the fishing pier. She then turned and trudged through the soft sand, leaving the kids alone.

Maggie tugged on the knit cap she wore whenever she left camp. "I said she's perfect."

With a cry of victory, Gator pulled a tick from between his toes. A bead of blood oozed onto his thumb. He cracked the insect between his ragged fingernails. Wiping his fingers on his khaki shorts, he said, "You reckon that blood is mine or the tick's?"

"I want that baby."

A blast of sour breath filled her nose as Gator laughed. "She ain't yours, Mags."

Now that the girls were sitting on the blanket she could see the older one was about ten while the baby was not a baby at all but a toddler with a full mouth of teeth. The ten-year-old threw a handful of sand on the little one's leg. Tears followed. From the corner of her eye, Maggie saw the mother running back from the restaurant clutching two ice cream cones. Going directly to her sobbing daughter, she handed her one. Appeased, the child grinned and took a lick.

That night Maggie lay on top of her sleeping bag next to Gator. Moonlight seeped through the nylon roof over their heads casting eerie shadows across the sharp features of Gator's narrow face. He snored, sucking in great gulps of air, his open mouth revealing a gap where a rotting tooth recently broke off. While she watched, Gator scratched his crotch.

Maggie sighed. While he left much to be desired, Gator was not as bad as some men she had been with and better than most. His greatest asset was the blue tent they called home. They lived in a wooded camp which they shared with a half-dozen other homeless people. For now at least, Gator's presence offered Maggie some protection. She knew the time would come when one of the other men would try something. As a precaution she kept an old fishing knife sharp by honing it on the sand and stored it under her pillow.

The hum of voices in her head kept Maggie awake. After tossing and turning for a few hours she jabbed Gator in the side with her elbow.

"Hey," Gator grumbled. "Hey! What'd you wake me for? I was havin' a real nice dream."

"I'm going crazy thinking about that little girl."

"You already crazy, Mags."

Maggie ripped the pillow out from under his head. He rose up on one elbow and glared at her.

"What is wrong with you, woman?"

"Nothing that having another baby won't fix."

Gator gave her a wicked grin. "You want a baby? I'll give you one right here, right now."

"No." Maggie shoved him away. "I want the one on the beach."

Gator studied her face. "You serious, ain't you?"

"I am."

He sat up and fumbled in his backpack for a cigarette. Striking a match, he drew the smoke into his lungs.

Maggie studied him. Gator was a physical wreck, underweight, lice infested and covered with scabs. But one thing was sure. His military training gave him skills that would come in handy for what she had in mind.

"Well, are you going to help me or not?"

"Stealing a kid is serious business, Mags. We can't just

walk up and grab her. Someone would see us for sure." Gator let the cigarette burn down to the filter before speaking again. "Besides, what makes you think they'll come back to the beach any time soon?"

"I've been watching them all week. They arrive at ten each day. Around noon their mother gives them sandwiches on the blanket and leaves them alone while she buys ice cream."

"Let me think on this a minute."

The minute and more went by before Gator spoke again. "Did you see the jewelry on that woman? Plenty of money there, I reckon. How much you figure she'd pay to get her kid back?"

Maggie sat up and slapped his arm. "I don't want money. I want the little girl."

"Can't rush into this thing. Gotta work out a few details first."

Maggie felt a glimmer of hope. "So, you'll do it?"

The corner of Gator's mouth turned up in a sneer. "I been waiting my whole life for something like this to come along."

Maggie recognized the glint in his eye. He was up to something, of that she was sure. She did not trust him for one minute but as long as he stole the child for her she did not care. Wrapping her arms around Gator she buried her face in his neck. In her excitement the voices in her head retreated to the corners of her mind. Maggie could still hear them—they were never far away—but for now at least, she could ignore their whispered warnings.

———————————

As the first rays of sun filtered through the blue tent, Maggie woke to the trumpeting sound of Gator's snoring. After a breakfast of peanut butter crackers and beer, she stuffed a bar of soap and her toothbrush into the pocket of her loose-fitting dress. Maggie slipped on her knit cap, tugging it down tight before heading to the public restroom on the beach. An hour later she returned to the camp to find Gator still sound asleep. Grabbing her sketchbook and a half-empty box of charcoals from her rusted shopping cart, she left. In the cloying mid-summer heat, her dress soon grew damp with sweat.

Maggie found a spot at the edge of the dunes with a clear view of the fishing pier. Pelicans dove into the water head first, plucking their catch from the Gulf. A group of sandpipers scurried along the sea foam. Except for an older couple sitting on beach chairs with their feet buried in the warm sand, Maggie was alone.

The young family arrived a few minutes before ten. The mother, struggling under the burden of beach bags and umbrellas, pointed to their usual spot on the sand. When the older girl kicked off her flip flops and ran ahead, the toddler followed. Their mother bent down to scoop up the abandoned sandals. She soon caught up to the girls who stood at the water's edge, cooling their burning feet. With a puff of breath, the mother blew the bangs off her forehead and spread the Disney blanket a safe distance from the rising tide.

Maggie opened her sketchbook and found an empty page. Selecting a stubby charcoal from the box, she began to frame the scene. She roughed out the figure of the mother setting up an umbrella while the children pulled their beach toys out of the bag. When Maggie looked up, the little one grabbed a bucket and ran on her short, chubby legs back to the water's edge. For a moment Maggie sat frozen with the charcoal poised above her sketchbook. She then began to capture the image of the child she already thought of as her own.

Voices raged in Maggie's head. She tried to concentrate, fighting to stay focused on her work. Someone cleared his throat and she looked up to see her old friend, Sam standing before her. His lined face broke into a grin. Something about that grin reminded Maggie of her father. Though she did not know exactly how old Sam was, she figured he was about the same age her father would be if he were still alive.

She returned Sam's smile. "You're blocking my light."

With creaking knees, Sam dropped down next to her. After studying the drawing in her lap he said, "Nice. You made her nose a little too small, though."

Maggie made the adjustment. "I was hoping to see you this morning. There's something I want to tell you."

Sam glanced in the direction of the children. "What are you up to, Mags?"

Unable to contain her excitement Maggie giggled. "See that little girl? I'm going to be her new mother."

"You can't be serious."

Maggie frowned. "Why not?"

"Where will you go? You can't raise a child in that camp of yours, that's for sure. They'll come and take her away. The same way they took Poppy."

"Not this time."

"You know they will."

"Stop talking like that. Don't you want me to be happy?"

"Of course I do. How long have we known each other?

"I don't know. A long time."

"Then you know I only want what's best for you. You may not like what I have to say but I'm telling you, this is a mistake."

"I don't have to listen to you!"

The old woman sitting with her husband turned at the

sound of Maggie's raised voice.

Maggie brandished her charcoal at her. "What are you looking at?"

Nudging her husband, the woman stood and dragged her chair several yards away.

Maggie looked down at her drawing. An angry black slash ran across the page.

"Now see what you made me do."

Sam pushed himself up from the sand. "No good will come from this, Mags."

Chapter 2

Before I begin, let me make one thing perfectly clear. I never intended to spend my so-called golden years working Detective Geri Garibaldi's cold cases. But when Geri called to tell me there was a disturbing development in a murder she investigated decades ago, I knew two things were about to happen. One, she was going to ask for my help. And two, I would say yes. Again.

Geri and I first locked horns when my nephew, Ben Shepherd persuaded me to get involved with one of his cases. Ben is my sister's pride and joy, a hot shot criminal lawyer who specializes in wrongful convictions. Geri was the homicide detective assigned to the case he was working. As things turned out, she had sent an innocent man to prison. To her credit, Geri swallowed her pride and worked with us to right the wrong. Now, only one year later she was back in my life.

With my phone pressed to my ear, I listened to Geri spin her story about the long-ago murder of a little girl. After three months in a shallow grave, nature took a terrible toll on Savannah Troy's body. Her remains yielded no clue as to who or what killed her. Yet the prosecuting attorney built a convincing case against a man named Randy Cousins. In his final statement, the prosecutor played on the emotions of the jury, demanding justice for the murdered child. Following a short deliberation, the jury's foreman stood with tears running down his cheeks. At the words, *We the jury find Randy Cousins guilty*, the mother of the victim collapsed to the floor. There wasn't a dry eye in the place.

When I asked Geri to get to the point of her story, she paused a beat before answering. "I have a bad feeling about this one, Cate. I'm beginning to have doubts. Randy Cousins may have been wrongfully convicted."

At the thought of another innocent man behind bars, my pulse quickened in anger. Still, I kept my voice devoid of emotion. "You know I'm retired from the law. If Cousins is looking for legal assistance, I suggest you put him in touch with Ben. His firm specializes in that sort of thing."

"Cousins isn't asking. He doesn't even know about Margaret Blue's dying confession."

"Who is Margaret Blue?"

"It's a long story, too long to explain over the phone. Let's meet at that restaurant on the beach tomorrow."

"Sharkey's?"

"That's the one. We can talk about this over lunch." With a click, she was gone.

While I sat looking at the phone, my cat, Rascal stared at me, the tip of his tail flicking back and forth. I put the phone down and reached for a box of treats. "I guess it won't kill me to listen."

I arrived at Sharkey's on the appointed hour to find Geri sitting at a table on the deck. When she saw me approach, she stopped licking the salt from the rim of her empty margarita glass. A bead of sweat ran down the side of her face.

She raised the glass and peered at me over the black frames of her sunglasses. "I started without you. Hope you don't mind."

"Since when do you drink while you're on duty?" I pointed to the gold detective's shield hanging around her neck.

Geri glanced down and pulled the lanyard over her head. "Forgot to take it off before I got here. I clocked out early so I could come and take another look at the scene." Looking up, she gestured for the waitress who was chatting with two teenaged boys at the table behind us. The girl acknowledged Geri with a nod and came over.

"Bring me another one of these." Geri tapped the stem of her glass and looked at me. "Chablis, right?"

I checked my watch. "It's a little early in the day, but sure, why not."

Geri chuckled as the waitress turned and walked to the palm thatched bar in the middle of the deck. She removed her blazer, folded it inside out and laid it on the bench next to her. My eye was drawn to the tattoo peeking out from under the sleeve of her tight T-shirt. She looked down and smiled when she caught me staring. Hooking her bleached bangs behind one ear she said, "What can I say? Lalo isn't worth what it would cost for me to have his name erased from my arm."

At the mention of her ex-husband, I felt little pin pricks up and down my arms. Lalo Sanchez, a freelance private investigator for Ben's firm, worked with me on that one-and-only case last year. Though he drove me crazy, we had a pretty good working relationship. I might even go so far to say it was more than pretty good.

Geri watched me closely. "Have you stayed in touch?"

I raised my hand to my mouth, remembering the press of Lalo's lips against mine as he said goodbye. "I haven't heard from him since he left for the Keys."

"I would have bet money you two would be together by now."

"I'm not ready to get back into that game. And even if I was, Lalo would be the last man I would want."

Geri stared into her empty glass. "Come on, Cate. How long has it been since your husband died? Two years? Three?"

"On Sunday it will be three years and two months."

"Don't you get lonely?"

Geri knew me better than I realized. There were a million and one reasons I missed Arnie but long, lonely nights was right up there at the top of the list.

I shook my head. "I don't want to have that conversation with you right now. We're here to talk about this guy, Cousins."

"Fine. But you're going to need Lalo." A wicked glint came into her eye. "With the case, that is."

"You haven't told me what the problem is yet."

The waitress returned with our drinks. She set the sweating glasses on the table and asked if we wanted anything to eat. I ordered the grouper sandwich. Geri told her to make it two.

"Take a look down there." Geri took a sip of her drink and tipped her head in the direction of the beach. "What do you see?"

I looked out to see the Gulf of Mexico stretching to the horizon, a pair of pelicans bobbing on the surface of the gray water. The teenagers sitting next to us got up and walked under the arch leading to the fishing pier. Below the pier, shaded from the scorching sun two young girls collected seashells. Their mother stood nearby, inspecting each treasure as they held them up. A frothy wave crept in and tickled their toes, eliciting screams of delight from the children.

"Cute kids," I said.

"How easy would it be to snatch one of those little girls

and take off with her?"

"Impossible. There are too many people around. And the mother is standing ten feet away."

"Right. Well, twenty-two years ago, Savanah Troy—the victim I told you about—and her sister were playing where those kids are now. Savannah was a blue-eyed, curly blond three-year-old."

I did not like the feel of where this conversation was going. Still, I couldn't resist asking. "Someone took her in broad daylight?"

"The guy walked right up, real friendly-like and sent the older sister back to Sharkey's to help her mother carry ice cream back to the beach. Then he picked up the little one—who never made a sound—and walked away. You've got to remember, back then Venice wasn't as crowded as it is now. There were only a few other people on the beach and they claimed they didn't see a thing."

Geri removed the straw from her Margarita and set it on the table.

"The Sheriff's office threw everything into finding Savannah. Within hours we had organized volunteer search crews to comb the beach and surrounding woods looking for anything that might give us a lead. Teams went door to door with her photo, asking if anyone had seen her. The Tampa news channels put Savannah's parents on air to plead for the return of their little girl. We even plastered the town with copies of a police sketch of the suspect based on the older sister's description. A few people called, hoping to collect the reward. They all claimed to have seen the man around town, but no one could tell us who he was or where to find him."

"What led you to Randy Cousins?"

"A few months after Savannah was abducted, right

about the time we were giving up hope, I got a call. Cousins claimed he was looking for loose change on Caspersen Beach when lo and behold, he discovered a small body in a shallow grave. He wanted to know how he could go about collecting the reward money for finding her."

Geri picked up her drink and took a sip. "He's currently serving a life sentence up in the Raiford State Prison for her murder."

"Presumably you had evidence linking him to the murder?"

"You mean other than the fact that he knew where the body was buried? Sure, though admittedly most of it was circumstantial. The prosecutor used it all but built his case around our one solid piece of evidence. The sister, Carrie Ann identified Cousins as the man who snatched Savannah from the beach."

"So, what's the problem? Case closed, right?"

"I got a call last week from a priest here in Venice. He was doing his rounds, visiting sick parishioners at the hospital when a nurse told him a homeless woman down the hall was dying. Naturally, the good father went to see what he could do. When he got there he saw this woman was in bad shape, totally out of her mind. It looked to him like she was counting her time on earth in minutes, not hours or days. The priest, Father Sullivan, offered to hear her confession. When he bent over to begin, the woman clutched his stole and started babbling."

"What did she say?"

"She told him her boyfriend murdered Savannah Troy."

"Did you speak with her?"

Gerri shook her head. "By the time I got there she was gone."

The waitress reappeared with our sandwiches and asked if we needed anything else. Geri waved her away and grabbed the ketchup bottle from the basket on the table. She squeezed obscene amounts all over her fries before popping one into her mouth. I knew where Geri was leading me, but I had to ask.

"Why are you telling me this?"

Geri reached for the salt and gave it a solid shake over the fries. "You're a lawyer."

"I'm a *retired* lawyer. My field was family law, divorces, wills, that sort of thing. Ben is the criminal lawyer in our family."

"Whatever. Do you know what a dying declaration is?"

The phrase sounded familiar, something I learned years ago in law school. Closing my eyes, I recalled the image of my professor firing questions about law of evidence into the packed lecture hall while I prayed he wouldn't call on me. From the depths of my memory I pulled out an answer.

"It's an exception to the hearsay rule." I opened my eyes to see her nodding confirmation.

"Exactly. Under certain circumstances, a dying person's confession can be admitted as evidence in court."

"It's a little late for that. The trial was held decades ago. Besides, you got the guy, right?"

"Like I said before, Carrie Ann gave us a positive ID so we never had any reason to doubt Cousins was guilty. But here's the thing. Before Margaret Blue died, she told the priest the name of the murderer."

I drained my wine in one swallow. "You're going to tell me it wasn't Randy Cousins."

"She said his name was Gator Pope." Geri paused. "Looks like we got the wrong guy."

One year ago, I bought a small bungalow close enough to the Gulf of Mexico for me to hear the waves from my lanai at night. My husband passed away two years before that, a victim of thirty years of smoking. Quitting my law practice and leaving the harsh New Hampshire winters behind seemed like the right thing to do at the time. While Venice was the perfect place to retire, I didn't realize how lonely I would be. I still missed Arnie as much as I did the day he died. Of course there were moments when I thought I could be happy again but then some trigger—a word, an anniversary, a flower in my garden—overwhelmed me to the point of tears. My grief counselor said the only thing to keep the sadness at bay was to stay busy. The problem was, I had no interest in the kind of activities the senior center in town had to offer. At this stage of my life I couldn't imagine joining knitting circles, or taking up Mahjong. Now, as I trudged through the soft sand by Geri's side, the thought of getting involved in another murder investigation got my adrenaline flowing in a way I hadn't felt since the last time we worked a case together.

Geri led the way slowly and with purpose, pausing occasionally to peer into the dense vegetation before moving on. Finally, after about fifteen minutes she stopped. "This way." She cut across the dunes and headed into the woods.

I followed close behind. Thick vines grabbed my legs. Thorny branches snagged my hair. When we emerged in a clearing, Geri looked around. The afternoon sun cast a curtain of light through the branches overhead. As I swatted a mosquito from my neck a gopher tortoise caught my eye. He blinked and stared back at me. I could hear the sound of the surf, suggesting we had circled through the woods to a spot near where we started. From the satisfied look on Geri's face, I knew she had found what she was looking for.

"What is this place?" I asked.

"An abandoned homeless camp. A few hours after Savannah was taken, Lalo came here on a hunch. I was at the beach, working the scene so I never got a chance to see this place for myself."

My senses went on high alert. "You didn't tell me Lalo was involved in the investigation."

"I thought I mentioned that."

"No, you definitely did not. You led me to believe this was your case."

"We worked on it together. Lalo took the lead." Geri smiled. "We were a shit-hot team back then, firing on all cylinders. As soon as we arrived at the scene of the crime, we rounded up all potential witnesses to find out if anyone saw what happened. Unfortunately, the beach was nearly deserted when the child was taken. Savannah's mother went to the restaurant to buy the kids ice cream. She was gone for about fifteen minutes. That suggested the perp was watching, waiting for a chance to snatch the kid. The only witness was Savannah's sister, Carrie Ann. The man said her mother needed help carrying the ice cream back to the beach. From the physical description Carrie Ann gave us, we figured he might be one of the homeless people who used to hang out around here."

"Let me guess. Cousins was one of those homeless people?"

"Homeless, yes. But he lived in a horse trailer parked a few miles away behind a plumbing supply shop on Seaboard Avenue. That's across the bridge, just off the island. Anyway, Lalo knew about this camp and thought it was worth checking out. When he got here, the place was deserted. As he started to leave the clearing, a crazy lady wandered in."

Geri glanced around. "There's nothing to see here now. We might as well head back."

"Wait." I searched Geri's face for confirmation. "You're going to tell me that lady was Margaret Blue, right?"

Geri stared at me from behind her mirrored sunglasses. "It's not a common name."

I pondered the information she had given me. Within hours of the abduction Lalo found Margaret Blue, the same lady who recently claimed her boyfriend murdered Savannah Troy. No wonder Geri had doubts about Randy Cousins' guilt.

"Why did you say she was crazy?" I asked.

"Lalo was convinced she was the key to solving the case so we brought her in for questioning. She was . . . I don't know, weird. Definitely not all there if you know what I mean. Even if she admitted knowing anything about Savannah— which she didn't—there was no way the prosecutor would put her on the stand. When Cousins popped up on our radar, we were told to drop all other lines of investigation and focus our efforts on him."

"Okay, for argument's sake, let's say Cousins is innocent. What do you need me for? You're the homicide detective. If you have doubts, re-open the investigation."

"Here's my problem." Geri gazed off to the distance, a frown on her lips. "We closed the book on this murder more than twenty years ago. Nobody in the department will have an appetite for taking another look. This was a high-profile case. The State Attorney put a ton of pressure on the prosecutor to get a conviction. Press coverage went national for about ten minutes until the O.J. Simpson trial kicked into high gear and sucked all the life out of the story."

"But you can't ignore Margaret's dying declaration. What if Cousins is innocent?"

"Exactly." One corner of Geri's mouth turned up in a snarky smile. "That's why I called you. And why you're going to call Lalo."

"What's that supposed to mean?"

"The people I work with wouldn't lose ten minutes of sleep over Randy Cousins. Still, I've got a bad feeling we made a mistake with this one. Lalo knows the details as well as anyone. The two of you worked together before. I figure with your legal background and Lalo's detective skills, you'll be able to find out if there was any truth to Margaret's dying declaration."

The bite on my neck began to itch. I swatted at another mosquito, squashing it in a pool of my own blood.

With a resigned sigh I said, "If I decide to get involved—and that's a big if—I want to check a few things out before dragging Lalo back from the Keys."

"I predict you'll call him sooner rather than later." Geri winked at me. "And when you do, he'll come running."

"You honestly think Cousins is innocent?"

Geri shrugged. "Who knows . . . I don't have to remind you Florida leads the country in wrongful convictions. I already have one with my name on it. If there's another problem out there, I want to get out in front of it before it bites me in the ass. The only question is, are you in or out?"

I thought about what she asked, understanding full well the commitment needed to investigate a murder that happened more than twenty years ago.

"Give me some time to think about it."

As she left the clearing Geri called over her shoulder. "Don't take too long."

Chapter 3

Cate, 2017

It was unusual for my sister to ignore me. Since moving from New Hampshire, I made it a habit to touch base with Nancy every Sunday night. Here it was, Monday evening and I still hadn't connected with her. On my last call, a computerized voice told me the mail box was full. Given the number of messages I left in the past twenty-four hours, I wasn't surprised.

There could have been a million and one reasons why Nancy didn't return my calls. But as time went by I began to wonder how else I could get in touch with her. A while ago she and her husband, Tim decided to cut costs by eliminating their land line and I never thought to ask Nancy for Tim's cell phone number. My only option was to try her son, Ben which wasn't a bad thing. I wanted to get his opinion about Geri's cold case anyway.

The sound of his voice at the other end of the line brought a smile to my lips. The television played in the background and I imagined him curled up with his girlfriend, Stephanie on the couch.

"Hey, Aunt Cate. What's up?"

"When was the last time you heard from your mother?"

"I don't know. A week ago, maybe two. Why do you ask?"

"She's not answering my calls."

The silence stretched between us.

"What is it Ben?"

"Nothing. Guilt that I haven't called her in a while, I guess. I'll give her a ring as soon as we hang up."

"When you do, tell her to call me back."

Ben chuckled. "I will. How's everything with you?"

"Great. You'll never guess who I saw this afternoon."

"Who?"

"Geri Garibaldi. She wants me to look into a local murder trial that may have resulted in a wrongful conviction."

Ben took some time to respond. In the background, I heard a door slam shut.

"Ben?"

"Sorry, Aunt Cate. You caught me in the middle of something. Can we talk about this tomorrow?"

"Sure. Don't forget to call your mother."

After speaking with Ben, I warmed a frozen dinner in the microwave and ate it standing at the kitchen counter. Glancing at the clock, I rushed out, arriving at my grief counseling session minutes before it was scheduled to begin I sat in my usual place in a back corner. With Nancy on my mind, I found it hard to concentrate. At the break I stepped out and reached for my phone. The group leader, Annie Murphy found me standing in the hall staring at the blank screen. In her hand she held one of her home-made brownies wrapped in a napkin. When she offered it to me I shook my head and mumbled something about watching my weight.

She threw me a sideways glance and took a bite. "I saw you eat two of Diane's cookies. If you don't like my brownies, just say so."

"The last time you gave me one of those I got high."

"Don't be ridiculous. I don't waste the good stuff on this lot."

With her tie-dyed kaftan, love beads and bangle brace-lets, Annie looked like she stepped right out of the sixties. She raised her hand, fingers splayed as she waved it in front of my face. "What's going on with you tonight? I feel a distur-bance in your aura."

"Nothing. All this talk about letting go of the past so we can live in the present is easier said than done."

Annie's smile revealed her chipped front tooth. "You need to work at it harder."

"What more can I do? After Arnie died I let go of everything. I even sold our house in New Hampshire and moved here to start over. That didn't seem to help much. I'll admit, I'm struggling."

"Sure, you nailed that part about letting go but you still aren't living in the present. You spend your days moping around the house, talking to your cat. Do something mean-ingful with your life. Get out more, meet new people."

I glanced at her from the corner of my eye. "As a mat-ter of fact, I had lunch with a friend today. Geri Garibaldi."

Annie scowled. "The dragon lady?"

I understood Annie's attitude toward Geri. As it happened, until now the only black mark on Detective Garib-aldi's service record was the wrongful conviction of Annie's grandson, Logan. After helping to get Logan exonerated last year, Annie and I developed a tight friendship. I considered telling her Geri may have played a part in condemning anoth-er innocent man to a life behind bars. But in the end, I decid-ed it was best not to.

"Geri's not as bad as you think. An acquired taste, maybe. I enjoyed seeing her again."

Annie popped the rest of the brownie in her mouth. "I'm having a few people over for dinner on Saturday. You should come. My friends are bringing their new neighbor. His name is Mike. He's from New Hampshire too."

"Maybe next time. I have plans for Saturday night."

Knowing she saw through the lie, I turned and walked away.

Chapter 4

After Sam left, Maggie brooded over what her friend had said. She knew he meant well, but he did not understand how desperately she wanted another child. And Sam underestimated Gator's ability to pull something like this off. One way or another, she knew Gator would find a way to get her that child. Maggie was sure about that.

Gator showed up at the beach around noon. Maggie stopped watching the children from her place in the dunes to see him strutting toward her. As he drew near she heard him whistling the theme song from Hogan's Heroes. He spread his sleeping bag on the hot sand before waving his arm in a sweeping gesture, inviting Maggie to join him. From his tattered backpack, he produced tuna sandwiches, two apples, a bag of chocolate chip cookies and a six pack of beer.

"This is nice." Maggie set her sketch book to one side, brushed the sand from her dress and settled next to him. "What's the occasion?"

Gator opened a beer and passed it to Maggie. He tapped his own bottle against hers in a toast. "We're celebrating. A few days from now, we're gonna be rich."

She sensed he was about to reveal another of his moronic schemes. Two months ago, Gator stole half of Maggie's disability pay to buy a bunch of Mega Millions lottery tickets. When he didn't hit the jackpot, he was perplexed. Not apologetic, mind you. Simply amazed that his number was not called. Maggie didn't speak to him for weeks. They survived on watered down beer and peanut butter crackers until her next check came in.

She now looked at him out of the corner of her eye, wondering what he was talking about. "I told you I don't care about the money. I just want that little girl."

Gator grew animated, pointing his bottle at her. "Yeah, yeah. Well, while you were sittin' here watching them kids I been working on that."

"You were sound asleep when I left."

He glared at her. "I said I been working on a plan. Came up with a good one, too. Wanna hear it or not?"

Maggie scooted closer. "Of course I do."

"How high do you reckon that pier is?"

Her eyes swept past the woman and her two children on the beach to the fishing pier beyond. "About ten feet."

"Maybe where it starts at Sharkey's deck. But I'm talkin' 'bout the height at the end."

"Probably twice that. Twenty feet or so."

He nodded in agreement. "That's what I figure. There's a two-foot tide this time of year so I'll have to take that into consideration."

From the slur of his words, Maggie guessed he had a head start on the booze. When he started talking nonsense like this, she knew it was best to let him ramble.

His smile sent a chill down her spine. "Aren't you gonna ask me what I'm thinking?"

"What are you thinking, Gator?"

"I'm thinking 'bout how I can swim two miles and back without coming up for air."

"No one can do that."

He thumped his chest. "When I was a SEAL I won prizes for best underwater distance."

Maggie sighed. His stories changed with every telling. On one of the many occasions when he'd had too much to drink he let it slip that he failed out of the SEAL program and served the majority of his time in the navy as a Seabee. Bracing for another long tirade about the asshole SEAL officers that ruined his life, Maggie stared out at the gathering clouds over the Gulf of Mexico.

"Hey, are you listenin' to me? I been workin' on this all day and you're sittin' there sippin' beer like I'm not even here."

"I'm listening, Gator. You were the best swimmer in the SEALs."

"Damn right, I was. I'll tell them to tie the money at the end of the pier, then wait until the tide rises so I can cut the bag and swim away without nobody seeing me."

Gator's speech picked up speed with every breath. Maggie was having a hard time keeping up with his train of thought. When she finally realized what he was talking about, her face flushed with excitement.

"Are you talking about ransom money?"

Gator squinted at her. "What'd you think I was talkin' about? We snatch the kid, make them pay to get her back, then we grab the money and run."

"And I keep the girl?"

Lines of annoyance creased his brow. "That's what I said, didn't I?"

"Well, I've been thinking too. A homeless camp is no place to raise a child. We'll have to find someplace to live. Someplace far away from here."

He tapped his temple with a dirty finger. "I'm still

working out the details. When I'm ready I'll let you know."

"Are you serious?"

"Serious as a heart attack." He popped open his second bottle of beer and guzzled half of it in one go.

While the children munched on their sandwiches, their mother rose from the blanket and brushed the sand from her tanned legs. Gator kept his eyes riveted on her as she walked across the sand toward Sharkey's. "Well I'll be damned. There she goes, just like you said."

Maggie's heart pounded with excitement. "Are you going to take her now?"

Gator snorted. "Ain't you listenin'? I'm still workin' on the details."

"But what if the baby cries out when you pick her up? What if someone tries to stop you?"

Gator's turned back to Maggie. "I'll figure out how to keep the kid quiet. Your job will be to watch her while I take care of business."

"What business?"

"What have I been talkin' about, Mags? I gotta mail the ransom note and take care of a bunch of other shit like gettin' me a boat. How much do you think we can get? Fifty grand? A hundred?"

"Nobody has that much money."

The look of annoyance returned to his face. "Look at those designer sunglasses that lady's wearing. And the gold chain around her neck. She's got the money all right. But now that I think about it, a hundred grand might be pushing it. I'll ask for fifty. Yeah, fifty will be good. That's what I was thinkin' all along."

Maggie felt herself get caught up with his plan. "How are you going to get a boat?"

Gator gave her a smug smile. "Simple, I'll jack one. After we grab the kid, you'll hide with her in the woods while I drop the ransom note in the mail. Then we'll all get on the boat and head out to the Gulf until they deliver the money. The cops will never find us there. At high tide, I'll bring the boat to within two miles of the pier, pick up the money and swim back. I figure the whole operation will take three, maybe five days max."

A few fat rain drops splashed on Maggie's cap. A bolt of lightning shot down from the black clouds followed by a distant rumble of thunder. Maggie caught sight of the mother running back to her children, the ice cream forgotten. Gathering the beach towels and stuffing them into her canvas bag, the mother herded the children toward the parking lot.

The rain grew steady. Maggie turned her attention to Gator. Though his plan had more holes than the socks on her feet, the thought of having that little girl for her own lifted Maggie's spirits.

"Can I give her a new name?" she asked.

Water dripped from her cap into her eyes. In the darkening light an eerie shadow crossed Gator's face. "Sure, whatever. Leave me be, now. I've got to work on this some more."

Chapter 5

The following morning, I woke up thinking about the circumstances surrounding Savannah Troy's murder. As I suspected from the start, Geri's story of a potential wrongful conviction piqued my curiosity. I couldn't help but wonder if in fact Randy Cousins was innocent. Not that I held out much hope for the man. Unfortunately, even if he was innocent, and despite Margaret Blue's dying declaration, Cousins had little-to-no chance for exoneration. From past experience, I knew when a guilty verdict was reached the burden of proof shifted to the convicted. I left Geri a voicemail promising to take a cursory look into the case. After a day or two of research, I hoped to put the whole thing behind me.

But first I needed to catch up with Ben. Since my nephew specialized in wrongful conviction law, I valued his opinion. I was also anxious to hear if he had spoken with his mother. If so, perhaps he could tell me why Nancy wasn't taking my calls.

"I spoke to my Dad last night," Ben told me when he answered the phone. "He said Mom has the flu."

"Thanks for letting me know. I'll give her a few days before I call again. Is this a good time to talk about the case Geri brought to me?"

"Sure. What's it all about?"

Before I finished explaining the situation, Ben started to chuckle.

"What's so funny?"

"You are." Ben's voice betrayed his amusement. "After a two-margarita lunch with Detective Garibaldi you dove head first into an area of the law you know nothing about."

"The only one drinking margaritas was Geri," I shot back. "How can I help?"

"You have access to Florida court documents, right?"

"Of course."

"I want to see a copy of the court summary. Cousins v. State. The trial took place in Sarasota in November, 1996."

I heard the click of Ben's keyboard as he searched the data base. While I waited, I turned on my own computer and watched the hour glass on the screen turn over and over.

"Got it, Aunt Cate. I'm sending the file now. You should have it in a few minutes."

"Thanks." I stared at my screen, knowing it would take more than a few minutes for my computer to finish booting up. "I'll let you know if I need anything else."

"Wait a sec. I just noticed something. Take a look at page six."

The icons popped onto the screen. "My computer is still warming up."

"How old is that thing?"

"Six years, give or take a few."

"Don't you think it's time to invest in a new one?"

"It just takes a little while to get going, that's all. I know firsthand that's what happens when you get old." When the mailbox finally appeared on the screen, I clicked to open Ben's message. "Okay, I got it. What am I looking for?"

"Did you know Lalo Sanchez was a witness for the prosecution?"

"Geri told me he was the lead homicide detective on the

case. I'm not surprised he testified at the trial."

"Have you spoken with him about this?"

I drew in a deep breath. "Not yet."

"Well, when you do, let him know that if he wants to come back to work for my firm, the door is wide open."

My cat, Rascal chose that moment to stroll into the room to demand breakfast. Hopping onto my lap, he reached up with a paw and batted the side of my cheek. When I tried to ignore him, he let out a loud yowl.

"When did you get a cat?"

"Lalo gave him to me last year."

"Must be good company, now that you're alone."

His words, well intentioned as they probably were, caught me off balance. I hastened to steer the conversation back to the business at hand.

"Thanks for sending the court summary. I appreciate it."

"Keep me in the loop, okay?"

"Of course."

Armed with a cup of black decaf, I tackled the job of printing Randy Cousins' court summary. My ink cartridge gave out near the end, spitting a few blank pages into the tray. A quick check on my computer showed nothing of importance on those two pages so I set the stack neatly on my desk next to two freshly sharpened pencils and a yellow highlighter. Of course I could have read the whole thing on the computer screen, but I'm guilty of working the old-fashioned way. I prefer to turn the pages with my fingers and mark up the document as I go. Despite the objections of my tree-hugging friends, I figured the Amazon forest wasn't going to vanish because of a few sheets of paper. I picked up a pencil, turned back the cover page, and started reading.

A few of the names on the list of players at the trial was familiar. David Hall, a freshman attorney at the time, prosecuted the decades-old case. I knew he was now ASA Hall, an assistant state attorney and rumored to be the next in line to replace his boss, State Attorney Phil Remy. Scanning the names of Hall's witnesses, Eduardo "Lalo" Sanchez jumped out at me. Carrie Ann Troy, Savannah's sister, was also on the list. If I decided to take this further, I would reach out and see if she would be willing to speak with me.

Randy Cousins' public defender was a lawyer named Grady Truman. I went back to my computer and typed in his name. The result of my search identified Truman as an attorney with an office on Nokomis Avenue in Venice. Knowing his input would be valuable I wrote his number in the margin next to his name and moved on to the next section of the summary, the description of the crime.

I read that on July 5, 1994 an unidentified man picked up three-year-old Savannah Troy from under the Venice pier. He walked away without anyone other than Savannah's older sister, Carrie Ann seeing him. Three months later, Randy Cousins discovered Savannah's body in a shallow grave a few miles south of the pier. He called the police to say he was walking along Caspersen Beach with his metal detector when he found what he believed to be human remains.

The next sentence described what was left of Savannah's body after three months in the sub-tropical climate. I closed my eyes and drew in a deep breath. Skipping ahead, I reached the part where Lalo brought Cousins in for questioning.

Since Cousins matched the general description provided by Carrie Ann Troy, the police took his photo and included him in a "six-pack" with five others. After making it clear that the abductor may not be in the pack, Geri asked Carrie Ann—ten years old at the time—if she could identify any of them as the man who took her sister. The little girl studied the faces for some time before pointing her finger at Cousins' image. Lalo then put him in a line-up and this time Carrie Ann chose Cousins without any hesitation.

As I continued to read, I learned that a little over two months earlier, the Troy family paid fifty-thousand dollars for the safe return of their little girl. Though the serial numbers of the bills were recorded, at the time of the trial only three twenties were recovered. That money was deposited by a local service station the day after the kidnapper picked up the cash. Once Carrie Ann identified Cousins as her sister's kidnapper, Lalo went back to the surveillance footage from the station and found Cousins' image smiling at the camera as he paid for gas. The video footage was admitted into evidence.

After four hours of deliberation, the jury unanimously came to a guilty verdict. Randy Cousins was sentenced to life in prison without parole. No appeals were filed.

By the time I finished reading, my coffee was cold. I glanced down at the cat who was curled up in a ball on a chair.

"Looks to me like Cousins is guilty as charged," I said.

With a great yawn, Rascal stretched his forelegs and shook his head. As I stared at the stack of papers on my desk, I decided the whole thing was a waste of my time. After what he did to Savannah and her family, Randy Cousins deserved to spend the rest of his life in jail. With a sigh, I rose from my chair.

I headed into the kitchen to pour myself a fresh cup of coffee, prepared to call Geri to say I didn't buy into her theory. I looked down to see Rascal staring at me with his green eyes.

"You're right. I should speak with Lalo first. Then at least I can tell Geri I covered all the bases before calling it quits." Reaching for my phone, I found the number. The sound of Lalo's voice carried me back to the last time we saw each other.

"Hey Cate. It's been a while. What's up?"

I heard a woman laughing in the background.

"Did I catch you at a bad time?" I asked.

"No, not at all."

"I'm calling about an old case of yours. It was a while ago but I'm sure you remember. The victim was a little girl named Savannah Troy."

I heard a click, the laughter muffled as Lalo closed a door. "Yeah, I remember. Why are you asking?"

"Geri thinks there's a problem."

"What kind of problem?"

"A woman has come forward claiming she knows who killed Savannah."

"Margaret Blue?"

After what Geri told me, I shouldn't have been surprised to hear him say the name.

"The thing is, the person Margaret mentioned isn't Randy Cousins."

"Listen, before you put too much weight behind what Maggie says, you should know she's not right in the head."

"Geri said something to that effect. Are you saying we shouldn't take her statement seriously?"

"Talk to Maggie. Then decide for yourself. Better yet, look up her caseworker, Sylvia Branch. She can give you a professional opinion."

"Maggie is dead."

The pause on the line told me he wasn't prepared for the news.

"Lalo? Did you hear me? Margaret Blue is gone, but

before she died she claimed someone named Gator Pope killed Savannah."

Lalo swore under his breath. "Sit tight. I'll get there as soon as I can."

Chapter 6

Maggie, 1994

Two days after the brief summer storm, Gator stared as the young mother headed toward Sharkey's restaurant. As expected, she left the two little girls alone while she went to buy ice cream.

"You know what to do, right?" Gator jumped to his feet, glaring down at Maggie.

Maggie glanced around. The timing was perfect. To her right, an elderly man reclined in his beach chair. His eyes were closed as the sun beat down on his leathery skin. A hundred yards away, a pair of teenagers played volleyball. There was no one else in sight.

Maggie met Gator's eyes. Taking in his greasy hair and beery breath, she began to have second thoughts. Recalling Sam's warning she said, "Maybe we shouldn't do this."

Gator growled in anger. "No screwing around here, Mags. Stick to the plan. When I grab the kid, you check to make sure the coast is clear. If it looks like someone notices, then you run interference to give me a head start."

"Okay, okay."

Maggie stared at the little girls. The older sister was showing the little one how to build a sand castle.

"Focus, Mags. Tell me what you're going to do after I grab the kid."

"I wait to see if anyone notices you."

"Then what?"

"If they do, I distract them, telling them I saw you run off in the opposite direction. If not, I walk to the end of Harbor Boulevard to Caspersen Beach where you'll be waiting."

Gator nodded agreement. "Just make sure no one follows you."

She watched as Gator approached the children. He said something to the older girl and pointed to the restaurant. After a moment of hesitation, she stood and ran after her mother. Gator then squatted down in the sand next to the toddler. Maggie's heart beat quickened, willing him to hurry. Gator smiled, pointed to his tattoo and let the child touch it. When he scooped her into his arms, the child opened her mouth to cry out. For a moment Maggie thought that would be the end of everything but Gator reached into his pocket and held a white cloth against the little girl's face. Within moments she went limp.

Maggie looked around. The elderly man still appeared to be asleep. The teenagers kept playing volleyball. The child's mother and sister had yet to reappear. No one paid any attention to Gator as he tucked the toddler in the crook of his arm and strolled along the beach at a leisurely pace. As Maggie watched, Gator crossed the dunes and vanished from sight. She stood and brushed the sand from her legs. Clapping both hands over her mouth, she stifled the laughter that rose in her chest. The voices in her head receded to a distant static buzz.

Maggie hummed to herself as she walked down the sidewalk toward Caspersen Beach. When the paved road ended, she entered the park, bearing left on the dirt path. Once she reached the empty parking area, she hesitated.

A public restroom sat at the far side of the lot. To her

right, a set of stairs lead to the boardwalk running the length of the beach. Recent storms had washed away most of the sand, resulting in steep cliffs dropping to the Gulf of Mexico. She jumped when a raspy voice called to her. Looking down on the beach she saw Sam waving at her.

"What are you doing down there?"

"Hunting for shark's teeth. Haven't found many yet. I may have more luck when the tide goes out." He started to climb the cliff to reach her.

"Not now, Sam. I don't have time."

"What's the hurry?"

"I need to use the rest room."

Sam's rheumy eyes stared back at her. "You're going through with this crazy plan, aren't you? I warned you Mags . . ."

She studied him for a moment. "You won't tell anyone, will you?"

"You know I won't."

"Thanks, Sam. If anyone comes looking, tell them you never saw me."

"I just hope you know what you're doing."

She waved goodbye and turned toward the public rest rooms. Except for the sound of dry twigs snapping under her boots, the air was deathly quiet. When she reached the cement block building, she paused.

"Gator? Where are you?"

The hiss of his voice in her ear made her jump.

"Keep it down! I'm right here."

She spun around, surprised to see him standing behind her. Gator roughly grabbed her arm and pulled her into the undergrowth.

"Did anyone see you?"

Maggie hesitated before answering. "Not that I know of. Where is she? Where's my little girl?"

"Shut up and follow me."

As they made their way deep into the woods, branches lashed Maggie's arms. The trail grew increasingly narrow, vines reaching out to trip her as she stumbled behind Gator. When she paused to catch her breath, a shaft of sunlight broke through the branches illuminating a thicket in the woods. On a blanket in the middle of the clearing, the little girl lay sleeping.

Chapter 7

I heard Geri chuckling on the other end of the line. "I knew Lalo would come running when you whistled."

"His truck just pulled into my driveway. Listen, is there any way I can get a look at the murder book? There may be something in the records of your investigation that will help."

"No problem. The binder is probably in the County archives collecting dust. I'll dig it out and make copies for you."

I peered out the window, wondering what was taking Lalo so long to emerge from the truck.

"Thanks. Call me when you're ready and I'll come pick them up."

Instead of Lalo, a diminutive young lady stepped out from behind the wheel. She hitched her sports bag onto one shoulder and came up the walk. When I opened the door, she brushed a lock of blue hair from her eyes and gave me a broad smile.

I looked at her in amazement. She appeared to be no more than twenty. Geri always hinted that Lalo liked younger women but this was going too far, even for him. Blocking the open doorway, I asked what she was doing there.

"I'm Bree."

"Who?"

She threw me an amused look. "Bree? Lalo's granddaughter. Who did you think I was?"

Now that I got a good look at the girl, I saw the family resemblance. The space between her front teeth was a dead give-away. "I . . . I wasn't expecting you."

Taking my cell phone out of my pocket, I dialed Lalo's number.

"Someone claiming to be your granddaughter is here."

"She made good time."

"Where are you?"

"Sailing up from the Keys on the *Chilanga*."

"You might have warned me. What would she have done if I wasn't home?"

There was a short pause before he answered. "Where else would you be?"

"I have a life, you know."

"But you are home, right?"

I heaved an exasperated sigh. "How long will it take you to get here?"

"There's bad weather heading this way. I'll have to stop at the marina in Cape Coral for the night. Depending on how quickly this system passes, I may have to stay put for a day or two."

I turned around and cupped my hand around the phone. "What am I supposed to do with Bree until then?"

"Feed her."

With that he was gone.

Hanging up my phone I said, "The guest room is down the hall. Make yourself at home while I fix us some dinner. I hope you like pasta."

Bree nodded. "Sounds great, I'm like, literally starving."

———

Over plates heaped with linguine smothered in my homemade tomato sauce, Bree talked up a storm. She told me she was majoring in computer science at the University of Florida in Gainesville. Her mother—Lalo's daughter with his first wife—lived with a boyfriend in Georgia. Bree made no secret of her feelings toward the boyfriend. She simply referred to him BHOF. When I asked what that meant she rolled her eyes and said it was shorthand for Bald Headed Old Fart. From the way she complained about him, I gathered BHOF was the main reason Bree decided to spend the summer with Lalo on his boat. She was heading back to school at the end of the month to begin her senior year in college. Her dream was to land a place in law school after she graduated in the spring.

"What kind of law do you want to practice?"

Bree answered without hesitation. "Like, literally everyone asks me that."

"You might consider Family Law. That's what I did."

"I know. Lalo told me about you."

I looked at her in surprise. Judging from Lalo's lack of communication over the past year I assumed he never gave me a moment's thought.

"I'm surprised Lalo dropped everything to come when I called," I said.

"Why?"

"It's complicated."

"Everyone says that when like, most things aren't complicated at all."

I looked at the girl, realizing she was right. "Let me explain. Last week, Geri Garibaldi called asking for my help with one of their old cases. It appears there may be a problem."

"What kind of problem?"

"It's possible they caught the wrong guy."

Bree pressed her lips together and shook her head. "Lalo doesn't make those kinds of mistakes."

Her belief in her grandfather's abilities was understandable. When I was her age, the people I cared for seemed infallible. Years of experience taught me otherwise. My husband, the man I loved more than life itself, scorned the tobacco company's warnings, promising we would grow old together despite his two-pack-a-day habit. I bought into his claim, never dreaming he would die at such a young age. Despite Bree's faith in Lalo, I wondered if he got it wrong this time.

"I hope you're right," I said. "Because if the man they caught is innocent, then the guy who murdered Savannah Troy must still be out there."

The following morning, Bree shuffled out of my guest room. Her blue hair stuck out in all directions, her eyes ringed with red. I thought perhaps she had been smoking weed until she pulled an inhaler out from her pajama's pocket. Raising it to her mouth she sucked in a lungful of spray.

"I can't even. Do you like, have a cat?"

I realized Rascal hadn't emerged from my bedroom. In fact, he had made himself scarce ever since Bree appeared.

"Allergies?"

In answer, Bree blew her nose into a sodden tissue.

"I'll keep him in my bedroom while you're here. There are some antihistamine tablets in the medicine closet which may help."

"Thanks. Tell me more about this case that Geri screwed up."

I started to say it was complicated but stopped myself before the word slipped out "Did Lalo tell you anything about it?"

"No. But after you called I could tell he was upset. He lit out of the Keys like, real fast."

I set a plate of blueberry pancakes on the table, two for her and two for me. She pulled the whole stack in front of her, doused everything with maple syrup and dove right in. I grabbed a box of cereal from the cabinet and poured myself a bowl. "I'll fill you in later. Right now I've got to leave for an appointment downtown. Make yourself at home until I get back."

"Best if I don't hang here too long. Cat allergies, remember?" She covered her mouth and coughed. "Let me come with."

I looked at her eager face and noticed another thing that reminded me of Lalo. Her almond-shaped eyes, full of mischief. Though I suspected the girl was a handful, I didn't see the harm in bringing her with me to meet Father Sullivan. As I raised my chin in assent, she erupted in a great sneeze. I passed her a tissue.

Our steps rang out on the marble floor as I glanced up at the blond wood ceiling high above. The modern design of the Epiphany Catholic church stood in stark contrast to the Colonial Spanish architecture of most other buildings in town. A weak light filtered through tall stained-glass windows, dust motes floated like fairies in the air. I felt vaguely uncomfortable in this place of worship. Bree dipped her hand into a holy water font and made the sign of the cross. At least one of us seemed at home.

Father Sullivan appeared from the back of the church, black garments swirling as he strode down the aisle to greet us. He suggested we would be more comfortable meeting in his office. We followed him outside and walked past a group of buildings connected by open walkways. I'd lived in Venice for a little over a year and never knew there was a school tucked behind the church. The oleander bushes were in full bloom, candy cane pink flowers peeking out from bright green leaves. Dark clouds gathered overhead, back-lit by distant lightning. I patted my handbag, checking to be sure I remembered my umbrella. The priest used his key to unlock a door before ushering us into a small room furnished with a desk and three chairs. Push pins tacked school children's crayon drawings to a cork bulletin board. I recognized Noah and his ark.

The priest sat behind the desk and waved at the two visitor's chairs. "Please take a seat. Can I offer you a coffee? I believe the sisters made a fresh pot a little while ago."

"No thank you, Father. We don't want to take too much of your time. As you know, I called to ask about a discussion you had with Margaret Blue prior to her death."

"I'm not sure what I can add to what I already told Detective Garibaldi."

"Let's start at the beginning," I said. "You were with Margaret in the hospital, right?"

"That's right. At first she didn't appear to be aware of my presence. She mumbled to herself like she was having a conversation with someone who wasn't there. I've seen it before with people who are near the end. When I placed my hand on her forehead she looked at me and went quiet. It was almost as if I pulled her back into the present."

"Then what?"

"She asked where she was. I explained she was in the hospital, that she had been found lying unconscious on Caspersen Beach. Seeing the condition she was in, I offered to hear her confession. She then grabbed my stole and pulled me down to whisper in my ear."

"And she told you about Savannah Troy?"

"Yes. She said someone named Gator snatched Savannah from under the Venice Pier."

Out of the corner of my eye I saw Bree lean forward. "So you already knew who Savannah was?"

The priest nodded. "Of course. Venice is a quiet town. Nothing like that ever happened here before." He made the sign of the cross. "Or since, thank God."

I was impatient to hear the rest of his story. "Is there anything else you can tell us?"

He shook his head. "Just that Gator lied to her. Apparently he promised to let Margaret keep the little girl. She told me several times that she tried to stop him from killing Savannah. I assured her God already knew that."

"You're sure you heard her say the man's name was Gator?"

"I heard her quite clearly. Gator Pope. Toward the end she became increasingly more confused. At that point all I wanted was to help Margaret leave this world in peace. Given the nature of her confession, I suggested it would be a sign of her penitence if she released me from the seal of confession."

"What does that mean?" I asked.

Bree piped up. "The only way a priest can discuss a confession with someone other than the penitent is to ask permission."

Sullivan beamed at Bree. "I see you were paying attention in Catechism class. That's exactly right. When I asked for permission, Margaret nodded. To be totally honest, by that time I'm not sure she was fully aware of her surroundings. I heard her say something about flowers . . . poppies maybe." Sullivan shook his head before continuing. "In any event, I gave her the last rites and stayed with her until the end."

I asked a few more questions, having him go over his

story once more to make sure I didn't miss anything. After thanking the priest for his time, Bree and I took our leave.

Outside a mass of black clouds rolled overhead. A great lightning bolt split the sky followed seconds later by a clap of thunder. We both dashed for the car, slamming the doors behind us as the deluge came pouring down.

Chapter 8

Maggie, 1994

Maggie tugged her woolen cap over her ears in a futile attempt to shut out the voices. She mumbled under her breath
as she stumbled along Harbor Drive. With every step she took,
the voices grew louder.

Maggie stopped in her tracks and clenched her fists.
"Shut up!" she screamed.

A pair of teenagers, towels over their bronzed shoulders, gave her a wide berth as they headed for the beach.

Maggie started walking again, picking up the pace.
Twenty minutes earlier, before he left the clearing to mail the
ransom note, Gator hissed a warning in her ear.

"Get over it, Maggie. This is how it always had to be.
Now stick to the plan. Five days . . . one week max and we'll
be fifty-thousand dollars richer and on our way to the Caribbean. You'd better be here when I get back or I swear to God . . ."

He didn't have to finish his threat for her to know he
was serious. But there was no way she could stay there. The
sight of the dead child wrenched Maggie's heart. She trembled
in fear knowing Gator would try to track her down when he
got back and found her gone. Her only hope was to get out of
town for a few days until Gator collected the ransom money.
Then hopefully he would head to the Caribbean and forget all
about her.

Maggie froze at the sound of Sam's raspy voice calling

her name. Glancing over her shoulder, she saw him walking toward her. He was winded, working hard to catch up. When he caught up to her he pressed his hands to the sides of her face, wiping her tears with his thumbs.

"Where are you going?" he asked.

"Back to camp."

"You can't. The cops are searching for the little girl."

Maggie heard the distant wail of sirens. Flashing red and blue lights were heading their way.

Sam gave her a half-smile. "They're looking for Gator."

Her eyes grew wide in fear. "The people in the camp know I was with him."

With his hands still holding her face, Sam gazed into her eyes. "That's why you can't go back there."

Maggie stepped away from him. Reaching into her sock, she checked to make sure what was left from her monthly disability pay was still there.

As if reading her mind he said, "Do you have enough for a bus ticket?"

"Yes."

"Then head straight for the station."

She knew he was giving her good advice. Still, before leaving town there was something she had to do.

"I need to pick up a few things first," she said.

Sam wagged his head from side to side. Concern and disappointment were written all over his face.

"I warned you not to take that child."

"Leave me alone, Sam."

"Where will you go?"

She squeezed her eyes closed, trying to focus. "I don't know."

"You'll let me know, won't you?"

Sam moved toward her, arms open. Giving him a wide berth, Maggie turned and walked away. As the distance grew between them he called out.

"Take care, Maggie Blue."

———————————————

When she reached the path to the camp she paused. The trip from Caspersen Beach had taken her longer than expected. To avoid the police, she took the long way around. Cops were still canvassing the area near the fishing pier but here all seemed quiet. Drawing moist air into her lungs, she pushed on. Rivulets of sweat dripped from under her cap, stinging her eyes. The only sound reaching her ears was the roar of waves hitting the beach.

She wiped the sweat from her brow with the back of her hand. An image of Gator—a wild look on his face—flashed in her head. He told her keeping the little girl was never part of his plan. Nothing she had said to him could change his mind.

Maggie ignored the branches that lashed her face as she stumbled down the path. The loose sole of her boot caught an exposed root throwing her face-down in the dirt. Cursing, she stood. A sharp pain shot up her leg.

Limping the rest of the way, she paused at the edge of the camp. Everything looked normal. The tents, the broken beach chairs, the community clothes line strung between trees. The tin pot Gator used that morning to make coffee sat at edge of the fire pit where he left it. The place appeared to be deserted save for Gator's mangy dog, chained to a stake in the ground. Hobbling now, she made her way to her shopping cart and reached for the bag holding her most precious items. Turning around, her heart stopped when she caught sight of a stranger striding toward her. He made a quick move to take something from his pocket.

Flashing the badge in his hand he called out. "Detective Sanchez of the Sarasota County Sheriff's Office."

Maggie froze. A bead of sweat ran down her back between her protruding shoulder blades. She stole a furtive glance at the detective. He was big, at least six feet tall, with broad shoulders and dark skin. His thick mustache turned down as he studied her.

"I'm looking for someone," Detective Sanchez said. "White guy, about my height, maybe fifty pounds lighter with long hair and a tattoo of a bee on his arm. Do you know anyone who looks like that?"

Maggie shook her head.

"He was seen wearing jeans and a green T-shirt with a tear right under the collar," The detective looked around. "I have a hunch he lives here."

Harsh voices filled her head like shards of glass.

The words tumbled out of her mouth as she tugged on the sides of her sodden cap.

"Leave me alone!"

The detective's lips were moving but it took a moment for his deep voice to cut through the other voices.

"Take it easy, no one's going to hurt you. Did you hear the sirens? A guy snatched a toddler from the beach and I'm trying to find him."

Maggie stared at the ground, trembling in fear.

"Do you understand what I'm saying? A man, about my height . . . You live here, right?"

She nodded.

The man studied her for a moment before approaching. He stopped only inches away. Maggie shrank back, colliding with her shopping cart before falling down. The pain in her ankle flared like fire.

"Hey, are you okay?" Sanchez reached down and touched her shoulder.

Maggie crabbed backwards in the dirt. "Don't touch me!"

"You're hurt." Sanchez bent to get a closer look. "You need a doctor."

"No!" Panic rose in her chest. Maggie started to cry, clawing the detective's pant leg.

He pulled out his radio and pressed a button. "Hey Laura, I have an injured female here in the homeless camp near the Coast Guard training center. Caucasian, estimated age around thirty. Potential witness with information about the guy who snatched the kid. Looks like she sprained an ankle. Send medical assistance ASAP."

"Please." Maggie closed her eyes, confusion and fear swirling in her brain. Her voice came out in a hoarse whisper. "Leave me alone."

Chapter 9

Cate, 2017

Three feet wide and loaded with menacing teeth, the fossil hung on the wall of Sharkey's restaurant across from the table where Bree and I sat.

"OMG, is that for real?" Bree asked.

"Probably. This restaurant is named for the shark's teeth that wash up on the sand. There's something about the tide that brings them here." I pointed to the fishing pier stretching over the blue waters of the Gulf. "Savannah Troy was snatched from under that pier."

"I can't even. How did that happen?"

I stared out the window. "Savannah and her sister, Carrie Ann were playing on the beach. Their mother told Carrie Ann, who was only ten at the time, to watch Savannah while she bought the kids ice cream cones. She only left them alone for a few minutes. But as soon as she left a stranger approached Carrie Ann and told her that her mother sent him down to tell her she needed help carrying ice cream back from the restaurant. He promised to watch her little sister until they returned. He then snatched Savannah and walked off without anyone noticing."

"That sounds impossible. There are tons of people here."

"Venice was quieter back then. Only a few people were on the beach at the time. No one heard or saw a thing. Carrie Ann was the only witness who could describe the kidnapper."

"The priest said the Troys are still in town. Have you spoken with Carrie Ann yet?"

I picked at the remains of my chicken Caesar salad, moving the croutons around on the plate. "I don't want to open old wounds unnecessarily. There's no reason to disturb the family until we're sure Randy Cousins isn't the man who killed Savannah. Right now I'm concentrating on Margaret Blue."

"But she's dead," Bree said.

"Of course. And we don't have much to go on." I held up my fingers as I made each point. "One, Margaret confessed—I guess you could call it a confession—to Father Sullivan that she wanted to raise Savannah as her own. Two, Gator Pope double-crossed Margaret and killed Savannah. And three, Geri and Lalo claim Margaret wasn't right in the head—whatever that means—so we can't believe anything she said." I went back to moving the food around on my plate. "Lalo gave me the name of Margaret's caseworker. I made an appointment with her for three this afternoon."

"What about tracking down this guy Pope? Maybe we can find him online."

I shrugged. "I googled him. Nothing."

"Did you check the social networking sites?"

"I'm not what you'd call an expert when it comes to those things. I'll ask Lalo to have a look after he gets here."

Bree burst into laughter. "Seriously? Lalo is like a Neanderthal. If there's anything about Pope out there, I can find it for you." Bree eyed my plate. "Are you going to finish that salad?"

Her cheeseburger and fries were long gone but my lunch proved far too much for me.

"Help yourself." I slid my dish across the table. "When we're finished here I can drop you at home. Your allergies may not bother you if you stay on the lanai while I meet with Margaret's social worker."

"Let me come with. Two is better than one."

I was tempted by her offer, but I preferred to have Bree work her magic on the Internet.

"You can be far more help searching for Gator Pope online."

Bree shrugged, picked up her fork and speared a piece of chicken. As small as she was, I wondered where she put all that food.

The first thing I noticed about Sylvia Branch was her hair. Thick, dark braids circled her head, a dozen or so colorful glass beads woven into an intricate pattern. Sunlight streamed through her office window, lighting the beads like crystals. Her clothes smelled of stale cigarettes. I caught a glimpse of nicotine-stained teeth behind her tight smile.

"What's this all about, Ms. Stokes?"

"Please, call me Cate. Detective Eduardo Sanchez sent me to ask about a former client of yours."

"Who might that be?"

"Margaret Blue."

She glanced at my business card. "It says here you're a lawyer." Her dark eyes met mine. "You know I can't discuss certain medical issues without the client's permission."

"Margaret is dead. Some questions have cropped up concerning a confession she made to a priest at the end."

Sylvia sat up straight in her chair. "Maggie is dead? I had no idea. Still, that doesn't change anything as far as the law is concerned. Do you have a subpoena for the information you want?"

"At this stage we're simply trying to determine if her

last words warrant further investigation."

"What kind of trouble was Maggie in now?"

"I didn't say she was in any trouble."

"No, but knowing Maggie, I'm guessing she was."

"Does the name Savannah Troy ring a bell?"

Sylvia's eyes opened wide. "The little girl they found on the beach? That must have been twenty years ago. You're not here to tell me Maggie had something to do with that?"

I could see by the look on her face that her initial concern about confidentiality was overcome by her curiosity to hear more.

"Would that surprise you?"

"When it comes to Maggie, nothing would surprise me. But I have to say, she was not a violent person. Deeply disturbed, but never violent."

"Margaret . . . Maggie had a friend. A guy named Gator Pope. Did she ever mention him to you?"

Sylvia shook her head. "No, I think I would remember a name like that."

"How long did you know Maggie?"

Sylvia cast her eyes to the ceiling. In the air her fingers counted the years like she was playing scales on a trumpet. "I picked up her case twenty-two years ago, right around the time of that kidnapping. Ever since then I worked with her on and off. My contact with Maggie depended on. . . well, frankly on her ability to stay in the program. There were long stretches of time when I had no idea where she was." She looked straight at me. "Not that I didn't care. I liked Maggie. But it isn't my job to go chasing clients who run off and disappear."

"When was the last time you saw her?"

"Oh, that must have been five, six months ago. Maybe more. I would have to check my records to be sure. Lalo found her living under the Circus Bridge and called to tell me where she was. I stopped by to see if she wanted any help but she told me to—pardon my French—she told me to mind my own fucking business." Sylvia smiled to herself and shook her head. "I didn't take it personally. I've heard much worse from other clients."

"In all the years you knew her, did Maggie ever mention Savannah?"

"No, of course not. I would have immediately reported something like that to the authorities. Our goal here is to help clients function in society as much as possible but we don't offer protection from legal violations." A sigh escaped Sylvia's lips. "You have to understand, some people we work with have addiction issues. Others are mentally challenged. To be honest, the majority fall into both categories. So naturally our clients get into trouble from time to time. We walk a fine line between offering aid and staying within the boundaries of the law."

"Can you tell me more about how your program works?"

"We provide food and housing for those who need it. Medical care and counseling for some who qualify. But I'll be the first one to admit the system isn't perfect. Our clients are . . . well, like I said, they're challenged. For example, Maggie suffered from schizophrenia." Her hand flew up to cover her mouth. "I probably shouldn't have told you that."

I smiled, trying to put her at ease. "Let's come at this from a different angle. Hypothetically, how would you go about helping a client who suffered from schizophrenia?"

"Right, I get it. Hypothetically, if a schizophrenic client stays on her meds and gets her monthly injections, she can function reasonably well. But things don't always work the way we intend. Sometimes the visiting nurses forget to drop

by or worse, they come too often. Clients themselves compli-
cate the situation by missing their appointments or self-medi-
cating. Maggie's drug of choice was alcohol. Vodka when she
could get it."

I pretended not to notice she mentioned Maggie by
name. "If Maggie was taking her medicine, would she be considered a reliable witness?"

"There's no way to tell. When she was off her meds
she suffered from paranoia, voices, even hallucinations. Everything would depend on the filter through which she saw
things at that time."

As she said the words, I realized Maggie Blue's confession could be dismissed as a fiction coming from a mentally ill
woman. If so, then the man serving time for killing Savannah
Troy could be guilty after all. Anything was possible. My disappointment must have shown on my face.

Sylvia placed her hand on mine. "I wish I could be
more help but honestly, there's no way to determine Maggie's
state of mind when she died."

I tried a new angle. "You mentioned your program
provided housing for Maggie. Didn't she have any family she
could stay with?"

Sylvia clicked her tongue. "Oh, circumstances didn't
allow for that."

"Can you tell me more?"

"You know I can't. But since you're working for the
Sheriff's office, I'm sure you have access to her criminal record.
You'll find the answer to your question there."

"Of course."

This was the first I heard Maggie had a record. I made
a mental note to ask Geri if she could shed some light on
Maggie's past.

Thanking Sylvia, I took my leave. All the way home I thought about Maggie Blue. Homeless, sick, alone in the world. I doubted she would have survived without the agency's help. But an overriding question rattled around in my brain. Given Maggie's schizophrenia, could I believe her when she said Gator kidnaped and killed Savannah Troy? Going into my meeting with Sylvia, I hoped she could answer that question. Unfortunately, I was no closer to the truth than before we met.

Chapter 10

Maggie fought against her restraints. Her thoughts were dulled, swaddled by whatever drugs they had given her. The last time they brought her to the hospital, things were exactly the same. She tried slipping the little white pills they gave her under her tongue and spitting them out when the nurse left the room. But after the first day they caught onto her trick. Now they shot the drugs directly into her body. All the voices were silenced.

The day nurse barged into her room, chirping as usual. "Good morning, Maggie. You have a visitor."

Maggie looked up, hoping to see her only friend, Sam. She knew she could count on him to help her get out of there. But instead of Sam, Detective Sanchez stood towering over the nurse's head. He smiled, exposing a gap between his front teeth. She gave him a guarded look.

"How are you feeling, Mags?"

His familiar tone did not sit well with her. She squinted at him, wondering why he was there. While she mulled this over, the nurse stepped close and jabbed her arm with a needle.

"Stop that!" Maggie tried to pull away but the nurse's fingers formed an iron cuff around her skinny arm. The plunger went down and Maggie felt the poison surging through her veins.

"I stopped by to see how you're doing," the detective said.

The mist in her brain cleared a little and she realized Detective Sanchez had not yet found Gator. If he had, then they would be having a different conversation.

She tugged again at the straps holding her arms. "Help me get out of here."

"Can't," the detective said. "They're holding you under the Baker Act. Your mother signed the papers."

The nurse paused from making notes on a clipboard and spoke up. "This is for your own protection, Maggie. We'll discharge you as soon as you're stabilized."

"Would you mind giving us a little privacy?" Sanchez asked.

The nurse looked relieved to be dismissed. The moment she left, Maggie felt exposed. The detective seemed friendly enough, but she knew not to trust him.

"How's your ankle?"

Her ankle hurt like crazy but Maggie refused to give him the satisfaction of an answer.

"I'm still looking for that little girl, Mags. Her name is Savannah Troy. My gut tells me you know something that can help me find her."

"I told you, I don't know anything about the girl."

"An eye witness got a good look at the man who took Savannah. I've been asking around and it seems someone matching his description was living with you in the homeless camp."

He reached into his back pocket and pulled out a police sketch. Maggie knew something about drawing portraits and this one was far from great. Still, whoever the artist was, he did a pretty fair job of sketching Gator.

The detective studied her face for a reaction to the sketch. "You were seen with him on the beach a few days ago."

Maggie turned her head away. "I don't remember. I've been sick."

She closed her eyes, hoping he would get the message and leave.

"Don't you want to know what happened to your dog?"

"What dog?" She opened her eyes to see Detective Sanchez had moved closer. He sat down on the edge of her bed, placing his hand on her arm.

"A pit bull terrier. I assume she's yours. When I got back to the camp, everyone had packed up and vanished. All that was left was a dog chained next to a blue tent. That and a shopping cart filled with plastic bags."

"Not my dog."

"What kind of person would abandon their dog like that?"

"How would I know?"

An awkward silence stretched between them.

"So, what happened to the dog?" Maggie asked at last.

"She's fine. The humane society is holding her. If you tell me her owner's name, I can let him know where she is."

"What did you do with my shopping cart?"

"I'm storing it in my garage until you're discharged. The tent too. But if you say that dog isn't yours, then maybe the tent isn't either."

Maggie stared at him, knowing full well he was playing a game of cat and mouse.

"I want the tent. And I'll know if you steal anything from my cart."

"Cross my heart." Sanchez made an 'X' on his chest. "I won't touch a thing. Help me, Mags. I need to find that little girl."

"How many times do I have to tell you? I can't help." Maggie rolled over, willing the detective to leave. A tear ran down her cheek as he closed the door behind him.

Chapter 11

Cate, 2017

I returned from my meeting with Sylvia Branch to find Bree on the lanai, her fingers flying over her laptop's keyboard. The rain pounded the flat roof, turning the screens translucent with moisture.

Bree looked up with a start. "I didn't hear you come in. How'd it go with Margaret Blue's caseworker?"

"Okay, I guess. She knew Maggie for years but she doesn't recall hearing her mention Savannah Troy. Gator Pope either. Have you had any luck searching the Internet for our mystery man?"

Bree gave me a big grin and hit a key on her laptop. She turned the screen so I could see the results. "There are literally one thousand and twenty-eight males with the last name 'Pope' living in Sarasota County."

"That's a lot." I squinted at the small screen. "Can you eliminate everyone under the age of forty? I'm guessing Pope had to be at least twenty at the time of Savannah's kidnapping. That would make him forty-two or older now."

Bree spun the laptop back around. She tapped a few more keys and leaned back with a satisfied air. "We're down to eight hundred and sixty-seven."

"It will take me weeks to check them all to see if one might be the Gator Pope we're looking for."

"That's what I figured. Maybe this will help." Bree hit

return with a flourish. I stepped behind her to peer over her shoulder.

"You found five guys named Gator Pope?" I looked at her in surprise. "That's incredible."

"Basic. While you were meeting with the caseworker I searched all the social networking sites. I got hits in Alabama, South Carolina, Texas, Georgia and Florida."

"Can you tell how old those men are?"

"Give me a minute. While I'm doing that, do you have like, anything to eat? Some potato chips or something?"

Having Bree around was like living with a swarm of locusts. When I returned from the kitchen with two glasses of iced tea and a bowl of pretzels, she was staring at the screen, drumming her fingers lightly over the keyboard.

"Anything?"

"The Alabama guy and the guy from South Carolina are under forty so I guess that rules them out." She stuffed a handful of pretzels into her mouth. "The other three are between fifty-six and seventy-two. I sent the list to your printer. Do you want me to shoot them each a message to see if one of them is our guy?"

"I'd prefer to wait for Lalo to see what he thinks," I replied.

Bree popped another pretzel into her mouth. "Oh, I forgot to mention. Lalo called. The weather is supposed to clear tonight so he should be able to get here sometime tomorrow."

I felt a little hitch in my chest at the thought of seeing Lalo again. Bree reached for a tissue and blew her nose. A loud yowl came from the house. Rascal wanted out.

"There isn't much in the house so after I feed the cat we can go out for pizza."

Bree pinched her nose in an implosive sneeze. "Sounds great. I'm starving."

We were lucky to get a table at Luna. The children's matinee at the theatre across the street had just ended and the restaurant was filled with boisterous kids. The couple at the table next to us had one little girl who I judged to be about three. She turned and gave me a shy smile. I smiled back and wagged my fingers at her. Bree dug into the loaf of warm bread the waiter placed on our table.

"How do you like living on Lalo's boat?" I asked her.

"Anything is better than staying with my mom right now."

"Because of the boyfriend, right?"

"Right from the start I knew Striker was no good. My mother thinks this might be her last chance at true love so she doesn't want to hear what I have to say." Bree stuffed a thick slice of the bread slathered with the restaurant's fiery tapenade into her mouth. She gave a little cough and reached for a glass of water. After she caught her breath she said, "Mom is literally SSINF."

"What does that mean?"

"So stupid it's not funny. She thinks Striker is some kind of genius. A true artist." As she said it, Bree wrote air quotes with her fingers. "I can't even. You know what kind of art he makes? He takes photos of naked girls and prints their image on coffee mugs and stuff. I decided to dipset when he asked if I would model for him."

"I'm sorry, are you speaking English? What's 'dipset'?"

"Leave, get out of there."

"Did you tell your mother what he wanted you to do?"

A shrug. "She wouldn't have believed me."

Our pizza arrived, enough to feed a family of eight. The smell made my mouth water. Bree's eyes lit up.

"So, what's the deal with you?" She asked after swallowing her first bite. "I see you're wearing a wedding ring."

"My husband died from lung cancer."

"Oh hey, I'm sorry. I didn't mean to—"

"That's okay. Tell me, do you smoke?"

Bree shook her head.

"Good. Don't start. I quit the day my husband died. Then a few months later I was back at it, smoking more than ever. I finally kicked the habit for good last year."

"Sorry about your husband."

"It was a long time ago."

We ate in silence for a while, Bree devouring most of the pizza. The family with the little girl got up to leave. The child turned around to look at me and I waved goodbye. She covered her eyes and giggled. It struck me that she was about the same age as Savannah when she was killed. I watched them leave, staring out the window until their car pulled away. Outside the rain finally stopped.

"I need to stretch my legs," I said. "Let's take a walk."

"Sounds great."

We strolled the length of Venice Avenue. I bought us each an ice cream cone which we ate at a sidewalk table. When most of the ice cream was gone, Bree bit the bottom of the cone and slurped what was left. She looked into all the shop windows, ducking into a souvenir store to buy a sweat shirt with "Venice Beach" printed on the front. While there she picked up a leather thong necklace with an inch-long shark's tooth dangling from a silver ring.

"Do you think Lalo will like this?"

I studied the thing with a jaundiced eye. "I'm sure he will."

After paying for her purchases, we left the store and headed back to the car. Though a fresh breeze came from the Gulf, the heat trapped in my Prius was stifling. As soon as I turned the key, the air conditioner blasted cold air.

"I'm sure you've seen your share of sunsets over the water," I said. "But the view from the South Jetty is something special, especially after the rain. If we head there now, we'll arrive in time to catch it."

Years ago, the Army Corps of Engineers built two jetties to keep the boat pass between Casey Key and Venice open. Bree and I joined the crowd waiting for the sun to go down. The storm clouds move out to sea as the blurred edges of the sun, egg-yolk yellow against a purple sky, melted on the horizon. A boat glided by, her sails forming a dark blot against the sky. I thought of my husband, Arnie, knowing he would love this moment. Closing my eyes, I tried to conjure his image. Instead, Lalo's smiling face came to mind. My eyes flew open.

The last rays of the sun painted the sky crimson.

"Red sky at night, sailor's delight." Bree smiled wide enough for me to catch a glimpse of the space between her front teeth. "Lalo will arrive tomorrow for sure."

Chapter 12

Maggie scanned the room, taking in the single bed, the electric stove, the pot-bellied couch shoved against the wall.

"This place smells." she said.

"It's the best I can do right now." Sylvia lit up a cigarette. "There aren't many rooms available on the list of qualified facilities. The agency will pay your rent directly to the landlord. If you stick to the rules, you can stay here indefinitely. Remember, no drugs, alcohol or tobacco are allowed on the premises. You must submit to random drug tests and attend regular Alcoholics Anonymous meetings. If you violate any of these rules you will be evicted."

Maggie hobbled on her crutches into the bathroom. A piece of cardboard covered the jagged shards of glass around the edges of the window.

"Can you get someone to fix that?" Balancing on one crutch she pushed back the shower curtain with the other. Black mold crept up the walls.

"I'll file a report with the manager," Sylvia promised. "Listen, the health care provider will be here the first Monday of every month to administer your medicine. If you miss even one injection you risk getting kicked out of the program. Tomorrow is food bank day so I'll stop by and show you where to get your groceries. Is there anything else you need before I go?"

"Cleaning supplies."

"There may be some here." Sylvia opened the cabinet under the sink. A cockroach ran out and scuttled along the baseboard. Maggie watched as the bug escaped through a crack in the wall. The cabinet was empty.

"We'll stop at Walmart on the way to the food bank." Sylvia flicked ash from her cigarette into the sink. "Put bug spray on your list."

After Sylvia left, Maggie laid down on the lumpy mattress and closed her eyes. Her thoughts turned—not for the first time—to Sam. She wondered if she would ever see him again. Her greater risk was Gator. There was no telling what he would do next. Thoughts of Gator brought her full circle to the child. The cop said her name was Savannah. A tear escaped from the corner of her eye and slid down her cheek.

Someone knocked on the door. Getting up, she hobbled across the room to see who it was.

Detective Sanchez's face broke into a broad smile. "You should check and see who it is before opening the door in this neighborhood."

"What are you doing here?"

If he intended to arrest her, now was the time. Instead, he pushed past her, parking the shopping cart in the middle of the room. A blue bundle she recognized as Gator's rolled-up tent was tucked under the detective's arm.

"I came to return your stuff."

"I warned you, Detective. If anything is missing, I'll report you."

"Call me Lalo." He set the tent down on the floor. "You'll find everything exactly as you left it. How's the ankle?"

"Better, thanks." Maggie stared at the detective. Though she was grateful to have her cart back, Lalo's presence made her uncomfortable. As she was about to ask him to leave, her stomach made a loud rumbling sound.

A look of concern crossed Lalo's face. "I was on my way to the Salty Dog for a burger and fries. Want to join me? My treat."

Maggie thought of the food Sylvia left for her supper. The lousy sandwich and carton of milk couldn't compete with the hot meal Lalo offered. She remembered an afternoon long ago when her father brought her to the Salty Dog for lunch. On that day Maggie delighted in watching the boats make their way from Sarasota Bay out to the Gulf of Mexico.

"If you're trying to get information from me about the man who took that little girl, I told you I don't know anything about him."

Lalo held up his hands in surrender. "Just lunch."

"Okay, then." Maggie plucked her woolen cap from the kitchen counter and pulled it down over her ears.

Lalo gave her a quizzical look, peering at her from under his thick eyebrows. "It's ninety degrees in the shade out there."

Maggie ignored him.

He tilted his head. "Have you been following the news about Savannah?"

During her time in the hospital, it was impossible to avoid television coverage about the child's disappearance. Savannah was the top story on every news channel across the state. Her mother and father made a heart-wrenching plea for the safe return of their little girl. The nurses and orderlies shared theories about where she was. Someone had leaked information to the press about a ransom demand. The authorities would neither confirm nor deny.

"I only watched my soaps in the hospital."

"Whoever took her sent us a ransom note demanding fifty grand for her return."

"I really don't want to talk about that. You said this was just lunch."

Maggie pulled the apartment door closed behind her.

"Fair enough. I suggest you lock up. I told you, this is a rough neighborhood."

She glanced at the surrounding area. The so-called apartment looked like it was once a run-down motel. The flat-roofed building was in a sorry state. Trash littered the parking lot. In place of curtains, some people had tacked sheets against their windows. Across the street, a group of teenagers slouched against a boarded-up building bearing a faded sign for the bar it once housed.

"They never gave me a key. Even if they did, the bathroom window is made of cardboard so anyone could climb right in."

"Let's see what we can do about that."

Lalo headed for the end unit where a MANAGER sign hung on the door. By the time Maggie caught up, the man in charge was standing in the open doorway, rubbing his bald head. Over his shoulder Maggie saw a half-dressed teenager scratching the crook of her arm. A smokey haze hung in the air.

"We don't issue keys to residents." The manager yawned. "They lose them."

"Then how do you expect Mrs. Blue to lock her door?"

"Sorry, fella. Those are the rules. If she don't like it, she can leave. Plenty more waiting for her bed."

"Her bathroom window is broken."

"Tell her caseworker to file a report."

Lalo sniffed the air, pulled out his badge and slammed

it against the startled manager's chest. "I have reason to believe there may be illegal drug use going on here. My guess is you don't want me coming into your place to see if I'm right. Mrs. Blue and I are going out for a bite to eat. Have her key ready when we get back. And I want to see that window fixed by this time tomorrow or I'll be all over you like the stink that's coming out of your apartment."

The manager blinked rapidly, his head bobbing in agreement. Lalo put his hand in the small of Maggie's back and guided her to where he left his truck parked in front of her apartment.

"I don't believe he's going to fix the window."

Lalo shrugged. "Call me if he doesn't."

Maggie reached up to touch her cap. "I don't have a phone."

Lalo reached into his breast pocket and took out a dog-eared card. "You can call me collect from the gas station across the street."

She ignored the card in his outstretched hand.

He tucked it in the pocket of her dress. "Take it. For when you're ready to give me the name of that guy who took Savannah."

Maggie spun around on her crutches and started hobbling back toward her apartment.

Lalo grabbed her arm and came around to face her. "Listen Mags. It's been almost two weeks. You, of all people know the hell Savannah's mother is going through."

Maggie wrenched her arm from his grasp and tried to hit his leg with one of the crutches. "You don't know me." She made her way back to the apartment, slamming the door behind her. Praying Lalo would not barge in, she lay on the bed and faced the wall. Tears of anger and regret ran down her cheeks as she prayed for him to go away. The engine of his truck roared to life. Slowly, her heartbeat returned to normal.

Her stomach rumbled.

Chapter 13

No matter what Geri thought, Lalo and I were not romantically involved. As a matter of fact, Lalo and I were so incompatible, so totally opposite in nature that I wondered how I put up with him at all. Now that I faced working with him again, I remembered the primary emotion that Lalo stirred in me. Frustration.

After Bree left to pick Lalo up from the marina, I buzzed through the house with the vacuum cleaner and polished all the glass tables. I then ran out to pick up rib eye steaks and corn on the cob for dinner. As an afterthought I threw half a dozen apples into the cart thinking a cobbler would go well for dessert.

The cat greeted me at the door, rubbing against my leg, nearly tripping me as I lugged grocery bags into the kitchen.

I felt a little guilty, ignoring Rascal for the past few days. Because of Bree's allergies I was forced to keep the cat isolated. Not that it seemed to do much good. Even with Rascal locked in my bedroom, Bree sneezed incessantly. I figured the three of us would have to eat dinner on the lanai.

I rushed around, popped the cobbler in the oven, husked the corn and tenderized the meat. By seven thirty, with the sun hanging low in the sky and the cobbler cooling on the counter, I still hadn't heard from Lalo. When the phone finally rang, I ran to pick up. Geri Garibaldi's name flashed on the screen.

"I've got that copy of Savannah Troy's murder book you asked for. Why don't you swing by and pick it up?"

"It's nearly eight o'clock."

"These days I can get more work done after hours. I'm on a particularly ugly case and the press has been all over me like a school of friggin' barracudas. The powers-that-be want me to make nice with the news crews so I spend half the day behind a podium giving updates to the leeches. I was thinking you and I could grab a bite to eat and go over that murder book together."

"I'm expecting Lalo and Bree for dinner any minute now."

"Bree? What's she doing in town? I thought she lived with her dead-beat mother in Georgia."

"Long story. The condensed version is that Bree moved onto the boat with Lalo for the summer. He wanted to bring the *Chilanga* back here so she drove up in his truck. She left a while ago to pick him up from the marina. I'm expecting them any minute now."

"I always liked that kid. Her mother is a piece of work but Bree is special. How is she doing?"

"Hard to say. Half the time I need a translator to figure out what she's talking about."

"What color is her hair?"

"Blue."

"Huh. It was pink the last time I saw her. She was just a skinny little thing back then."

"Still skinny, but that girl can eat up a storm."

I heard Geri chuckle on the other end of the phone. "Well, stop by my office tomorrow then. And tell Bree I said hello."

At eight thirty I started to worry. Picking up the phone I called Lalo to see what was keeping them.

"Problem? Nope, everything's good. Why?"

"I expected you for dinner hours ago."

"We already ate."

"What?"

"My port engine blew black smoke all the way up from Cape Coral so I decided to change the fuel filter. Bree ordered a pizza."

I closed my eyes and counted to ten.

"You could have called," I snapped.

In the old days I would have slammed down the receiver. As it was I had to settle for throwing my cellphone on the couch. It bounced, landing with a soft thud on the carpet. When Lalo's caller ID lit up the screen, I let the phone vibrate until he gave up.

Geri's office was located in the Sarasota County Justice Center. In winter when the population spikes in Florida, parking is a nightmare. But this was mid-August, long before the snowbirds arrived in their out-of-state cars for the winter. I found a great spot for my Prius right in front of the building.

Having been there before, I knew the routine. After passing through security, I headed for the bank of elevators and punched the button for Geri's floor. The sign on the door read, "County Investigative Bureau." I found Geri sitting in a cubicle that served as her office. When I approached she looked up, acknowledging me with a half-smile. Sticking a pencil behind her ear she grabbed a three-ring binder from her desk and pushed back her chair. She gestured for me to follow her down the carpeted hall to a small conference room with a window overlooking the street below. I settled into a seat with my back to the wall. The room filled with the smell of Geri's perfume when she closed the door. She didn't waste any time on small talk.

"Thanks for jumping right on this thing. What do you think so far? Did we screw this one up or not?"

"I don't know yet." I glanced at the thin binder she set on the table.

"I was sorta hoping you could tell me I had nothing to worry about."

"I'm just getting started. The priest didn't have any-thing new to say. And Maggie's caseworker wasn't much help either. She said we shouldn't consider Maggie a reliable witness. Apparently, everything depends on her state of mind when she died." I pointed at the binder. "Is that all you've got? It seems to me the records for a murder investigation would be much more substantial."

Geri shrugged. "Lalo was a helluva a detective but paperwork wasn't his strong suit. During the investigation, I tried to document his interviews after the fact but running af-ter him was like pinning jelly to the wall." She tapped the blue cover with an acrylic nail. "One thing's for sure, *my* records are all here. Interview summaries, crime scene reports, photos, whatever. I don't have lab results, autopsy reports, and all the other stuff that was handled outside this office. Those things will be in the archives. You'll have to find another way to get your hands on them. I can't risk raising eyebrows around here by pushing too hard. Not yet anyway. As for the FBI files . . . good luck getting your hands on those."

At the mention of the FBI I did a double take. "What did the FBI have to do with this?"

Geri removed the pencil from behind her ear and tapped the table with the eraser end. "As soon as the ransom note showed up in the mail—before the case turned into a murder investigation—the Sheriff decided to call in the FBI. The feds assigned Steve Prane to take the lead. Something about Steve rubbed Lalo the wrong way. One thing you probably already know about Lalo—he doesn't play well with others. He probably still believes we didn't need outside help but the absolute truth is, we wouldn't have nailed Cousins without Steve."

I was about to ask her more about the FBI's involvement when the door to the conference room swung open. A breath of fresh air rushed in. Standing before me was a young man wearing a polo shirt with the Sheriff's office logo embroidered on the breast pocket. Geri stopped tapping the table, looked up at him and scowled.

"What do you want?"

"The Captain wants to see a copy of today's press release."

"Can't you see I'm in the middle of something here? I'll send it up later."

The scowl remained on her face even after he backed away and closed the door. "Sorry about that."

"Did that have something to do with the case you mentioned earlier?"

Geri nodded. "Last month some guy accidentally killed his son at a shooting range on Bee Ridge. Terrible thing, really terrible. Bad enough we've got people killing each other on purpose but when something like this happens . . ." She shook her head.

"I read about it in the paper."

"You know, some days I really hate this job." She closed her eyes and rubbed a hand over her forehead. "Where were we?"

"The FBI."

"Right. Listen, I need to get back to work." She slid the binder across the table. "This will keep you busy for a while. Call me if you learn anything new."

As I stood to leave, Geri placed her hand on my arm. "I almost forgot to ask. What does Lalo have to say about all this?"

"I don't know. He was a no-show last night."

A sly grin crossed her face. "I'll bet next month's paycheck he didn't bother to call."

My expression must have said it all.

Geri barked a laugh. "Some things never change. Listen, I don't care how you do it, get that man on board with this investigation."

"He's impossible."

Geri nodded. "True, but I'm telling you, we need his help. Read his interview reports and you'll see why."

"What are you talking about?"

"Before Cousins was a suspect, Lalo was hot on the trail of someone named Gator."

"Gator Pope?"

Geri shrugged. "I don't think he ever caught a last name but how many Gators do *you* know? Like I said, Lalo never documented half of what he did. But one thing's for sure, he kept going down that road long after Prane told him to quit. There wasn't a lot of love lost between those two."

"Do you think Lalo agreed to help us because he has something to prove to this FBI agent?"

"That's a distinct possibility. But if that's what's going on in Lalo's head, then tell him to get over his issues with Steve Prane. Tell him whatever the hell you want. Just bring him on board."

Chapter 14

Maggie, 1994

Maggie's tongue was dry as dust. Sitting up in bed, a wave of nausea washed over her. She crossed the room for a glass of water, grabbing the sink to stop everything from spinning.

The nurse who came to her apartment the previous day insisted she was due for her monthly Haldol injection. It seemed to Maggie only two weeks had passed since her last shot but who was she to question what day it was. Most days she spent watching television, too tired to even think about cooking a meal. Not that she was hungry. Thanks to the food bank she had stocked up on her favorites, peanut butter crackers and Cheez Whiz. She spooned the Cheez Whiz right out of the jar and chased the crackers down with tap water. She figured the best thing about being in Sylvia's program—aside from having a solid roof over her head—was having a full belly.

In her waking hours she thought about Gator. Based on what Detective Sanchez told her, Savannah's abductor had disappeared into thin air. Maggie could only speculate. It was unlikely that he was still hiding out near Caspersen Beach. If everything went according to Gator's plan—he was always going on about his plan—he had stolen a boat and was biding his time in the Gulf of Mexico. He said it would take five days, max but that day had come and gone. When the time did come, Maggie hoped Gator would grab the money and run, forgetting all about her. By now he probably realized she hadn't spoken to the police. And she had every intention of keeping it that way.

Earlier that day she plucked a copy of the *Herald Tribune* from the trash can outside the manager's office. During the first week she was out of the hospital, the front page carried stories about the little girl and her family. With every passing day, the articles became shorter and shorter, the last blurb relegated to the back page. Today she did not find mention of Savannah Troy anywhere.

Maggie managed to swallow a few mouthfuls of water and hobble back to bed. She could not understand why she was so tired. An irresistible urge to close her eyes overwhelmed her. It seemed only moments later when she rose to consciousness. Someone was knocking on her door.

The only people who ever came to see her were Sylvia and the visiting nurse. As she was expecting neither, she wondered who it could be. She rose from the bed to open the door. Lalo Sanchez stood before her clutching a stack of mail in one hand and a brown paper bag in the other.

"I told you to look out to see who it was before opening the door. Did the manager give you a key?"

Maggie nodded. "He fixed the bathroom window too."

"Good. Call me if he gives you any more trouble. Or if you need anything else for that matter." He cast a glance over her shoulder, his eyes coming back to rest on her face. She felt uncomfortable under his intensive stare.

"What are you doing here, Lalo?"

"Helen asked me to deliver your mail."

A guarded look darkened Maggie's face. "When did you see my mother?"

"I dropped in this morning. She's concerned about you."

A scornful laugh erupted from Maggie's lips. "I don't believe that for a minute. In fact, Helen prefers to pretend I never existed."

A glimmer of a smile appeared in Lalo's eyes. He held up the brown bag. "She mentioned you like chili. Extra spicy."

Grabbing the bag, Maggie swiveled on her crutches and shoved the food into the overflowing trash can under the sink. She turned back to face him.

"I hate chili."

The smile spread to Lalo's mouth.

Maggie gave him a poisonous stare. "Does Helen know where I am?"

"'Course she does. Your caseworker told her."

"Sylvia had no right to do that."

"Helen is your legal guardian, remember?"

Maggie snatched the stack of envelopes from his hand and threw it on the table.

"She also asked me to give you this." Lalo handed her a framed photo.

Maggie stared at Poppy's face, her eyes filling with tears as she pressed the image to her heart. "My little girl."

"She's a cute kid. When I told her I was coming to see her mama she insisted on drawing a picture for you." He pulled a folded paper from his back pocket. "Not exactly a Rembrandt but I figured you'd want to have it."

Fighting the tight feeling clutching her heart, Maggie studied her daughter's preschool artwork.

She choked back a sob. "Poppy was only two when they took her from me."

The silence stretched between them for a few moments before she trusted her voice not to break. "Thanks for stopping by but I'd like you to leave now."

"I was hoping you would tell me where to find Gator."

Maggie clenched her teeth, focusing on a spider crawling up the wall. "Who told you his name?"

"Your mother. She said you brought him to her house."

"That was years ago. I haven't seen him since."

"Funny, she said the two of you showed up last month asking for money. Your lies are catching up with you, Mags. That was Gator with you on the beach, wasn't it? For God's sake, tell me where I can find him."

"I don't know!"

"What's his real name?"

"He never said."

"He's demanding fifty thousand dollars in exchange for Savannah's safe return. The FBI is now involved and trust me, those guys don't play nice. You're better off telling me what you know before they catch up with you."

A high-pitched ringing pierced Maggie's ears. She bit her lower lip, panic rising in her chest. She needed to warn Gator that the FBI was onto him. It was a long shot but maybe his sister Lizzy would know how to reach him.

"I'm sorry." She forced a mask of concern on her face. "I really am. But I can't help you."

Maggie closed the door and twisted the deadbolt with a satisfying click. Standing next to the window with her back pressed against the wall, she waited until she heard Lalo's truck leave the parking lot. Though her stomach churned with nerves, she retrieved the bag of chili from the trash can. Spicy and hot, exactly the way she liked it. She grabbed a spoon and dug in. Fifteen minutes later she bent over the cracked toilet and brought it all back up.

That afternoon, Maggie wrote the letter to Gator's sister. Peering out the window to make sure no one was looking, she pulled on her cap and hobbled down to the manager's office. Hands shaking, she dropped the letter in the outgoing mail slot.

Four days later, Sylvia took her to the hospital where they declared her ankle healed. As soon as Sylvia dropped her back at the apartment she walked to the liquor store and bought a liter of vodka. By the next day the bottle was empty. That was when she read the news. The ransom was paid, but the authorities had not recovered the child. There was no sign of the kidnapper either. An official spokesman from the Sheriff's Office did his best to spin the story, saying a joint task force was working 24/7 to get Savannah back. The FBI was now in charge of the investigation.

Maggie could read between the lines. Gator grabbed the money and was on his way to some island in the Caribbean. To celebrate she went back to the liquor store, bought another bottle and drank herself into a stupor.

She woke up on her apartment floor, her teeth chattering uncontrollably. Lalo sat by her side. She reached out and touched him to make sure he was real. When her calf muscle spasmed, she cried out in pain. Stomach wrenching, she vomited all over the detective's white shirt.

"Maggie? Mags, do you hear me?"

His question cut through the voices in her head. She moaned in response.

"Oh Maggie, what have you done?" Lalo's face hovered over hers, his mustache turned down in disappointment.

"Leave me alone."

"Hang in there, Mags. The EMTs are on their way."

She closed her eyes as Lalo stroked her forehead, just like her father used to when she was a child.

"We're going to get you out of here."

She opened her eyes and shook her head. "Where's my hat?"

"I've got it right here." Lalo slipped the wool cap on her head. "Anything else you want to bring with you?"

She pointed a trembling finger at the photo of Poppy on her nightstand. With a nod, Lalo picked up the frame and put it into her outstretched hand.

Then everything went black.

Chapter 15

Cate, 2017

I thumbed through Geri's murder book, figuring it would be best to get an overall feel of the investigation before reading each report in detail. When I reached the end, I went to the kitchen to refill my coffee mug. Before I made it back to the office, the phone rang.

"Hi Ben, I was just thinking about you. You'll never guess what I've got sitting on my desk right now. A copy of Detective Garibaldi's—"

I heard the strain in his voice. "Sorry to cut you short, Aunt Cate. I don't have a lot of time. I'm calling for a favor."

"Anything, you know that. What's wrong?"

"I want you to come with me to New Hampshire to help my mother."

"I thought she only had a bad cold."

"That's what my father said." Ben took a deep breath. "Yesterday he found her passed out on the bathroom floor. When the EMTs arrived, they took one look at the needle in her arm and gave her something to get her breathing again."

"What needle?"

"She was shooting heroin."

My brain was slow to process his words. "That's not possible. Nancy isn't a drug addict."

"She did a pretty good job of hiding it from all of us. Dad insists he can handle the situation by himself but I think he's in over his head. Mom needs professional help. Listen, I've booked us seats on a flight out of Gainesville to Hartford."

"Give me a few hours to get to the airport. I'll meet you there."

The moment I stepped out of the searing heat into the air-conditioned airport, I spotted Ben towering above the crowd. My nephew's hair, chestnut brown like his mother's, fell over his eyes. He sported a scruffy day-old beard. Ben pulled his messenger bag's strap over his head and bent down to crush me in an embrace.

"Thanks for coming."

I reached up and brushed his bangs to one side. "You knew I would."

"I can't believe I didn't see this happening."

"When did it start?"

"I'm not sure. Maybe as far back as three years ago after her car accident. Dad admits knowing she kept taking the pain pills long after she should have stopped, but he says he doesn't know when she turned to heroin."

I sat silent, thinking back to the day of Nancy's accident. Arnie was home in bed, struggling to breath. As the hours dragged by he grew increasingly weaker. When I picked up the phone to call for an ambulance, Arnie stopped me, insisting he wanted to die in his own bed. I gazed outside, my vision blurred by a winter fog and the tears I fought to hide.

Unable to bear the vigil alone, I called Nancy. We took turns sitting by Arnie's side as he drifted in and out of consciousness. I fed him ice chips, held his hand, and offered what little comfort I could. His breathing became intermittent. Before long he lay still, mercifully at peace.

The mist turned to sleet, covering the roads with black

ice. I asked Nancy to stay the night. She refused, saying her husband would want her home. At the bottom of our street her car spun out of control, colliding with a pickup truck that came from the opposite direction. At first it seemed she escaped with only a broken wrist. Her back and neck problems surfaced later, the pain growing intolerable with time.

I looked at Ben. "You're saying she became addicted to the pain medicine?"

He nodded. From the look on his face I could tell he was annoyed. "I can't believe Dad didn't know."

Even if Nancy shot heroin right in front of her husband, he might not have noticed. I always felt my sister could do better than Tim. His favorite pastimes were drinking with his friends and stomping through the woods with a hunting rifle slung across his arm. Yet Nancy seemed content in her marriage. Being Ben's mother was enough to make her happy.

I reached over to pat Ben's arm. "Don't blame your father. This isn't his fault. This isn't anyone's fault. The important thing now is to get your mother the help she needs."

"That's easier said than done. Mom is in a state of denial. We went around and around until finally she agreed to check into the rehab center in Gainesville. She's telling all her friends that she's coming here for a visit." Ben threw me a glance. "By the way, she doesn't know you are coming with me today."

"What?"

"She made me swear that I wouldn't tell you what was going on. But I figured you have a right to know. And if she tries to back out of going into rehab, you can help me convince her."

We sat next to each other on the plane, avoiding the subject of my sister by chatting about Savannah Troy's murder.

After we landed, Ben was quiet during the two-hour drive from Hartford to Keene. I gazed out the window, lost in my own thoughts. Though the end of August was still weeks away, there were signs that summer was drawing to a close. Amid the dark green foliage, a few sunlit birch leaves turned a dying yellow. As we crested a hill, the town appeared before me in the valley below. Everything seemed unchanged. I could see the outline of the old textile mills transformed into shopping malls, shoe factories converted to high tech manufacturing plants, and—a sign of modern influence—big box stores sprouting like mushrooms on the outskirts of town. A single word popped into my mind. *Home.*

We passed the college campus where nearly forty years before Arnie reached under his graduation robes and pulled out the engagement ring that I still wore. At the head of the Square, the white spire of the Congregational church pierced a cloudless sky, the same sky that rained with rice as we left the church on our wedding day.

Ben turned onto Court Street, driving slowly by my old law office. I glanced down a side street to see the leaky garage apartment where Arnie and I first lived. We started out poor but happy, burning tanks of heating oil we could barely afford in a futile attempt to keep the pipes from freezing. A few blocks down, we passed the Victorian house where Nancy and I sat vigil by Arnie's side.

My nephew's voice broke into my ruminations. "Aunt Cate? Don't be upset if Mom doesn't seem happy to see you. She's not herself right now."

I gave Ben a weak smile as he pulled up in front of Nancy's little Cape Cod.

As soon as she saw us, my sister ran out to give Ben a big hug. She then turned to look at me, her face flushed red.

"Isn't it just like Benny to surprise me by bringing you for a visit. How long will you be staying?"

Ben and I exchanged glances. "Aunt Cate knows, Mom."

Nancy brushed off his comment with a wave of her hand. "Oh, that little fall I took? I'm fine now. But I've had second thoughts about coming to Florida. You know how your father is. He can't handle being alone. Maybe we'll come for a visit after the snow starts to fly."

I took my sister's hands in mine. "Stop pretending, Nancy. Ben and I came to take you to the rehab center in Gainesville."

Nancy's eyes, thin bands of brown encircling dilated pupils, welled up with tears. "I can't."

Drawing her close, I wrapped my arms around her trembling body. "Yes, you can. I'll be there for you, the same as you were for me when I needed you most."

Chapter 16

Cate, 2017

Despite the warm welcome she received from the staff at the rehab center, Nancy trembled like a frightened puppy when I hugged her goodbye. I promised to visit often but the admitting nurse shook her head.

"Nancy isn't allowed to have any visitors for the first two weeks. After that, you can come to see her between noon to three on Sundays. No exceptions."

I felt Nancy stiffen under my embrace. Rubbing her arm, I spoke to her in soothing tones. "I'll call you as soon as I get home."

The nurse thrust a sheet of paper at me. "Sorry, ma'am. No phone calls, no emails, no video calls. In case of emergency, you may contact the office."

I glanced down the list of items I could and could not bring on visitation day. Photos were allowed, paperback books, writing paper and pens. No food or beverage of any kind. Electronic devices including phones, tablets or computers were strictly forbidden. All items were subjected to inspection prior to the patients receiving them.

Feigning a smile I didn't feel, I turned to Nancy. "Look at it this way. Over the next few months we'll see each other more than we did in the last year."

"Months?" Nancy turned to Ben. "I only agreed to stay here for a few weeks."

Ben gently pried me away and kissed his mother's cheek. "Let's see how it goes, Mom."

As the nurse led her away, the sound of Nancy's sobs wrenched my heart.

The visit left me emotionally drained. After I returned home, to keep my mind off my sister's problems I pulled out Geri's murder book. Starting at the beginning, I absorbed the details of the investigation as it unfolded. Following a close look at the transcript of the initial 911 call, I read Geri's first report. Within minutes of arriving at the crime scene, Detective Garibaldi began interviewing potential witnesses.

Melanie Troy claimed to have put her older daughter, Carrie Ann in charge of watching Savannah while she bought the girls some ice cream. She denied sending the stranger to ask Carrie Ann for help. When Carrie Ann showed up in the restaurant, panic set in and Melanie ran to the beach only to discover Savannah was gone. I set that first interview summary aside and moved on to the next report.

After speaking with Melanie, Geri sat down with Savannah's sister, Carrie Ann. At the top of page, Geri noted the time, date, location and Carrie Ann's full name. In her neat penmanship, she jotted a comment in the margin. "Kid is scared to death. Need to get a child specialist involved." After reading the note, I turned my attention to the body of the report.

Witness states suspect was tall, Caucasian male, long, brown hair tied in a ponytail. Suspect wearing shorts, pale green T-shirt with tear at the collar, and flip flops. When asked if she could remember any identifying marks, witness states the suspect had a tattoo of a

bumble bee on his right arm. (Note: witness
initially appeared undecided about which arm
but when asked to role play, she pointed to my
right.)

The next few interview summaries were also written
by Geri. Unfortunately, there were only a few people on the
beach when Savannah was snatched, none of whom noticed
anything out of the ordinary. At the time a handful of others
were eating on the deck overlooking the pier. One lady remembered seeing the man who picked up the little girl but she
said the child appeared to be sleeping and she thought he was
her father. When questioned further, the lady admitted that
she couldn't see very well as the sun was in her eyes. Geri had
very little to show for her effort. After several hours all she
had was a sketchy description of the perpetrator provided by
ten-year-old Carrie Ann Troy.

An impression of the hours following Savannah's abduction took shape in my mind. While Geri interviewed witnesses, Lalo and a host of law enforcement officers searched
for the little girl in the surrounding area. Going on a hunch,
Lalo headed to a homeless camp north of the pier.

His report of what followed was included in Geri's
binder. As I struggled to decipher his handwriting, I realized
that within a few hours of Savannah's abduction Lalo met
Margaret Blue. Though some words of his report were difficult
to understand, the message that Lalo felt Maggie knew something about the man who snatched Savannah came through
loud and clear. Skipping ahead I saw Geri's binder included
several other summaries written by Lalo. Most expressed frustration that Maggie continued to withhold potentially valuable
information. When my doorbell rang, I put down a report

summarizing Lalo's interview with Maggie's mother and went to see who was at the door.

Lalo's year in the Keys had done little to change him. New strands of silver ran through his coarse, black hair and it seemed he was a bit heavier than the last time I saw him but the mischievous glint in his eye and wide grin were exactly as I remembered. *Salty* is the word that jumped to my mind as I stared at him. He wore a broad brimmed hat populated with fishing lures and an untucked Hawaiian shirt over a pair of cargo shorts. Leaning in, he planted a kiss on my cheek. Speechless, I reached up to touch where his new beard scratched against my skin.

Maya, Lalo's loyal Rottweiler stood by his side. Her stubby tail beat a happy rhythm when she saw me. She leaped up, her paws braced against my shoulders as she washed my face with her tongue. I couldn't stop smiling as I pushed the dog back on all fours and wiped my cheek with the back of my hand.

Lalo studied me from a distance. "You look great."

"You should have called the other night. I had to throw out the food I prepared."

"This is for you." Lalo held up a dead fish by the tail.

"Do you honestly expect all is forgiven because you showed up here with something you hauled out of the Gulf?"

"It's a red snapper."

"Hardly what I'd call an apology."

"You like snapper."

"That's not the point. Where's Bree?"

"She's on the boat, surfing the Internet." He waved the fish in the air. "Are we going to eat this or not?"

I eyed the snapper, turned on my heel and lead the way into the kitchen. Lalo slapped the fish down on my granite counter and asked where I kept the corn starch. When I pointed to an upper cabinet, he put his hand against my back and gently moved me out of the way. While he prepared the fish, I uncorked a bottle of Chablis. Together we sipped wine while the snapper sizzled in butter.

"Haven't we done this before?" Lalo said.

Though I didn't reply, I remembered that night with Lalo all too well. How at the end of the evening I closed my eyes, waiting for his kiss. And the disappointment I felt when it never came. My face flushed with the memory.

Lalo forked the tender pieces of fish onto a serving plate. I looked down, amazed to see Rascal rubbing against Lalo's leg. Maya stood in the doorway, a thin line of drool hanging from her mouth.

"Rascal isn't usually this friendly."

"He must smell the fish."

Plucking a scrap from the plate, Lalo threw a morsel to Maya who caught it in mid-air. He then bent down and set some in front of Rascal. The cat sniffed in distain and looked up at Lalo with his green eyes.

I picked up the plates. "Let's eat before you give it all away."

The fish was delicious. Though Lalo kept reaching across the table to top up my wine glass, I only took small sips. At the end of the meal I zapped the two-day-old apple cobbler in the microwave and served it with ice cream for dessert. As Lalo licked his spoon clean, I went back into the kitchen to brew a pot of coffee. I caught a whiff of aftershave and turned to find him standing close behind me.

"You haven't finished your wine."

I took the glass of wine he offered and set it on the counter. "We can drink our coffee on the lanai."

I grabbed the pot. A late summer rain hit the flat roof with a steady drumming sound. Lalo flipped on the outside lights. The water in the pool glowed Caribbean blue.

I blew across the surface of my mug, trying to read the expression on his face. "Can we discuss the case now?"

One side of his mustache curled up in a half-smile. "You haven't changed. Still all business."

"I read in the murder book that you continued to meet with Maggie Blue even after you were told to drop that line of investigation."

Lalo leaned back in his chair and stretched out his long legs. "I did, yeah."

"You believed Maggie knew Savannah's abductor but no one would listen to you."

"That's one of the reasons I decided to come back."

I looked up, startled by his comment. "Was there some other reason?"

"Bree's classes start again in a few weeks. I need to get her back to Gainesville."

I peered at him over the rim of my coffee mug.

His bushy, black eyebrows rose up on his forehead. "Why else should I have come back?"

"I don't know . . . maybe you grew tired of fishing in the Keys?"

His explosive laugh cleared the air. "You got me there. But I'll be honest. There is another reason I came back. I missed working with you."

We sat in silence. I watched the rain drops create overlapping circles on the surface of the pool. Rascal curled up in Lalo's lap. Maya lay at my feet, snoring. I suppose if someone saw us from a distance we would look like an old married couple. In some ways that's exactly what it felt like.

Lalo yawned and stretched his legs. "I guess I should be getting back to the boat. Bree will start to get ideas about us if I stay too late. By the way, she likes you."

"I like her too. She's got her head screwed on straight."

Lalo chuckled. "She sure does."

"You were good to let her stay with you this summer. The situation with her mother's boyfriend sounded dangerous."

There was something about the controlled way Lalo lifted his head. He drew in a long, slow breath and turned to stare at the lighted pool. His expression grew dark, a storm cloud on the horizon. "What are you talking about?"

I shifted uneasily in my seat. "You should ask Bree."

Lalo tipped back his mug, draining the coffee. "Thanks for tonight. We'll start work tomorrow."

He raised my hand to his lips. I felt the bristle of his mustache as he planted a soft kiss on my palm. We stood facing each other until I awkwardly pulled away. With a nod he turned and whistled. Maya followed him out the door.

Chapter 17

Cate, 2017

The next morning Lalo appeared in my doorway freshly shaved, decked out in clean cargo shorts and a bright yellow shirt with a fish logo on the pocket. His Tampa Rays baseball cap completed the outfit. Maya sat by his side, lips curled up in a smile, her tongue lolling out the side of her mouth. I caught a glimpse of Bree standing behind him, her head bent to the phone cupped between her hands as her thumbs flew over the glass.

"Have you had breakfast?" I asked.

Bree piped up without missing a beat. "What have you got?"

"Bacon and eggs."

Lalo turned to his granddaughter, his eyebrows drawn together. "We ate on the boat."

"That was like an hour ago." Bree stepped around him, her focus still fixed on the phone as she came inside.

Lalo removed his cap and smoothed his coarse, black hair with a swipe of his hand. Maya brushed past and followed Bree into the kitchen.

"I don't know where she puts all that food," Lalo muttered under his breath.

Stepping aside, I waved him in. "I just put on a fresh pot of coffee. We can talk about the investigation while Bree eats."

When we entered the kitchen, I saw Bree was still working on her phone. "Hey guys, look at this."

I peered over her shoulder to see a bewhiskered man on the screen. His pale blue eyes stared back at me from under a floppy-brimmed camouflage hat. As Bree scrolled down the page, I caught sight of the tattoo.

"Who is that?"

"Gator Pope from Texas," Bree said. "He just accepted my friend request."

Taking one step back, I bumped into Lalo who was watching his granddaughter page through several photos of Gator Pope on her phone. Most were shots of the blue-eyed man drinking beer with his friends. One particularly offensive image showed him bending over to expose his butt crack.

"He sure looks creepy enough to be a killer," Bree said. "Get a look at that gun."

The sight of him gripping a semi-automatic sent a chill up the back of my neck. "Does this guy know you're looking at his Facebook page?"

"No prob. I created a fake profile. If he takes the time to check, he'll discover I'm a fashion model named Kiki who lives in Nashville. Kiki is into guys who ride Harleys."

I grabbed the phone from Bree's hand. "Let me see that first picture again."

A tattoo of a smiling alligator with pointy teeth stood out clearly against the man's tanned skin.

Lalo peered over my shoulder. "No one could mistake that as a bumble bee."

I turned to him. "Did Maggie ever talk about Gator?"

"Maggie's mother, Helen was the first one to mention his name," Lalo replied. "Maggie brought Gator to her house one day. They left when she threatened to call the police."

"Why would she do that?"

"There was a restraining order to keep Maggie from having contact with her little girl."

"Maggie had a daughter?"

Lalo nodded. "The State took Poppy away after Maggie drove her car into the Gulf of Mexico with the kid strapped next to her in a baby seat. Helen was awarded full custody."

"That explains why Maggie didn't live with her family." Staring at the image on Bree's phone I could feel my pulse kick up a notch. I knew what our next step must be. "It wouldn't hurt to run this photo by Helen to see if he's is Maggie's Gator."

Lalo shrugged. "His body type fits the description. But aside from the tattoo being all wrong, Carrie Ann said the guy who took her sister had brown eyes."

Heat rose to my cheeks. "You're right. I read that in my copy of Geri's murder book." My voice was flat with disappointment. "I guess we can rule out Texas Gator."

Lalo rested a hand on Bree's shoulder. "It might be a good idea to unfriend this guy."

While Bree erased Texas Gator, Lalo studied me with his almond-shaped eyes.

"Let's get started with this investigation. Grab the murder book. We're going to see Helen Blue."

"Can I come too?" Bree asked.

"I want you to stay here with Maya," Lalo replied. "You can make yourself that second breakfast."

I climbed into the passenger side of Lalo's pickup, wrinkling my nose at the cloying smell of dog. The truck was filthy, cluttered with candy wrappers and empty soda cans. As Lalo hit the gas pedal, I reached for my seatbelt.

"I don't get it." I opened the window a crack to let

some fresh air into the cab. "Why did you ask me to bring the murder book?"

Lalo, glanced in the rear view mirror as we sailed through a yellow light. "Our only witness, Carrie Ann Troy worked with a police artist to develop a sketch of the man who abducted her sister. There should be a copy of that sketch in the binder."

"There is. Along with a hand-written one-page report you filed after you showed that sketch to Helen. Although she said it looked something like Gator, she was unable to positively identify him."

He cocked his head to one side in surprise. "I filed a report?"

"One of very few. In most cases Geri wrote up your interviews for you."

"Oh, right. Well, after we brought Cousins in we included his photo in a six-pack and asked Carrie Ann if any of those guys looked like the man who took her sister. She didn't hesitate. Pointed to Cousins immediately. Then later, she picked him out of a lineup, confirming that Cousins was the man who abducted her sister."

"I know all that. What I don't understand is what this has to do with Helen Blue."

"If you compare the original sketch—the one I showed to Helen—you'll see there's a world of difference from that sketch to the photo in the six-pack. I didn't think much of it at the time given the artist was working with a kid who was traumatized. But I realize now I never went back and showed Helen the photo of Cousins."

I fished around in my purse for an alcohol wipe and started to clean the inside of the windshield on my side of the truck. Lalo threw a quick glance in my direction.

"What are you doing?"

I kept wiping. "There are dog nose prints all over the glass. So let me get this straight. You want to show Helen that photo now? Why? She had nothing to do with Cousins."

"Helen is the only person we know who met Gator. If she tells us Cousins doesn't look anything like him—"

"Oh, now I get it." I stuck the spent wipe in my pocket and fished around in my purse for another. "If they don't look alike then it is unlikely Carrie Ann Troy got the two of them confused."

"Exactly." He gave me an approving smile.

"On the other hand, if Gator bore a resemblance to Randy Cousins, then Carrie Ann could have mistaken one for the other. In legal terms that's called witness misidentification. It can be a basis for wrongful conviction."

The excitement must have shown on my face.

"Don't get your hopes up yet," Lalo said. "If that's where this investigation takes us, it will all boil down to who the court believes; a ten-year-old kid who identified Cousins as the man who snatched her sister or Maggie Blue, a dying homeless woman suffering from schizophrenia. You get one guess who they'll choose."

Lalo pulled up in front of a cement block house on a quiet street in a mature neighborhood of South Venice. After he cut the engine, moist, suffocating air filled the truck within minutes. I followed Lalo's gaze to the overflowing recycle bins sitting at the curb.

"Looks like she's home." He reached back to retrieve the murder book from the back seat. As we stepped out of the truck he handed it to me. "Let me do the talking while we're in there."

He knocked on the front door. A pretty young girl with light brown hair and wearing a cropped T-shirt answered the door.

"Is Helen home?" Lalo asked.

"Who are you?"

"Detective Sanchez."

"She's not feeling well right now. Is there something I can do for you, Detective?"

"You must be Poppy. Tell your grandmother I've come to see her. She'll remember me."

Poppy's eyes darted from Lalo to me and back again.

"May I see some ID please?"

I waited to see what Lalo would do. He calmly reached into his pocket, produced a business card and passed it to her.

"Says here you're a *private* detective."

"I am now. I used to be with the Sheriff's Office."

Poppy tapped the card against her bottom lip. She finally nodded, telling us to wait outside while she told Helen we were there. I shifted my weight from one foot to the other while I listened to the murmur of voices inside. When Poppy returned, she waved us in.

The living room smelled musty. The furniture, upholstered with a faded palm tree print showed signs of wear. An empty glass sat on a coffee table marked with water rings. The face of the woman sitting in the rocking chair was the same pale yellow of the flowers on the peeling wallpaper behind her. Helen was dressed in a high-necked flannel nightgown wearing a shiny blond wig that sat off kilter on her head. Her hands were nothing but skin and bones, her cheeks sunken. A cat sat curled in her lap. Though Helen was only a few years older than I, she looked ancient.

"Nice to see you again, Detective Sanchez." She didn't

get up but offered a skeletal hand in greeting.

Lalo went over to her and took her hand. He gave her one of his most charming smiles. "I'd like you to meet a friend of mine, Cate Stokes. We've come to offer our condolences for your loss."

Helen focused her rheumy eyes on Lalo. "You know as well as I do, Detective. Maggie was lost to me long before she left this earth." After a few beats she turned to me. "You may not understand but I find it hard to grieve for my own child."

Poppy crossed the room and placed a hand on her grandmother's shoulder.

Lalo pulled up a footstool and sat directly in front of Helen. "Maggie lived her life on her own terms."

"Of course. But I don't believe you came by just to offer condolences. Tell me the real reason you're here, Lalo."

"I need your help. I'm looking for Gator Pope."

Poppy cleared her throat. "Who?"

"No one important." Helen waved a dismissive hand in the air. "One of Maggie's boyfriends. Tell me, Detective. What do you want with Gator?"

"He's a person of interest in an investigation I'm conducting."

Helen's eyes opened wide. "That good for nothing bum." She broke into a coughing fit, bringing a ruddy brightness to her cheeks. Poppy patted her on the back until the older woman caught her breath. "What did he do? Rob a bank?"

"This has to do with the Savannah Troy case."

"Savannah?" Helen closed her eyes. I watched the pulse in her temple, wondering if she was drifting off to sleep. When she looked up at me, I saw a clarity that wasn't there before.

"I remember, of course. The Troys went to our church. If I'm not mistaken, Melanie and her daughter, Carrie Ann still live in town. Poor Melanie never got over losing that little girl. To make matters worse. her marriage broke up because of it. But I thought the man who killed Savanna is behind bars."

"That's right," Lalo said. "But some new information has come to our attention and we now believe Gator was involved."

The color drained from Helen's face. Blue spider veins stood out on her translucent skin.

"You're upsetting her." Poppy took a few steps toward Lalo. "I think you should go."

"No!" Helen covered Poppy's hand with her own. "Tell me the truth, Detective. Was my Maggie tangled up in that ugly business too?"

Lalo looked her in the eye. I knew him well enough to see the lie. "I don't believe so."

"I wish I could help you but I have no idea where Gator is. I haven't seen him since that day Maggie brought him here. Let me see . . . that must have been more than twenty years ago. Have you spoken with Sam? Maybe he can tell you where to find Gator."

I perked up at the mention of the new name. "Who is Sam?"

"Another homeless friend of Maggie's. But Sam was nothing like Gator. He was much older for starters. She told me he reminded her of her father. It seemed he was a good influence on Maggie."

"Gan you give us his last name? Or can you tell us where to find him?"

She shook her head. "No idea. You might try checking the shelters but to be honest, your chances of finding Sam are not good. Remember, we're talking about twenty years ago and he was already an old man back then."

I pulled out the photo of Randy Cousins from the blue binder and passed it to Helen. "Do you know this man?"

Helen peered at Cousins' photo for what seemed like a long time. "No, I don't think so. Though this fellow looks quite a lot like Gator. Is he related somehow? A brother perhaps?"

My chest felt tight. I searched for something to say but Lalo beat me to it, taking out the original police sketch.

"You saw this the first time we met. Do you remember?"

Helen sighed, nodding assent. "You asked if that was Gator and I told you it looked something like him but I couldn't say for sure."

"What's different?"

"The eyes. They were half-closed all the time. Gave Gator a mean look. You could see it in the shape of his mouth too."

"Could it be Sam?"

"No. I told you, Sam was much older."

I could see she was tired, worn down by our visit. Nudging Lalo's arm, I suggested it was time to go. Lalo stood, mumbled a word of thanks and kissed Helen on the cheek.

"You've been a great help, Helen. Please call me if anything new comes to mind."

As we made our way to the front of the house, Poppy spun around, blocking the door. An angry look flashed across her face. "What's going on? And don't give me the same crap you gave Helen. Where did this new information about Savannah Troy come from?"

When Lalo didn't volunteer an answer, I spoke up. "Before she died, Maggie told a priest that Gator killed Savannah."

Poppy's eyes opened wide. "You can't believe a word she said. Maggie was a chronic liar not to mention she was a certifiable nut case."

Lalo's voice was uncharacteristically gruff. "What if

she was telling the truth this time? We owe it to Maggie to follow up on her claim."

Red blotches bloomed on Poppy's neck. "I don't owe Maggie a damned thing."

Before either of us could respond, she slammed the door in our faces.

Chapter 18

Maggie, 1994

Voices crept around the edge of her consciousness as Maggie fought her way out of a drugged sleep. A beeping sound broke into the dark dreams, the voices growing louder with every passing moment. She blinked against the white, florescent light, struggling to figure out where she was. Her mother's face loomed inches from her own. Tired of the effort, Maggie closed her eyes and let the voices swirl around her.

"What is taking so long?"

Maggie wondered if she was still dreaming. Or if this was something playing out in her head.

"It takes time to flush the Haldol out of her system, Mrs. Blue."

"I don't understand why the blood levels were so high."

"You'll have to take that up with the doctor."

Everything started coming back to her. The last person Maggie remembered seeing was Lalo. He was looking down at her, stroking her forehead, his face creased in concern. Or was that a dream? Maggie cracked open an eye and her mother came into focus. She wore an expression Maggie knew all too well. Concern tinged with disappointment.

"Hey, baby. How are you feeling?"

"Mama? What are you doing here? Where am I?"

"You're in the hospital." Helen's face twisted into a frown. "How many times have I told you? You can't drink alcohol while you're taking your medicine. If that detective didn't find you when he did, I don't know what would have happened."

Maggie closed her eyes, wishing her mother would go away.

"Don't be too hard on her, Mrs. Blue," the other voice said. "The best thing for your daughter is to arrange a consultation with her caseworker."

"Lot of good that will do," Helen said. "I've had it with those agency people."

Maggie spoke from behind closed eyes. "Give it a rest, Mama. Sylvia has been good to me. She puts a roof over my head and gives me food. That's more than you do."

"Oh baby," Maggie felt the pressure of her mother's hand on her arm. "You know I worry about you every minute of every day. I'm grateful to Sylvia for getting you off the streets, I am. But I wonder . . . is it wise for you to live alone? Maybe a group home would be better, you know, in case something like this happens again. Or in case that Gator shows up and drags you off somewhere."

Maggie opened her eyes to see the deep crease between her mother's brow. The wrinkles on Helen's face and the premature gray in her hair made her look older than her years. Recognizing her concern, Maggie felt a pang of guilt.

"Gator is gone, Mama."

"Well, that's a blessing, I suppose. I didn't want to upset you but that detective, the one who found you yesterday, he came to my house last week asking about him."

"So it wasn't a dream."

"What?"

"Nothing. What did Lalo say?"

"He told me Gator is in some kind of trouble. Didn't I

warn you? Good riddance to yesterday's trash, that's what I say."

Maggie closed her eyes again. An image of Gator sitting on a Caribbean beach and sipping rum popped into her head. In her mind, he turned to her with a wicked grin on his face.

"Maggie? Baby, did you hear me?"

Maggie looked at her mother. "What?"

"I said I've got to pick up Poppy from preschool. Did the nice detective give you the picture I sent?"

"Yes, thanks." Reaching out to touch her mother's arm, Maggie thought she'd try one more time. "I'm better now, Mama." She lifted her head, her voice cracking with emotion. "Do you hear? I'm better."

Helen opened her mouth, but no sound came out. Maggie tightened her grip on her mother's arm. "Whatever happened to me this time isn't my fault. It's those drugs they're giving me. Let me come home with you. Please, I want to be with Poppy."

Maggie saw her mother's back stiffen. "Oh baby, look at you. They carried you in here, drunk as a skunk. I can't risk . . . that is, Poppy's psychiatrist says she was too young to remember but . . . Don't you see? It's best for Poppy if you stay away for a while longer."

Tears streamed down Maggie's cheeks. She turned her head, gazing through the window at the blurred image of a palm tree. "You know I didn't mean to hurt her. You know that, right?"

"I know, I know." Now Helen's tears were flowing too. "Listen baby, I've got to go. You take care of yourself, okay? I love you."

By the time Maggie turned around to tell her mother that she loved her too, Helen was gone.

"Where are the rest of your things?" Sylvia glanced down at the plastic bag clasped in Maggie's hand.

"I didn't have time to pack before they strapped me to the stretcher and rolled me into the ambulance." Maggie held up the bag and shook it. "The nurse gave me these things to use while I was here. Shampoo, a toothbrush, a bar of soap."

"Do you want to stop on the way home to pick up groceries?" Sylvia pushed the elevator button for the parking garage level.

"I left my Assistance Program card at home."

"The food bank has your SNAP number in their system. You don't need the card as long as you have some ID."

Maggie climbed into Sylvia's car and slammed the door. "Well, I don't have any ID either. I told you, I was out cold when Lalo found me. I don't even remember the ride to the hospital. Unless that horrible manager stole my purse while I was gone, everything is still in my apartment."

Sylvia eased her car out of the hospital garage. "No need for sarcasm. Can't you see I'm trying to help? Let's go to McDonald's for lunch. My treat."

Maggie closed her eyes and leaned back against the headrest. "Thanks, but I'd rather go straight home."

They rode in silence. Sylvia sucked on a cigarette, flicking ash out the open window every few minutes. Tapping a new one out of the pack, she cleared her throat.

"The nurse told me your Haldol levels were off the chart so I looked into your medical records. Turns out the nurse who came to give you your shot was two weeks early. I filed a report and sent it up the chain of command but with the turnover in staff . . . well, there's no guarantee it won't happen again. Let me give you some advice, Maggie. Start taking responsibility for yourself. Keep track of your injections. Mark the dates on a calendar or something."

Maggie was too tired to argue. "Whatever you say."

"There's one more thing."

"What?"

"The booze. You know the rules. No alcohol in the apartment. I'll overlook it this one time, but if you slip up again . . ."

Maggie looked up to the ceiling and counted to three. "I won't."

After she got back into the apartment, she flopped down on her bed and pulled the vodka bottle from under the mattress. Tipping back her head, she swallowed the last mouthful. The AC unit blew warm air. With a sigh she picked up the television remote. Her favorite soap opera was about to start but when the TV came on there was nothing but static on every channel. She let her head drop back on the pillow. Out of the corner of her eye she caught a cockroach crawling up the wall inches away. Too tired to bother chasing it, she rolled over.

The next morning, she packed her things and left.

Chapter 19

Cate, 2017

As time went by it became increasingly clear that despite her mental illness, I had to take Maggie's dying confession seriously.

Looking at the situation from a legal standpoint, I knew the most damaging evidence against Cousins was the testimony offered by Savannah's sister, Carrie Ann. A few short months after Savannah was snatched from the beach, Carrie Ann looked at the six-pack of photos and identified Randy Cousins as the kidnapper. Hours later, she stood behind a two-way mirror and picked Cousins out of a line-up. At the murder trial, the prosecutor asked Carrie Ann to identify the man who took her sister. With tears streaking down her cheeks, she stood and pointed a trembling finger at the accused. Given three opportunities to change her mind, the only person to see the man who took Savannah never wavered.

I decided to give my nephew, Ben a call. If anyone could help me untangle this Gordian knot it was him. He picked up on the first ring. Before jumping into business, I asked about Nancy.

"Have you heard from your mother?"

"I called the center yesterday. They told me she's doing well. I checked in with my dad too. He's managing."

By "managing" I figured Ben meant Tim was living on fast food and donuts. Though I never said anything to Ben, I thought it was terrible that Tim didn't come with us to check Nancy into rehab. I wondered if he even bothered to call the center to ask about his wife. Keeping my thoughts to myself, I said. "Glad to hear it. How are you holding up under all this?"

"I'm keeping busy at work. What about you?"

"We're working that case I told you about."

"Did you say 'we'?"

"Lalo is helping me."

Ben waited a few beats before responding. "That must mean there's something to this."

"He has a personal stake in the case. The man Maggie mentioned on her death bed, Gator Pope, surfaced as a suspect in Lalo's original investigation. But when the evidence against Cousins started stacking up, Lalo's captain—under pressure from the FBI—told him to drop that angle of investigation and concentrate on getting Cousins convicted. Listen, I need some expert advice. Have you ever encountered a situation where a witness mistakenly identified the wrong guy?"

"Sure. Eyewitness misidentification is one of the leading causes of wrongful convictions. It's a factor in over seventy-five percent of the cases I've handled."

"And from what I've learned so far it's a real possibility in this case too. The problem is, I don't know how to convince Carrie Ann Troy she may have been wrong."

"Sounds to me like you're approaching this all wrong, Aunt Cate. If you want to help Cousins, you need to take a step back. What evidence did the FBI have against him?"

"Cousins led the police to where the body was buried on Caspersen Beach."

"That's not evidence," Ben said. "He might have found the body by accident. There must be more than that."

"There was a surveillance video proving Cousins was

in the gas station's convenience store on the day some of the ransom money surfaced."

"Were his fingerprints on the money? What about DNA on the body? Did the police find anything from the victim in Cousins' possession?"

I found myself getting a little annoyed. "There was nothing like that. The body was so badly decomposed that they couldn't even determine cause of death. The case against Randy Cousins was purely circumstantial. It's a little late for all this now. The man was convicted. It's up to us to prove he's innocent."

"So how are you going to do that?"

Ben reminded me of my law school professors, prompting me to think logically. The answer to his question was obvious. "I have to re-examine the evidence. One way or another, if Randy Cousins didn't kill Savannah, there must be a way to poke holes in the prosecutor's case against him."

"Exactly. Keep me in the loop, okay? I'm here if you need anything."

I drove up and down Casey Key looking for the marina where Lalo kept his boat. After taking directions from a bikini-clad pedestrian, I spotted the sign on a gravel drive between two mega-mansions that I had passed at least twice before. At the end of the drive was a squat wood-clad building with peeling yellow paint. Nailed to the door was a weather worn sign reading, "Wet Slips." A rack sporting four orange bicycles sat out front. I got out of the car and followed the crushed shell path to the back of the building where a handful of sailboat masts pointed to the sky like giant telephone poles. Calling this place a marina was generous. The boat basin boasted a mere ten slips, several of which were empty. The

Chilanga, a forty-foot trawler that had seen better days floated at the end of a splintered pier.

Lalo sat on the back deck, waving his coffee mug at me. Maya wagged her stubby tail in greeting, beating a tattoo against the teak floor. Lalo gestured to the empty deck chair next to him.

"Welcome aboard."

I eyed the boat rocking gently in her slip. "No thanks. I came to tell you that I've been going over the evidence against Randy. There's something about the gas station surveillance tape that I thought you could—"

Bree's face appeared from behind the cockpit's glass doors. My mind flashed back to the day Maya came crashing through those doors while I was held at gun point in the cabin below. If Lalo hadn't rescued me that day . . . a shiver ran down my spine at the thought. Bree's voice broke through the sound of blood pounding in my ears.

"Cate? Why are you standing there? Come on board and join us for a cup of Mexican coffee. I make it with cinnamon. It's amazeballs."

I shook my head.

Lalo spoke up. "Cate is afraid of boats."

I felt the blush rise to my cheeks. "I am not."

Lalo gave Bree a knowing wink. "No time for more coffee anyway. We need to get going."

I backed off the dock, happy to place my feet on solid ground. "Where are we going?"

"Helen called. She wants to see us."

"Right now?"

"Of course now."

"What if I didn't happen to stop by?"

"But you're here, aren't you?"

"I'm just saying. Helen called asking to see us and I find you here, drinking coffee on the back of your boat like you don't have anything better to do."

He pulled keys from his pocket and jangled them in the air. "We should go."

"Did Helen happen to mention why she wants to see us?"

"She thinks she found something that may lead us to Gator."

"Why didn't you say so?"

"I just did."

I wanted to scream, my frustration with the man reaching a new high.

He stepped off the boat with a big grin on his face. I followed him to the truck, watching the way his shirt strained against the muscles in his broad back. He held the door for me, supporting my elbow as I climbed onto the seat. When Lalo gave the truck some gas, we shot out of the parking lot onto the two-lane street that ran down the length of the key. Tires screeching, he turned onto Albee Road, skidding to a sudden stop behind a gate as the narrow bridge opened for a sailboat. When the light turned green he stepped on the gas and the truck lurched forward.

At the next intersection, Lalo turned south onto Tamiami Trail. Traffic was light, no out-of-state plates in sight. It was that time of year when the kids were back in school and the snow birds hadn't yet arrived for the winter. The sky was clear, a welcome break from the summer rains yet the air was still heavy with moisture.

I picked at my chipped nail polish. "I came by to ask about the surveillance tape."

"Shoot."

"You were able to get a subpoena because a few bills

from the ransom money turned up at that gas station."

"Right."

"How did you know that?"

"The FBI traced the cash."

"The bills were marked?"

Lalo turned to look at me. He held my gaze until the wheels of the truck hit some gravel on the shoulder. Turning his attention back to the road, he gave the wheel a quick turn to set us back in the middle of our lane. He picked up the conversation without missing a beat.

"Not exactly. Agent Steve Prane was the jackass in charge. The kidnapper demanded the ransom in used, unmarked twenty-dollar bills and that's exactly what he got. What he didn't know is that Prane had the serial numbers scanned. When the money hit the bank, the FBI system threw up a red flag. Within twenty-four hours we knew where those bills came from."

This was all news to me. "Didn't Agent Prane embed a tracking device in the bag itself? That would have led him straight to the kidnapper."

Lalo nodded. "Yeah, that didn't work out too well."

There was still so much I had to learn about what went wrong when the ransom was paid but for now I wanted to stay focused on the surveillance tape.

"If the FBI was in charge, why were you the one to take the stand when it came to presenting the evidence to the jury?"

"Because I was the one who sat through sixteen hours of video, looking for someone who fit Carrie Ann Troy's description of the man who snatched her sister. You know how those surveillance systems worked back in the 90's, right?"

"Did they use a video recorder?"

"Yeah, a VCR. The camera was mounted on the wall

behind the cashier, pointed at the customers in front of the counter. The machine was set to record every sixteenth frame. That way they could squeeze an entire week's worth of film onto one tape. I saw two different guys in the store on the day Savannah was killed. Both fit the Carrie Ann's description. A few months later, she confirmed that one of them—Cousins—snatched her sister."

The long delay between when Lalo first watched the video and when he showed it to Carrie Ann surprised me. "Why didn't you show Carrie Ann the tape when the image of the kidnapper was still fresh in her mind?"

Lalo threw me an annoyed look. "I did show her. All I got from the kid was that either of those two guys could have been the man who took her sister. Because of the machine setting, the images flickered like an old-time silent movie. Not to mention the whole thing was out of focus so she couldn't tell one guy from the other. It was only after she picked Cousins out of the lineup that she ID him as the second guy on the tape."

Lalo stopped the truck in front of Helen's house and turned off the engine. He stared straight ahead, drumming his fingers on the steering wheel. "After the kidnapper got away with the ransom, I blamed myself for not standing up to Prane." He jabbed the air with his finger and thumb an inch apart. "I was this close to catching the perp when I saw that tape. I wasn't getting anywhere with Prane so I took the initiative to leak the images to the media." Lalo chuckled under his breath. "I nearly lost my badge but I figured it was worth it. The press printed the images of both guys in the paper the next day and the local TV stations ran the clip on the evening news. We set up a hotline but like I said, the faces were so blurred it was impossible for anyone to tell who those guys were."

"Where is the tape now?"

"Should still be in the evidence locker at the station."

"Can Geri get it for us?"

Lalo pulled the keys out of the ignition and turned to me. "You should ask her. Geri isn't inclined to do me any favors. Not since the last time."

"When was that?"

"After I left the force and started working as a private detective. I needed her to get me some information for a client and it's possible that I may have led her to think it was all above board. Turns out she got caught with her hand in the cookie jar, so to speak."

With a deep sigh I shook my head. "I'll bet you were a juvenile delinquent when you were a kid."

He broke into a big grin. "The worst sort."

Chapter 20

Maggie marched to her own music, pushing her shopping cart down the middle of Tamiami Trail, belting out songs she loved when she was a kid. Cars flew by in both directions, horns blaring, angry drivers hurling curses at her. Suddenly the song caught in her throat. She froze and looked around, wondering where she was.

"Hey!"

She turned to see a man yelling at her from the side of the road. He waved his arms over his head, bringing the oncoming traffic to a stop. As he approached, he continued shouting at her.

"Hey, lady! Are you trying to get yourself killed?"

He grabbed her cart with one hand, tugging her arm with the other. A bit of gravel stung Maggie's face when a car sped up and passed. The driver flashed her the finger.

The man dragged her behind a horse trailer hitched to a rusty pick-up truck. He stood by her side, peering at her from behind long, greasy bangs. Stealing a glance, she saw his skin was deeply tanned, marked by scrapes and scabs. Despite all the car exhaust, she could smell the sweat on him. Tugging her wool cap over her ears, she turned away.

"You okay lady?" the man asked.

She nodded, not trusting herself to speak.

"Want a lift? I can take you as far as Venice."

"That's where I want to go but . . ." She gestured at her shopping cart.

"I got plenty of room for that." The man opened the trailer's tailgate. Maggie peered inside to see one half jammed with a battered riding mower. On the other side she noticed an army cot, a few cardboard cartons and a rusty bicycle.

"I thought this was a horse trailer," she said.

"Used to be. You wanna ride or not? No problem squeezing in your stuff."

She gave him a hesitant nod and watched him roll her shopping cart up the ramp and into the trailer. The man slammed the tailgate closed and walked around to the driver's side of the truck. Maggie scrambled in next to him.

"What's your name?" he asked.

"Maggie."

"Pleased to make your acquaintance, Maggie. I'm Randy. Randy Cousins."

Maggie reached into her pocket and drew out a flask. Unscrewing the cap, she took a swig. The vodka burned her throat all the way down. She offered him a sip.

Randy eyed the flask but shook his head. "I'm sixty-three days sober. Each and every blessed day is a struggle but Jesus will see me through."

Maggie listened to the voices coming to life in her head. She hummed along with them.

Randy's smile revealed a mouth crammed with crooked teeth. "You sure picked a hot day to be walking down the middle of the Trail wearin' that wool hat. Good thing I stopped to pick you up. The lord sure does work in mysterious ways, don't he?"

"There's no horse back there."

"That's right." He laughed and slapped the steering

wheel. "I do believe you've got a touch of the heat stroke, Maggie. Like I said, this used to be a horse trailer but now it's more like home-sweet-home." He turned the key in the ignition and the truck roared to life. Gospel music blared from the speakers. Maggie clasped her hands against her ears. When Randy reached over to turn the volume down, she noticed the tattoo on his arm.

"Navy?"

A furrow formed between Randy's brows until he followed her gaze to the image inked into his skin. He nodded in understanding. "Did my tour on the USS Enterprise during Vietnam. Good times. Best 365 days of my life as a matter of fact."

The tattoo reminded Maggie of Gator. He rarely spoke about his stint in the Seabees, preferring to brag about his short time with the SEALs. She did not believe all of his stories. If it weren't for the ring on his finger, she might not have believed he was in the military at all.

She offered the flask to Randy again. "You sure you don't want a drink?"

Randy licked his lips and shook his head. "That stuff will kill you, little lady." He gunned the engine and eased the truck onto the road.

Maggie drained the last of the vodka and swallowed.

"So what's your story, Maggie?"

"Story?"

"Everyone has a story. A lady pushing a shopping cart down the middle of the Trail . . . well it seems to me you could use a little help getting your life together. If you give yourself to the Lord, Jesus will guide you."

"I'm okay, thanks."

Maggie ignored his steady stream of preaching, letting her thoughts roam. She stared out the window as they passed one car dealership after another. It felt like a lifetime ago when her father brought her to one of those lots and told her to pick out a graduation present. She chose a candy apple red Mustang. How she loved that car. Then four years later he was gone and she drove straight into the Gulf of Mexico with Poppy strapped in the baby seat next to her. Maggie felt a chill run down her spine. Her hands started to shake. Memories had a way of twisting her up inside.

Randy's nasal voice broke into her thoughts. "Friend of mine lets me keep my rig parked behind his plumbing shop on Seaboard Avenue in Venice. That anywhere near where you want to go?"

"Close enough."

"There's an AA meeting tonight at a church around the corner. You interested in joining me?"

Maggie shook her head and started humming, hoping he would get the message and shut up. She got to the end of a John Denver song and started again at the beginning. Over and over she hummed until she saw the sign welcoming them to Venice. They were only a few blocks away from Seaboard when Randy pulled into a gas station.

"I'll be right back," he said. "Need to take a leak and pick up a carton of smokes."

Maggie watched him disappear into the shop and decided it was time to get out. She checked the cab for loose change, hitting a jackpot of quarters and dimes in the ash tray. Dropping the coins in the pocket of her loose-fitting dress, she went around to the back of the trailer. With a grunt she managed to open the tailgate and drag her cart onto the pavement. As she crossed the street, a black SUV hauling a cabin cruiser pulled out of the gas station. She looked up, catching a glimpse at the driver of the vehicle as it sped away.

"Can't be," she mumbled.

An hour later, she arrived sweaty and bone tired at her destination. The clearing in the woods was deserted, the cold fire pit and scattered trash the only indications that people used to live there. She yanked off her cap, fished a plastic bag from her cart, and sat down against a tree. Pulling a jar from the bag, she scooped some peanut butter into her mouth. A few daylight hours remained before she needed to pitch Gator's blue tent.

She looked up through the trees, remembering the last time she saw Gator. It was hard for her to keep track of the time. Was it only a few months ago? So much had happened to her since that day on Caspersen Beach. A shiver ran down her spine at the memory.

Chapter 21

Poppy helped Helen into a wheelchair and tucked a lap blanket around her legs. Helen waved a gnarled hand in the air, complaining that her granddaughter should stop fussing over her. Poppy ignored her, taking a hold of the wheelchair's handles to push Helen to the screened lanai. Lalo and I followed.

As we sat together in awkward silence I looked around. Fruit trees populated the small yard backing onto an algae-infested canal. A large blue heron appeared from around the corner, approaching us on spindly legs. Soon a pair of white ibis climbed up from the bank. Muddy brown baby feathers peeked out from their sleek adult plumage. Lifting their curved bills, they stared through the screen.

"They look like they want something," I said.

Helen turned to Poppy. "Did you forget to give them breakfast?"

With a scowl on her face, Poppy got up to go inside, returning with a dish of hot dogs cut into coins. She opened the screen door and tossed some meat to the birds. I heard her calling to them by name, speaking in soft tones, gently admonishing the heron for trying to steal from the smaller birds. When the food was gone, the heron took flight with a flap of his wings. Poppy stood a while longer, waiting while the ibis strutted back to the canal.

"They're beautiful," I said.

Poppy returned to the chair next to me. "They're orphans. An alligator got their parents when they were still chicks. I moved the nest up here until they were old enough to fend for themselves. They are capable of catching fish now, but I guess we spoiled them with the hot dogs."

"What about the heron? Did you raise him too?"

"It's a she," Poppy corrected. "But no, that heron is a moocher. I suppose others will show up eventually. At some point we will have to stop feeding or the neighbors will complain about having too many birds around."

Silence settled over us once again. I was about to broach the subject of why we were there when Poppy turned to Helen.

"You don't have to talk to these people about Maggie. It will only upset you."

"Not as much as it apparently upsets you, Poppy."

"Well, you know how I felt about her. You always said she couldn't help the way she was but she had a million chances to get her life together and blew it each and every time."

"We're not here to judge Maggie," Lalo told her. "We only want to find the man who killed Savannah Troy."

"You're basing your investigation on the word of a woman who was a chronic liar."

"I'm aware of that. Still, the more we learn about the situation, the more it looks like Maggie told the truth—this time at least."

Poppy sighed. "Even if she wasn't lying, you can't trust she was in her right mind at the time. Her caseworker told us she had been off her meds for some time."

I looked at her in surprise. "When did you speak with Sylvia?"

"When she dropped off Maggie's things." She turned back to Helen. "That's what this is all about, isn't it?"

Helen's eyelids, paper thin fluttered shut. Her words came out in a whisper. "Yes. I want to show Lalo."

Since Maggie was destitute and homeless, it never occurred to me that she owned anything worth passing down to her family. I sat up straight in my chair, hoping there was something among her belongings that could help our case.

"What did you find, Helen?"

Poppy sputtered. "It was all junk. Old rags, shoes, empty jars, a few sketch books. We threw most of it away. I would have chucked everything in the trash but Helen insisted on keeping a few things."

"Like what?"

"I'll get them. Wait here."

As Poppy went back to the house to retrieve the remnants of Maggie's life, a faint glimmer of hope rose in my chest. Slim though the odds may be, it was possible that among Maggie's belongings we would find a photo or some other clue that would lead us to Gator. Poppy returned holding a shoe box in her hands. She removed the lid and pulled out a stack of papers. After setting them on the table between us, she reached into the bottom of the box and extracted a framed photo. Behind the cracked glass, an image of a little girl smiled up at me.

"Is that you?" I asked.

"She was four when I took her to the mall to get that picture taken," Helen said with a smile. "That dress with the little hearts on the collar was her favorite."

Poppy rifled through the stack and pulled out a folded square of thick paper. On it was a child's drawing of a little girl in a red dress. She stared at it, her demeanor softening.

"Let me guess. That's one of your early masterpieces," I said.

Poppy laughed out loud. "Seems my love of art started early. I teach at the high school now but all my childhood work looked like this. Helen tells me I inherited my talent from Maggie. She majored in art at college until she dropped out. But she kept drawing, even after she became ill. Portraits, mostly. Helen kept all of Maggie's sketchpads. They're in her bedroom." She stared at the picture in her hands, the smile still playing at the corners of her mouth.

Helen pointed a finger at the stack of papers still sitting on the table. "Let me have those."

Poppy passed everything to her and watched as Helen thumbed through the pile. She set aside few more of Poppy's childhood drawings and a copy of her kindergarten report card. Coming across a small, brown envelope she paused. After peering inside she passed it to Poppy.

"See? All those years your mother lived on the streets, she held onto this lock of your baby hair. If that isn't proof that she loved you I don't know what is."

Near the bottom, she found what she was looking for. An envelope addressed to Maggie at Helen's address. The letter was post marked Beaufort, South Carolina. The date caught my eye.

"What's that?" Lalo reached over and took the envelope from Helen's hand.

Poppy peered over his shoulder. "I thought I threw it out with all the other junk."

"That's what I wanted to show you, Lalo," Helen said. "There was something about that note . . . the fact that Maggie kept it for more than twenty years struck me as odd. I thought you should see it."

Lalo pulled out a single sheet of paper and read it to himself before passing it to me. I scanned the letter, reading it out loud.

"Dear Maggie,

Sorry that I cannot help you. I haven't seen my brother in years. Your letter said Waylon is in some kind of trouble again. If you find him, tell him to keep away from me and my family. He's not wanted here.

Lizzy Holt"

"Who is Lizzy Holt?" I asked.

"No idea," Helen replied. "And I never heard Maggie mention anyone named Waylon either. That letter probably means nothing but I thought . . ."

"You never know," I said. "Would you mind if we held onto it for a while?"

Helen nodded. "Keep it." She looked down at the pile of papers left in her lap. "Lord knows Poppy doesn't want any of this stuff. After I'm gone I'm sure she'll throw it all away."

"Really grandma, I hardly knew my mother." Poppy's eyes filled with tears. She took both of Helen's hands in hers. "This whole business about Maggie is taking a toll on you."

I dropped the letter into my purse and stood. "We should be going."

Lalo bent over to whisper in Helen's ear. "Don't blame Poppy. She didn't know Maggie like we did."

When I stepped on board, the *Chilanga* shifted under my feet. Maya bounded out through the cabin's open doors. Taking a deep breath, I told myself there was nothing to fear. After all, the boat was safely tied up to the pier in water that was probably only four feet deep. Following Lalo into the cockpit I noticed that except for the green light on the ship's radio, the instrument panel was dark. The pilot's chair was bolted to the floor behind a polished mahogany steering wheel. A murder mystery novel sat on the leather seat. Maya trotted past me and scrambled down the steps to the cabin below. Lalo held my elbow as I took the stairs one at a time.

Taking another deep breath, I looked around. The teak floor, slippery with blood a year ago had been bleached and scrubbed. The spatter on the walls and mahogany cabinets were also wiped clean. All evidence of the struggle that occurred back then was washed away. I exhaled slowly.

Bree sat with her elbows propped on the table, a crease on her brow. "My phone's blowing up."

I looked at the phone in her hand. "What's wrong with it?"

Lalo laughed. "She's getting lots of emails."

"The LSAT results are out." She looked up at me, her dark eyes filled with concern. "Some of the kids who prepped with me this summer got their scores this morning. I can't even. What am I going to do if don't get into law school?"

"I'm sure you did fine," Lalo replied. "Anything else going on?"

"Oh, I almost forgot." Bree's thumbs flew over her phone's screen. She passed it to Lalo. "Another Gator Pope accepted my friend request. If this isn't the face of a murderer, then I don't know what is."

Lalo sat down next to me and laughed. I peered over his shoulder. The profile picture on the screen was an image of an alligator with blood dripping from his mouth. The cartoon reptile was sprawled out in a sand trap, a lone golf club lying next to him. I shook my head and smiled.

"This guy lives in Palm Beach." Bree took her phone back. "Every item in his news stream has to do with golf.

There's a ton of photos of him with his wife, living it up in their clubhouse."

She brought up a series of photos showing a six-ty-something man and his trophy wife raising martini glasses for the camera.

"We can cross him off our list," Lalo said.

"Are you sure?" I pointed to what looked like a tattoo peeking out from under the man's short sleeve shirt. "What is that?"

Lalo bent down to get a closer look. "Looks like the Marine insignia. Gator was a Navy man. Besides, this guy has no neck."

I picked up Bree's phone from the table and swiped through the golf fanatic's photos. "You're right. No way that's him."

Bree shrugged. "Now what?"

"Cate and I are going to pay Geri a visit," Lalo said. "We need to get another look at the surveillance video."

Bree's phone pinged. She looked down and took a moment to read her message before letting out a victory whoop. The look on her face said it all.

She was heading to the University of Florida's Levin College of Law.

Chapter 22

I felt like an invisible spider on the conference room's wall. Lalo and Geri argued like they were still married. With an impatient huff, Geri shoved her pencil behind her ear. A shock of blond bangs fell across one eye as she leaned in. She pursed her lips—hot pink to match her tee-shirt.

"Don't give me any of your bullshit." The gold cross hanging around her neck bounced when she jabbed her finger at him. "Back in the day you wasted a helluva lot of time with Maggie. You never came up with one solid shred of evidence. It's not my fault things went sideways."

In contrast to Geri's display of vitriol, Lalo sat with one arm slung over the back of his chair, an amused smile on his face. "Admit it, Geri. You had your nose so far up Prane's butt you didn't want to listen to me. He didn't believe Maggie knew anything about Savannah's kidnapping and you went along with him for the ride."

Geri's upper lip curled. "That is a cheap shot, even for you. I sided with Steve because he presented a good case against Cousins. I don't need this shit. I wish I never asked Cate to get you back here."

Lalo's face grew serious as he reached across the table and took her hand. "You're a damned good detective, Geri. Always were. Your instincts tell you Maggie was telling the truth. Just because we got it wrong back then, doesn't mean we can't make it right now."

Maybe it was the way he looked at her, maybe his half-whispered words. Whatever it was, Geri slowly relaxed. She pulled her hand from his grip and leaned back, the gold cross coming to rest against her tanned skin.

"Was she? Telling the truth, that is."

"We both know she was."

Geri stared at him, a crease forming between her brows.

Now that the steam appeared to be spent between them, I figured it was safe to chime in. "We need to check the surveillance video to get another look at the second man in the gas station."

Geri looked at me like she suddenly remembered I was in the room. She removed the pencil from behind her ear and set it on the table. "I can't just waltz into the evidence locker and pull that tape. I'd need a case number so the evidence guys can book it against an active investigation."

"So use one of your other case numbers." Lalo said. "Always worked for me."

"I'm not you. Besides, I seem to remember it took you days to scan every frame of that video. Unlike you, I have a real job. I can't waste time on something that may or may not pan out."

"Won't take that long. I tagged the locations on the tape where I found the two different guys who matched Carrie Ann's description. We're betting the other man was Gator."

"I don't know. . ." Geri spoke more to herself than to either of us. "If word leaks out that I'm having another look at this case, Dave Hall will go ape shit. Last thing he wants right now is to have his record tarnished with a wrongful conviction. He will do everything in his power to shut me down rather than risk losing his bid for State Attorney."

Lalo stood up, his imposing figure towering over her. "You started this, Geri. If you're telling me you have cold feet, I'll have to find some other way to get the job done."

I looked up with a start. It never occurred to me that Geri would want to quit. Or even more surprisingly, that Lalo would threaten to forge ahead without her.

Geri stood to face Lalo, meeting his steady gaze without blinking. "I'm just saying I need to watch my back. Hall has got a lot of clout around here and if he gets wind of this he will come after me like a rabid dog.

"You're the best detective on the force," Lalo replied.

"You got that right."

"So what are you going to do?"

She drummed the table with her painted fingernails. "I will figure something out."

I breathed a sigh of relief, knowing Geri was still on board with the investigation. With a curt nod, she stood, signaling that she was done.

I remained seated. "There's something else we need to ask you."

"What now?"

"Have you ever heard the name Lizzy Holt? Or do you know anyone called Waylon?"

The pencil was back in her hand, lightly tapping the table.

"I don't think so. Why?"

"Helen Blue found a letter among Maggie's things. It was signed 'Lizzy Holt' and postmarked shortly after Savannah's kidnapping."

Geri shook her head, certain now.

"Nope. Doesn't ring a bell."

"Okay," I said. "There's just one more thing."

She threw me a look of pure annoyance. "Make it quick. I'm late for a meeting."

"Hear me out. If Randy Cousins didn't kidnap Savannah, then that means someone—presumably Gator Pope—did."

"Obviously," Geri said.

"So what did he do with the money? Lalo explained to me that the FBI had a way of tracking the bills. Was any of the ransom recovered *after* Cousins' incarceration?"

"Steve Prane would be the one to ask. But I gotta believe he would have told me if that was the case."

"Nothing in the FBI rule book says Prane needs to share information with you," Lalo said with a smirk. "And Prane is all about following rules."

"Okay, maybe he doesn't have to tell me if anything new pops up, but I think he would. Out of professional courtesy, that is."

"I wouldn't bet on it. Give him a call. Let's see what he says."

Geri glared at Lalo, her ice blue eyes brimming with anger. For a minute I thought she was going to fire off a snarky reply, but instead she reached for her cell phone and dialed a number from memory.

"It's me," she said. "Something new has turned up regarding the Troy case. Did any ransom money surface after Cousins was locked up?"

I watched the color rise to her face.

"And you didn't see fit to tell me? . . . don't be a prick, Steve. Shut up and listen. I'm sending someone over to see you . . . yes, now . . . Cate Stokes. She'll fill you in when she gets there."

As Geri hung up a young officer opened the door and cleared his throat.

"What do you want?" Geri shouted.

The officer shrank under her glaring eyes. "They sent me to find you, Detective. The meeting in Conference Room A started five minutes ago."

"Tell them I'm on my way." As the officer backed out and scooted down the hall, Geri pinched the bridge of her nose.

"You forgot to tell Prane that I'll be there too," Lalo said.

"Because there's no way that's going to happen." Geri turned to look at me. "The two of them can't be in the same room without getting into a grade-school pissing match. The FBI office is on the sixth floor of the building around the corner. When you see Steve, tell him what's going on then ask about the money. Shit, I thought he would have told me . . ."

"Don't forget the surveillance tape," Lalo said.

"I'm not some rookie you can push around," Geri shot back. "Get out of here. I have work to do."

As the conference room door closed behind her, Lalo and I stood facing each other.

"Good call about the money," he said. "I should have thought about that before. Let's listen to what Prane has to say."

"You heard Geri. Better if I handle this alone."

Lalo shook his head. "The minute you bring Prane into this investigation we lose control."

"We were never in control. I sometimes wonder if I'm cut out for this kind of work. Family law was so much easier to handle."

Lalo smiled, easing the tension between us. "You're perfect. Get ready to meet the biggest asshole you ever saw. I never could understand what Geri saw in the guy."

"Is he anything like you?"

"Total opposite."

"That would explain it, then."

The sound of Lalo's laughter echoed down the empty hall as we left the building.

Chapter 23

Maggie, 1994

Maggie sat on a rotting log and gingerly peeled off her socks to examine the puffy, red blisters on her heels. Limping barefoot to her shopping cart, she slid her hand down the side and pulled out a pair of sandals. The thongs were not her favorites but they would have to do until the blisters healed. Shoving her boots into the cart, she tucked everything back into its rightful place.

Slipping into the sandals she discovered a tick, fat and swollen on her ankle. Reaching down, she plucked it off, wiping the bead of blood with her thumb. With a shake of her head, she shoved her cart into the dense underbrush and covered it with fallen branches. Standing back, she viewed the result. Satisfied everything was hidden as well as possible, she set off on the twenty-minute walk to the local grocery store.

Ignoring the rude stares she drew from the other shoppers, Maggie stood in the aisle, studying the vast selection of insect repellent on the shelf. Dirty strands of hair fell from under her wool cap and covered her eyes. Her fingernails were broken and dirt encrusted, her face streaked with grime. Maggie wore a dress two sizes too big and threadbare from use. It fell loosely to her ankles on her thin frame. The pockets proved useful when she went shopping. When no one was looking, she slipped a can of insect repellent with DEET into one of the pockets. She then shuffled to the refrigerator section of the store, relishing the cool, moist air coming from the beer aisle. She picked up a six pack and lugged it to the check-out counter.

If the lady behind the register noticed the bulge in Maggie's pocket, she did not say. "Hey Maggie. We haven't seen you in a while. Where have you been?"

Maggie's eyes darted back and forth until she came up with something.

"I've been on vacation."

The lady laughed at her. "I didn't mean to pry. Listen, I know times are tough. If you go around to the back of the store you'll find some produce that's past its prime. Help yourself if you want anything."

"I don't take charity."

"Suit yourself. Just trying to help."

Sharkey's beach was empty. Wiggling her toes, Maggie burrowed her sore feet into the warm sand until only the tops of her arches showed. She sat watching the pelicans dive for their lunch. A pair of young boys raced by kicking up sand in their wake. The parents followed, the mother toting a large canvas bag stuffed with towels, the father lugging an umbrella over his shoulder. The boys paused long enough to pull their shirts over their heads and cast them aside before splashing into the sea. Maggie watched as the parents staked out their spot a healthy distance from where she sat.

"Hiya Maggie."

She looked up with a start to see Randy, the man with the horse trailer standing in front of her. Randy glanced at the cans of beer by her side.

Maggie reached for one. "Have one, they're cold."

Randy licked his lips. "Nah, I have an AA meeting

tonight. Sixty-four days sober. I wouldn't mind keeping you company, though." Without waiting for permission, he dropped down next to her. He laid the device he carried, a long stick with a disk attached at the end, by his side.

"What is that thing?" Maggie asked.

"A metal detector." Randy patted the handle. "Last week this baby found me a silver ring on the beach. Take a look."

He held out his hand, showing her a ring that looked exactly like the one Gator wore.

"Where did you get that?"

"On Caspersen Beach. Whoever lost it served in the navy. See? That's the Seabee insignia. Same group I was in."

Maggie shook the sand from her feet and slipped them into her sandals. "I have to go."

Randy touched her sleeve. "Are you going to run off on me again? I thought we had some kind of connection here."

Maggie jumped up and took two steps back. "Don't touch me."

Randy raised both hands in the air. "Take it easy. I just wanted to invite you to the AA meeting tonight. They say we should reach out to fellow drinkers."

"No thanks."

"Suit yourself."

"I don't need saving." Maggie reached down to retrieve her beer. "People who try to save me only make things worse."

"They'll have free coffee and donuts at the meeting."

The temptation was strong. Maggie lost track of how long it had been since she ate. But with the promise of filling her stomach with beer, she hugged the cans to her chest and trudged down the beach in the direction of home.

Back in Gator's tent, Maggie wondered for the hundredth time if Gator's sister ever received the letter she sent weeks ago.

Gator did not talk much about his family. It was only from the little he did say that Maggie knew about his sister, Lizzy Holt. Gator was drunk at the time, and his fond memories of his sister turned bitter when Maggie asked about their parents. His father skipped town—gone before Gator was out of diapers—and his mother did not bother filing for divorce before marrying a man who eventually chased Gator out of the house at the wrong end of a shotgun.

Maggie also knew Gator had one son. When she pressed him for more information about the boy and his wife, he grunted and told her it was none of her business.

Her thoughts were interrupted by the sound of branches snapping. A deep-throated voice called out.

"FBI. Come out with your hands up."

Chapter 24

I didn't need to read the sign on the door to know I had arrived at the FBI offices in Sarasota. The decor was '80's government style. Cork boards were covered with wanted posters and Federal notices. A framed photo of the President of the United States hung on the wall. Brochures touting the benefits of working for the FBI were fanned out on a table. Behind the Formica counter in the reception area I saw a row of closed doors. The receptionist, a trim lady with a tight perm, picked up the phone to notify Special Agent Steven Prane I was there to see him. Prane appeared from behind one of the doors, eyeing me up and down.

Pale blue eyes, pale skin to match, he looked more like a Scandinavian than a Florida resident. His head was Kojak-bald, his eyebrows chalky white. In his dark blue polo shirt with the FBI insignia embroidered on the chest, all he lacked was a shoulder holster to complete the stereotype. I handed him an old business card from my NH law firm.

He glanced at the card, his face a blank mask. "What's this about, Ms. Stokes?"

"I am investigating Savannah Troy's murder."

We stood close enough for me to see a thin scar cutting across his right eyebrow. He took one step back and folded his arms across his chest. "That case was closed a long time ago."

"Does the name Margaret Blue mean anything to you?"

The eyebrow with the scar rose a fraction of an inch. "It sounds vaguely familiar. Why?"

"According to Maggie, someone called Gator Pope killed Savannah."

He blinked once, a slow, give-me-time-to-think-about-that blink. "Why don't you bring Maggie in so I can speak with her myself?"

"That would be rather difficult. Maggie is dead."

That got the reaction I hoped for. His eyes opened wide and he leaned forward.

"Step into my office, please."

The hazy light of a humid, summer afternoon seeped through the window. I saw no evidence of Prane's personal life anywhere. No photos, no coffee mugs claiming he was the world's best dad, nothing. His desk was cluttered with paperwork, his trash can full of empty fast-food wrappers and soda cans. A display of his achievements including diplomas in law enforcement, finance and a law degree hung on the wall together with several framed accommodations for his years in service. Behind his desk, two blown up maps with the Google Earth logo in the bottom corner were tacked to the wall. The first one, an image of the Florida peninsula was populated with red, green and blue dots. Miami was dense with all three colors while the other areas—Venice, Fort Myers and Naples—had only a few. The other map showed a section of the South Carolina low country.

Prane pulled out a pack of nicotine gum and popped a piece into his mouth. He then reached for a fat file from a metal cabinet and dropped it on his desk. The yellowing label on the folder read, TROY, S.

"Okay, Ms. Stokes. Let's get down to it. Why are you here?"

It took a few minutes to explain. I told him about Maggie's dying confession and how Geri took it seriously. I assured Prane that Lalo and I were hot on the trail of the mysterious Gator Pope and based on what we had learned, we suspected Randy Cousins was wrongfully convicted.

"This Lalo fellow you're talking about, would that be Detective Eduardo Sanchez?"

I nodded. "He's a private investigator now."

"Protocol dictates that if a case in which the FBI was involved is reopened, we need to be officially informed. Tell Detective Garibaldi if she wants my cooperation, she needs to go through the proper channels. Sending a civilian with second-hand information is not the right way to go about this."

My blood pressure spiked. It took every ounce of my self control to keep a civil tongue in my head. "The case is not reopened. Not officially, anyway."

The springs in his chair groaned as Prane leaned back. "I see. And since you are here, can I assume that despite your best efforts you and Detective Sanchez haven't come up with the evidence Geri needs to initiate that action?"

I met his cold gaze without wavering. "We're working several angles simultaneously. I am here today to ask you about the ransom money."

"What about it?"

"Two days after the ransom was picked up, three twenty-dollar bills surfaced at a gas station in Venice. That money was used as evidence in Randy Cousins' trial. Today you told Geri more bills have turned up since Cousins' incarceration."

Prane glanced at the ceiling and rubbed the crown of his bald head.

"Yes, Mrs. Stokes. Some—not all—of that money has turned up over time."

"How do you explain that? Cousins has been in prison for twenty years."

"I don't have to explain anything to you. But as a courtesy, since you've come in good faith, I would say my working theory is Cousins had a partner. That's a guess, mind you. I have no proof."

I took a moment to process what he said. "Do you have any idea who that partner might be?"

Prane pointed to the map behind his desk. "What do you see there?"

Realizing the dots represented recovered ransom money, I took a closer look. "Most of the ransom money turned up in South Florida."

"Most, not all."

My gaze shifted the other map on the wall. A cluster of dots were concentrated around a single city. I slipped a hand into my purse and fingered the envelope from Lizzy Holt. "Is that Beaufort?"

The springs on his chair groaned again as he sat up straight. "What do you know about Beaufort?"

He stared at the envelope I slid across his desk. When he looked up, there was a hint of a smile on his face.

"Where did you get this?"

"It was among Maggie Blue's belongings at the time of her death."

Prane took a minute to read Lizzy Holt's letter before slipping it into the top drawer of his desk.

I held my hand out. "I didn't intend for you to keep that."

"I work for the FBI, Ms. Stokes. The letter is potential evidence in an ongoing investigation."

My heart raced. An ongoing investigation? That explained why Prane kept the two maps on his office wall. And if Prane thought the note from Lizzy Holt was important, that meant we were on to something.

"I'm not leaving here without that letter."

The sound that erupted from Prane was more like a snicker than a laugh. "We'll see about that. What else can you tell me about Lizzy Holt?"

"Nothing."

Pulling his lips back in a grin, he nodded slightly. "If and when Geri re-opens the investigation into Savannah's death, I'll send her a copy of that letter for her files. In the meantime, you and Detective Sanchez can continue wasting your time searching for Gator Pope. I've been on the man's trail for twenty years. And if I can't find him, you never will."

I found Lalo leaning against his truck in the parking lot across the street from the FBI building. Behind him clouds darkened the horizon, a roll of thunder in the distance. I crossed the road to join him.

He opened the passenger door for me.

"I can open my own door."

"There you go with that liberated woman crap. Get in the truck and tell me how it went with Prane."

"Suffice it to say your opinion of the man is accurate."

"Asshole, right?"

"I need a drink."

Lalo smiled as he walked around to his side of the truck and settled in behind the wheel. "We'll pick up some wine on the way back to the boat. Bree texted me while you were in with Prane. You're invited for dinner. Nothing fancy. Burgers at the North Jetty Park."

"It looks like rain."

Lalo cranked his head to look up through the windshield. "Not to worry. The wind from the east should keep those clouds out to sea. So tell me, what did Prane say?"

"There were maps on his office wall showing where the ransom money surfaced. A great deal turned up in Florida, mostly Miami. Prane thinks Randy Cousins had a partner. And he said since he hasn't been able to find Gator, we won't either."

Lalo's eyes scanned the road ahead of us. "I never considered the partner angle. Could be Gator and Cousins worked together."

"I agree. But if that's true and Gator is still in Florida, why hasn't Prane been able to find him?"

Lalo remained quiet with his brow furrowed. "Something doesn't add up here."

"Do you remember that letter from Lizzy Holt?"

"Yeah. What about it?"

"It was postmarked Beaufort, South Carolina."

Another lapse of silence filled the truck. When we came to a red light, Lalo turned to look at me. "So?"

"Well, we both agreed that letter was Lizzy's answer to a letter sent by Maggie. In it she wrote that she didn't know where her brother was."

"Yeah, Waylon. You and I talked about this on the way back from Helen's. We figured Waylon was Gator's given name."

"I have to tell you something."

"What?"

"Promise you won't get mad."

A flick of his eyes in my direction warned me there would be no such promise. I took a deep breath and dove in. "I showed Prane the letter."

Lalo faced forward, staring at the light which remained red. I could see his jaw working overtime. "Why would you do that?"

"Because Beaufort was one of the towns where Savannah's ransom money surfaced. I figured there has to be a connection."

The light turned green and Lalo hit the gas. "I can't believe you showed Prane that letter!"

"Don't yell. I thought he might know something about Lizzy Holt. If he does, he didn't say. He took the letter from me and refused to give it back."

The knuckles on Lalo's hands turned white as he gripped the steering wheel. He reached for his phone and tossed it into my lap. "We should have done this earlier. Google Lizzy Holt."

I typed in her name and got thousands of results. When I narrowed the search to those living in South Carolina, I hit pay dirt.

"I think we just got the break we've been looking for. Lizzy is still living in Beaufort. You don't suppose Gator moved back there, do you?"

"Doubtful."

I gave it a try anyway. My heart began to race when one Waylon Pope popped up in Beaufort. With a single click, I landed on the man's Facebook page. I looked at Lalo in surprise.

"You're not going to believe this."

Chapter 25

Maggie, 1994

Maggie froze, her heart thudding against her rib cage. Her first impulse was to run, even if it meant slicing the back of the tent to make a mad dash through the woods. With a sinking feeling, she realized her knife was still in her cart, stashed in the underbrush at the edge of the clearing. Gripped by indecision, she bent over and started keening.

"Easy there, I'm coming in."

She flinched at the touch of a hand on her back. The man grabbed her legs and pulled. Kicking and screaming, Maggie tried to resist as he dragged her out of the tent. When he finally let go, she curled into a ball and tucked her head in the crook of her arm.

"No one's going to hurt you. I'm FBI Special Agent Steven Prane. I only want to talk."

She felt a tap on her shoulder. When she opened her eyes, she caught a glimpse of the badge he flashed under her nose. He jerked his hand away when a cockroach crawled out from a pile of pine needles and scurried off. Taking one step back he cleared his throat.

"I'm investigating the abduction of Savannah Troy. Witnesses say you know the man who was seen running off with her."

Maggie shook her head.

"Okay then. Have it your way. I'm sure you won't mind if I take a look around."

Keeping her head down, she listened to the sound of dried branches snapping until she realized what he was doing. After dragging her cart into the open, he started rooting through her things, pulling out plastic bags, dumping their contents. With a crash, Poppy's picture hit the ground. Shrieking in anger, Maggie jumped to her feet and reached into her pocket. As Prane spun around to face her, she fired.

He wailed when the insect repellent hit his face.

Maggie dropped to the ground, grabbing Poppy's photo. She stroked the cracked glass, tears blurring the sight of her little girl.

"What's going on here?"

Maggie glanced up to see Lalo standing at the edge of the clearing. She scrambled to pick up the can. Keeping her finger on the trigger, she pointed it at the detective.

Prane rubbed his eyes. "That crazy bitch hit me with pepper spray," he shouted.

Lalo stepped toward Maggie and held out his hand. "Give it to me, Mags."

She glared at him.

"You can have the can back after we leave."

As the FBI agent moaned, she allowed Lalo to pry the insect repellent from her grip. Maggie turned to see Prane blindly pointing an accusatory finger. "Arrest that woman."

Eyes wide with panic, Maggie looked at Lalo. He winked at her, his face breaking into a wide grin. "On what grounds?"

"Attacking a Federal agent." Prane, tears streaming down his face, continued to rub his blood shot eyes.

"Did you attack this agent, Mags?"

Maggie ignored Lalo's question as she groped around in the dirt, picking up the dust covered items that Prane dumped on the ground. As she stuffed the precious mementos from her daughter back into the bag, she saw the brown envelope was stuck at the bottom. With a sigh of relief, she clutched Poppy's things to her chest.

"What are you waiting for Sanchez?" Prane asked. "Cuff her."

"Seems to me she was protecting her belongings from an intruder," Lalo said. "In defense she hit him with a lethal dose of bug spray."

"What?" The color rose to Prane's bald scalp as he stared open-mouthed at the orange can Lalo held in his hand.

"Do you have a search warrant, Special Agent Prane?" Lalo asked.

Prane sputtered. "You said it yourself, she knows the kidnapper. I'm bringing her in for questioning."

"Lotta good that will do." Lalo squatted down next to Maggie. "You want a hand putting your things back in the cart?"

She shook her head.

"Okay then." He handed the can back to her. "How 'bout if I drive you down to Sharkey's for a burger?"

Maggie's stomach growled. She stole a look at Prane through her greasy bangs and shook her head again.

With a soft grunt, Lalo stood. He touched the brim of his cap and gave her another wink. "See you around, Mags."

She sat watching as Lalo took Prane by the arm to lead him out of the clearing. Waiting until the sound of their arguing voices faded to nothing, she finished packing her things into the plastic bags. When she was done, she reached into the cart and pulled out her knife. Exhausted, she returned to the tent, slipped the knife under her pillow and curled up on her sleeping bag.

Maggie woke to the sound of Sylvia's voice shouting her name. Outside the tent the caseworker stood with her arms folded across her chest, a scowl on her face. Maggie resisted the urge to scratch the bug bites on her arms as she came out to face her. She jumped at the sudden movement of Sylvia swatting a mosquito on the back of her neck.

"I hope you don't expect me to come looking for you every time you decide to run off," Sylvia said.

"I suppose Lalo told you where to find me?"

Sylvia nodded. "He's worried about you. I'm worried too. It seems you're the only person who is not concerned about your wellbeing. What are you doing here?"

An easy lie came to her lips. "Sam told me it was time to come home."

"You're old friend? How did he know where you were?"

The lies kept flowing. "I wrote him a letter. He promised to look out for me if I came back."

"I see." Sylvia gave her a dubious look. "So, Sam picked you up and brought you here from Sarasota?"

"No. Someone gave me a lift in his horse trailer."

"A horse trailer, huh? Listen, Maggie. You don't have to lie to me. I get that you're angry. But if you do what I told you and start to keep track of your injections, that screw up with your meds won't happen again. Come back now and we'll pretend this . . ." Sylvia waved her hand in the air. "We'll pretend this little camping trip never happened."

Maggie clamped her hands over her ears.

"Are the voices back, Mags?"

She nodded. An expression of concern crossed Sylvia's face. The caseworker slapped another mosquito, leaving a smear of bright red blood on her dark skin. With a grimace, she flicked the remains of the dead insect from her arm.

"I'm getting eaten alive here, Maggie. Last chance. Lalo is sitting in his truck, waiting for my call to come and drag your stuff out of here."

Maggie glanced around the clearing. As bad as the apartment was, at least she could lock the door if that FBI man came back. With a resigned shrug she turned to Sylvia.

"Take me home."

Chapter 26

As I stepped onto the sandy parking lot of the North Jetty Park, Maya ran to greet me. She nudged my hand until I reached down to scratch behind her ears. Her deep brown eyes, rimmed with gold, closed in an expression of ecstasy.

Bree brushed back her blue bangs from her eyes. "What took you so long? I'm famished."

"We had some business downtown," Lalo said.

Bree peeked into the grocery back in the back seat. "Where's the dessert?"

"We can go to Sweet Melissa's for an ice cream." Lalo reached in and handed her one of the bags. "Here, make yourself useful."

I took another bag and followed Bree to the picnic table. Lalo brought enough to feed a dozen people. Hamburger patties, hot dogs, corn on the cob and potato salad. He even remembered to pack barbecue sauce. While Bree set the table, I shucked the corn. Lalo grabbed a bag of charcoal and stepped aside to light the grill.

"How'd your meeting with Geri go?" Bree asked. "Did she agree to check the surveillance tape to see if Gator was in the gas station that day?"

"She wasn't too thrilled about it but Lalo sweet-talked her into trying," I replied.

Bree lowered her voice to a stage whisper. "I think Geri

still has the hots for him."

"What makes you say that?"

"I saw them together when I was a kid. Couldn't keep their hands off each other."

Lalo looked up from the grill and pointed a finger at Bree. "That was a long time ago. Before I came to my senses and realized I couldn't stand the woman."

I caught his eye and smiled. No matter how much he denied it, I could tell by the way he and Geri argued that they were still fond of each other.

"I hope she finds that tape," I said.

"There's no way of knowing if it's still there until she checks the evidence locker," Lalo replied. "How do you like your burgers cooked?"

"Medium rare. Do you want to tell Bree what we found or shall I?"

"You mean the letter you gave to Prane?"

Bree looked up from slicing tomatoes. "Who?"

"The FBI agent assigned to investigate Savannah's kidnapping." I cast an annoyed glance at Lalo. "I didn't say he could keep it."

I explained to Bree how Geri put me in touch with Steve Prane. Leaving out my opinion of the man, I told her how we came into possession of the letter Lizzy Holt wrote to Maggie.

"What did it say?" Bree asked.

"It sounded like a reply to a letter Maggie sent to her. Apparently Lizzy is Gator's sister."

"OMG, that's mongo!"

"Mongo?"

"You know, big, humongous."

"Show her," Lalo said.

Pulling out my phone, I found the Facebook page of

Gator Pope. I passed the phone to Bree and waited for her reaction.

"Get out!" she said. "This is one of the guys I found like, days ago. You know, the one from South Carolina. You said he was too young to be the guy we're looking for."

"He's thirty-four." I took my phone back from her. "Which makes him twelve when Savannah was killed. He's Gator's son, Waylon Pope, Jr."

Bree picked up the uncooked hot dogs and brought them to where Lalo tended the burgers. "Now what do we do?"

Lalo laid the hot dogs and the foil-wrapped ears of corn on the grill. "*We* don't do anything. In case you forgot, I'm driving you to Gainesville tomorrow so you can get settled into the dorm before classes start."

"Gainesville is half-way to Beaufort," I said.

"Yeah, I thought about that already."

"The hamburgers are burning." I took the spatula from his hand and moved the burgers to the edge of the grill. "You aren't thinking of visiting Waylon Jr. and Lizzy without me, are you?"

"It's a long drive to speak with people who may know nothing about Savannah Troy."

"It can't be a coincidence that some of the ransom money surfaced in his home town."

"How do you know that?" Bree asked.

"Prane had a map on his office wall that showed where the ransom money turned up."

Bree dipped a plastic fork into the potato salad and started eating.

"He's probably already found Lizzy Holt too."

"It is possible," I agreed. "Bree, hand me a plate. The burgers are ready."

"Aren't you going to toast the rolls?" she asked.

Lalo took the spatula back from me and moved the burgers back to the center of the grill. "You women drive me crazy."

Bree shoved the last of the potato salad into her mouth. "If you want to see Lizzy before Prane beats you to her, you'd better get going."

Lalo placed our food on the table. I poked at my burger. The red juices bled onto my plate. I glanced up to catch him looking at me with a smug smile.

"I've been thinking," I said. "Maybe we should let Prane take it from here. He's better positioned to catch Gator than we are."

Lalo wiggled his dark eyebrows before forking another burger and two hot dogs onto a clean plate. Dousing everything with barbecue sauce, he set the plate on the ground. Maya finished her meal in three bites and turned her brown eyes to Lalo, begging for more. With a laugh, he tossed her a piece of roll from his own plate.

"Prane might be better positioned, but after ten years of looking for Gator all he's got to show for his effort is a map on the wall. That and the letter you gave him."

""I told you, I didn't give it to—"

"We'll continue on to Beaufort after we drop Bree at school tomorrow."

I thought about that for a minute while I ate my burger.

As if he could read my thoughts, Lalo said, "You're still in, right?"

"For now at least. We can decide how much further to take this after we speak with Lizzy and Gator Jr."

"We have a long day ahead of us. I'll pick you up at eight."

———————————

I found Rascal waiting by the front door, his tail snapping in anger. When I stepped into the house, he trotted ahead of me to the kitchen. Instead of rubbing against my leg as he usually did, he kept his distance while I dished out his dinner from the can. He stared at me, unblinking until I left the room.

After the events of the past few days, it appeared my part in this investigation was almost over. Tomorrow Lalo and I would drive to Beaufort to meet Gator's sister and the man we assumed was his son. Depending on how that meeting went, the FBI could take the case from there. As it was getting late, I decided to call Geri and fill her in on our latest discoveries in the morning.

The air on the lanai was charged with electricity. Muffled thunder rolled in the distance. Lalo's prediction was right. With the wind coming from the east the rain stayed out to sea. Easing into the chaise lounge, I took a sip of wine and closed my eyes. It occurred to me that I was getting too old for this game. The sound of the distant surf lulled me to sleep.

An insistent ringing woke me. I groped for my phone, holding it at arm's length to read the caller ID. Ben's voice, full of excitement came through loud and clear.

"Hey, Aunt Cate. I've spent some time looking into Cousins. Did you know he had no prior arrests and no history of violence? His service record was clean too. No doubt he had fallen on hard times but there's nothing in his background that fits the profile of a man who could murder a child in cold blood. On top of that, there was no physical evidence that tied him to the crime. Carrie Ann Troy's testimony was the solitary nail in Cousins' coffin. My boss wants us to be on the lookout for exactly this kind of case. If Cousins petitions the Project for legal assistance, there's a good chance we'll accept him. What are you doing tomorrow?"

"I'm going with Lalo to Beaufort, South Carolina."

"Why?"

"We located Gator's sister and a young man who is probably his son."

There was a pause on the line while I waited for Ben to digest the news. "Let Lalo handle that. You're coming with me to speak with Carrie Ann Troy."

"Savannah's sister?"

"I told her there was new evidence suggesting Randy Cousins was innocent and that the Project was considering accepting him as a client. Carrie Ann went ballistic, told me Cousins was a monster. She only agreed to meet because she wants to convince me to drop the case. I think having you with me will help calm her down."

"But Lalo—"

"Listen, Aunt Cate. Don't take this the wrong way, but you need to stop thinking like a private investigator and approach this case from a legal perspective. If Randy Cousins is an innocent man—and I understand that's a big 'if'—the only way he's going to win his freedom is through a legal challenge. Leave the detective work to Lalo. I need your help to determine if there is a basis to file for a wrongful conviction."

As usual, Ben was right. For weeks I had been chasing leads like an amateur sleuth when I should have been doing legal research to see if Cousins was wrongfully convicted. I cleared my throat before speaking. "I'll call Lalo and tell him to go to Beaufort without me."

"Great. I'm leaving for Venice first thing in the morning. See you around noon."

Chapter 27

Cate, 2017

I reached across my kitchen table to brush Ben's bangs away from his eyes. "You need a shave and a haircut."

Ben grinned. "The girls in the office think I'm sexy."

"Don't let Stephanie hear you talk like that."

Stephanie and Ben had been together for a little over one year. A tall, red-headed beauty, she was also whip-smart. Just the kind of girl to keep Ben on his toes.

Ben took a deep breath. "I've been meaning to tell you. Stephanie was accepted at FSU Law in Tallahassee. She starts classes next week."

"That's great. She'll make a wonderful lawyer."

"Here's the thing, Aunt Cate. The next three years are going to be a grind for Steph. You know how intense law school can be. And with her living two and a half hours away, we decided it would be best to cool things between us for a while so she can concentrate on her studies."

"You broke up with her?" I stared at Ben in disbelief.

"More like she broke up with me."

"Oh, Ben." I stood to pour him a second glass of iced tea. "As terrible as it seems right now, I promise you, other girls will line up to take her place in no time."

Ben smiled. "I'm in no hurry. Between the Project and my routine at the gym, I keep busy."

I sat down and passed him the bread basket. "How's your mother?"

"The nurses tell me she's doing well. I still have to wait another week before I can visit."

"It would be best if you go alone the first time. I'll drive up the following week."

Ben removed two slices and set them on his plate "So, tell me what you learned from the FBI agent. What makes him think Cousins had a partner?"

While we ate our sandwiches, I filled him in on the meeting with Steve Prane. I also explained that Geri promised to check the evidence locker for the gas station surveillance tape. A loud ping came from his pocket and he pulled out his phone. While I sat there with a scowl on my face, he started tapping a message.

"What's so important that can't wait until after lunch?"

I heard a swooshing noise and Ben looked up with a big grin on his face. I expected he would pocket the phone but instead he slid it across the table to me. A familiar face filled the screen.

I drew in a sharp breath. "Where did this come from?"

"Lalo. He's with Lizzy Holt. She gave him a photo she took of Gator thirty years ago. If you check your phone, you'll see he copied you."

I stared at a different version of Gator than the police sketch posted around town after Savannah was abducted. In the poster Gator was pictured as a man in a torn tee shirt with stringy hair and an untrimmed beard. Lizzy's photo showed her clean-shaven brother with short hair wearing a white, button-down shirt. As I compared the two, I noted the shape of his face, his skin color and his big ears were exactly the same in both images.

I couldn't contain my excitement. "This is mongo!"

Ben laughed. "What did you say?"

"You know, humongous, mongo."

"Where did you pick up that expression?"

"From Lalo's granddaughter, Bree. Now that you're single, I should introduce you."

Ben raised one eyebrow. I had to smile.

"What? I can't fix you up with a pretty, smart girl your own age?"

Ben took back his phone and slipped it into his pocket. "I told you, I'm not looking for anyone."

"There's more to life than work and going to the gym, Ben."

"It's enough for me right now. Lalo says he'll call after he checks into the hotel. His timing is perfect. We can show Carrie Ann Troy this photo."

"Do you think she'll recognize him as the guy who snatched her sister?"

"Not necessarily. Since Randy looks so much like Gator, there's a good chance Carrie Ann simply made a mistake. But getting her to admit that won't be easy. We've got a lot of experience with this sort of thing at the Project. Legally it's called 'unconscious transference.' When presented with a group of images, if an eyewitness isn't sure, he or she will often pick the next best one. Once that image is fixed, the brain creates a false memory of the event. It usually takes additional evidence to convince the witness he—or in this case she—was wrong."

"What if Carrie Ann stands by her original testimony?"

"Then we'll need something else that will give us a legal foothold so we can file for a wrongful conviction. You know the list of causes. In addition to eyewitness misidentification there's improper forensic science, prosecutorial misconduct, bad lawyering, false testimony by an informer—"

"I know, I know. But there was no informer. And from what I saw in the court records, Cousins' public defender did a good job. Do you know he found a witness who claimed Cousins was in Sarasota at the time Savannah was snatched? The only problem was, the prosecutor convinced the jury to disregard the man's testimony."

A deep furrow formed between Ben's eyebrows. "What was name of the witness?"

"Bob something." I closed my eyes, running through the letters of the alphabet to jog my memory. "Wickes," I said. "The man's name was Bob Wickes."

Ben glanced at his watch. "That might be worth digging into. Right now we need to go. I don't want to be late for our appointment with Carrie Ann."

I picked up our empty plates and set them on the counter. "Give me a minute to get the cat in from the lanai."

As I locked the door behind me, I saw Ben sitting behind the wheel of his old BMW checking his phone once again. Climbing into the car, I saw he was typing an address.

I took the phone from his hand. "We don't need a computer to get us there. I know my way around town."

Carrie Ann Troy Roberts met us at the door with an infant on her hip. The child chewed on a plastic ring, the bib around his neck soaked with drool. He gave me another toothless grin far more welcoming than the hostile frown on his mother's face.

"I know I promised to meet with you today but this isn't a good time," she said. "Jason woke up late from his nap and he hasn't had his lunch yet."

"No problem," Ben said. "We can talk while you feed him."

Jason grabbed his mother's hair with his sticky fingers. She took his hand in hers before raising it to her lips. She hesitated before agreeing to Ben's suggestion. "I guess that would be okay." Pushing her pink-framed glasses up the bridge of her nose she stepped aside and waved us in.

She led us to the kitchen through a maze of baby toys littering the living room floor. After plunking the child in his high chair, she used her arm to sweep a mound of magazines and newspapers to one end of the table. She gestured for us to sit down. "Don't mind the mess. I haven't had a moment to myself since the baby started teething."

Jason started fussing, waving his arms in the air while his mother spooned baby food into a Winnie-the-Pooh bowl and popped it into the microwave. I glanced at the dirty dishes piled high in the sink, the overflowing trash can, the counter cluttered with unopened mail. Rising from my chair I gently eased the spoon out of Carrie Ann's hand and sat next to Jason. "Allow me. I love children. And it's been a long time since I had an opportunity to feed a baby."

The microwave pinged. Carrie Ann removed the dish and stuck her finger into the food. Satisfied with the temperature, she handed the dish to me with a tentative smile. "I guess that's okay. It will give me a chance to load the dishwasher while you two tell me what this is all about."

With one hand I kept Jason's fingers away from his lunch while I offered him the first spoonful. Some of the food dribbled out the side of his mouth. I scraped it off his chin and shoved it right back in. Carrie Ann watched me for a minute, giving a slight nod before turning to face the sink.

"We appreciate your willingness to talk to us today," Ben said. "As I said on the phone, we have new information concerning your sister's abduction."

Carrie Ann paused, a dirty glass suspended over the sink. "Murder," she said. "Savannah wasn't only abducted, she was murdered."

"Of course." Ben cleared his throat. "But we have reason to believe someone other than Randy Cousins was involved."

Carrie Ann spun around to face Ben. "What?"

"A person of interest at the time of the investigation recently passed away. On her deathbed, she admitted to planning the kidnapping with a man named Waylon Pope. We are looking into her claim to see if there is any truth to her statement."

"Who was this 'person of interest?'"

I scraped the last of the food from the dish and offered it to Jason. He sealed his mouth shut with a shake of his head and pushed the spoon away. I used the bib to wipe his chin before turning to Carrie Ann. "Her name was Margaret Blue."

The color drained from Carrie Ann's face. "Poppy's mother?"

"How do you know Poppy?" Ben asked.

"This is a small town, Mr. Shepherd. Poppy and her grandmother live near here. I heard recently that Helen isn't doing well."

All the while Carrie Ann spoke she cast nervous glances in my direction. When Jason raised his hands to signal he wanted to be picked up, she dropped a spoon in the sink and reached for the baby.

"I can hold him," I offered.

"He doesn't like strangers."

The child gave me a toothless smile.

I stood and stepped out of her way. "Sit here. I'll finish loading the dishwasher."

Carrie Ann dropped into the chair and bounced the baby on her knee. Turning to Ben she said, "You know Maggie was crazy, right? I never met the woman but from everything I've heard, you can't believe a word she said."

"We're currently working to confirm her statement." Ben tilted his head. "Do you remember Detective Garibaldi?"

"She spoke to me right after . . ." When Carrie Ann paused, I looked over my shoulder to see her fiddling with the baby's teething ring. Casting her eyes to the floor she spoke just above a whisper. "Geri is a hero in my eyes. She and Special Agent Prane were wonderful. I'll always be grateful to them for bringing that monster to justice."

I crammed the last dish in the dishwasher and searched under the sink for the detergent. Finding the box, I dropped a pod into the soap compartment. I closed the door, pushed the Start button and turned to face Carrie Ann.

"Geri thinks Maggie was telling the truth."

The teething ring slipped out of Carrie Ann's fingers and hit the floor. Jason began to whimper. His mother's knees ceased bouncing. I bent down to picked up the ring and rinsed it under the tap. The baby took it from my outstretched hand and shoved it into his drooling mouth.

Carrie Ann looked up at me. "You have no idea what we've been through. My parents . . ." Carrie Ann's eyes opened wide. "This would literally kill my mother."

Ben reached across the table and lightly rested his hand on Carrie Ann's arm.

"Carrie Ann, we don't know for sure if Waylon Pope had anything to do with your sister's murder. But we do have reason—aside from Margaret Blue's dying confession—to believe someone other than Randy Cousins was involved. I know this must be difficult for you, but I want to show you a photo of the man in question. Maybe you can tell us if you've ever seen him before."

Carrie Ann's eyes darted from Ben to me and back again. When she gave a little nod, he pulled his phone out of his pocket and held it for her to see. Her brows drew together as she stared intently at the photo of a young Waylon Pope. For a few beats I actually thought she was going to tell us he was the man who took her sister. She closed her eyes and shook her head.

"No," she said. "I've never seen that man, not ever."

"Take another look," Ben said. "This photo would have been taken a few years before you saw him. Try to picture him with long hair and a beard."

Carrie Ann cast a passing glance at Ben's phone and looked him in the eye. "I'm absolutely certain. Randy Cousins took my sister, not this man."

I expected Ben to press the issue further but instead he put his phone away and stood. Bending down, he offered his pinkie to the baby who grasped it with his wet fingers. When Ben gave Jason's hand a gentle shake, the child giggled. Turning to Carrie Ann, Ben said, "Thanks for your time. Don't bother getting up. We can see ourselves out."

"Wait, what happens now?" Carrie Ann asked.

"We have a few other details to nail down before we can put this one to bed. We'll be in touch if anything comes up."

"Promise me one thing. If you want to contact anyone else in my family, call me first. My mother . . . well, my mother is fragile. And my father abandoned us soon after Savannah died. I tracked him down after Jason was born but he didn't want to see us. Don't you see? Losing Savannah destroyed our whole family."

"I understand." Ben took his pinkie back from Jason and placed his hand on Carrie Ann's shoulder. "Thanks again."

Back in Ben's BMW, I heard a muffled ping come from my purse. As Ben put the car in gear, I dug the phone out from the bottom of the bag and checked the screen.

"Anything important?" Ben asked.

I nodded, too shocked to answer.

*

Chapter 28

Cate, 2017

I stared at my phone. The screenshot from Geri showed Waylon Pope looking straight into the gas station's surveillance camera nine minutes before Randy Cousins arrived. When I told Ben, he didn't seem surprised.

"Too many things about this case point to Gator's involvement." Ben stopped for a red light and turned to look at me. "You told me Special Agent Prane thinks Randy Cousins worked with a partner. If they were in on this together, then Cousins is right where he belongs and it's not up to us to bring Waylon Pope to justice. That would be Prane's job."

I mulled that over in my mind for a few minutes. While Ben's words made perfect sense, it didn't feel right. When the light turned green I mentioned something that had been bothering me from the start. "Why do you think Randy never filed an appeal?"

Ben shrugged. "It may have come down to money. The State is only obliged to provide legal assistance for Death Row appeals. Cousins is serving a life sentence. That leaves him with three options. He could hire a lawyer, file an appeal on his own or remain in prison for the rest of his life."

"He was destitute at the time of his arrest, living in the back of a horse trailer parked behind a plumbing supply shop. I'm sure he didn't have the resources to hire a lawyer."

"I think it's time to contact Cousins and see if he'll agree to a meeting."

"What can I do?"

"Check out his alibi. Find out why the jury didn't believe Bob Wickes, the man who saw Cousins in Sarasota at the time of the kidnapping."

"I'll jump on that tomorrow."

Ben checked his watch. "I need to get back to Gainesville to meet with a colleague."

I tried to keep the disappointment out of my voice. "Is there any way you can reschedule? I thought you'd like to see the beach where Savannah was taken. Then later, I was hoping to take you to Sharkey's restaurant for dinner."

Ever since Arnie passed away, I couldn't bring myself to dine out alone. Sitting by myself in a public place, surrounded by happy couples rubbed my emotions raw.

Ben shook his head. "My colleague, Marc is our resident expert on eyewitness misidentification. It's time to get him involved with this case."

I started to protest but Ben held up his hand. "Next visit, I promise."

After he was gone, the silent house closed in around me. I looked down at Rascal who rubbed against my leg. For once, his presence didn't make me feel any less lonely. Phone in hand, I wandered out to the lanai. I turned the pool light on and listened to the crickets raise a racket. The phone vibrated and I remembered I had turned off the ringer while visiting Carrie Ann. I looked down to see Lalo was calling.

"How'd it go?" he asked.

"Nothing we said changed Carrie Ann's position. We even showed her Gator's photo. She still insists Randy Cousins snatched her sister."

"Yeah, well she's wrong. Gator is our guy."

"What did Waylon Jr. tell you?"

"He wasn't much help. The kid was only ten when Gator abandoned him and his mother. Eventually his mom remarried a guy who Waylon Jr. considers his real father. By the way, the mother is deceased. Died of breast cancer last year."

"I saw the photo Lizzy gave you."

"At first, when I said I wanted to speak with her about her brother she refused to see me."

"What changed her mind?"

"I told her Gator's illegitimate son hired me to try and find him."

Just when I thought there was nothing Lalo could say or do to shock me, his blatant lie left me speechless. "Lalo . . ."

"What? Lizzy would never have spoken to me if I told her the truth. She's a nice, church going lady but I doubt she'd be willing to turn in her brother if she knew finding him meant he'd spend the rest of his life in prison. But when she thought she had a blood relative that she never knew about . . ."

I clicked my tongue. "One of these days your lies are going to catch up with you. Does Lizzy have any idea where Gator is?"

"Not a clue. When I told her we had a copy of the letter she sent to Maggie, she opened up a little. Said Maggie had written to her first, warning her that the FBI was looking for Gator. Sometime later Lizzy got another envelope in the mail with a thousand dollars and no return address. She figured it was from Gator and gave the money to her church."

"Now we know how that part of the ransom surfaced in Beaufort."

"There's one more thing."

The crickets grew quiet. The dark night seemed to hold its breath in anticipation of what Lalo was about to say.

"She told me Gator was an excellent underwater swimmer. He could stay under for miles by using a rebreather, something he learned during SEAL training. That explains how he collected the ransom without us seeing him. Forget Prane's partner theory. Gator is our man."

My friend Annie shoved her canvas bag into the back of my Prius and slammed the hatch closed before climbing into the seat next to me. She called earlier in the day asking for a lift to our grief counseling meeting. Her Volkswagen Beetle was out of commission. Something about a cracked engine block. Sounded serious to me.

Traffic on the island was light. I loved this time of year when half the population went up north to their second homes while we full-time residents enjoyed our quiet little town. I knew it was only a matter of months before the snowbirds returned in force but for now traffic was light, taking me only ten minutes to arrive at the Community Center. Annie and I were first to show up, a good thing given she needed time to get ready for the meeting.

While she taped her laminated GRIEF GROUP sign to the door, I arranged chairs in a semi-circle. This was a safe space where I came to learn how to deal with the loss of my husband. The carpeted floor and padded chairs made the windowless room cozy. People started drifting in. Though we knew each other well, not a word was spoken. I settled down in my usual seat in the corner.

I stared straight ahead at Annie who wore her signature tie-dyed kaftan. Her face was deeply tanned and wrinkled by the sun. White age spots marked her arms. It was difficult to tell exactly how old Annie was but my best guess was somewhere north of seventy.

As people took their seats, she set a box of tissues on the floor in the middle of the room. I watched as she fished a book out of her tote bag and thumbed through the pages until she found the passage she sought.

For the most part our gathering of a dozen or so didn't change from one month to the next. From time to time some dropped out. A few weeks ago I bumped into one of those people downtown. Walking hand-in-hand with an older gentleman, she glowed like a schoolgirl on her first date. I couldn't imagine ever feeling that way again.

Annie cleared her throat and smiled broadly, revealing her chipped tooth. "Last time we met we spoke about the importance of recognizing when it's time to let go. Before we move on to a new topic, does anyone have anything to add?"

A hand shot up. Diane, who never lacked for words spoke.

"After I left here I got to thinking about my husband's shirts. They were all still in our closet, hanging exactly like they were on the day he died. Don't ask me why I never cleared them out. They gave me comfort, I guess." Her eyes brimmed with tears as she choked out the words.

A murmur went around the room as several people encouraged her to go on.

"Anyway, all that talk about shedding the past to make way for the future . . . It occurred to me his clothes were holding me back. The following day I gave them to the hospital charity shop."

Diane took a deep breath before continuing. "I'm sorry. This is so hard for me. I know it was time to move on. And I do feel like a burden has been lifted from my shoulders but still . . ." She reached for the box of tissues.

Annie nodded in sympathy. "That was brave of you, Diane. Anyone else?"

Except for the sound of Diane sniffling, the room fell silent. Annie waited a few minutes. She glanced at the dog-eared paperback on her lap and began to read.

"*You know the feeling. Suddenly you feel off center, thrust into a state of anxiety, depression, guilt or shame. The process of identifying what your triggers are, getting to know and understand them, will help you heal.*"

Annie eased the book closed and waited again for someone to speak. A few people shifted in their seats.

"I thought I was doing well," Diane said at last. "You know, moving on with my life. But while I was packing my husband's shirts, I saw the photo album I keep on the top shelf of my closet. I've looked at those photos a hundred times since he died, but for some reason, when I saw him standing on the beach with a can of beer in his hand and that big goofy grin on his face, I lost it."

Annie spoke in a soothing voice. "Photos can be a comfort, a reminder of the good times with our loved ones. But as we just heard, an emotional trigger can knock you off center. Have you looked at those photos since?"

Diane held a fresh tissue to her tearing eyes and shook her head.

"Take your time. If looking at the photos makes you sad, leave them on the shelf. You know best what is healthy for you and what isn't."

Gill, a well-dressed woman whose designer shoes matched her handbags spoke up. "On my way to the dry cleaners yesterday an old song came on the radio. I'm sure most of you remember 'Stairway to Heaven.' Anyway, Denny and I danced to that song at our high school prom. Right there, on my way to the hairdressers I burst out crying. Until then I thought I was past all that. Denny has been gone for over a year now. Is it ever going to get better?"

Several people in the room said they understood. Annie gave Gill a sympathetic half-smile. "Part of healing means we're going to relapse now and then. It happens to all of us."

Tracy, the youngest one in our group touched the locket around her neck. "I'm glad to hear I'm not the only one. Most of you know I started seeing someone a few months back. He seemed nice, took me out to nice restaurants and stuff like that. I actually felt like everything was going to be okay again. There were whole weeks when I didn't even think about my husband. Some of you probably noticed I stopped coming to Grief Group."

She glanced around the room and though I hadn't missed her at all I found myself nodding with everyone else. Drawing encouragement to go on, she continued.

"After a while this guy started to get possessive. You know what I mean. He kept pressuring me to take off my locket. I don't know, maybe wearing my husband's ashes creeped him out. At first I agreed to take it off but then I realized if I wanted to wear my husband's ashes that was my business and nobody else's. So I put the locket back on and here I am, alone again, feeling like crap. I keep thinking things will never be the same as they were before my husband died."

As she finished speaking, the door opened. I looked up to see a silver-haired man dressed in a button-down shirt and chinos. He spotted the empty chair next to me and sat down.

"After shave."

Every head in the room turned to look at me. Heat rose to my cheeks as I hurried to explain my outburst.

"Whenever I come across someone wearing my husband's after shave, for a split second I forget he's gone. I expect to see him standing there, right next to me. It catches me out every time."

Gill reached over and placed her hand on mine. "When did your husband die?"

"A little over three years ago."

A few people looked at me in surprise. Most had struggled with their loss for much less time. Here I was, three years later and still unable to completely shed my grief.

Annie tipped her head to the side. "The important thing is to be aware of these emotional triggers. They're random so don't even try to avoid them. You have no control over the radio station's playlist or what aftershave someone is wearing. If you have an emotional reaction, all you can do is try to figure out why, what the trigger is and go with it."

Annie glanced at her watch. She reached for the other book still in her bag. "I'm afraid we're out of time tonight. Let's wrap things up with a quote. Who wants to pick the page?"

Tracy, still grasping her locket, called out. "Seventeen."

"Is there some significance to that number?" Annie asked.

"My wedding anniversary."

"Let's see now . . ." Annie thumbed through the book looking for the page. Clearing her throat, she began. *Give sorrow words. The grief that does not speak whispers the o'er-fraught heart and bids it break.*

"Oh, that's perfect," Tracy squealed. "That's why we're here. To give our sorrow words so our hearts don't break."

A deep voice next to me spoke out. "Isn't that Shakespeare?"

Annie beamed at Button Down. "That's right, from Macbeth. Remember everyone, if you feel overwhelmed, use the tools we spoke about a few months ago. Deep breathing exercises, meditation, whatever works for you. Most of all, be kind to yourself. And remember, you are not alone. We are on this transitional journey together."

I jumped up, anxious to leave. As I started stacking chairs, Button Down reached out to take one from my hands.

"Let me do that."

"No, really. I can manage."

"This is no work for a lady."

I bristled at his comment. Making a point of grabbing the last chair, I slammed it on top of the stack.

Button Down rubbed his palm against the side of his pants and extended his hand to me. "I'm Mike."

I grasped his hand firmly. "Cate Stokes."

Annie approached with a leather-fringed purse slung over her shoulder, the heavy tote bag hanging at her side.

"Mike is the guy I told you about, Cate. He recently moved here from New Hampshire." Annie flashed him a smile. "Cate's from New Hampshire too."

Mike turned to look at me. "It's very nice meeting you, Cate. I hope to see you again next time."

Later, after parking in front of Annie's house I removed her things from the car's trunk. Following her into the house, I set the tote bag on the foyer's cracked floor. She headed straight for the kitchen, calling over her shoulder.

"Stay for tea."

Annie's idea of tea was a concoction of crushed nuts and broken twigs steeped in warm water that ended up tasting like dirt.

"No thanks. I've got work to do."

Her voiced reached me from the kitchen. "Work? Since when did you get a job?"

"I'm doing some pro-bono work for my nephew, Ben."

Annie stuck her head around the corner, eyes opened wide. "When did that start?"

"Remember I told you Geri Garibaldi and I met for lunch last month?"

Annie nodded.

"Well, some new evidence in one of her old murder cases surfaced. The more we look into it, the more Ben and I are convinced the convicted man is innocent."

"I'm sure your nephew won't mind if you take a tea break. After all, I want to know what you think about Mike, the guy who wears Arnie's aftershave."

Chapter 29

Downtown Sarasota buzzed. Artist from all over the country came for the annual Fall Art Festival on Main Street. The smell of grilled onions and sausage drifted from the food vendor's booths. People jammed the sidewalks, sweating under the glaring September sun. Some clutched bubble-wrapped artwork under their arms while most browsed the artist's exhibits empty-handed. I sat sipping iced tea at an outdoor cafe while waiting for Geri.

A flash of pink caught my eye. Looking up I saw the detective towering over me, her lips painted to match her tight-fitting t-shirt. She took a seat and peered over the top of her mirrored sunglasses. "You picked a helluva time to come downtown."

"I forgot about the Festival."

She caught the attention of a waitress who struggled under the burden of a tray loaded with dirty dishes. "Bring me some sweet tea, will ya? And a glass of extra ice on the side."

The waitress glanced over her shoulder, a weary expression on her face. Her eyes opened wide at the sight of the gold badge hanging on a lanyard around Geri's neck. "Oh hey, Detective. Give me a sec. I'll be right with you."

I looked at Geri in wonder. "I sat here for twenty minutes before she gave me a second look."

The waitress returned with Geri's tea and two menus.

"Sorry to keep you waiting, Detective. The boss said to tell you lunch is on the house."

Geri gave her a tight smile. "Thanks but no thanks. What do you recommend today?"

"The salmon quiche is fresh. I'd stay away from the tomato flatbread."

"I'll take the quiche. What about you, Cate?"

"Make it two. And please bring me another unsweetened iced tea when you come back."

I smiled as the girl ran off. "Do you get this kind of service all over town?"

"Only when they see the badge." She glanced at the steady stream of people passing by. "Actually, this is one of my favorite places for lunch. It's usually a quiet spot but with all this going on . . ." She waved her hand at the crowd of people. "After lunch we should probably go back to my office."

I nodded agreement. Discussing a case in public, especially one as politically charged as this one, was not a good idea. The waitress came back with our lunch and two sweating glasses of tea filled to the brim.

The quiche was delicious, filled with chunks of flaky salmon. As I took a second bite, I noticed an emaciated lady dressed in rags staring at me. I felt uncomfortable, torn between offering her something to eat or ignoring her. Before I could make up my mind she shuffled across the street, heading for a trash can on the sidewalk. Bending down, she fished out the rumpled pages of the *Sarasota Herald Tribune*. Weaving her head from side to side, she tucked the paper under her arm and melted into the crowd.

Geri caught me looking. "We call her Crazy Betty. I have no idea what her real name is. Every now and then she wanders into a shop and makes a nuisance of herself. By the time the cops respond to the call she's gone. I've seen her a few times on a park bench in Five Points Park. Maybe she's heading that way now to read the paper."

"Is she homeless?"

"Probably."

"Like Maggie Blue."

Geri sighed. "Exactly."

After we paid for lunch, she led the way through a side street to Ringling Boulevard. When we entered the lobby of the County Building, Geri flashed her badge and the security guards waved us through. We rode the elevator to her office floor in silence. As soon as we settled into the same conference room where I sat with Lalo a few short weeks ago, I pulled my phone out and showed her the photo of Waylon Pope.

The corners of Geri's mouth turned down. "That's the guy I found on the surveillance tape. You're going to tell me this is Gator, right?"

I nodded. "His real name is Waylon Pope. Lalo got this photo from Gator's sister in South Carolina."

"Where's Pope now?"

"No one knows. Back in 1994 Pope sent his sister a package in the mail. Inside she found a thousand dollars in twenties. No note, no return address. That was the last she heard from him."

"How did you find her?"

I shifted in my seat. "There was a letter mixed in with Maggie's things."

"A letter from Pope?"

"No, his sister, Lizzy Holt. Lalo drove up to Beaufort to meet her and Gator's son."

"You're losing me." Geri picked up a pencil and started tapping it on the top of the table. "Back up and start over."

I told her about seeing the maps in Special Agent Prane's office. When I explained that some of the money turned up in Beaufort, Geri stuck the pencil behind her ear, leaned back in her chair and stared at the ceiling.

"So Steve knew about Gator all along."

I gave her a weak smile. "And now he knows about Lizzy Holt."

"Let me see that letter."

"Prane has it. He said you could get a copy after you opened an official re-investigation."

Geri sat up straight and pounded the table. "Damnit."

"Don't take it personally. He strikes me as someone who holds his cards close to his vest. By the way, while I was there I saw all the other places marked on his map."

"Like where?"

"South Florida, mostly. Miami, Fort Myers . . . This may not mean anything but he marked the locations where the money turned up with three different colors."

"Okay, I get the connection between this letter Maggie had and the ransom turning up in Beaufort. But how did you track down Gator's son?"

"We found him on the Internet together with an address for Lizzy Holt. Lalo drove up there, gave Lizzy a story about why he was looking for Gator and . . ." I cleared my throat. "Anyway, Waylon Jr. didn't know anything about his dad but Lizzy had this photo of Gator when he was much younger."

Geri grabbed the pencil from behind her ear and started tapping again. "Maybe it's time for me to speak to my captain about re-opening the investigation."

"That would be a good idea. You need to move fast if you want to beat Prane from speaking with Lizzy. Or for that matter, Ben from signing Randy Cousins as a client."

"You're not serious, are you? The Project sets a pretty high bar before taking on a new client. I wouldn't have thought you had enough evidence for them to take the bait."

I felt the heat rising to my cheeks. "Ben is planning to set up an exploratory meeting with Cousins."

"Great. The whole world is going to know about this now."

"Isn't that why you came to me in the first place? By the way, Ben asked me to find out more about Bob Wickes."

"Cousins' alibi?" Geri drew in a deep breath and pressed her fingers to her temple. "I wondered how long it would take you to get around to Wickes."

"Tell me about him."

"He owned a liquor store in Sarasota that Cousins frequented. Wickes gave sworn testimony that Cousins came into the store that morning to buy a liter of gin."

"If Randy went to the store often, how could Wickes be sure that was the day Savannah was taken?"

"Because Cousins was more drunk than normal. He backed his beat-up horse trailer into the side of the building when he left."

"Sounds like a good alibi to me. So why did you go ahead and charge Randy with Savannah's murder?"

"Because of the time stamp on the store receipt. Cousins paid for the gin thirty-two minutes before Savannah was snatched which gave him plenty of time to get from Sarasota to Venice." Geri shook her head. "Besides, at that point Cousins was all we had. With every day that passed, the political pressure to solve the case got more and more intense. Anyway, at the end of the day it wasn't my call. That was up to the prosecutor. Dave Hall believed the rest of the evidence was enough for a conviction so he went ahead and filed the charges."

Remembering Ben's admonition to find a legal foothold in the case, an idea popped into my head. A legal procedure known as discovery required the prosecutor to share
essential evidence with Cousins' lawyer in advance of the
trial. If the prosecutor violated that procedure it would give
Ben something to sink his teeth into. I sat up straight in my
chair. "I didn't see the store receipt listed as evidence in the
trial summary. Did the prosecutor include it in the discovery
package?"

Geri shrugged. "I assume so. I turned it over to Steve.
He probably passed it along to Dave Hall. I don't believe either one of them would risk the case by withholding evidence
from the defense."

"You're saying you saw the receipt with your own two
eyes?"

"I'm the one who found it under the driver's seat of
Cousins' pickup truck. And before you go all 'legal loop hole'
on me, I assure you the search was legit. Steve arranged for the
warrant."

"Can you help me get a look at the Public Defender's
records?"

Geri reached for her phone and pressed a number. I
heard Dix Powers, the Public Defender Administrator answer.

"Hey Dix. I need a favor. Remember the Savannah Troy
murder? . . . That's the one. Any chance Cate Stokes can get a
look at your case file? . . . Right, the same Cate that worked on
the Murphy case last year . . . Great. I'll tell her."

She pocketed her phone and turned to me with a smile.
"Dix remembers you. She said to drop by tomorrow afternoon.
I don't know whether to hope that receipt is in the PD's files or
not. Dave Hall will throw a fit if we accuse him of intention-
ally suppressing evidence. Listen, now that I'm going to start

rattling cages around here, I need to stay on top of this thing. I don't care what time of day or night, call me if you learn anything new, okay?"

As I drove south on Rt. 41, I tuned my car radio to NPR. A specialist on climate change claimed this year's active hurricane season was the result of mankind's disregard for the amount of fossil fuels we burned. Hurricane Harvey was presently churning in the Gulf of Mexico while another storm system was forming off the coast of Africa. According to the expert on the radio, we could expect many more violent storms if we didn't take global warming seriously. As I crossed the bridge to Venice, I found myself mentally checking out. I'd heard it all before and my immediate concern took priority. All I wanted was to get home, kick off my shoes and unwind from a long day.

Turning onto my street, I saw Lalo's empty truck parked in front of the house. In the flower bed by the front door, I noticed the fake rock where I hid a spare key had been moved. Inside the house I found a bag of potatoes sitting on the kitchen counter next to two thick steaks swimming in marinade. When I stepped into the living room, Maya raised her head, her stumpy tail beating the rug. Lalo sat on my couch facing the television, a half-empty wine glass in his hand. Rascal lay curled up on his lap.

"I see you've made yourself at home."

When he looked up, the sight of Lalo's face stole my breath away. His eye was swollen shut, the raw skin surrounding it a deep shade of purple. I reached down to brush my fingers against the side of his cheek.

"Who did this to you?"

He winced at my touch. "I want to hear the weather report first. Grab the bottle and join me."

I returned to the living room with a clean glass and the half-empty bottle of wine. He took the bottle from me and filled my glass before topping up his own. I plopped down next to him on the couch, watching as the weatherman described hurricane Harvey's progress. Overnight the storm had developed into a massive storm. Because the Gulf's temperature was above average, the expectation was the Harvey would continue to gather strength. The latest forecast was that it would hit landfall somewhere in Texas as a Category 4 hurricane. The weatherman ended his report by forecasting cloudless skies in Venice throughout the week.

"It doesn't seem we have anything to worry about," I said.

"That hurricane is still a long way off. There's no way to predict where Harvey will go or how bad the storm will be once it hits."

Talk about distant storms and global warming didn't interest me at the moment. I took the remote control out of Lalo's hand and turned off the television. "Okay, now tell me how you got that black eye."

Chapter 30

Maggie sat in Five Points Park sipping her morning vodka through a straw. These past two months she had been glad to have a roof over her head but the meds made it difficult for her to concentrate. She almost forgot what she was waiting for until a stranger emerged from the library and dropped his newspaper in the trash. Rising from the bench, Maggie shuffled across the street and reached into the can. She pulled out the paper to find it neatly folded, free of spilled coffee or greasy donut crumbs. With a satisfied grunt she tucked the paper under her arm and stepped out of the wilting humidity into the cool, dry air of the library.

The librarian looked up. Maggie knew the gray-haired lady would leave her alone as long as she did not overstay her welcome. Casting her eyes to the ground, she moved to a quiet corner, sat down and unfolded the paper. The headline gave her a jolt.

BODY OF CHILD FOUND ON CASPERSEN BEACH

She sat frozen, staring at the words. Below the headline she saw the picture of a man who looked vaguely familiar. Fighting to recall where she had seen that face before, she closed her eyes. The man remained nothing more than a foggy memory. She scanned the article with a morbid dread, turning to the inside page where she learned the body was found by the man in the picture. An investigation was underway to determine if the remains were those of Savannah Troy.

Maggie was filled with rage. If only Gator had let her keep the child. With all that ransom money, they could have lived the rest of their lives in luxury on some Caribbean island. Now Gator was free as a bird while she was practically a prisoner in her motel apartment. Given the unsavory neighborhood—not to mention the sleazy manager—she kept her knife safely tucked under her mattress. She was careful not to be caught with alcohol in her apartment. By day Maggie drank in the park or at the water's edge overlooking the sailboats moored in the bay. At night she drank on the steps of the abandoned Children's Museum where nobody paid any attention to the group of homeless people who gathered there.

She took her time reading the article again. In the last paragraph, the reporter said he contacted the police to ask if there were any recent developments in the Troy case. Detective Eduardo Sanchez replied, "no comment."

Maggie re-folded the paper. With a slurping noise, she sucked up the last drop of vodka. Touching her wool cap for reassurance, she left the library with the newspaper clutched in her hand. An hour later she stepped off the bus and staggered the few short blocks home. In her addled state she never noticed the pickup truck parked in front of her door. While fumbling with the key, she heard Lalo's voice.

"Hello, Mags."

Maggie spun around, the key slipping from her hand.

"Thought I'd drop by to see how you're doing." In one hand Lalo gripped a white paper bag from the deli, in the other a stack of letters. "On the way I stopped at your mother's house to pick up your mail."

Maggie stood up straight, trying to appear sober. "It's all junk."

Lalo held up the bag. "I also brought sandwiches."

Maggie picked up the key and unlocked the door, leaving it open behind her. Lalo followed and sat down at the small table crammed into a corner.

She crossed the room to her bed and dropped the mail on the blanket. Shoving the newspaper under her pillow she turned to face Lalo. "What kind of sandwiches?"

In the two months since she last saw him, the detective seemed to have lost weight. He looked tired, dark circles under his eyes, his straight black hair grown over the back of his collar. He reached into the bag and pulled out two wrapped sandwiches. "Your choice. Philly cheese steak or chicken Caesar wrap."

"I'll take the chicken wrap." Maggie sat down across from him and pointed to the bag. "Please tell me you have beer in there."

The detective removed two cans of soda and set them on the table. His eyes drifted to the mattress. "I noticed you picked up a copy of this morning's paper."

Maggie took a bite of her sandwich. "So?"

"So you know we found Savannah's body."

Maggie swallowed hard, the food caught in her throat.

Lalo's thick eyebrows drew together. "A man named Randy Cousins found her."

The image of the man in the paper leapt out from her memory. Randy, the man with the horse trailer.

The lie came easily. "Never heard of him."

"Funny how you keep forgetting people you know. Cousins says he met you a few months ago. Found you wandering down the middle of Route 41 with your shopping cart. He gave you a ride to Venice."

"Oh, him. He never told me his name."

The look in Lalo's eyes told her she wasn't fooling anyone. "Cousins claims he was looking for loose change on Caspersen Beach when he saw a bone sticking out of the dunes. We're waiting for DNA confirmation but you and I both know it's Savannah."

"How would I know that?"

"Don't play dumb, Maggie. You have to trust me. I'm not here to arrest you. I only want to catch the bastard who killed that little girl."

"How many times do I have to tell you? I don't know where Gator is."

"Do you have any idea what three months in the Florida heat did to Savannah's body? What the animals didn't get, the insects finished off. All that's left of her clothes are a few wormy scraps. We found her skull six feet away from her jaw bone."

Maggie clamped both hands over her ears. "Shut up!"

Lalo reached across the table and gently pushed her hands down. "Cousins meets the description of the man who snatched Savannah from the beach but there's something about the guy . . . Anyway, the powers that be have decided to charge him with Savannah's murder."

The news took Maggie by surprise. She quickly recovered, feigning indifference with a shrug. "Congratulations."

Lalo stared at her for a few beats, his face void of all expression. "Cousins doesn't strike me as a man who collected fifty thousand dollars three months ago. The guy still works cutting lawns. He lives in a broken-down horse trailer parked behind a friend's plumbing shop. The poor idiot thinks he's going to get a reward for finding Savannah when right now the State Attorney is planning to send him away for life."

Maggie couldn't hide the tremor in her hand when she reached for the soda. Pulling it back, she gripped the edge of the table.

Lalo studied her. "Talk to me, Maggie."

Maggie rose unsteadily to her feet. "I don't have anything to say to you."

"Tell me where Gator is."

"How would I know? I haven't seen him since . . ." She caught herself mid-sentence. Running her palms down the front of her dress, she gripped the back of her chair. "I don't know where he is. He's gone."

As she stood there, her eyes fell on the stack of mail on the bed. At the top of the pile was a hand-written envelope from Lizzy Holt.

Lalo continued to probe her for information about Gator but Maggie shook her head in response to every question. Before long, he gave up. As soon as the door closed behind him, Maggie picked up the envelope. Hands shaking, she tore open the flap. Inside, she found a single sheet of paper. On it Lizzy Holt wrote, "Sorry that I cannot help you. I haven't seen my brother in years. Your letter said Waylon is in some kind of trouble again. If you find him, tell him to stay away from me and my family. He's not welcome here."

With the letter dangling from her fingers, Maggie felt a wave of relief wash over her. If his own sister didn't know where Gator was, then he must be gone for good. As she stood there, the window air conditioner kept up its death rattle. The place was a dump. There were brown marks under the window where the rain leaked in, rust stains in the bathtub and a mouse trap under the kitchen sink. Aside from the healthcare worker who gave her weekly injections, the only person Maggie had spoken to in days was Lalo. Her caseworker, Sylvia

Branch was not due to check in on her until the end of the month. It would be so easy for her to leave this place. To go back to Venice where she could sneak past Poppy's school now and then and catch a glimpse of her daughter during recess.

Her gaze landed on the framed photo on her nightstand. Poppy smiled at her from behind the cracked glass. Maggie picked it up, ready to start packing. Something held her back. If she left now, Sylvia would kick her out of the program. And that meant Maggie would never regain visitation rights of her daughter. With a sigh, Maggie set the photo down. Returning Lizzy's letter to its envelope, she stuffed it in the bag with Poppy's things.

That night she woke to the sound of a child screaming. Heart pounding, she got up to turn on the light. Maggie had no memory of the day she drove with Poppy straight into the Gulf of Mexico. She only recalled a sense of dark desperation that compelled her to end it all. Helen told Maggie that when they pulled her out of the car, Poppy was strapped in the seat next to her, screaming in fear.

Returning to bed, she pulled the covers to her chin, hoping the light would keep her demons at bay.

Chapter 31

Cate, 2017

I grabbed a bag of peas from the freezer for Lalo. A groan of relief escaped his lips as he pressed them against his damaged face. He reached for the remote and turned the volume up.

"Are you going to sit there and watch the weather channel all night?" I asked.

Lalo turned to look at me. "The folks on the Texas coast are in for a few bad days."

"What about that other storm?"

"Still out in the Atlantic. Nothing to worry about yet."

"So tell me, who gave you the black eye?"

"Striker."

"Your daughter's boyfriend?"

Lalo nodded. "I stopped on my way home back from Beaufort. My daughter, Marilena answered the door with her arm in a cast and a nasty bruise on her cheek. This wasn't the first time Striker hit her but it damned well better be the last."

"Is he gone?"

Lalo sat up straight to look at me. "For now. He's probably still getting stitched up in the ER. I've been through this kind of thing with Mari before. Same story, different guy."

"I'm sorry."

"Yeah, me too. At least Bree is safe."

"Is she happy to be back at school?"

"I think she'd rather be here helping with the case."

"Lean back and keep that bag of peas on your eye. I'm going to start dinner."

I went into the kitchen, took one look at the beef and pulled out my largest skillet. Opening the refrigerator, I removed the beans I picked from my garden that morning and started peeling potatoes. With the vegetables cooking on the stove, I turned my attention to the meat. Soon the aroma of sizzling beef filled the room. Maya sat watching with slobber hanging from her jowls. I cut a chunk from one of the steaks, set it on a plate and placed it on the floor in front of her. The meat disappeared down her throat with one gulp. When I returned to the living room to tell Lalo dinner was ready, I found him sitting up on the couch, looking at my phone.

I held out my hand. "Coming into my house when I'm not home is one thing but I draw the line with you reading my email."

"It's from Dix Powers."

I took the phone and glanced down to read Dix was holding Randy Cousins' records for me at the Public Defender's office. Looking up I glared at Lalo. "What if this message was something personal?"

Lalo tilted his head. "A note from Dix? Come on."

"You're missing my point."

"How did you convince her to give you access to the file?"

"Geri arranged it. I'm going there tomorrow. Do you want to join me?"

He shook his head. "Pouring over a bunch of legal documents is more in your line of work than mine. I've got other things to do."

"Suit yourself. Turn off that TV and come to dinner. We can talk about the case while we eat."

With a soft moan Lalo settled into a kitchen chair.

Between bites of food, I filled him in on everything that happened while he was gone. By the time I got around to talking about the visit with Savannah's sister, Lalo had polished off a full bottle of my best Pinot Noir and was working his way to the bottom of a second.

"If Ben signs Cousins as a client, he'll have his work cut out for him," he said, topping up his glass. "Eye witnesses rarely change their story."

"Ben's firm has a lot of experience in that area."

"You know as well as I do—better even—that he has an uphill battle, legally speaking. Cousins' best bet is for me to find Gator."

I nodded agreement. "At least now we know how Gator took the money from the pier without anyone seeing him. Can you explain how he got away? I didn't see anything about that in Geri's notes."

"The ransom operation was Prane's baby. I'm sure he documented everything but he's not into sharing. I never got copies of his reports."

I moved the food around on my plate, wondering if Lalo's problem with Steve Prane was rooted in something personal. Deciding not to stir up that hornet's nest, I stuck to the business of learning what I could about the ransom payment.

"Okay, then tell me what you do know. When did Gator first make contact?"

Lalo took a sip of wine and stared into space. "His letter arrived at the Sheriff's office by mail two days after Savannah was taken. The instructions were written on plain white paper with a ball point pen. There were no prints on either the envelope or the paper itself."

"What did the note say?"

"He told us he had Savannah and included a lock of

her hair as proof. We were instructed to put the money in a canvas satchel and on the appointed day—three days after the letter arrived—we were to tie the bag to an eighteen-foot rope and drop it from the end of the fishing pier."

"I assume Special Agent Prane had a team watching the pier?"

Lalo grabbed the bottle and refilled his glass, taking a healthy swallow before answering. "Sure. Gator threatened to abort if we got within a hundred yards of the drop but Prane positioned his men out of sight on the beach and in the restaurant. He also brought in the Venice Marine Unit to assist. I rode along on one of their boats in the Gulf while Geri rode on the other. We monitored the situation from a hundred yards out, equipped with night-vision binoculars. I wanted Prane to put a few divers in the water but the arrogant prick thought he knew better. He spewed some garbage about divers being in harm's way if the perp came in by boat."

"Then how did he propose catching the guy?"

"Prane put his trust in the transmitter he had sewn into the lining of the bag. He figured if something went wrong at the drop, he could follow the money. So while everyone else kept their eyes on the pier, Prane sat watching the transmitter's position on a screen."

Maya nudged my leg under the table. I slipped her a piece of steak while watching Lalo. "But the transmitter didn't work?"

"Worked great. But Gator was two steps ahead of Prane. He waited until high tide when the bag was submerged, swam in and removed the cash. Must have transferred it to another bag before swimming away."

"Nobody saw him?"

"Believe me, I kept my sights on the pier the whole time and never saw a ripple. After meeting Lizzy I know why."

I leaned forward. "Explain that again."

"According to Lizzy, Gator learned to swim before he took his first step." Lalo shook his head. "The guy trained with the friggin' SEALs for Christ sake. He could swim underwater for miles, navigating with a compass while measuring the distance by the number of kicks he made. He must have used a rebreather because I didn't see any bubbles on the water's surface."

"How did a Navy SEAL end up living in a homeless camp?"

"I didn't say he was a SEAL, just that he trained with them. Failed out of the program and ended up as a Seabee." Downing the contents of his wine glass, Lalo reached for the bottle. "Pisses me off just talking about this."

It was uncharacteristic for Lalo to drink so much. Under the glare of the overhead light his ravaged face looked haggard. After consuming two full bottles of wine, I knew he wasn't in any condition to drive.

"You're sleeping here tonight," I said.

He gave me a wicked grin. "Thanks for the invitation."

I removed the empty bottle from his grasp. "You can sleep in the guest room."

His lined face broke into a full-blown smile. "My things are in the truck."

At first light, I woke to find both Maya and Rascal in bed with me. Maya lay stretched on her side, taking up more than half the bed. Rascal rested on my chest, eyes shut, purring up a storm.

The house was still, not a peep coming from the guest room where Lalo slept. I donned my bathrobe and retrieved the newspaper from my driveway. For the third day in a row, the front page was filled with the story of Snooty, a manatee who lived a record-breaking sixty-nine years in Tampa's aquarium before dying as a result of a tragic accident. Coverage of hurricane Harvey was relegated to page three. There was a small article below which gave passing mention of the other developing storm, still thousands of miles away in the Atlantic Ocean.

While I poured my first cup of coffee, Lalo appeared in my kitchen wearing boxer shorts. Never having seen him without a shirt before, I stared for a moment at the thick, carpet of black hair covering his chest. His unshaven face seemed worse than the night before. The injured eye was swollen shut, the skin around it split and bruised. From that wounded face, a weak smile emerged.

"Got any aspirin?"

I poured him a cup and pointed to the bottle sitting on the table. "Way ahead of you."

Lalo shook out three pills and washed them down with the steaming coffee.

Suspecting he was in no mood for food, I offered anyway. "Can I fix you some breakfast?"

Before I could answer, the doorbell rang. Maya jumped to her feet, hackles raised. I looked up. "Who could that be at this time of day?"

I followed Maya into the foyer. Grabbing her collar, I opened the door to see Mike, the newest member of my grief group. With a swift movement I shoved Maya back into the house, stepped outside and closed the door.

"That's quite a dog you have."

I glanced over my shoulder, realizing Mike got a clear view of Lalo standing half naked in my kitchen. The heat rose to my cheeks as I hastened to explain. "The dog belongs the man you saw in my kitchen."

Mike appeared unsure. "Annie never told me you were in a relationship with someone."

I burst out laughing. "A relationship? Me and Lalo? Never in a million years."

"Then what is he doing here?"

"Not that it's any of your business but Lalo and I are just friends. What can I do for you, Mike?"

"I stopped by to invite you to dinner Monday night. I figured we could go to our Grief Group meeting together and grab a bite later."

The invitation hit me by surprise. "I . . . that is, thanks but I offered to give Annie a ride. Her car is still in the shop."

He hesitated only a moment. "No problem. I'll swing by here a few minutes early, then pick Annie up on the way to the meeting."

I accepted, telling myself it was not a date, simply dinner with friends. As I turned to go back to the house, the curtain in the front room shifted to reveal Lalo's prying eyes. Smiling to myself I went inside.

Chapter 32

Cate, 2017

I arrived at the Public Defender's office downtown on the appointed hour. When I pressed the button, a disembodied voice wanted to know the nature of my business.

"My name is Cate Stokes. Dix Powers is expecting me."

"Fifth door on the right."

I thanked the voice and waited for the buzzer to sound before pulling the door open.

The smell of burnt coffee greeted me. I walked down the hall, my footsteps muted by the gray, industrial carpet. After passing the first four offices, I rapped on the door with Dix's name on it. From inside I heard her familiar voice. Based on the one-sided conversation it was obvious to me that she was on the phone.

"I need more hours, Larry . . . don't give me that bull crap. You've got like, what, a hundred attorneys working for you? . . . Sure, I know they're busy. We're all busy. But do you want Judge Gold to hear your public defender hours are down forty percent over last year? . . . All right then, I'll have the case files ready when she gets here. And Larry? . . . Thanks."

I raised my hand, prepared to knock again when she shouted out. "What are you waiting for? Get in here."

My smile faded when I saw Dix pressing her fingers to her temple. She ran her fingers through her hair, the tight, black coils springing back as she looked up at me. Reaching into her top drawer she pulled out an orange prescription bottle, popped two pills into her mouth and swallowed them dry.

"Good to see you again, Dix."

"Same here but I gotta tell you, I'm a little surprised. How did you get involved in the Troy case?"

"Geri asked me to take a look. Unofficially."

Dix made a sound that could best be described as a growl. "Shit. I thought she'd be over it by now. All right then. Come with me. The files you're looking for are in the conference room."

We walked down the hall in mute silence. Obviously Dix was still upset about something, but I had no way of knowing what. When we got to the end of the hall I peeked through the conference room window to see a middle-aged man sitting on one of the plastic chairs at the long, wooden table. As I watched, he removed the cover of a cardboard file box with Savannah's name and trial date on the side. Below the date someone had written the word, "CLOSED" in black ink.

The man stood when we entered. He scanned me top to bottom with his hooded gray eyes. Thrusting out his hand he didn't wait to be introduced. "Grady Truman, Randy's defense attorney."

My mouth hung open for a few seconds while I gathered my wits. "Dix didn't . . . that is, I wasn't aware you would be here today."

"That's because I asked her not to tell you."

"Why?"

Dix cleared her throat. "After Geri said you wanted to see the Troy file, I realized you were probably angling for a wrongful conviction. Am I right?"

"Yes, but—"

"So I figured it's only fair to let Grady be part of this. It was his case after all."

"You're barking up the wrong tree if you think you're going to pin this one on me, Ms. Stokes," Grady said. "I gave Randy a perfectly competent defense. The guy could have had F. Lee Bailey for a lawyer and it wouldn't have made a damn bit of difference. The local press convicted my client long before I stepped foot in that court room."

Something about him rubbed me the wrong way. "Let's get one thing straight, Mr. Truman. If I find you did not serve your client well then I will not hesitate to get Randy Cousins exonerated by blaming you."

"All right, then," Dix cut in. "Nobody is suggesting Grady did a crap job here. I thought maybe the two of you would work together on this. Come on now, Grady. You never believed your client was guilty, right?"

"You think Randy is innocent?" I asked.

"I'm sure he is." Grady exchanged glances with Dix. "Most of the people who end up here are guilty as charged. But from the start I believed Randy was in the wrong place at the wrong time and took the blame for something he didn't do."

"Then help me prove it."

Dix cleared her throat. "Okay you two. You're going to have to play nice without me. I'm up to my ankles in alligators out there. Between that guy who accidentally shot his son to death and the bastard who murdered two security guards on Longboat Key, my office is stretched to the limit."

For someone who ran the Public Defender's office I thought her choice of words was strange. "Don't you mean *allegedly* murdered two guards?"

Dix dismissed my question with a wave of her hand. "He did it all right. After he shot them, the idiot looked right up at the security camera, waved his gun in the air and grinned. Best I can do is keep his ass off Death Row."

Grady took Dix's elbow and led her to the door. "I'll take this from here."

After Dix left to deal with her alligators, Grady sat down and gave me a cold stare. "You aren't going to find anything to use against me here. I filed all the right motions, deposed all the prosecution's witnesses and spent more time than I probably should have working a case that was doomed from the start."

"Let's start with the discovery documents."

I sensed Grady's demeanor soften. He cocked his head. "You're not basing your case on incompetent legal representation?"

I shook my head. "Just checking all the bases."

Grady extracted a thick Manilla folder from the box. "As far as I know, everything is here. Names and addresses of Dave Hall's witnesses, copies of police reports and the transcript of Randy's statements at the time of his arrest. The coroner's autopsy report is here somewhere too. There wasn't much left of the body so the forensic evidence was sketchy. Dave made good use of the photos, though. At the trial he reduced the jurors to tears."

I reached for the folder and started flipping through the pages. "Did Hall share any exculpatory evidence?"

Grady's eyebrows shot up. "Is there something in particular you're looking for?"

"The search warrant return for Randy's truck."

"Sure, that's in there along with everything else. If memory serves correctly, the cops didn't find anything Dave could use in court so I didn't put a lot of time into that."

"Detective Garibaldi told me she found a liquor store

receipt that backed up Randy's alibi. She gave it to Special Agent Steven Prane."

He scratched his head. "I remember speaking with the store's owner . . . his name was Bill or Bob something."

"Bob Wickes."

"That's the one. Anyway, Bob was pretty clear about the time and date Randy came into the store but unfortunately, we didn't have any way to prove it. Nobody told me about a receipt."

While we spoke, I found the warrant granting permission to search Randy's property. Putting on my reading glasses, I went down the list of items removed from the truck and horse trailer. I squinted at the signature at the bottom of the form. Sliding the paper across the table, I asked, "Can you make out these initials?"

Grady picked up the paper and studied it for a few moments. "Looks like SP. That would be Steven Prane. There's no liquor store receipt listed here. Are you sure Detective Garibaldi isn't confused? This was a long time ago. She must have worked dozens of cases since."

"How well do you know Geri?"

Grady stared at me. "Good point. That's not the kind of mistake she would make."

I ran the legal implications through my mind. If Prane withheld exculpatory evidence—evidence that benefited the accused—then Randy's chances for a wrongful conviction hearing were good. I looked up to see Grady still staring at me.

"I'm no expert," I said. "But I think we've got something here."

"I thought you *were* the expert. Dix told me you've done this before."

I couldn't contain my laughter. "I spent the majority of my career in family law. Last year I helped my nephew with a case, though. He's with a firm in Gainesville that specializes in wrongful convictions."

"The Defender Project?"

"You've heard of them?"

"Of course, they do good work." Grady checked his watch. "Listen, I know you're just getting started here. Take your time with these records. All I ask is you give me the courtesy of a phone call if it looks like this thing is going to bite me in the ass." He extended his hand across the table. "Do we have a deal?"

After we shook on it, he reached into his pocket and pulled out a business card. I looked down to see he was a principal partner in a personal injury law firm. An ambulance chaser.

I suppressed a smile. "I see criminal law isn't exactly your area of expertise either."

He pushed back his chair and stood. "I usually assign our first-year associates to handle pro bono work. Since this was a high-profile case, I took it myself."

Slipping his card into my purse, I turned my attention to the task at hand.

At four thirty Dix poked her head in the door. She gave me a sheepish grin. "Grady seemed happy when he left. Sorry to spring him on you without warning. The lawyers that work for me . . . most of them are great guys. The ones who depend on this work for a living put in long hours for crappy pay. The others, guys like Grady work for free. It's my job to watch their backs, you know?"

"I understand."

"All right then. Find anything interesting?"

I removed my reading glasses and rubbed my tired eyes. "Maybe."

"Geri called a few minutes ago. She wants you to stop by her office before you leave."

I figured she wanted an update. Since the detective's office was only a few floors up, I nodded agreement. "Would you mind if I made some photocopies first?"

"No problem. When the copier asks you to enter a billing code, use 999." She pulled out a chair and sat down. "Tell me what you found."

"There may be an issue with the discovery documents that we can use. Off the record, I want your take on something Grady mentioned. He said Cousins was in the wrong place at the wrong time. Do you know what he meant by that?"

Dix pointed at the files strewn across the table. "Randy found Savannah's remains on Caspersen Beach. Since the prosecution didn't have anything better, they ran with that. As far as I could tell, there was no tangible evidence to prove he murdered the kid."

"You're familiar with the forensic evidence?"

"I checked the file before you got here. There wasn't much left of Savannah by the time they found her." Frown lines creased her tanned face. "Real life is nothing like you see on TV with the victim's skeleton laid out neatly on a table. Never happens, certainly not in this case. They only recovered about a third of her bones. Animals must have made off with the rest. Seems the prosecution didn't have much to work with. Just dental records for a positive identification. That and a trace of chloroform in her remains but the specialists say that could have been naturally occurring."

"So the cause of death wasn't conclusive."

She looked at me from the corner of her eye. "Based on what was left of her lungs and the toxicology report the medical examiner suggested suffocation possibly due to an overdose of chloroform."

I shook my head. "To be exact, he said the evidence 'was consistent with' suffocation as a cause of death. In legal terms, consistent with does not constitute proof."

"I think Grady tried to make that point in court. Obviously, it didn't matter much to the jury."

Her words rang true. Though there was plenty of room for doubt in this case, the jury reached a guilty verdict after deliberating for less than an hour. I gathered up the interview summaries and autopsy report. "I'll go up to see Geri after I run these copies."

Dix stood to leave. "If my office failed Randy Cousins the first time around, I will take that personally. All I ask is that you don't spring any nasty surprises on Grady."

I nodded. "I promise."

"All right then."

Thirty minutes later I turned off the conference room lights and waved to Dix on my way out. While waiting for the elevator, I checked my phone for messages. I only had one, Ben confirming our meeting with Randy Cousins on Saturday. He suggested we get together for lunch at a fast food place in Starke before going to the prison. When the elevator door opened, I was surprised to see Lalo standing inside. The tight skin around his eye had turned eggplant purple. Maya sat by his side wearing a yellow vest with the letters S-E-R-V-I-C-E D-O-G printed in black.

"What are you doing here?"

Lalo took my hand and pulled me into the elevator.

"Geri called. She wants to see us."

I watched the digital lights mark our ascent until the elevator lurched to a stop. Maya rose to her feet. Several office workers waited for us to step out before they pushed their way in. One of them glanced down at Maya's vest, hesitating before squeezing into the elevator with the rest of the crowd.

When the doors closed I turned to Lalo. "You should be ashamed, passing Maya off as a service dog."

"I figured you'd be upset if I left her alone in your house."

"Have you moved in without telling me?"

"I wanted to get some work done."

"Last I heard you lived on your boat."

He shook his head like I was an idiot. "Your wi-fi is faster."

I pinched the bridge of my nose, thinking I could use one of Dix's pills. "Do you know what Geri wants?"

Lalo opened the door to Geri's office. "I have a pretty good idea."

At the sight of Geri, Maya's stubby tail began to wag. Whining, she broke free of her leash and ran to Geri. The detective laughed, roughing the fur around Maya's neck.

"Damn, Lalo. Maya looks great." She tucked her loose bangs back behind an ear. "You, on the other hand look like shit."

Chapter 33

From inside her cell, Maggie struggled to keep Sylvia's blurry face in focus. When she rolled over on the cot, shooting pains stabbed her behind the eyes. She propped herself up on one arm, peering through the bars at her caseworker. "What am I doing here?"

"You threw a vodka bottle at the nurse when she came to give you your injection." Sylvia sounded angry. "Luckily you missed or you'd be facing an assault charge on top of everything else."

Maggie dropped back on the cot and took a deep breath. She fixed her gaze on the ceiling. The dingy white cement had cracks in it. If she squinted just right, she could make them disappear. "I don't remember that."

"The public defender asked me to come down and speak on your behalf. Apparently he found my name in your file. At least you landed a lawyer who cared enough to check. You're due to appear before the judge in an hour. Helen is on her way with her checkbook."

At the mention of her mother, Maggie sat bolt upright. She pressed her fingers to her temple. "You shouldn't have called her."

"What choice did I have? Who but Helen is going to bail you out? Listen Maggie, every time you do something foolish it makes my job more impossible than it already is. I don't think I can protect you this time."

"Protect me from what?"

"The nurse filed a report. My supervisor wants to kick you out of the program."

Maggie glared at Sylvia through her blood-shot eyes. "What do I care? You can tell them to take their stinking apartment and shove it where the sun doesn't shine."

"The only way you can regain visitation rights to see Poppy is by sticking with the program."

Her words hit Maggie hard. Head bent, she watched the tears fall on the thin fabric of her dress. When Sylvia spoke again, the sharp edge of her anger had vanished.

"I'll do what I can. But don't expect the judge to go easy on you. This isn't your first offense."

Maggie listened to Sylvia's heels clacking down the corridor until the sound faded and disappeared. She leaned back, banging her head over and over against the cement wall.

A uniformed guard escorted Maggie into the courtroom. She scanned the room to see if her mother was there. In the back row, Helen sat next to Sylvia, her back stiff as the wooden bench on which they sat. Maggie's lawyer, a public defender with an acne scarred face stood to greet her. He pointed to the empty chairs on the side where they both took a seat. Her attention was drawn to the gray-haired attorney standing next to a disheveled man in front of the judge's bench. The lawyer was arguing to have the charges against his client dismissed. The client looked familiar. Possibly one of Maggie's fellow homeless who hung out at the park. Turning to the accused, the judge spoke.

"I do not take disorderly intoxication lightly, Mr. Samson. Yelling obscenities and throwing trash at people in the park is not acceptable behavior. Having said that, since this is your first time before me, I am letting you off lightly. Six months' probation."

The attorney nudged his client in the side with his elbow.

"Thank you, your honor," Mr. Samson mumbled.

"As a condition of your probation, you will submit to random drug testing as directed by your probation officer. Do you understand what I'm saying?"

"I have to pee in a cup when they tell me to."

"That's right. And if any substance that doesn't belong in there shows up, you will immediately land right back in my court. If that happens, I promise things will not go well for you."

Mr. Samson studied his broken finger nails. His lawyer thanked the judge and they left the courtroom. The gavel came down with a bang. "Who's next?"

The court clerk checked her list. "Margaret Blue, your honor."

At the mention of her name, Maggie's young lawyer gestured for her to get up. He took her by the elbow and walked with her to the front of the courtroom.

The judge peered at the paper his clerk placed before him. "I see this isn't your first rodeo, Ms. Blue."

Maggie's public defender spoke up. "If it pleases the court, we have several character witnesses to appear on behalf of my client, your honor."

The judge gave Maggie's lawyer an amused look. "Getting a little ahead of yourself, aren't you counselor? As you're new to this game, I'll give you a little help. The way we do things here is to let the prosecuting attorney state his case first. After that I get to ask him a few questions. Then you can speak. Not before."

A scarlet blush crept up the neck of the public defender. "Sorry, your honor."

The prosecutor spelled out the events leading up to Maggie's arrest, ending with the flying bottle of vodka that narrowly missed the health care provider. The judge asked if the nurse was present to testify on her own behalf.

"No, your honor. Her child is home sick with the chicken pox. She wasn't able to arrange for childcare."

"Huh." The judge's lower lip stuck out. "Okay, counselor, *now* it's your turn."

Maggie's lawyer took a deep breath. "My client suffers from schizophrenia, your honor. At the time of the alleged attack, she believed she was being threatened. We would like to cite Florida's 'Stand Your Ground Law' in this case."

Maggie glanced over her shoulder to see if her mother was paying attention. When she saw Sylvia waving her index finger in a circle, she turned back around to face the judge.

"Threatened by whom? The health care provider?"

"Well, your honor. The law states that if my client reasonably believed she faced great bodily harm—"

"Hold it right there, counselor. I know what the law states. Did you say your client suffers from schizophrenia?"

"Yes, your honor."

The judge peered over the rim of his reading glasses and raised an eyebrow.

"Is there anyone here who can speak to your client's mental state at the time of the attack?"

"Ms. Blue's caseworker, Sylvia Branch is present today."

At the mention of her name, Sylvia stood.

"Well, Ms. Branch. What do you have to say?"

Sylvia threw her shoulders back, the glass beads in her braids sparkling under the overhead lights. She looked the judge squarely in the eyes and said, "It is entirely possible that Maggie believed her health care provider was attempting to harm her."

"It is also possible that she was hallucinating at the time?"

"Yes, your honor. That is a possibility."

"Thank you, Ms. Branch. You may sit down."

The judge looked down at the paper before him. Maggie shifted from one foot to the other. A low-level of static crept into her brain. When the judge looked back up, his eyes held Maggie in an intense stare.

"I cannot see how you are covered under the Stand Your Ground Law, Ms. Blue. There is no proof that you had reason to believe you were being attacked. In addition, the blood alcohol level at the time of your arrest confirms you were intoxicated when you threw the bottle. In the state of Florida, intoxicated disorderly behavior carries with it a maximum sentence of thirty days in jail and a five hundred dollar fine."

"I don't have five hundred dollars," Maggie said.

"I'm not through. Since the health care provider isn't here to give us her version of events, I have no choice but to dismiss these charges." Lifting his eyes to Sylvia he added. "And perhaps, Ms. Branch, you should look into having your client's medication increased so this doesn't happen again."

With a bang of the gavel, Maggie exhaled.

Outside the courtroom, Maggie shrugged off her mother's attempt to give her a hug. "You shouldn't have come here, Mama."

Helen looked up, anger sparking in her eyes. "Is that the thanks I get for coming all the way down here to bail you out? I have a child to look after, your child as a matter of fact. Every time you do something stupid like this it cost me money for a baby sitter."

Before Maggie could respond, Sylvia approached. The broad smile on her face faded as she glanced from Maggie to

Helen and back again. Taking a drag from her cigarette she turned her head to blow the smoke over her shoulder.

"Well, Maggie, that went better than I thought it would. That judge usually throws the maximum sentence at second-time offenders. If the nurse showed up to testify, you would be spending the next thirty days in jail instead of going back to your apartment."

"I thought you were kicking me out of the program."

A frightened look crossed Helen's face as she turned to face Sylvia. "What is she talking about? You don't expect *me* to take her in, do you?"

Sylvia put a reassuring hand on Helen's arm. "Let me see what I can do. Since the case was dismissed, I might be able to convince my supervisor to give Maggie another chance. I'll make some calls this afternoon."

The twenty-minute ride to her apartment passed in silence. When Sylvia's car came to a halt, Maggie stepped out without so much as a backward glance. Slamming the apartment door behind her, she dropped down on the bed and covered her ears with the palms of her hands. Bits of conversations in her head broke through. She squeezed her eyes shut, trying to block the noise.

"Shut up! I need to think."

She wiped a bead of sweat from her brow and looked around. The room was sweltering. As her gaze landed on the opposite wall she realized why. The long-suffering air conditioner was finally dead. She took it as a sign.

Getting to her feet she pulled one plastic bag after the other from her cart and dumped their contents on the floor. At the bottom she found a tattered backpack. One by one, she made her selections. First into the backpack went the pink hospital wristband from the day Poppy was born. Right behind came Poppy's drawings, the framed photo with the cracked glass, and the lock of curly blond hair. Hesitating for only a moment she added the letter from Lizzy Holt. There was plenty of room left for a spare dress, a few pairs of underwear and her hair brush. Sorting through the various shoes on the floor she selected a pair of sandals that seemed to have some life left in them. On top of everything she squeezed her sketch book, colored pencils and the half-empty can of insect repellent.

Hoisting the backpack over her shoulders, she picked up her sleeping bag and tucked Gator's blue tent under her arm. As she scanned the room for anything she missed, she remembered the knife. Bending down she retrieved it from under the lumpy mattress. Feeling the blade with her thumb she nodded approval. Tucking the knife into the rolled sleeping bag, she pulled on her cap and closed the door behind her. In a final goodbye, she slid the key under the door, turned and walked away.

Chapter 34

Cate, 2017

Maya sat on Geri's feet, her brown eyes closed in ecstasy as the detective scratched the dog behind her ears. I wondered why Geri summoned us to her office. When she gave Maya a final pat, the dog lay down with a grunt. It seemed we were about to begin.

"Good call on those other kidnappings," Geri said. "Could be him."

I looked at her in confusion. "What other kidnappings?"

Geri gave me a knowing smile. "Tell her, Lalo."

"I followed a hunch." Lalo shrugged. "An uptight guy like Prane does everything for a reason. When you said he used different colored dots on his map, I figured they might represent different cases." He winked at me. "With your high-speed Internet, it didn't take me long to find them. Since Savannah, there have been two other children kidnapped within a hundred miles of here. The perpetrator used the same M.O."

I looked at him in surprise before turning to Geri. "Did you know that?"

Geri scowled. "Of course not. The FBI isn't obliged to notify us when an investigation falls outside our jurisdiction."

"Stop making excuses for your boyfriend," Lalo said.

"How many times do I have to tell you? Steve is not my boyfriend."

The banter between Lalo and Geri wasn't getting us

anywhere. And the lines drawn between different law enforcement agencies who worked in adjacent buildings made no sense to me. "Can we focus on why we're here? Where and when did these other kidnappings occur?"

"Eight years after Savannah was killed, a two-year old boy was snatched from the beach in Naples," Lalo said. "Six years later a little girl was taken in Ft. Myers. The newspapers covered both stories until the children were reunited with their families. No arrests were made."

The image of Steve Prane's map was still clear in my mind. A cluster of blue dots appeared around Naples while green ones were concentrated in the Ft. Myers area. Large quantities of both colors joined Savannah's red dots in Miami. "Did you say the children were returned unharmed?"

Lalo nodded. "After the ransom was paid. If Bree were around I would have asked her to hack into the Sheriff's system. Since she's at school, I called Geri instead."

Geri rolled her eyes. "I'll pretend that hacking comment was a joke. When I pulled the files, I learned the Lee and Collier County Sheriff's Departments put one and one together and determined the two cases were related. The perp's ransom demands were identical, right down to the collection method."

I leaned forward in my seat. "Let me guess . . ."

Geri nodded. "Fifty thousand dollars in used twenties, placed in a duffle bag and tied to the end of a pier. He got away clean."

"I'm surprised they didn't connect those kidnappings with Savannah's."

Lalo chimed in. "Savannah's killer was locked up. The guys in Lee and Collier probably figured they were dealing with a copycat."

"My guess is, you're right," Geri said. "And remember,

the M.O. wasn't exactly the same. Those cases didn't involve murder."

My head was spinning from the realization that Gator had kidnapped two other innocent children. "Special Agent Prane is way ahead of us on this. And now that he has the letter from Lizzy Holt, it's only a matter of time before he figures out Gator's name is Waylon Pope."

Geri shrugged. "That wouldn't be a bad thing. But in the meantime, we have to work every angle available to us. What did you learn at the PD's office this morning?"

"The liquor store receipt that you found in Randy's truck was not included in the discovery documents. Either the prosecutor didn't turn it over to Randy's defense lawyer like he was supposed to or Prane withheld the evidence. I won't go so far as to say he held it back on purpose but—"

With a wave of her hand, Geri brushed the idea away like an annoying fly. "I know Steve and believe me, he would never withhold evidence. The receipt probably fell through the cracks. Stuff like that happens. And don't forget, Randy didn't exactly have an iron-clad alibi. It was summer time. There isn't much traffic at that time of year. That gave Randy plenty of time to drive from the liquor store to Venice."

I didn't want to argue with her, but the missing receipt seemed important to me. Ben and I were scheduled to meet the following day. I planned to raise the issue with him before we went to the prison to see Randy Cousins. Having dismissed the missing receipt, Geri returned to the subject of Special Agent Prane's map.

"With all that money turning up in Miami, my guess is we'll find Gator there."

"Doubtful," Lalo said. "My bet is he left the country."

"Why do you say that?"

"If he was still in the States, Prane would have found him already."

I thought of all the times Arnie and I traveled overseas. "To get through immigration, Gator would have needed a passport. And every time you come and go they enter your number into their database. Don't you think Prane had access to that information?"

Lalo pursed his lips. "I've left the country plenty of times without a passport."

"How?"

"By boat."

It was then that it hit me. I don't know why I didn't think of it before. Ninety miles off the coast of Florida there was a place where someone could escape from the US authorities and never be found. In that country, fifty thousand US dollars would last for years. A hundred and fifty would enable someone to live like a king.

Lalo locked eyes with me. "I took the *Chilanga* to Cuba a few years back. The folks at the marina there were happy to take my dollars with no questions asked. Pretty much everyone there has relatives in Miami. I'm sure some of that money made it back here."

Geri tapped the table with the eraser end of her pencil. "I know what you're thinking, Lalo. Don't even go there."

Lalo held up his hands in surrender. "Did I say anything about going to Cuba?"

"You didn't have to. I know how your mind works."

My eyes darted between the two of them, wondering if Lalo was crazy enough to try something that stupid. Even if he were, I realized that if he wanted to sail down to Cuba, there would be no stopping him.

After the meeting, I went straight home to pack for my trip to Starke. Ben and I agreed to meet at a fast food restaurant before driving to the Florida State Prison where we would speak with Randy Cousins. Ben was coming prepared with the paperwork necessary for Randy to file a petition asking the Project to accept him as a client. He didn't yet know about the missing liquor store receipt, but I knew he would be happy to add that to all the other information we had gathered.

Since I planned to visit my sister in the rehab center on Sunday, I needed to bring enough clothes for the whole weekend. Though I had been busy with the case, Nancy was never far from my mind. In the two weeks since Ben checked her in, I hadn't heard a word from her. I was anxious to see how she was doing.

Rascal sat on the bed watching as I threw a few things into my overnight bag. He followed me around the house all evening, sticking close, complaining in a loud voice. I went to bed at my usual time but stayed awake, reviewing my notes on the case. Sometime after midnight I fell asleep with the cat curled on the pillow next to me and copies of the public defender's file spread all over the covers.

Chapter 35

Cate, 2017

At the crack of dawn, I was on the road keeping my Prius to the official limit as I drove across Florida. While I passed through small towns notorious for their speed traps, the car's GPS guided me to the hamburger joint down the road from the prison. Ben sat at a table in the back of the restaurant, his head bent to his cell phone. When I stood by his side and cleared my throat, he looked up with a start.

"Hey, Aunt Cate. I didn't see you come in. How was the drive?"

"No problem," I replied. In truth the journey was tedious. I forgot to bring along my CDs and had nothing to keep me company but static, Spanish music and religious talk radio for the final hour of the trip.

"Are you hungry?"

I could almost feel the grease in the air as the deep fryers bubbled in the back of the restaurant. "Not really. I could do with a cup of coffee, though."

While Ben went to the counter to place our order, I slipped an alcohol wipe from my purse and washed the table. He soon returned with an orange tray loaded with a paper-wrapped burger, a carton of fries and two large coffees. I removed the plastic lid and took a sip. To my surprise, the coffee was absolutely delicious, better than I could have made myself.

"I thought it would be helpful to review the case before we head to the prison," he said between bites of his burger.

I took a look around. Ben had chosen a table away from all the other customers on purpose so no one would overhear our conversation. "Good idea. But before you begin, tell me how your mother is doing."

Ben drew in a deep breath. "Not well. She keeps calling my father, telling him that she wants to come home. He was ready to fly down and bring her back to New Hampshire today but I talked him out of it. Now she's mad at both of us."

"She'll get over it. I have no doubt you're doing the right thing. Even if she doesn't see that now, she will after she gets well again."

"I hope so." Ben popped the last fry in his mouth and washed it down with a slug of coffee. Glancing at his watch he said, "I guess we should get down to business. When I spoke with Randy Cousins about today's meeting, I told him some new information has come to our attention that suggests he might have been wrongfully convicted. Naturally he asked for details. I told him we'd go over everything when we see him."

I drained the last of my coffee and set the paper cup on the table. "I met Cousins' trial lawyer at the Public Defender's office yesterday. He gave me access to his case files."

"Did you find anything?"

"Maybe. A while back Geri Garibaldi found a liquor store receipt in Cousins' truck that placed him twenty miles away from Venice Beach thirty-two minutes before the kidnapping. That receipt should have been included with the discovery documents but there was no record of it on the search warrant return. Geri says it wasn't an iron-clad alibi anyway but it strikes me as strange that the receipt went missing."

Ben squinted his eyes and stared into the distance.

"Hmmm. Failure to disclose exculpatory evidence. Anything else?"

"Nothing specific. Lalo found two other child abductions in Southwest Florida that fit the same pattern as Savannah's. The difference is those kids were returned safe and sound after the ransom was paid."

"Did they take place before or after Savannah was killed?"

"After."

Ben glanced at his watch. "And did they catch the guy?"

"Nope."

"Interesting." Ben stood and picked up the tray with the trash. "Don't mention any of this to Randy when we're with him. Let me do the talking."

We left my car at the restaurant and rode to the prison in Ben's BMW. Passing under the archway leading to the Florida State Prison, I caught sight of the double row of chain linked fence that circled the complex. Coils of razor wire topped the fence, making it impossible for anyone to climb over. A shiver ran down my spine at the memory of visiting Logan Murphy in prison a year earlier. Since Logan was on Death Row where visits are strictly non-contact, he sat manacled and cuffed on the far side of a Plexiglas partition while we spoke. This time would be different. Though Randy was classified as a maximum-security prisoner, Ben and I would meet him face to face in a room reserved for attorney visits.

Abiding by prison rules to avoid tight-fitting or sexy clothing, I wore a loose blouse over a pair of chinos. Ben looked smart in his business suit, a striped tie knotted under the collar of his white shirt. We checked into the visitor's office where our briefcases were searched and our bodies frisked. Ben filled out all the paperwork, checking boxes and signing his name at the bottom of the forms. A guard led us down a cement block hallway. A series of gates opened and closed automatically. At every juncture we waited for one gate to close before the other opened. Finally, with sweat trickling down my back, we were shown into a meeting room with a square table bolted to the floor. Four seats were suspended from the table like something in a public park.

Ben caught me staring. "They don't take any chances," he said. "This way, if tempers get hot, the inmates can't throw the chairs around."

That didn't exactly engender confidence in me. After all, neither one of us had every met Randy so we had no way of knowing what sort of temperament he had. The guard reassured us there would be someone stationed outside the door the entire time he was in the room with us. While that person could not hear our discussion, the glass windows kept us in sight. Until that moment, whenever I thought of Randy I viewed him as an innocent victim of the justice system. But when the guard pointed to the red button we could use in case of emergency, the fact that we were meeting with a convicted murderer serving a life sentence sent chills down my spine. I took my seat next to Ben in the stifling room and braced myself for whatever was about to happen.

Through the window I saw Randy Cousins approach. He walked with a swinging gait, standing a full head taller than the correctional officer who escorted him. Though he still wore his hair the same way he did twenty-two years ago when his mug shot was taken—parted down the middle and tied in a pony tail at the base of his neck—his once brown hair had turned white. He dressed in standard prison blues, a short-sleeved button-down shirt with matching trousers. In his left hand he clutched a black book.

Randy stepped into the room. He remained standing for a moment to get a good look at us. Wiping his palm on his trousers, he accepted the hand Ben extended to him.

"Pleased to meet you, Mr. Cousins. This is my associate, Cate Stokes."

Now that we were up close I noticed Randy's arms were covered with scabs. As he reached across the table to shake my hand I saw a row of blue-black crosses tattooed on his knuckles. After releasing my hand, he took a seat. My eyes were drawn to the dog-eared book he set down on the table between us. On a soft, black leather cover, the title of the book was embossed in gold letters. "The Holy Bible."

"Thanks for seeing us today," Ben began.

"Not like I have anything else to do." Randy shrugged. "What's this all about?"

"I'd like to help you."

"You're a little late, aren't you? I asked you people for help twenty-two years ago. Got a form letter back saying I didn't qualify."

Though I was caught off guard by this information, Ben seemed to take the news in stride. "Unfortunately, Mr. Cousins, our resources are limited. We receive over a thousand petitions for assistance each year. All those years ago, when our attorneys reviewed your case, they couldn't determine a legal path to overturning your conviction."

"So why now? You got something I can use?"

Ben leaned forward and locked eyes with his potential client. "Someone recently confessed to knowing who killed Savannah. After looking into it, we believe her claim could be credible."

"What's the name of this person?"

"Margaret Blue."

A flicker of surprise crossed Randy's face. "Maggie?"

"You know her?" I asked.

Cousins shifted his gaze to me. "Met her a few times, that's all. The first time I saw Maggie she was walking down the middle of a busy road with her shopping cart loaded so high I couldn't believe it didn't topple over. She was never going to make it alive the way she was weaving in and out of traffic like that. So I threw her things in the back of my trailer and gave her a lift. When I stopped for gas, Maggie left without so much as a thank you or God bless." Randy turned back to Ben. "Who is this other guy Maggie mentioned?"

"Does the name Waylon Pope mean anything to you? Friends called him Gator."

I watched for his reaction. If Steve Prane's theory was correct about Randy working with a partner, I figured the mention of Gator's name would prompt a reaction. Randy simply looked down at his tattooed knuckles, his brow creased in concentration. If he had heard the name before, he showed no sign of recognition. "Never heard of him."

Ben switched back to asking about Maggie. "When was the next time you saw Maggie?"

"Let me think . . . it was a few days after I gave her that lift to Venice. I was on the beach looking for loose change with my metal detector and there she was, drunk as a skunk sitting in the dunes. I asked her to come to a meeting with me but she had no interest." He looked up with a grin that revealed a mouth crowded with crooked teeth. "Maybe now she's ready to set herself straight. God must have placed her in my path all those years ago, just like he sent you folks here today. Does all this mean I'm going free?"

"It's not that simple," Ben replied. "We can't use Maggie's statement as evidence in court. She passed away right after confessing."

"What about this Pope fella? What does he have to say?"

"We haven't been able to track him down. Not yet, anyway."

"So where does that leave me?"

Ben reached into his messenger bag and pulled out a sheet of paper. "The first step is to resubmit a petition for help from the Defender Project. Since Cate has done most of the research, she will handle the paperwork. All you have to do is sign this form and give us permission to proceed."

When Randy picked up the paper and began to read, I shot my nephew a look saying he should have asked before volunteering my time.

With a nod of approval, Randy set the paper on the table. "Do you have a pen?"

Ben reached into his suit jacket and handed one to him. As he reached across the table to take it, Randy caught me staring at his arm.

"Skin cancer," he said, glancing at his scabs. "The docs here tell me it's from working in the sun. I used to mow lawns, you see. And of course I spent a lot of time at sea while I was in the Navy."

"I noticed your tattoo. It is exactly like the one Carrie Ann Troy described."

Randy's ponytail swung back and forth as he shook his head. "Nothing unique about my tattoo. Lots of Seabees have them."

Ben glanced up briefly before stuffing the signed form into his messenger bag. "When did you serve?"

"I did my tour on the Constitution in '74. Stayed out in the Gulf of Tonkin the whole year. I've got good memories from that time, mostly. Lucky I didn't join the Marines. Man, they went through a meat grinder."

Having what we came for, Ben waved to the guard to come and collect his prisoner. As Randy walked away, I believed I saw a spring in his step that wasn't there when he first came in to meet us.

Chapter 36

Cate, 2017

I waited for about ten seconds after we left the prison grounds before launching into Ben.

"In case you don't remember, my legal expertise is limited to filing divorce papers and drafting wills. I don't know the first thing about preparing a petition for the Defender Project."

A slow grin spread across Ben's face. "It wouldn't exactly be kosher if my name was at the bottom of that petition, would it? I'll send you a sample that you can use as a template. Shouldn't take you more than a day or so to put everything together. Besides, what I said back there is true. At this point you know more about the details of this case than I do. All you have to do is present the evidence supporting Randy's innocence."

"I saw that expression on your face when you asked Randy about his time in the Navy. What was that all about?"

"It's probably nothing. When I get back to the office, I want to check Gator's service record to see when he served."

"Randy said he never heard of Waylon Pope."

"True, but we shouldn't take his word for it."

I turned the possibilities over in my mind. Prane's theory about Randy working with a partner nagged at my brain. "Do you think Randy might have had something to do with Savannah's murder after all?"

"I simply think it would be prudent to cover all our bases before we get too far down this road. Clients lie, Aunt Cate. I'm not saying Randy is guilty, but in this line of work it's better to check and double check everything before proceeding."

When we arrived back at the fast food restaurant, Ben let his car idle while I gathered the keys from my purse.

"What do you think? Is Randy guilty or not?"

"My gut tells me he's innocent. We just have to prove it."

The next afternoon we arrived at Nancy's rehab center on the stroke of one. Without Ben I would have been hard pressed to find the place. The visitor's building with its picket fence and well-tended gardens filled with colorful hibiscus blooms looked more like an elegant private residence than the main entrance to a rehab center. There was no sign, no street number, nothing that revealed the facility's purpose.

The solidly-built nurse behind the front counter asked for my purse. I handed it over, expecting her to check for drugs or contraband. Without bothering to look inside, she stuffed the bag on a shelf under the counter. Ben gave her his cell phone, wallet and car keys, then signed a form acknowledging the rules and regulations of the facility. As we turned to leave, the nurse called out a reminder to be off the premises by 3:00pm.

We strolled through the winding paths of the campus, past a number of small buildings resembling vacation cottages. Ben spotted Nancy sitting in a rocking chair on a porch. Though we were in plain sight, she seemed unaware of our presence. It was so quiet I could hear the squeak of the wood as she rocked back and forth. Ben and I settled into the two empty chairs next to her.

Ben was the first to break the silence. "It's good to see you, Mom. You look great."

The torment of the past two weeks had taken a toll on my sister. Nancy's vacant eyes were ringed with dark shadows, her skin chalky white. Her hair, a beautiful chestnut brown with red highlights, lay flat against her skull, the gray roots marking the weeks she had been in rehab. The words that came out of her mouth made this woman, my own flesh and blood, sound like a stranger.

"I look like shit, Benny." She glared at him. "Where's your father?"

Ben and I exchanged glances. We had this conversation earlier. Nancy's husband kept coming up with excuses for not visiting. He couldn't get time off of work, the tickets were too expensive, he would come down in a few weeks' time. None of them made sense to me but there was nothing Ben could say or do to persuade him otherwise.

I took her hand in mine. "He's having a hard time getting away from work, that's all."

Nancy whipped her hand away. "I don't need you to make excuses for my husband." She turned back to Ben. "Tell Dad to come and get me. I want to go home."

Ben took a frustrated breath through his nose. "We've talked about this before. You're not ready."

"How much longer are you going to force me to stay here?"

"The doctors recommend a few more weeks."

"Are you kidding? Two more weeks of group sessions, diaries, head shrinkers? Do you have any idea what this place costs?"

"It's for your own good," I said. "If you need some help, I'll be happy to pay—"

"How dare you? The only help I need is to get out of

here. Will you take me with you?"

"You know I can't."

"Then get out and don't come back!"

My legs trembling, I rose to my feet and whispered in Ben's ear that I would wait for him out front.

When the nurse in reception saw my tear-streaked face, she reached under the counter and passed me a box of tissues. "If your sister said something to upset you, don't take it personally."

I blew my nose. "I know."

"Nancy's still in denial but with time and counseling, she'll be able to face the emotional issues that landed her here."

"Emotional issues? She's here because she got hooked on heroin."

The nurse came around the counter and put her hand on my shoulder. "Her physical dependency to opioids is behind her. During her first two weeks we slowly weaned her off the drug. But her addiction, the uncontrollable desire for more, comes from someplace else. The only way for her to address that is through therapy. Did she say she wants to go home?"

I nodded, choking back the tears.

She shook her head "Well, that's what they all say at this stage of rehab. Don't worry, whatever she said to upset you, she didn't mean it. In situations like these we usually recommend giving the patient time to cool off. Skip a few visits and try again. The important thing is to keep Nancy here until the doctors say she's ready to go home."

I grabbed a clean tissue and blew my nose once more. Passing the box back to the nurse, I forced a smile I did not feel.

Chapter 37

Cate, 2017

As soon as I got back in my car I took my phone off airplane mode to discover I had two messages. The first was from Annie, telling me she didn't need a ride to Grief Group after all Her mechanic found a used engine at a junk yard and her VW Beetle was back on the road. Her message was followed by one from Mike saying he would pick me up fifteen minutes before the meeting. For a fleeting moment, the tone of his deep voice sounded familiar. After listening a second time, I decided he didn't sound like Arnie after all. When I hit the call back button, I went straight into voicemail.

"Hi, Mike. It's me, Cate Stokes. Listen, I'm sorry to cancel on such late notice but—" I didn't get the whole sentence out before my phone started vibrating. With a glance I saw it was Mike calling me back.

"I was just leaving you a message," I began.

"Are we still on for dinner?"

"Sorry Mike, I have to cancel."

I let the seconds tick by in silence, waiting for him to respond.

"May I ask why?"

"I'm going to skip the meeting tonight. Annie called to say she doesn't need a ride and frankly, I'm exhausted. For the past few days I've been dealing with a difficult family issue."

"Sorry to hear that. Is there anything I can do to help?"

I thought he was sweet to ask.

"Thanks. But what I need most right now is a good night's sleep."

"How about meeting me for lunch tomorrow? I heard there's a great place on the water in Osprey. Casey's Fish House or something like that."

"The Casey Key Fish House. Unfortunately, I'm going to be tied up for the next few days doing some work for a client," I said. "Are you free next Tuesday?"

"Perfect. And Cate? Whatever your family crisis is, I hope everything works out okay."

After we hung up, I felt a flutter of nerves in my stomach. It had been a long time since I'd been on a first date—if indeed that's what this was. I almost reached for my phone, ready to call Mike and cancel. Then I pictured his smiling face in my mind, and realized how much I needed someone to talk with about Nancy. With a shake of my head, I turned my thoughts to Randy Cousins and his petition for help from the Defender Project.

I sat at my desk, wondering where to begin. Randy's case bore little resemblance to the sample petition Ben sent me. There was no DNA evidence we could use to exonerate him, no recanting of witness testimony and no confession of the crime by another party. Everything hinged on our belief that Randy had been mistakenly identified by the prosecution's star witness. But as long as Carrie Ann Troy stood by her original statement, it would be her word against Randy's.

After a few false starts, I opened a blank worksheet on my computer, titled the first column, "New Evidence," and began listing everything Ben could use to justify a judicial hearing. When I was done, I leaned back and looked at the result.

<u>New Evidence</u>
- Maggie Blue's dying declaration
- Portion of ransom money sent to Lizzy Holt nee Pope
- Helen Blue's identification of Waylon 'Gator' Pope on the surveillance tape
- Liquor store receipt missing from discovery documents
- Similar kidnappings in Lee and Collier Counties while Cousins was incarcerated

Seeing the evidence in black and white, I realized how thin our case was. Against every item on the list, the State could proffer a strong legal argument. For starters, Maggie's dying declaration was inadmissible. And as Geri continued to say, the time stamp on the liquor store receipt—even if it was included in discovery—would not provide an iron-clad alibi for Randy. Nothing we had met the burden of proof needed to convince a judge of Randy's innocence.

With a sigh, I picked up the phone and called Ben.

"We need to convince Carrie Ann Troy that she made a mistake."

Ben laughed. "That would be great, but highly unlikely at this stage of the game. I think we have enough to get started without that. Listen, Aunt Cate, don't worry about Carrie Ann. Once we get the petition approved, our legal team will deal with her."

His message was clear. I was meant to step aside to let the lawyers at the Project take over. I imagined Lalo's reply if I told him as much. Smiling to myself, I knew we would keep going no matter what the Project decided to do.

"Did you get a chance to look into Randy's service record?"

"I did. No overlap with Gator. By all accounts they didn't meet while they were in the Navy."

"So there's nothing we have so far to suggest the two of them knew each other?"

"Right. Which follows that they probably didn't work as partners. Let's keep going on that premise and plow ahead with the petition."

Before letting Ben go, I asked the question that had been on my mind all day. Struggling to keep my voice from breaking I came out with it. "I can't stop thinking about your mother. Has she changed her mind? Will she let me visit her?"

"I'm afraid not."

"Did she explain why she's so mad at me?"

"No, but whatever it is I'm sure she'll get over it."

"I hope so," I said. "When you see her next weekend, tell her I love her."

The moment I hung up the phone it rang. Thinking it was Ben calling back to tell me he forgot something, I was surprised to hear Lalo's deep voice at the other end of the line.

"Open your door."

"What?"

"I said open your front door."

My footsteps rang out on the foyer tiles. Lalo, the phone pressed to his ear, stood on the front porch grinning at me from under the brim of a Baltimore Orioles baseball cap.

"What are you doing here?"

"I thought you might want to come with me to see Helen."

He pushed his sunglasses to the top of his head. While the swelling around his eye had gone down, the bruise had turned a sickly purple. I cringed.

"You look awful."

Chuckling, Lalo slipped the dark shades back on.

"Well? Are you coming or not?"

Stealing a glance in the hallway mirror I realized I didn't have any makeup on. In a feeble attempt at making myself presentable, I ran my fingers through my hair and grabbed my purse.

"It would have been nice if you gave me some advance notice."

He turned and headed back to the truck, waving his phone in the air.

"I called, didn't I?"

Chapter 38

Cate, 2017

Despite Lalo's lead foot on the gas pedal, road repairs slowed our progress across town. Fortunately, that gave me plenty of time to describe my trip to the State Prison with Ben. When I got to the part about Randy's reaction—or lack thereof—at the mention of Gator's name, Lalo nodded.

"Yeah, the more I think about it, the more I believe Prane got that part wrong. It's pretty clear that Gator could have pulled this off by himself. He had the ability and know-how to pick up the ransom without anyone seeing him. Any why would Cousins let his partner get away with the money while he's spending the rest of his life in prison?"

"Not only that, I can't help but think Randy doesn't fit the mold of a murderer. He's too . . . I don't know, religious or something."

"Could be repentance."

"Could be," I agreed. "But I don't think so. By the way, he knew Maggie."

A slow smile spread across Lalo's face.

"You already knew?"

"Yeah, sort of."

He drummed the steering wheel with his fingers.

"Leroy Lamb is meeting with us on the *Chilanga* tomorrow."

"Your friend in the Ft. Myers Sheriff's department?"

"I figured he might give us the inside scoop on their investigation."

"If you're talking about the child who was kidnapped a few years ago then you know that case fell under the jurisdiction of the FBI."

Lalo nodded. "Prane took the lead. But he would have depended on support from the local Sheriff's office. If we play it right, Leroy will tell us what he knows about it."

Sitting in the late summer sun without the engine running, I felt the temperature in the cab rise. A wave of claustrophobia washed over me at the mere thought of being trapped inside the bowels of the boat. Wiping a bead of sweat from my forehead, I made a suggestion.

"Wouldn't it be better if we meet him at his office in Ft. Myers?"

Lalo continued to stare straight ahead, fingers tapping lightly against the wheel. "I want to keep it unofficial. Remember, the perp was never caught. Last thing we want is having the Lee County Sheriff asking us to form a joint task force or something. Better to get Leroy out of his office and a drink or two into him. That will make him more inclined speak openly."

As the sun beat through the windows, the smell of dog intensified. Unable to stand being in the cab another minute, I reached for the door handle and pulled. The heat outside hit me like a blast furnace. A movement in the house caught my eye. Pushing the curtain aside with her boney hand, Helen peered out at us.

Lazy dust motes drifted on a beam of light filtering through the blinds. Helen sat in the same rocking chair where I saw her on the first day we met. Her wig was gone, replaced by a scarf wrapped like a turban around her head. An oxygen tank sat on a trolley next to her rocker, a coil of clear tubing hanging from a hook. Though Helen was still painfully frail, her skin didn't appear as pasty as before. Lalo and I sat across from her on the thread-bare couch.

The Hospice nurse who showed us into the house touched Helen's shoulder and bent down to whisper something. Helen shook her head and waved the woman away. As soon as the nurse left the room, Helen reached for the oxygen tubes and plugged them into her nose.

"You're looking better than the last time we saw you," Lalo said.

Sticking a finger under her scarf, Helen scratched her head. "I decided to stop chemo last week," she said. "No point fighting the inevitable. I figure why go through all that misery when the end result will be the same?"

"I'm sorry," I murmured.

"Don't be. We all gotta go sometime. My husband passed a long time ago and now with Maggie gone . . . I do wish I had more time for Poppy, though. I'm all she has left."

"Where is she?" I asked.

"She's at school. Her students started back to class this week. I didn't want her around while we have this little talk. There are certain things Poppy doesn't know about Maggie and I am determined to keep it that way."

"What things?" Lalo asked.

Helen pointed to a small stack of sketch books sitting on the coffee table. "Hand those to me, will you?"

I jumped up and placed the books on Helen's lap. She stroked the top cover while she continued talking.

"Maggie was a beautiful child. Of course everyone says that about their own babies, but there was something special about that girl. She was so talented, smart too, top of her class. Her illness changed all that."

"When did you first notice something was wrong?" I asked.

"Mid-way through her second year of college. Out of the blue Maggie came home, moved back into her bedroom and closed the door. All day long I heard her talking to herself, gibberish, mostly. When I asked who she was talking to, she said her friends. At first I thought she was putting me on but after a while, I realized the people in her head were as real to her as you are to me."

Helen's chin dropped down to her chest. Her lungs wheezed with every breath. I was about to call the nurse when finally, the old lady looked up and blinked.

"Where was I?" she asked.

Clearly Helen was in no hurry to explain why she asked us there. I knew she would get around to it in her own time.

"You were telling us about Maggie's imaginary friends."

"Oh yes. Things went from bad to worse. Drinking, drugs, in and out of trouble with the police. Sometimes she'd disappear for days without letting me know where she was and God forgive me, at those time all I felt was relief that she wasn't in my house. Eventually Maggie would come back without so much as a how-do-you-do or worse, the phone would ring and it would be the police telling us to come and get her."

"When did Poppy come along?" I asked.

Helen's face broke into a smile, the skin around her eyes folding in a thousand wrinkles.

"I do believe God gave me Poppy to even up the score," she said. "After Maggie found out she was pregnant, she settled down for a while. She never did say who the father was. Truth be told I suspect she didn't know. With all the drugs and alcohol she took, I was worried sick, but Poppy came out fat and healthy. Screamed at the top of her lungs the minute she entered this world. And for the first few months my Maggie was a good mother, fussing over and caring for Poppy. I even thought for a while that maybe having the baby cured Maggie of her illness but of course that's not how it works. Despite the terrible thing she did to Poppy, Maggie loved that child." Helen turned to Lalo. "That's the truth, right Detective?"

Before Lalo could answer, the nurse returned with a full glass of chocolate milk and a thimble-sized paper cup holding two pills. She eyed the oxygen tubes stuck in Helen's nose and gave an approving nod.

"Time for your pain meds, Helen," she said.

Helen took the pills, popped them in her mouth and took a sip. With a grimace, she set the glass down on the table next to her.

The nurse pressed her lips together. "All of it."

"Later," Helen said. "I can only stomach a little bit at a time."

With a grunt and a scowl, the nurse left.

Helen picked up the glass and drained it. "No sense making things easy for her," she said with a wink. "This stuff is supposed to help me put back some of the weight I've lost. Doubt there's enough time for that, but it does taste pretty good."

With a great sigh she set the glass back on the table. "I suppose you want to know why I asked you here."

Lalo pointed to the sketch books balanced on Helen's knees. "I assume it has something to do with those."

Helen resumed stroking the top cover. "Mostly what

you'll see in here are drawings of people Maggie met on the streets. There are some of Poppy too, of course."

Her hand stopped moving. She swallowed hard before continuing. "After you came around asking about Gator, I got to thinking. Some of Maggie's drawings of Poppy didn't look right to me."

Helen sat frozen, pausing a moment before adding, "And then there's this."

She turned back the sketchbook cover and pulled out a small brown envelope, the kind banks used to put coins in. Inside was a snip of blond curls.

"Poppy showed that to me," I said. "She said it's a lock of her baby hair that was among Maggie's belongings."

Helen shook her head. "It isn't Poppy's. From the moment that child came into this world, Poppy's hair has been straight as a board."

Lalo met her gaze without blinking. "Let me see those drawings."

Chapter 39

Sam gave Maggie the silent treatment as they walked down Harbor Boulevard under the blazing August sun. They had argued earlier. He insisted that returning to the place where Savannah's body was discovered was a bad idea. She told him to mind his own business.

The straps on her backpack bit into her shoulders. Her feet screamed in protest as the vinyl strap on her last pair of sandals rubbed her heel raw. As she passed the airport Maggie looked up to see a small plane descend from the sky. She tugged the sides of her cap, cowering under the shadow of the wings. When the plane taxied away, she squinted into the shimmering waves of heat rising from the landing strip. A faded sign, "Flight Instructions at Reasonable Rates" was nailed to the side of the building. Maggie dropped down in the weeds and pulled out her flask. She paused, sensing a slight tickle as a fire ant crawled up her arm. Feeling the burning prick of the insect's sting, Maggie squashed it against her skin. Sam resumed nagging her.

"Why don't you listen to me? You know I'm right."

"You're not always right, you know."

"What if that detective shows up?"

It had been six weeks since Maggie last saw Lalo but deep down inside she knew the detective could appear without warning at any time. She tipped her head back and drained the flask. The last drop of vodka barely wetted her tongue. Maggie peered down the empty road.

"I can handle Lalo."

"You're playing a dangerous game, Maggie."

She snorted a laugh. "I managed just fine without you the whole time I was in Sarasota."

"Are you still mad at me?"

A sigh escaped Maggie's lips. "Leave me alone, Sam."

With a soft moan, she picked up the backpack and started walking. Glancing over her shoulder, she checked to make sure Sam wasn't following. He wore a sad look on his face, waving goodbye before turning around and walking away. Maggie wiped the sweat from her brow with her sleeve and headed to Caspersen Beach.

Leafy branches formed a green canopy over the road. Where the pavement ended, a sign welcomed her to the park. To her right, a wooden walkway snaked along the length of the beach. Maggie slurped lukewarm water from the fountain next to the restrooms.

The place was empty. Curious, she glanced around but with the police tape gone, she had no way of knowing exactly where Gator buried the child. She made her way to the clearing in the woods where she last saw Savannah. Despite the heat, a chill ran down her arms.

Maggie returned to the beach and sat on one of the benches overlooking the Gulf. She opened her sketchpad. A warm wind caressed her damp face. She closed her eyes and tipped her face to the sun, drawing a deep breath of salty air. In her mind's eye she recalled the moment before Savannah woke. The sleeping child wore a smile on her face, her cheeks pink from the heat.

Holding on to that sweet image, Maggie began to draw. After sketching a rough outline of the child, she started filling in the details. Lost to the world around her, she jumped at the touch of a hand on her shoulder. At first, she thought it must be Sam come to apologize. Instead, she looked up to see a white-haired woman admiring the drawing. A small, towheaded child dragging a wire basket attached to a pole stood next to the woman.

"I didn't mean to interrupt. My granddaughter and I came to search for shark's teeth on the beach."

"I want to find the biggest one ever!" the child said.

The woman pointed to the drawing. "You have a real talent. Your daughter looks a lot like Jessie here."

Maggie clutched the sketchpad to her chest and stood. As she walked away she heard the woman speaking to the little girl.

"I don't know why she's wearing that funny hat, Jess. Some people are just not right in the head."

After stopping at the liquor store, Maggie made her way back to the deserted camp. Sitting cross-legged inside the blue tent, she brought out the sketch book and turned back the cover. In the safety of her nylon home, Maggie took a sip from the bottle and studied the images she had drawn. Her art often came from a place deep inside, her hand propelled by an unknown force. This day's results were no exception.

Portraits of Savannah covered the page. In one sketch, the child sat on the beach under the pier, her head bent to the task of filling a bucket with sand. Wisps of fine hair blew in the wind, the expression on Savannah's face one of studied concentration. Another showed the little girl laughing, her mouth crowded with baby teeth. As Maggie's attention shifted to a smaller image, she frowned. Savannah, wide-eyed and frightened stared back at her.

A veil of sadness descended upon her. Taking another sip of vodka, she put the book away and lay down. Outside her tent, the last rays of the sun cast strange shadows against the blue walls.

Closing her eyes, Maggie began humming to herself. She hoped for once that she could sleep without being awakened by the voices that plagued her.

Chapter 40

Cate, 2017

Maya pricked up her ears when Deputy Leroy Lamb stepped on board the *Chilanga*. Before extending his hand to Leroy, Lalo caught my arm and helped me regain my balance on the swaying boat.

The Rottweiler let out a groan as she rose to her feet. Ambling over to Leroy, she stuck her nose in his crotch. The deputy took one step back. "Friendly dog you've got here," he said, reaching down to push her head away. Maya looked up at him, her stubby tail wagging.

"Mostly." Lalo called the dog to his side where she dropped to a sitting position. "Coffee's hot if you want a cup."

"Maybe later." Leroy's gaze swept the boat. "You don't see many trawlers like this around here. Spanish built, right?"

Lalo gave him an appreciative grin. "That's right. Starting to show her age a little."

"Aren't we all? Do you mind if I have a look around before we get down to business? Didn't get much of a chance the last time I was here."

I might as well have been a deck chair for all the attention they paid me. They chatted like two old friends, discussing the benefits of diesel engines and comparing their favorite fishing holes down in the Florida Keys. Lalo asked me to step aside so he could open a trap door in the deck beneath my feet. When they scurried down into the engine room, I climbed down the steps to the main cabin and poured myself a glass of wine. Maya followed, jumping onto the bench next to me where she rested her head on my lap.

I hated being back on this boat. As a non-swimmer, not only did I have a healthy fear of water, I found it hard to block the memory of being held at gunpoint on the *Chilanga* one year ago. As I stroked Maya's warm, black fur, I sent a silent thanks to her for saving my life that day. She took the bullet for me and had a ragged scar on her side to prove it.

After a while the men returned. Leroy, a head taller and about fifty pounds lighter than Lalo, ducked before entering the cabin. He removed his Lee County Sheriff's cap, running his fingers through his shaggy, salt and pepper hair. Up close I could see his weather-worn face, marking him as a man who spent a great deal of time outdoors.

His eyes met mine for the first time. "Lalo tells me you're a lawyer."

"Cate Stokes."

The calloused skin on the palm of his hand pressed hard against mine. "Pleased to meet you, Counselor."

Lalo set two glasses with ice on the table. Reaching into the refrigerator he pulled out a can of Coke. Before sitting down, he reached for the bottle of rum on a shelf over the sink.

"Call me Cate," I said. "I assume Lalo told you about the case we're working?"

Leroy poured his glass half-full of rum and reached for the soda. After adding a splash of cola to his drink he picked up the glass and nodded a toast.

"He said you're thinking of re-opening the Troy murder investigation."

Lalo took the bottle from Leroy, poured a shot into his

own glass and filled it to the top with Coke. "I hate to admit it, Leroy, but it looks like we caught the wrong guy."

"I'm in the process of preparing a Defender Project petition on behalf of Randy Cousins," I explained. "Recent evidence suggests Savannah Troy's murder might be linked to an old case of yours."

Leroy peered at me over the rim of his glass. "'And what case might that be?"

"Jade Wilson."

"I figured as much." Leroy said with a note of annoyance in his voice. "When I heard you were poking around in the Troy case I put two and two together. The bastard who kidnapped Jade was a copy-cat. Used the same M.O. as your guy. Snatched Jade from the beach in broad daylight and demanded fifty grand for her safe return. Then he retrieved the drop at the end of the pier without so much as breaking the surface. One big difference, though." Leroy shrugged before downing half his drink. "My guy didn't kill nobody."

"We're also aware that there was another kidnapping in Naples a few years before Jade Wilson was taken," I said. "What can you tell us about that?"

"Same perp for sure." Leroy turned to Lalo. "Let me get this straight. Are you suggesting you nailed the wrong guy for Troy's murder?"

Lalo shrugged. "Looks that way."

"That puts a whole new spin on things."

Lalo ran his finger down the side of his sweating glass. "You know how it feels when an unsolved case gets under your skin?"

"You bet I do. Sticks in my gut, knowing the bastard who snatched Jade got away."

"Are you still working the case?"

"Technically, the case belongs to the FBI. You ever crossed paths with a guy named Prane?"

Lalo grimaced.

"Right. Couldn't agree more. Anyway, Prane was glad for my help when he needed it but after we got Jade back my captain told me to stand down." Leroy winked at me. "Funny thing, though. Sometimes I see the Cap's lips moving but can't hear a word."

The hum of an engine reached my ears as a boat passed by. The *Chilanga* rocked gently in her slip. I grabbed the bottle of Pino Grigio and continued stroking Maya's head with one hand while filling my glass with the other. Thanks to the wine, being on a floating death trap was not freaking me out the way it usually did.

Lalo leaned across the table. "I think we're both looking for the same guy."

"Just because the Cap told me to move on, that don't mean I can't work the case in my own time, you feel me?"

Lalo nodded in agreement.

Leroy finished his drink and set it down on the table. The two of them appeared to be fast friends, brothers in a shared profession. I relaxed, letting Lalo ask the questions while I sat back and listened.

"Let's back up a little. How did Jade's kidnapping go down?"

"The perp snatched Jade from the beach, you know, the same as in Naples." His eyes opened wide. "Same here too. Anyway, a few days later the ransom note arrived, telling us when and where he wanted the money delivered. He collected the cash at the drop without a hitch. A few hours later, a good Samaritan found Jade wandering around the outlet mall and called 911. Prane didn't have anyone local who was trained to interview kids so he asked us to bring in our child services officer."

"Remind me." Lalo reached across the table and poured more rum into Leroy's glass. "How old was Jade when this happened?"

"Four. The Naples kid was only two so when it came to getting information about the perp, the little guy was about as useful as teeth on a chicken. But since Jade was old enough to answer our questions, we caught a break. She said she was kept on a boat with a lady who spoke a foreign language. The man who snatched her came and went. We tried to get composite sketches of the two of them but it's hard with a kid that age."

"Could Jade describe the boat?"

Leroy picked up a can of cola, then changed his mind and set it down. "Not really. She was kept in a cabin with blue curtains on the window. Said when she peeked out, all she saw was water. The boat bounced around a lot so my guess is they were out in the Gulf the whole time. She doesn't remember getting on or off the boat and has no idea how she got to the outlet mall. Our medical team checked her out as soon as she was recovered. They found a high level of antihistamine in her blood."

I sat up straight. "Cold medicine?"

"Right. We figured the perp used that stuff to put Jade to sleep. From what she told us, she was pretty much out of it most of the time."

"Was there any trace of chloroform in her blood?"

"I know what you're thinking. That's another area where our cases differ. Sorry, Counselor. No chloroform."

"Cate."

"Right. Cate."

Lalo took the first sip of his drink. "You didn't have a lot to go on."

Leroy broke into a broad grin and reached for his phone. "Well, we got this . . ." He thumbed through his photos and passed the device to Lalo. I looked over his shoulder to see a slip of paper with gold hologram stripes on the top and bottom. Between the stripes, I saw the image of an Indian head stuck between the words *Cuba Cohiba*.

"Jade found this stuck between the mattress and the cabin wall," Leroy said. "Said she pocketed the thing because she liked the way it sparkled."

Lalo's face lit up in recognition. "That's a Cuban cigar band."

"I already figured that out," Leroy added straight rum to his drink this time. "Like I said—no one said I couldn't work the case on my own. Now and then I take my boat down to Cuba, buy the locals a few drinks, ask questions. You know how it works."

Lalo and I exchanged glances. I couldn't contain my excitement. "Have you found him?"

Leroy's eyes flicked in my direction.

"Seems to me I'm doing all the talking here. You gotta name for this guy we're looking for, Counselor?"

"Waylon Pope. Goes by Gator."

"What else can you tell me?"

As I met Lalo's gaze, an unspoken agreement passed between us. I began to tell Leroy everything we knew about Gator. When I got to the part about Maggie's dying confession, the detective whistled softly.

"Last time I was in Cuba I heard about an American who showed up several years ago with a boat load of US twenties. Maybe he's still there. Maybe not. But based on what you just told me, I'm thinking I'll go back there to check it out."

"Do you want company?" Lalo asked.

"Any time." Leroy turned to me. "You coming too, Counselor?"

"Cate."

"Right, Cate. Will you be coming with us?

Lalo frowned. "Cate stays here."

I bristled. "I can make my own decisions."

"'Course you can. But if we get caught entering Cuba illegally, you can kiss your license to practice law goodbye. And that's a risk I won't let you take." He turned back to Leroy. "When do we leave?"

"I'm good to go Tuesday afternoon. My boat will get us to Key West in under three hours. We can spend the night there, refuel and leave for Cuba at first light Wednesday morning. That will put us in Vista del Mar before sundown."

"I'll bring some new DVD players and a few dozen movies," Lalo said.

Leroy nodded. "I can see you're no stranger to Cuba."

The look on my face must have betrayed my confusion.

"For the locals," Lalo explained. "DVD players cost a small fortune in Cuba. And the latest videos are only available on the black market. Those things help get the skids greased."

That made sense to me, knowing about the trade barriers that had been in place between the U.S. and Cuba for over seventy years. Leroy finished his rum and slammed the glass down. "Let's go fishing!"

I remained in the cabin with Maya while Lalo went upstairs to send Leroy on his way. The dog looked at me from under her brown eyebrows and blinked. The smile on my face faded as the flaws in their plan hit me. Lalo and Leroy were about to enter Cuba illegally. They had no jurisdiction and no local support if anything went wrong. Even if they found

Gator—a long shot at best—apprehending him would not be as easy as Lalo made it sound. I was still mulling over the problems when Lalo reappeared in the doorway.

"Let's get out of here," he said. "A breath of fresh air will do us both good."

I stood, reaching for the edge of the table to steady myself. Though there was no sound of a boat passing, the cabin floor rocked under my feet. Lalo placed a hand in the small of my back, the warmth of his skin passing through the thin fabric of my blouse. Guiding me up the stairs, he took my arm and helped me off the boat. Maya followed.

"Where are we going?"

"To the North Jetty so we can get some food into you," Lalo said.

Though I only had two glasses of wine, I felt a little dizzy. At the mention of food, I realized I hadn't eaten since breakfast. With Maya trotting by my side, we cut across the road and stepped onto the soft sand of Nokomis Beach. The sign at the edge of the dunes clearly stated no dogs were allowed. I stole a glance at Lalo knowing there was no point in calling the sign to his attention. The beach was deserted anyway.

Looking at the dog, something occurred to me.

"What are you going to do with Maya while you're in Cuba?" I asked.

He gave me a silly grin. "I figured you could . . ."

The protest died in my throat when I saw his face break into a full-blown smile.

"You're only going to be gone for a few days, right?"

"Depends."

"On what?"

"On what we find when we get there."

Lalo kept his hand pressed against my back. By the time we reached the Tap & Grill, I felt steady enough to pick up the pace. Lalo let his arm drop down to his side. He gave our order to a man behind the counter and we sat at a picnic table overlooking the jetty. I watched in silence as a sailboat floated in from the Gulf. A large black cloud cast a shadow across the unfurled sail.

"Maybe you and Leroy should delay the trip for a few days," I said. "I heard the storm in the Atlantic has been upgraded to a hurricane."

Lalo paused as a teenager wearing a soiled apron approached with our food. After setting down the tray, the kid mumbled a word of thanks for the crumpled dollars Lalo pressed into his hand. Lalo broke one of the three burgers into bite-sized pieces and smothered the whole thing with barbecue sauce before setting the plate on the ground in front of Maya. As the dog wolfed her lunch down, Lalo shook off my suggestion.

"The forecast is for the system to turn north and stay out in the Atlantic. We should be fine."

I took a bite out of my burger, happy to see it was cooked the way I liked it—medium rare. Maya followed with her eyes as I picked up my drink and took a sip.

Lalo squirted sauce on his own burger the same way he prepared the dog's meal. "By the way, it will be best not to tell Geri about Cuba."

"I promised to keep her updated."

"She doesn't need to know."

"Are you worried she'll tell Prane?"

"I wouldn't put it past her."

I took a deep breath before voicing my own concern. "Have you thought about what you'll do if you actually find Gator?"

"I'll deal with that when the time comes."

"When will you be dropping Maya off at my house?"

"Around noon on Tuesday."

"I won't be home."

"Why not?"

"I have a date . . . well, not a date, exactly. I'm meeting Mike for lunch."

Lalo's dark eyebrows shot up on his forehead. "Mike?"

"From my Grief Group. You saw him at my house the other day."

"How is that not a date?"

There was something in Lalo's voice I never heard before.

"Don't tell me you're jealous."

"Why would I be?"

"No reason. Anyway, I should be home by two. You can drop Maya off any time after that."

Lalo looked at me from the corner of his eye and tore into his burger.

Chapter 41

Cate, 2017

Mike sat behind the wheel of his Lexus in his button-down shirt, his eyes following the mast of a sailboat as it slowly passed in front of us. After the boat cleared the bridge, a horn sounded. We remained stationary on the narrow road, waiting for the bridge to swing shut before he could move forward. Mike eased the car over the single lane, the tires clacking on the metal grill. Drivers coming from the opposite direction backed up for half a mile waiting for their turn to cross.

"I never saw a swing bridge like this before," Mike said. "Feels kind of rickety to me. Can't be very safe."

I replied with a laugh. "There isn't enough money in the County budget to replace it so they close it now and then to make repairs. When that happens, anyone who wants to come to the Fish House has to drive five miles south, cross the only other bridge to Casey Key, then drive five miles back to this end of the island."

We pulled into the crushed shell parking lot and stepped out into a slice of "old Florida." Small pleasure boats lined the dock, their owners sitting outside under a Tiki hut clutching cold beers. Next to the boat launch, a brightly painted stand advertised kayak rentals. Black Anhingas perched on low-hanging mangroves, their wings spread to dry in the sun. A lone Egret stalked the deck railing, waiting for someone to ignore the sign that said, "DO NOT FEED THE BIRDS."

"I know it doesn't look like much," I said. "But trust me, the fish sandwiches here are the best around."

Mike grinned. "As long as I'm with you it will be perfect."

The waitress seated us at a table on the outside deck overlooking a salt-water cove. Mike followed her with his eyes as she sashayed to the kitchen with our order.

"This reminds me of a place I used to take my wife, Tricia." By the time our sandwiches arrived, he had told me how much he missed her and all about his three grown children. As he droned on, I tried hard to maintain interest in what he was saying. When he started in on the litany of his grandchildren, the only thing remaining in my food basket was a handful of French fries.

"You should eat before your fish gets cold," I said.

Mike looked down at his untouched lunch with an embarrassed grin. "I'm afraid I've been monopolizing the conversation. Now it's your turn. Tell me, how long have you lived in Venice?"

"A little over one year," I replied.

He took a bite of his sandwich. "Annie told me you're a lawyer."

"Technically I suppose, but I'm retired from practice. I do a bit of volunteer work now and then. Currently I'm working on a project with my nephew. He's a lawyer at the Defender Project."

"My son is a lawyer too," Mike said. He droned on for the next fifteen minutes, boring me with his children's accomplishments and his own career as an accountant. When he started to pull out his phone to show me photos of his grandchildren, I struggled to keep the polite smile on my face.

"Tricia always said she waited all her life to be a grandmother." Mike paused, staring at the photos. "I miss her."

What started out as a promising lunch was turning south. The last thing I wanted was to be a shoulder for Mike to cry on.

"I miss Arnie too but life goes on, right?"

Even as I said it, I realized I missed Arnie less and less. Though I would always love him, I was learning to manage on my own.

Mike reached across the table and placed his hand on mine. "Maybe this is the beginning of something new for both of us."

I sputtered, his unexpected comment catching me off guard. Thankfully, the waitress stopped to ask if there was anything else we wanted. Mike pushed his unfinished lunch to one side and asked for the check.

"Make that two checks, please," I said.

"A gentleman never lets a lady pay on the first date." Mike pulled out a wad of cash and handed it to the waitress. "Keep the change, sweetie."

As I began to protest he put a finger to my lips. "Invite me back to your house for a cup of coffee and we'll call it even."

"But I have some work to do for my nephew this afternoon."

"One cup, that's all I ask. I'm sure your nephew will understand."

Maya met us at the front door, her tail wagging in greeting. The smell of freshly brewed coffee filled the air.

While I scratched Maya behind the ears, Mike kept his distance. "Your friend with the dog is still here?"

"I'm watching Maya for a few days while Lalo goes out of town on business." The half-truth came easily. It seemed wiser to call what Lalo was about to embark upon as a business trip than a fool's errand. The smell of coffee suggested he was in the kitchen. I raised my voice loud enough for him to hear. "We're back, Lalo."

At the mention of his name Lalo appeared with an empty coffee mug in his hand. "Did you kids have fun on your date?"

I glared at him. "I didn't expect you to drop Maya off until later."

"I decided to get an early start." Lalo handed me his mug. "Don't let me interrupt you two lovebirds." Grabbing me in a tight hug, he planted a kiss on my cheek. His breath tickled my ear as he whispered. "Be good."

After he left I tried to hide the blush on my face by turning toward the kitchen. "How do you take your coffee?" I asked Mike.

"Cream and sugar."

"Milk okay?"

"Sure. Hey, does this dog bite?"

I peered into the living room. Mike stood exactly where I had left him. Maya kept her eyes trained on him from a distance.

Calling the dog to my side I said, "Make yourself at home. I'll be back in a minute."

Maya followed me to the kitchen and back. Mike sat with one hand stretched along the back of the couch. As I set his coffee on the table, he pointed to one of the photos I kept on my mantle.

"This is a great picture of your son. He looks just like your husband. That is your husband in the picture, right?"

"Yes, but that is my sister's son standing next to him, the one who works at the Defender Project." I glanced at the photo that caught his attention. "I think Ben was about twelve when that one was taken."

I took another look at the photo. Ben was decked out in his baseball uniform, the bill of his cap turned to the side as he grinned from ear to ear with a trophy in his hands. Arnie had his arm around him, smiling for the camera. I had no memory of attending that particular game. As a matter of fact, I never knew the photo existed until after Arnie died and I started clearing out his desk. Inside I found another photo that caught me by surprise.

"Ben adored my husband." I said, haltingly. "It hit him hard when Arnie died."

Mike picked up his mug, cradling it between both hands. "You never had any kids of your own?"

I shook my head. "No."

"You and your sister must be close."

I heaved a sigh, remembering the hate in Nancy's eyes when she said she never wanted to see me again. "We used to be. She's going through a difficult time right now."

Mike smiled politely but didn't ask for details. "That's too bad. Me, I've got three brothers, all in New Hampshire. Tricia and I had a tradition of inviting the whole family for Thanksgiving dinner at our place."

A warning bell went off in my head as I realized he was about to launch into another long story about his family. Fortunately, Maya picked that moment to ask to go out. She stood before me, her whole body wagging.

"I guess she's trying to tell me something." Snapping on her leash, I rose from the couch.

Mike stood, making an awkward move to pull me into a hug. Maya's forelegs stiffened as a low rumble sounded in her throat. Taking one step back, Mike looked down at her in surprise.

I corrected her with a sharp pull on the leash. "She can be a little overprotective until she gets to know you."

"So I see." Keeping one eye on Maya, Mike slowly

reached for my hand. "Listen, I had a nice time this afternoon. When can I see you again?"

"Oh, well . . . I'll be tied up for a few more weeks with the project I'm working on."

"You have to eat sometime. How about Monday night? We can go to dinner together after Grief Group."

As I opened my mouth to protest he added, "I won't take no for an answer."

With a nod and a wave, he sauntered down the front walk. I watched as he backed the car out of the driveway. Glancing at Maya, I saw her smiling up at me.

I shook my head. "What have I got myself into now?"

Chapter 42

Two days later Geri agreed to meet me at Sharkey's for lunch. This time I arrived early, securing the same table where we sat the day Geri first told me about Savannah Troy. I stared at the menu while my mind revolved around Lalo. At that moment he was on a boat with Leroy, heading for Cuba. A few hours earlier, while sipping my morning coffee, I listened to the Weather Channel, learning the storm in the Atlantic had been upgraded to a hurricane named Irma. The weatherman, arms waving, gestured to a radar image of the system churning hundreds of miles away in the Eastern Caribbean. The projected path of the storm still showed the eye shifting north before moving along the east coast of Florida. It seemed Lalo had nothing to worry about.

Here in Venice the weather was picture perfect. A brilliant sun blazed in the clear, blue sky. Looking out from my place on Sharkey's deck I saw colorful blankets and umbrellas lining the beach. A few bathers splashed in the Gulf of Mexico where the temperature was a tepid eighty-four degrees. The level of activity suggested some early snowbirds had arrived for the winter season. Though it was early September, most of the restaurant's tables were full.

Geri arrived wearing none of her usual makeup, her face deeply tanned under her bleached blond bangs. She slipped onto the bench across from me and eyed my glass of soda. With a swift glance at her watch, she waved the waitress over and ordered a beer. Tucking her bangs behind one ear, she said, "Five o'clock somewhere, right?"

I plucked a laminated menu from the basket on the table and passed it to her.

"Thanks for meeting me here. I could have come to your office to update you on our investigation but I thought you might want a break from work."

Geri nodded agreeably. "Good idea." She set the menu down and looked over her shoulder. "Where's Lalo?"

"By now he's probably in Cuba. He went by boat with a friend."

A look of alarm crossed her face. "There's a monster hurricane in the Caribbean."

"The storm is expected to steer clear of where they're heading."

"Lalo should know hurricanes have a mind of their own. No telling where Irma is going next. Did you see the news this afternoon? She slammed into the island of Barbuda this morning as a category five storm. A few hours later she hit St. Maartin. The satellite images show there's debris everywhere. Total destruction. The authorities are evacuating the coastal areas south of Miami."

I saw something about that in the morning news but as the forecast was for Irma to turn north before she ever came near the east coast I figured the latest measure was taken in an abundance of caution. I trusted Lalo knew what he was doing and told Geri as much.

"You have more faith in that man than he deserves. What is that fool doing down there?" She squinted one eye at me. "He's looking for Gator, isn't he?"

Despite Lalo's fear that she might tell Prane, I believed

Geri had a right to know. "He's following a lead with Detective Leroy Lamb."

Geri leaned across the table, meeting my stare. I saw the flash of anger darken her features. "Then that makes two fools. I take it they went on more than a hunch?"

"We met with Leroy a few days ago to find out what he knew about the Ft. Myers kidnapping. Even though the case is officially in the hands of the FBI, Leroy has been investigating the case on his own time. He thinks Gator is in a town called Vista del Mar."

The waitress came back with Geri's beer and took our lunch orders. After Geri took a long drink, she smacked her lips and carefully set the glass back on the table. "So what happens if they find him? Even Lalo must realize they have no jurisdiction in Cuba."

Though I shared her concerns, knowing Lalo was no stranger to bending rules, I shrugged. "I'm sure he'll figure it out."

Geri snatched a French fry from the basket of food the waitress set down and stuffed it into her mouth. Chewing thoughtfully, she took another swallow of beer to wash it down. "My captain wasn't too happy when I told him I wanted to re-investigate Savannah's murder. He told me I didn't have enough evidence to open that particular can of worms. At least he stopped short of forbidding me from working on the case. So the gloves are off and I'm here, ready to go."

"That's great news. By the way, our meeting with Randy went well on Friday. Ben wants to sign him as a client."

Geri's eyebrows rose a fraction of an inch. "Things are moving faster than I could have predicted."

"I imagine it will take a while for the Project's team to ramp up. You know what they say, the wheels of justice turn slowly. But in the meantime, Lalo and I came across this." I picked up Maggie's sketchbook from the bench next to me and placed it on the table.

Geri glanced at it. "What is that?"

"A collection of Maggie's drawings. It was found with her personal belongings when she died." I turned back the cover and slid it across the table. "Take a look."

Geri sucked in her breath, her gaze slowly rising to meet mine. "These drawings are all of Savannah."

"Maggie wasn't lying, Geri. Your instincts were right. Randy Cousins is an innocent man."

"Let me play devil's advocate here." Geri tapped the sketch with an acrylic nail. "This doesn't prove anything. Maggie could have drawn Savannah from a distance."

"Look at that one portrait of her sleeping. That wasn't done from a distance. And how do you explain this?" I pulled the little brown envelope out of my pocket and handed it to Geri. "This was also among Maggie's things."

"Geri peered into the envelope. "A lock of hair? Could be from anyone. Didn't Maggie have a little girl of her own?"

"Helen Blue insists this didn't come from Poppy. Don't you see? This could be exactly what we've been looking for. Evidence to prove Maggie was in direct contact with Savannah Troy. But first we need to compare the DNA from this hair to a sample from a family member. Can you help with that?"

Grabbing her cellphone, Geri dialed a number. After several rings, Savanah's sister, Carrie Ann answered.

Carrie Ann Troy kept a close eye on me while I held her baby on my knee. Jeremy reached up with his sticky fingers and tried to poke me in the eye. I gently took hold and blew raspberries into his damp palm. Giggling, he thrust his hand against my lips, begging for more.

Carrie Ann looked from Geri to me and back again.

"This can't be happening."

"Our investigation has raised too many unanswered questions," Geri said. "If there is any chance Randy Cousins didn't kill Savannah, then don't you want us to find out who did?"

"Of course but . . . I know it was him!"

"Do you remember that day we first met?" Geri asked.

"How can I forget?"

"You were so brave, holding it together while you described the man who took Savannah. But now it looks like we got it wrong. I need to make this right."

Carrie Ann nodded hesitantly. By the look in her eye I could tell she was suspicious about where Geri was going with this.

Geri removed two photos and set them on the table for Carrie Ann to see. I recognized one as the young Gator Pope—the photo Lizzy Holt had given to Lalo. There, in stark contrast on Gator's pale forearm was an inked image of an angry bee toting a machine gun. Next to that photo sat Randy Cousins' mug shot. Carrie Ann's eyes flicked up to meet Geri's gaze. A look of defiance crossed her face before jabbing a trembling finger at Randy's image.

"That is the man who killed Savannah."

"Are you sure?" I asked.

"I know what you want me to say. This other guy looks a lot like him. They even have the same tattoo. But I was there. I saw Randy Cousins with my own two eyes."

With a slight nod from Geri I pulled out Maggie's sketchbook. Bouncing the baby on my knee, I reached down and removed the book from my briefcase. Geri took it from me and flipped back the pages to where Maggie drew the little blond girl. Carrie Ann gasped as her hand shot to her mouth.

"Where did you get this?"

I ignored her question. "Do you recognize the child in the drawings?"

"That's Savannah but how—"

"This sketchbook was found among Maggie's belongings."

Carrie Ann kept staring at the likeness of her sister.

Geri took Carrie Ann's hand and gently squeezed, drawing her attention away from the sketchbook. "This must be terrible for you. But on her deathbed, Maggie told a priest that she and this man . . ." Geri pointed to Gator's photo. "She and this man planned Savannah's abduction together."

The baby chose that moment to cry out. I glanced down to see he had dropped his teething ring. Carrie Ann jumped up. Holding out her arms, she lifted the child from my knees and held him close against her chest. Jeremy struggled against her tight grip, pushing against his mother with both hands as his face turned red. I bent down and picked up the ring, washed if off at the sink and placed it in his damp hand. He immediately threw it across the room and began to bawl.

His young mother looked like she was about to burst into tears too.

"Carrie Ann," Geri said softly, "You were only ten years old."

With a violent shake of her head, Carrie Ann fought back the tears. "I still see his face in my dreams."

Geri drew in a deep breath. "I know."

The baby's cries died down to a whimper when Carrie Ann relaxed her grip and patted his back. This time when I handed him his teething ring he shoved it directly into his mouth.

"We also discovered a lock of blond hair among Maggie's things. If we can prove it came from Savannah, then we'll know for sure she came in contact with your sister at some point."

Carrie Ann shot me a hostile look. "Why can't you people let this go? Do you have any idea what that man has done to my family? When Savannah died, part of us died with her. My father left, my mother started drinking to forget and I . . ." She turned to Geri, pleading. "I've been in therapy most of my life. The guilt is still there. I know it wasn't my fault but I keep thinking that if I didn't leave Savannah on the beach with that man . . . Even my husband doesn't understand. He accuses me of being too protective with the baby. I simply cannot shake the fear of losing him too."

Geri pulled the envelope with the lock of blond hair from her pocket. She explained that we needed Carrie Ann's cooperation in order to determine if it was Savannah's or not. I watched as the floodgates opened and Carrie Ann looked at the hair and started sobbing. I pulled a clean tissue from my purse and handed it to her. Geri already had the DNA swab kit in her hand.

"How accurate is this test?" Carrie Ann passed the baby back to me, blew her nose and gulped a few times.

"Things in real life are not like what you read in crime novels," Geri explained. It looks like this lock of hair was cut with scissors. There are no roots so we can only test for mitochondrial DNA."

"What does that mean?"

"We'll be looking for a match between people who have the same mother. If we get a positive result, the hair is either yours or one of your siblings."

"If you prove the hair is Savannah's, will Randy Cousins go free?"

"Not necessarily. Ultimately, it will be up to a judge to decide if that is enough to grant Randy a hearing."

Carrie Ann opened wide and held still while Geri

swabbed the inside of her cheek. Hitching the baby high on her hip, her bottom lip trembled. She repeated the words I heard earlier.

"This can't be happening. I saw him with my own eyes."

Chapter 43

Cate, 2017

Geri sat behind the wheel of her car, shoulders slumped. She stared straight through the windshield at the empty street ahead. After a few minutes of silence she finally spoke.

"I wish I could do something to make things easier for Carrie Ann. This whole screw-up is on me."

"Don't be so hard on yourself. According to my nephew, eyewitness misidentification is common. In fact, it happens a lot."

Geri blew her bangs away from her eyes "Lalo and I showed Carrie Ann the six pack of photos together. I made it clear that the man who took her sister was not necessarily in the pack, but she probably assumed one of them did. Maybe she sensed I *wanted* her to pick Randy."

"Randy wasn't convicted on Carrie Ann's testimony alone. I'm sure the fact that he was in the gas station the day some of the ransom money turned up swayed the jury."

"True, but I should have listened to Lalo. Right from the start he tried to slow the investigation down. He insisted Maggie knew who snatched Savannah. And he kept saying we shouldn't ignore the other guy on that surveillance tape who matched Carrie Ann's description. At some point, just to shut Lalo up, Steve agreed to bring Maggie in for questioning. Strangest interrogation I ever witnessed. It was like Maggie was having a totally different conversation with people who weren't even in the room with us. After that, Steve blew Maggie off and directed us to focus the investigation on Randy."

Geri turned the key and cool air immediately blasted out of the vents. I didn't know what to say. Maybe Geri did share some of the blame for the way things turned out. But the important thing now was to correct the potential injustice done to Randy Cousins, a man who spent half of his life behind bars for a crime he probably didn't commit.

I knew the ball was now in Geri's court. "Now what?"

"I'm going to tell my captain about the hair sample. Hopefully he won't make me wait for the DNA results before giving me the green light to re-open the investigation. In the meantime, I'll get the paperwork ready." She pulled to a stop in front of my house and turned to look at me. "And as soon as it's official, I'll personally go to Steve's office and tell him it's time to play nice."

I woke that next morning feeling more tired than before I fell asleep. Reaching for the phone on my nightstand I checked to see if there was any word from Lalo. Nothing. Maya pounced on my bed with her forelegs, leash hanging out from both sides of her mouth. She dragged it around while I got dressed.

"You are a pain in the neck, you know that?"

She answered with an enthusiastic wag of her entire back end. I clipped the leash to her collar and headed outside. A neighbor approached with a smaller dog. Catching sight of us she gave a small wave before crossing to the other side of the street. Maya paid no attention to them as they walked by, her nose pointed straight ahead, her big paws slapping the tarmac as she set a brisk pace.

After only twenty minutes, rivulets of sweat ran down

my back. The street we were on ended at the beach where we took shelter from the morning sun under a Tiki Hut. Maya dropped onto the sand, panting. Someone left a pet bowl next to the water fountain which I filled and set down in the shade. Without rising to her feet, Maya lapped the bowl dry.

The beach was deserted. As I sat gazing over the calm waters of the Gulf I thought of Lalo. Reaching for my phone, I checked again for what seemed the hundredth time. I knew he wouldn't have phone service while at sea but I thought by now he would have called or sent a text to let me know he had arrived safely in Cuba. The previous day I assured Geri that Lalo knew what he was doing but deep down inside I was worried. After all, he and Leroy crossed rough waters in a small boat to enter a hostile country illegally. With a sigh I stood. Maya rose to her feet and together we returned home.

The whole day stretched ahead of me. After weeks of running around, I found myself with nothing to do. While waiting for the DNA results Geri pushed to officially re-open the investigation. Lalo and Leroy were in Cuba looking for Gator. Ben had received Randy's petition and was presenting it to his boss that afternoon. Feeling restless, I poured myself a cup of coffee and stepped onto the lanai. On the other side of the screen my vegetable garden, choked with weeds, wilted under the brilliant sun. Only a few short months ago I would have been delighted to spend a day working outside. Now as I gathered my tools, all I felt was the burden of a chore I would prefer to skip.

For the rest of the morning I pulled weeds and salvaged what I could from the bug-infested tomatoes. My arms were covered with mosquito bites, my hair plastered to my scalp with sweat. Standing at the kitchen sink, I held my hands under a stream of cold water. When the phone rang, my heart skipped a beat as I thought it must be Lalo. Grabbing a dish towel, I glanced down to see Ben's name and number. When I put the phone to my ear, someone knocked on my door. I followed Maya to the foyer.

Reaching for the handle I listened to Ben's voice on the phone. "Good news, Aunt Cate."

A twinge of excitement ran through my veins. If my guess was right, the petition I so carefully prepared for Randy had been approved.

Through the glazed sidelights flanking the door I saw a blur of color.

Hang on a second, Ben. Someone's here."

My smile soon morphed into a jaw-dropping look of surprise. Bree, her blue hair now streaked with pink high-lights, gave me a gap-toothed grin.

I waved her in and pointed to the phone in my hand. She nodded understanding, dropping her backpack on the floor before bending down to give Maya a big hug.

"I'm back, Ben. That was Bree at the door. Tell me, did you get the approval?"

"I wanted you to be the first to know. Greg signed off on the petition a few minutes ago. Listen, I'll call you back later. I'm going to tell Randy now."

I hung up and turned to Bree. "What are you doing here? You're supposed to be at school in Gainesville."

"I know, right? The governor shut down the state colleges because of Irma. I caught a ride to Venice with a friend. When we got to the *Chilanga,* everything was locked up tight. I figured Lalo must be here."

I took a few moments to imagine the hurricane's projected path in relation to where Gainesville was located. Something didn't add up. "Last I heard the storm was staying out in the Atlantic."

"That was like, yesterday's news." She rose to her feet, pulled out her phone, tapped the screen and passed it to me. "Check it out."

Sure enough, a red line on the map showed Hurricane Irma had shifted to the west. The storm was now projected to hit U.S. landfall near Miami. Gainesville, together with most of central Florida fell inside a pink cone which illustrated the potential path of the storm.

She took the phone back from me and looked around. "So where's Lalo?"

I stared at the dot indicating Irma's present location. "In Cuba."

Bree frowned. "He picked a bad time, what with the storm and all. What's he doing down there?"

"Following a lead. Listen, I was about to fix myself some lunch. Are you hungry?"

"I thought you'd never ask. I'm starving."

While I washed and sliced tomatoes, I filled Bree in on everything that had happened since she left for school. I didn't want to worry her, but as I slid two grilled cheese sandwiches onto her plate, I couldn't stop myself from sharing my concern for Lalo.

"He left four days ago. I haven't heard from him since."

"Did you try texting?"

"Several times. He doesn't answer."

She started tapping on her phone. "He's bad about this stuff but we have a deal. When either of us reaches out we text right back."

I glanced at the screen to see she sent a four-word message to Lalo. "R U OK." Moments later, her phone pinged. She looked up at me in triumph.

"He's fine," she said.

The feelings that roiled inside me were a jumble of relief, frustration and anger. "Well, he could have saved me a few sleepless nights of worry if he told me so. Ask him if he found Gator."

Bree was already busy typing. She spoke to me while her thumbs flew over the glass. "Give me a sec. I'm telling him about school closing and all."

When she finished the message, we both sat staring at the phone, waiting. While we sat, heads bent in anticipation, Rascal strolled into the room. Bree jerked her leg away when he rubbed up against her.

"Oh man, I forgot about the cat."

"Let me put him in the bedroom. We can eat on the lanai."

I grabbed a box of tissues and met Bree outside where she was reading Lalo's latest message. When she finished, she passed the phone to me. He was brief and to the point.

Gator gone. Stuck here because of storm.

I puzzled over the cryptic reply. "What does he mean, 'Gator gone?'"

Bree erupted in a big sneeze. I pulled a tissue out of the box and handed it to her. After blowing her nose she said, "I don't know. I guess that mean's the guy is FOT."

After three weeks away at college, Bree's language was as bad as ever. I was about to ask for a translation when I saw the look of concern on her face.

"He'll be fine," I said. "Like he said, he has to wait for the storm to pass before he heads home."

"We should drop by the marina to tie a few extra lines to the Chilanga. You know, just in case."

"First ask Lalo what he meant when he said Gator was gone."

After another brief exchange of text messages, I had my answer.

Left Sunday. No idea where he is.

Bree met my gaze. "Like I said, Gator is FOT. He got the eff outta there."

In all the excitement with Bree suddenly appearing, I almost forgot Ben's promise to call me back. We were on the way to the marina when he reached me.

"How did Randy take the news?" I asked.

"To say he's happy would be an understatement. He's probably still praising Jesus as we speak."

I could picture Randy, a wide smile on his face as he looked up to the cement ceiling of his cell, thanking his lord. "Hey, that's great. I've got some good news for you too. Geri is pushing to get the investigation re-opened."

"When will that happen?"

"Hopefully soon."

"So why is Bree there? I thought she was back at school."

At the mention of her name, Bree piped up. "They closed the college because of the hurricane."

Ben paused before speaking again. "Aunt Cate, maybe it's time for you and Bree to get to a shelter."

"The storm isn't coming anywhere near here."

"Don't risk it. The projected path continues to drift west."

"Really Ben, we'll be fine. Besides, what would we do with Maya and Rascal? At this point the pet shelters are full of people who evacuated from the east coast."

"Well, if the situation changes, promise me you'll get in the car and drive north."

"You're as big a nag as your mother. I'm telling you, we'll be fine."

Ben sighed. "Speaking of Mom, that's another reason I called. She wants to see you."

The news came as a welcome surprise. "That's great. As soon as the storm passes, I'll drive Bree back to school. We can meet up then."

"Come early so the three of us can grab a bite to eat before going to the rehab center."

Bree turned to me, her head bobbing approval.

"Sounds great. See you soon."

When we hung up, I patted Bree on the leg. "If you're interested in doing an internship at the Project, Ben may be able to pull some strings."

She sat back in her seat, an irrepressible smile on her face. "That would be amazeballs."

The whole time Bree and I worked to secure Lalo's boat, the sun beat down from a crystal blue sky. There wasn't a cloud in sight. I noticed every slip in the marina was now full. We weren't the only ones making sure our boats were secure. The man on a sailboat next to us waved, saying he had been on his way to Tampa but came into port seeking safe harbor from the storm.

While I stowed away the loose items in the cabin, Bree dragged thick ropes out of storage lockers to double-up on the lines that tied the boat to the dock. From the engine room she produced several extra bumpers—she called them fenders—and passed them up to me. We secured the fenders to the outside of the boat to cushion the *Chilanga* from rubbing against the dock. While taking one last look around I caught sight of the small American flag hanging limp in the oppressive heat. I rolled it up and tucked it into my purse.

"I guess that's everything." Bree said as she locked the cabin door.

A muffled tone came from my purse. After fishing around, I found the phone under the flag. I managed to answer on the third ring. Geri didn't waste time on niceties.

"Where are you?"

"On the *Chilanga* with Bree."

"Bree? What's she doing there? I thought she was in Gainesville."

"She was evacuated along with every other college student in the state. What's up?"

"How quickly can you get to my office?"

"Why?"

"Steve Prane wants to see us. Now."

Chapter 44

Maggie, 1994

Maggie shivered in the chill of the air-conditioned room, blinking against the glare of fluorescent lights. She kept her hands folded in her lap, resisting the urge to touch her cap for reassurance. Sliding her foot under the chair, she checked to make sure her backpack was still there. Two people stared at her from the other side of the table. Lalo, sitting to her left, stood up and draped his jacket over her shoulders. Maggie grabbed the sides and pulled them tight, savoring the residual warmth from his body.

Across from her, Special Agent Prane wrote something on a pad of paper. Remembering the day when the FBI man pulled her from her tent, Maggie shrank into Lalo's jacket in fear. She stole a peek at the only other person in the room, an attractive woman with blond hair. The gold badge hanging on a chain around her neck identified her as a detective with the Sarasota County Sheriff's Office. The female detective kept her eyes trained on Prane. Lalo introduced her earlier but Maggie was so distracted by the woman tapping her pencil on the table that she didn't catch her name.

Voices drifted down from the ceiling like soft rain. She smiled, glad to have her friends join her.

Maggie sensed Lalo watching her. She briefly met his gaze before averting her eyes.

"Are you hungry, Mags?"

Maggie's hand flew to her rumbling stomach. She tried to remember the last time she had anything solid to eat. As far as she could recall, it had been at least three days.

The legs of Lalo's chair scraped the tiled floor when he stood. "I'll be right back."

Prane looked up. "Where are you going?"

"Across the street to pick up some food."

"Get me a bottle of water while you're at it."

Lalo glared at Prane for a few beats before departing. Left alone with the other two, Maggie rocked back and forth, keening softly.

Prane cleared his throat. "As I told you earlier, Ms. Blue, you are not the subject of this investigation. However, you are entitled to call an attorney—at your cost—to represent your interests."

Maggie shook her head. "I don't have money for a lawyer."

"Very well." Prane slid a piece of paper across the table and set his pen on top of it. "In that case, we'll need you to sign this waiver indicating you are willing to speak to us without an attorney present."

Without reading a word, Maggie picked up the pen and scrawled her signature. At the sound of the door opening, she turned to see Lalo slip back into the room. He set a six pack of beer on the table. From his pocket he produced several packages of cheese crackers. He removed a sweating can from the cardboard carrying case and passed it to Maggie.

"Where's my water?" Prane asked.

"Get your own water."

Prane reached across the table to snatch the beer out of Maggie's hands. "No alcohol allowed."

Lalo stepped over to Prane, towering over the agent

who remained seated. He grabbed the can back. "I'll hold it for her until we're finished here."

Prane's pale skin flushed red. Pressing a button on his phone he shouted into the microphone. "Sally, could you bring us a few bottles of water, please?"

Lalo went back to his seat and slipped the beer back into the box. Maggie smiled. Out of the corner of her eye, she caught the lady detective stifle a laugh with the back of her hand.

"Let's get started," Prane said. "Ms. Blue, when did you first meet Randy Cousins?"

Maggie gave him a blank stare. "Who?"

"Randy Cousins, the man accused of murdering Savannah Troy. You admitted to Detective Sanchez that you met him on several occasions."

An image of Randy popped into her mind. "The man with the horse trailer."

"That's right. When did you first meet him?"

"He gave me a ride."

Prane leaned across the table. "When was that?"

"I don't know, exactly."

"Yesterday? A month ago? When?"

Maggie's fingers curled around thin fabric of her dress. "I don't know."

Lalo's deep voice interrupted. "That's enough."

Lowering his voice, he turned to Maggie. "After he gave you that ride, you spoke with Randy once more, right?"

Maggie nodded her head so hard it ached. A glance at the six pack sparked a memory.

"I was drinking beer on the beach when he showed up with a metal detector."

The lady detective leaned forward in her seat. "What did you talk about?"

"He wanted me to come with him to an AA meeting."

Lalo nodded encouragement. "What else?"

"He showed me a ring he found. It looked like Gator's."

Someone knocked on the door. A skinny girl in a business suit entered with a pitcher of water and four glasses. She set everything on the table and retreated. The only sound in the room came from the lady detective tapping the table with her pencil.

Maggie flinched at the touch of Lalo's hand on her back. "What ring, Mags? Describe it for me."

Maggie stared at the lady detective. "Stop doing that!"

"Sorry," the detective said. "Bad habit."

After the room grew quiet, Lalo handed her a package of crackers. She tore it open and shoved a handful into her mouth. Choking, she reached for the water.

Prane beat her to it, filling a glass and sliding it across the table. "Is Gator a friend of Randy's? Tell me how we can find him."

After taking a swallow, Maggie set the glass back down, spilling some water on the table as her hands shook. Pulling Lalo's jacket tight around her shoulders she started rocking again.

The sound of Prane's fist hitting the table made her jump in her seat. "Answer the question. Does Gator know Randy Cousins?"

Maggie squeezed her eyes shut, her heart pounding in her chest. Prane was sneaky. He had tricked her by letting her believe he wanted to talk about Randy when the whole time he was really looking for Gator. She started to hum to herself.

"Maggie? Mags?"

Lalo's voice seemed to come from a great distance. Rising unsteadily, she let Lalo's jacket drop to the floor. Bending down to pick up her backpack, she shrugged the straps over her shoulders and headed for the door.

"Where do you think you're going?" Prane demanded.

Maggie took another step and pulled the door open.

"Hey, get back here. I'm not finished with you."

"We can't hold her against her will," the lady detective said.

Maggie glanced into the empty corridor. In a state of rising panic, she had no idea which way to turn.

At the touch of Lalo's hand this time she did not flinch. He guided her gently through the maze of hallways until, with a sigh of relief, she saw sunlight streaming through the glass doors. Pulling her woolen cap down over her ears, she stepped outside. Without a word Lalo led her to his truck where he helped her into the passenger seat.

"Get me out of here," she whispered.

On the way to the camp Lalo did all the talking. Maggie paid no attention to what he said. Peeling off the plastic packaging, she nibbled on the crackers. As the wrappers piled up on the floor of the detective's truck, her mouth grew dry with thirst.

They came to a halt. She looked around to see they were in the Coast Guard training center's parking lot. Steps away from where she sat, she could see the trail that led back to camp. She got out, anxious to go home and crawl into her tent where no one could bother her. Lalo reached into the back seat of the truck. He handed her the full six pack of beer.

"Did you hear me? The residents who live near here are raising a fuss about bottles and other trash in your camp. The County Parks Commissioner has vowed to clear it out. You're going to have to find another place to live. Soon."

"I don't have anywhere else."

"Sylvia will find you something."

Maggie thought about how terrible the apartment was, the mold, the broken A/C unit, the nurse who shot her full of poison. Here in the woods she could live as she liked, eat what she liked, drink as much as she liked. Best of all, Poppy's school was nearby. Maggie liked to sneak into the park across the street and watch her child play. Poppy never even knew she was there.

"This is my home."

"Staying here is not an option."

Maggie stood still, listening to the sound of the waves breaking on the beach.

Lalo gazed across the dunes with a scowl on his face. "Tell me, Mags. Just between the two of us. Was Cousins working with Gator?"

Maggie looked down at her feet. "I don't think Randy even knows Gator."

"Well, at this point they have enough to indict him for murder." Lalo held up his fingers as he made each point. "He was at the gas station on the day some of the ransom money turned up. Three months later he calls 911, claiming the reward for finding Savannah's body. Minutes ago you told me he showed you a ring like Gator's. But something is missing. Where's the rest of the money? Randy sure doesn't have it. What can you tell me that will keep an innocent man from taking the fall?"

"I can't help you."

Lalo sighed. "Well, as things stand now, unless we find Gator, Cousins will spend the rest of his life in prison."

"You will never find him."

Maggie adjusted the weight of her backpack to ease the

pain shooting down her spine. Clutching the leftover beer, she turned and started down the path. Lalo followed. As Maggie stepped into the clearing, she drew a sharp breath.

Lalo swore softly under his breath. "I didn't think they'd move so fast."

The camp was gone. Her tent, the rusted beach chairs, Gator's old tin coffee pot, every scrap of paper, broken glass and rusted can that cluttered the area a few hours earlier had been cleared away. In a panic, Maggie dropped down to the ground, grabbing fists full of leaves, heaving dry sobs.

She felt Lalo's presence standing over her. His warm hand rested on her shoulder. "Take it easy, Mags. I'll call Sylvia in the morning to ask where you can find temporary lodging until she gets you set up with something more permanent. You'll have to check into a shelter for tonight."

He gently took ahold of her arm and pulled her to her feet. In a daze, she stumbled behind him. From somewhere behind her she heard Sam calling her name. Turning around, she paused.

"Are you coming, Mags?"

Nodding, she followed.

Chapter 45

Cate, 2017

Prane sat behind his desk, making us wait like school children while he flipped through documents in a thick file. I fought an overwhelming urge to fill the silence. As if reading my mind, Geri nudged me with her elbow.

"What's going on Steve?" she asked. "We've got better things to do than sit here watching you shuffle papers."

Prane's voice was smooth, bordering on smarmy. "It's time we have a chat about Savannah Troy. What do you know about Waylon Pope?"

I caught Geri's eye. She gave a small shake of her head, telling me to let her do the talking. "I suspect by now you know as much as we do."

Prane slid a letter—the one he took from me—across his desk. "I've spoken with Gator's sister, Lizzy. To be honest, she wasn't very helpful. I won't mince words with you, Geri. I need to find this guy."

"Why?" Geri shrugged indifference. "Twenty-some years ago you were convinced Cousins was guilty of killing Savannah Troy."

Prane wiped a bead of sweat from his upper lip. He ignored Geri's question and turned to me. "Perhaps I gave you the wrong impression the other day. In my line of work, it's imperative to verify information before acting on it. When you came in here with your story about Margaret Blue's dying confession, I pulled the notes from an interview we had with her after Savannah's body was recovered. I'm sure Detective Garibaldi recalls that meeting."

He paused, waiting for Geri to nod confirmation. "At the time Margaret appeared distracted, confused. Nothing she said made any sense. But when I went back to my notes, I saw she mentioned a ring Cousins wore. She let slip that Gator had one like it. On a hunch, I checked the list of personal property taken from Cousins at the time of his incarceration. Sure enough . . ."

Prane reached into his top drawer. Tossing a plastic bag across the desk he said, "Take a look."

The silver ring bore an image of a machine-gunning bee on its flat surface. Slipping on my glasses, I inspected the inside of the band.

I read the initials out loud. "W.L.P."

"Waylon Lee Pope." Prane confirmed with a nod. "See the maps on my wall? The colored dots represent recovered ransom money from three different kidnappings. I've come to believe Gator was involved with all three. I have been on that man's trail for twenty-two years, a trail that dead-ended outside of my jurisdiction."

I stared at him in amazement. "All this time you knew Randy is innocent but never said a word?"

"Innocent?" Prane snorted. "I don't know about that. My working theory has always been that he and Pope were partners. When Gator took the money and ran, Cousins tried to make the best of a bad situation by claiming the reward for finding Savannah's body. Since then Gator has kidnapped three more kids and this time I aim to catch him."

I wondered if I heard him correctly. "*Three* kids? Your map only shows two others."

290

His eyes darted between Geri and me. Reaching for the file on his desk, he extracted a hand-written note. He passed it to Geri, giving her a moment to read before answering.

"A few days ago, another child went missing. That ransom note arrived in the mail this morning. Our instructions are to tie a bag containing fifty thousand dollars to the channel marker at the end of the North Jetty on Wednesday night. That gives me four days to find Gator before he gets away again."

Geri, her face ashen, handed the letter to me. "Tell him."

I explained how Lalo and Leroy chased Gator to Cuba only to find he was already gone.

At the mention of Lalo's name, the thin scar crossing Prane's pale eyebrow twitched. He pushed back his chair and rose to his feet. Leaning across the desk, he towered over me. "Where is Lalo now?"

"Still down there, waiting for the storm to pass before he can return."

"How can I get in touch with him?"

I jotted Lalo's cell phone number on a piece of paper. "You can try texting."

We sat waiting while Prane typed. As soon as the swooshing sound confirmed the message went out, he set his phone on the desk. Prane continued to pummel me with questions. I told him what little I knew. That Gator left a marina in Cuba a little over a week ago but Lalo did not know where he went from there. Prane also wanted every detail of our investigation but his nods and grunts suggested he already knew most of what I had to say. Every few minutes his eyes wandered to his phone. From where I sat I could see there was no reply from Lalo.

When I reached the end of my story, Prane stood.

"Listen to me," he said. "This is an active FBI investigation.

Any further interference from either of you could endanger the life of the child who was kidnapped. Go home. If Lalo contacts you, call me immediately. Otherwise, stay out of my way."

Before we could say a word, he dismissed us with a wave of his hand.

Outside in the building's courtyard, Geri pulled a pack of cigarettes from her jacket pocket. I shook my head when she offered me one.

"I quit a year ago."

"Me too. Twice. Terrible habit." She cupped her hand around the lighter to shield the flame from the breeze. "Beats me what I ever saw in that man."

"Who, Lalo?"

She took a deep drag, turning her head to blow the smoke away. "No, Steve."

"I thought you and Lalo were married back then."

"We were but we let the job get in the way of our marriage. Lalo and I couldn't agree on the direction of the investigation. He was convinced Gator killed Savannah while I sided with Steve believing Randy was guilty as charged. Then one day—the last day of the trial—Steve invited me out for a celebratory drink. That's all it was at the time, one drink. A few months later, after I caught Lalo in bed with a rookie cop half his age, I picked up the phone and . . . well, you get the picture. Steve and I didn't last long. More of a rebound thing than anything else. After a few months we parted as friends."

"Does Lalo know?"

Geri dropped the half-smoked cigarette to the ground, grinding it out with the toe of her shoe. "I never admitted any-thing but I'm sure he suspects. And like I said, our marriage was pretty much over by then anyway. Listen, you did good in there. Gator won't get away from Steve this time around."

"What makes this time different?"

"The FBI knows the guy's playbook. They'll have divers in the water waiting for him when he tries to pick up the money."

———————————————

On my way home, the low fuel light on my dashboard lit up. Though the Prius could take me miles on a thimble of gas, I started to look for a gas station. One after another, they were all closed, the fuel pumps covered with plastic yellow bags. As I drew close to Venice, I noticed several empty car lots. Where hundreds of new vehicles were usually parked, there was nothing but black asphalt.

Inside the house I found two gallons of water and an unopened package of AA batteries on the kitchen counter. Bree, her attention riveted to her phone, looked up when I stepped out on the lanai.

"I see you went shopping," I said.

As soon as the words left my mouth, both our phones sounded an alarm. A public service message scrolled across my screen. The storm had continued to shift westward. An evacuation order was in effect for the Florida Keys. While Miami was now in the clear, the entire west coast of Florida was under a hurricane warning. I ran inside to turn on the news. What I saw made my heart pound.

The swirling icon representing Hurricane Irma's core rotated like a buzz saw over the north coast of Cuba.

Our eyes met, hers wide with fear. "I haven't heard from Lalo all day."

I tried to swallow my own fears. "The cell phone towers must be down."

"What do you think? Should we leave?"

That was exactly the question rattling around in my brain. Then I remembered the tens of thousands of people who fled Florida's east coast to wait out the storm on our side of the state. The hotels and shelters were full of those evacuees, all of whom were probably regretting their decision to leave their homes. I realized it was too late to leave. The roads north would be clogged with people trying to escape the hurricane.

"At this point we don't have a choice," I explained. "The service stations have run out of gas and I don't have enough in my car to get us out of Sarasota County, much less the state. We'll be fine here. I just need to run out to pick up some more groceries while the stores are still open."

Bree forced a smile. "They're already closed. When I got there most of the shelves were empty. I bought their last jar of peanut butter and two boxes of crackers."

A nervous laugh escaped my lips. "Well, we won't starve."

I could feel Bree's whole body tremble as she gave me a hug. Despite my words of reassurance, I was on the brink of panic. Drawing a deep breath, I peered over her crown of blue hair to catch another glimpse of the news. The buzz saw continued to rotate with Lalo trapped in the teeth of the monster storm.

The order to evacuate Venice Island came the following morning. I had only a passing acquaintance with most of my neighbors but we spilled out into the street, chatting nervously with each other about what to do. Everyone agreed it was too late to outrun the storm but we were all concerned about the possibility of a storm surge that threatened to cut us off from rescue vehicles. Some people, like myself had already decided to take a chance and brave out the hurricane in their own homes. Those who opted to take refuge in the shelters on the mainland hurried back to their houses to pack the few belongings they were permitted to bring with them. As I turned to head inside, I caught sight of Annie, kaftan whipping around her legs, striding down the middle of the street toward me. A photo album was tucked under one arm while an enormous tote bag hung from the other.

"I'm staying with you if that's all right. Won't be much left of my house if this storm is as bad as they say. One strong gust of wind and the roof will fly right off."

I took the tote bag from her, peering inside to see it was stuffed with plastic containers of food. She handed me the photo album saying, "Take this. I'm going back for more."

She soon returned, bearing a tattered suitcase and a horrible, large abstract painting. It was impossible to tell what the subject was supposed to be. Since she chose this painting above all the other possessions she might have saved, I could only think it held some sentimental value.

Annie caught me staring. "Beautiful, isn't it?"

"Let's put it in my bedroom closet for safe keeping," I replied. "I hope you don't mind sleeping on the sofa bed. Bree has the guest room."

At the mention of her name, Bree appeared. She took one look at the artwork and said, "Oh hey, Annie. That painting is so *not* basic."

Annie glanced down at the painting, a blank look on her face.

"She means it's different . . . in a nice way," I translated.

"Right, like it's totally lit," Bree insisted.

I took hold of Bree's shoulders and pointed her down the hallway. "Annie is staying with us until the storm passes. Get some clean sheets out of the linen closet and make up the sofa bed in my office."

"What can I do?" Annie asked.

"It would be great if you could go outside and pull

some carrots from the garden. They'll go well with the chicken I'm roasting for dinner."

Annie scrunched up her nose. "You know I don't eat flesh. There's homemade kimchi and brown rice in my tote bag."

Bree called over her shoulder from halfway down the hall. "Awesome. Kimchi and rice, my fave food ever!"

Sunday morning found the three of us glued in front of the television watching the Weather Channel. The news trickling out of Cuba was terrifying. One hundred and eighty-five mile an hour winds had mowed down trees and power lines, knocked out cell towers, ripped roofs from buildings. Chest-high water flooded the streets of Havana. Hundreds of houses across the small island country were destroyed, leaving unknown numbers of people injured and homeless. Though Bree sent text message after text message to Lalo, he did not reply.

The eye of the storm was a few hundred miles away but the wind outside whistled through the trees as the rain pelted the windows. For lunch I set out peanut butter sandwiches and chunks of cheddar cheese. I pulled a bottle of wine from my refrigerator and filled three glasses to the brim. Annie picked up the bottle to inspect the label. I figured she wanted to see if it was 'organic' or not. It wasn't but that didn't stop her from downing a healthy gulp. She set her glass on the table and announced she was going home to pick up a few more things. As she stood to leave, a thunderous crash shook the house. We all rushed to peer out the window, surprised to see a palm tree had fallen on my front porch.

"Maybe I'd better stay here," Annie said, topping up her glass.

We kept the television on as Irma bore down on the Florida Keys. The on-site reporter grabbed at her yellow rain hat, too late to keep the wind from snatching it away. She yelled into the mic but we barely heard her voice above the roar of the storm. The image cut to the network studio where the weather man informed us it was too dangerous to continue broadcasting on location.

We lost power at 2:30pm and with it our television access to the news. By that time information about the damage wrought by the storm in the Keys had started to come in. Punishing winds felled trees, heavy rains forced drivers to abandon their cars on flooded streets. The body of an unidentified man was found in the rubble of a building. All the news reporter could tell us was that the victim was an "older white male with gray hair and a beard."

I realized we may be without electricity for days. To conserve our batteries, I suggested we use only one phone at a time. Bree took the first shift, following the storm on a weather app. Annie began to pace. Maya rested her head on my lap, an occasional whine escaping from her throat. I stroked her velvet fur, as much to offer reassurance as to comfort myself. Around three o'clock Bree called out, declaring Irma was battering Marco Island which lay off the coast of Naples. With the eye of the hurricane ninety miles away, the outer bands of wind whipped the palms in my front yard to a frenzy.

We were in for a bad night.

Chapter 46

Late in the afternoon Bree's phone died. After I turned mine on the three of us crowded around the small screen, listening to the weather man warn about a storm surge six to eight feet or more. I caught Annie's eye. The Gulf lay a few short blocks from my front door. The rising waters would flood the streets, seep into my house and destroy my furniture. Too late, I realized my decision to stay was a terrible mistake.

Maya lay under the table, her chin resting on my feet. Reaching down to give her a reassuring pat, I went to check on Rascal. The poor cat, banished to my bedroom since Bree arrived, cowered under the bed. I coaxed him out, cradling him in my arms to offer a few moments of comfort. Stepping to the sliding door I peered outside. The fury of the storm was deafening. The shredded screens on my pool cage flapped in the wind. Tree branches danced wildly as Irma drew near. I shuddered to think what the next few hours would bring.

When a bolt of lightning split the sky, Rascal squirmed out of my arms and scurried back under the bed. Maya looked up when I returned to the kitchen. Bree's attention remained riveted to the radar image of the approaching storm. Annie, her brow furrowed in thought, concentrated on four colorful cards laid out on the table.

I placed another bottle of wine in front of her. "What are those?"

She looked up with a start. "Tarot. I thought it would be a good time to consult the cards."

That got Bree's attention. "For real? A girl in my dorm plays around with that stuff. She claims she's a witch."

"This isn't a game," Annie said. "The cards only work if you take them seriously."

"Will you tell my fortune?"

Annie shuffled the deck eight times and told Bree to cut. Drawing the top card from the pile, she laid it face down on the table. She dealt three more cards, creating the same diamond pattern I saw her staring at earlier. Pushing her wild hair away from her face, she turned over the first card to reveal a picture of an angel blowing a horn.

"Ah . . . this is a good sign, Bree. Your first card is Judgement, a major arcana card. You are about to experience a positive change in your life."

Bree grinned. "How did you know? I'm going to UF's Levin College of Law next year."

Annie returned her smile. "Congratulations. Let's see what the other cards have to say."

The second card contained the image of a young boy wearing a cape. He held a rough staff that looked like a branch cut from a tree.

"The Page of Wands," Annie said. "This indicates you have boundless energy, a love of learning and deep loyalty. That should serve you well at law school."

Annie flipped over Bree's third card to reveal an elaborate image of a king on a throne. The crowned figure held a golden chalice in both hands. Annie seemed pleased. "The King of Cups."

"What does that mean?"

"The suit of cups deals with emotions. Feelings, relationships, that sort of thing. The King represents someone who will aid you in achieving emotional goals."

Bree bit her lower lip as she thought about this for a while. "I guess that would be Lalo. But to be honest, he isn't into talking about emotions and stuff like that."

"Your king could be any person of authority in your life, not necessarily a man." Annie stole a glance in my direction. "Think about this for a while. You'll figure it out."

On Bree's last card, two figures, a man and a woman faced each other holding golden chalices in their hands.

"Another card from the suit of cups," Annie said with a broad grin. "It seems your future is heavily influenced by emotions. The Two could represent a partnership, friendship or even a deeply emotional love affair. Whatever the case, this will be a source of great happiness for you."

A snort escaped my lips. Both Annie and Bree looked up. Covering my mouth, I tried to hide my amusement.

"Sorry, Annie. Romance? That would be a good reading for Bree no matter what card turned up."

Annie glared at me while she reshuffled the deck. "Let's see what your cards reveal." She set the deck in front of me, indicating it was my turn. I hesitated.

"Go ahead," Bree said. "I want to hear this."

As the rain lashed the windows, the battery powered lantern on the kitchen table cast shadows. Annie dealt my four cards, leaned back and placed her palms on the table. "Are you ready?"

When I nodded, Annie turned over the first card.

I didn't know what to make of the image. A pale moon hung in a deep blue sky. Two dogs—possibly wolves—howled. There was something ominous about the expression on the face of the moon.

"Interesting," she said.

"What?"

"The Moon indicates deception. It may mean someone you trust is hiding something from you." Annie drew a deep breath. "Or it could be you are fooling yourself. We spoke about this in Grief Group. After the loss of a loved one, our minds play tricks on us. The good times in your marriage may not have been as good as you remember and the bad times not so bad."

Though I still thought this was all nonsense, Annie's words touched a nerve. I forced a smile. "It's true that Arnie and I hit a few rough patches over the years. All marriages do, don't they? But I never doubted Arnie loved me."

"Of course. Just remember the message of the Moon."

The picture on my second card showed three swords piercing a red heart. Dark rain clouds filled the sky above. While I had no idea what that meant, it didn't look good.

"The Three of Swords. Absence, sorrow and grief." Annie cleared her throat. "Don't look at me like that."

"Arnie again? Fortune telling is easy if you know the person well enough."

She sighed. "Cate, I'm only reading your cards, not telling your fortune. Do you want me to keep going or not?"

I nodded. "But if you turn over the grim reaper, I'm done."

When she flipped the next card over, I saw what looked like a tailor hammering on a work bench.

"This should make you happy," Annie said with a grin. "The Eight of Pentacles shows you have the ability to learn quickly. It usually refers to an apprenticeship of sorts."

"Apprenticeship?"

Bree piped in. "You know, like volunteering at the

Defender Project after a career in family law."

Annie's eyebrows shot up on her forehead. "There is something else I forgot to mention. Unlike the rest of the suit, the Eight isn't about money. He's all about spiritual reward."

"All I'm getting from this investigation so far is frustration."

Annie gave me a smug grin. "You're missing the point. You're a volunteer. That's your spiritual reward."

She turned over the last card. We stared at the image together. When she didn't offer an explanation, I asked her what it meant.

Annie tipped her head to one side as if she was trying to work things out in her head before speaking. "What do you see?"

"I see a man struggling with a staff while six other people are rising up against him."

"The Seven of Swords. It means you are facing a great challenge."

"No kidding. We're in the middle of a Category 4 hurricane."

The lights chose that moment to flicker. On the third try they stayed on. The microwave clock blinked red. A moment later the television came back to life. From the kitchen I heard the weatherman say something about the storm shifting inland. I exchanged glances with Annie and we got up to see what was happening. Maya rose to her feet to follow us into the living room.

After leaving a wake of destruction on Marco Island, Irma took a hard turn inland. When the weatherman said the storm's eye-wall began to fall apart as soon as it made landfall, Annie let out a whoop. I glanced through the curtains to see the storm already seemed to be lessening.

Bree plugged in her phone and checked for messages.

Her eyes filled with tears. Wrapping my arm around her thin shoulders, I pulled her close.

The tears spilled over, running down her cheeks. "I still can't find him."

I didn't need to ask who she was talking about. In fact, I was as worried about Lalo as she was. They had their phones set to track each other's locations and the map on her phone was blank. Where Lalo should have turned up as a red dot, there was nothing.

I fought back my own tears and held on tight. Drawing in a ragged breath, Bree buried her face in my shoulder.

Maya padded behind me as I went through the house blowing out candles. Annie wanted to return to her own home but with the rain still pouring down and the street littered with debris, I convinced her it would be better if she stayed the night. The three of us nibbled on peanut butter crackers and polished off the rest of the wine. Though I kept the television on, we soon lost interest in the storm. Bree went to her room saying she wanted to check her social media sites. Annie, her eyes glazed over from the wine leaned over to whisper something in my ear. I didn't quite catch what she said so I asked her to repeat it.

"The Seven of Wands wasn't about the storm."

"What are you talking about?"

"The presence of the Seven is serious. There may be danger ahead. Be careful, Cate. The cards are never wrong."

Chapter 47

Monday morning dawned bright and clear, the blue sky showing no trace of the previous day's storm. Maya pounced on my bed, leash hanging from her mouth. I laughed, roughing the fur around her neck.

"Give me a minute to get dressed before we go for a walk."

Emerging from my room, I realized Annie was gone. She left a brief thank you note on the kitchen counter saying she was cancelling Grief Group that evening. Maya tugged on the leash, anxious to go out. When I opened my front door, the fallen tree blocked my way

I left through the lanai, noticing the shredded screens of the pool cage flapping in the light breeze. Walking along the side of my house, I checked for other damage. With my attention elsewhere, I didn't see Mike standing in my front yard. A growl rose in Maya's throat. She came to heel when I gave her leash a stern snap. Her tongue hung out the side of her mouth as she panted in the heat.

Mike kept his distance. He stared at the fallen tree. "That palm missed your roof by inches."

I nodded, surveying the situation around me. Broken branches littered the front yard but the rest of my landscaping was intact. "The pool cage needs new screens," I said. "Everything else seems okay."

He pointed to Maya. "I see you still have the dog."

"Lalo got stuck in the storm. I'm not sure how long it will take for him to get back."

The news seemed to please him. He flashed me a smile. "Annie called to cancel Grief Group so I guess that means it will just be the two of us tonight."

I had completely forgotten my dinner date with Mike. Shaking my head I said, "I'll have to give you a raincheck. Lalo's granddaughter is staying with me now."

"He asked you to babysit his granddaughter *and* the dog?"

I bristled at his tone. "I'm not 'babysitting' Bree. The university sent their students home because of Irma and I wasn't about to let her stay on Lalo's boat through the storm."

Mike raised his hands in surrender. "Sorry. None of my business. But if the granddaughter is a college student, then surely she can fend for herself while we go out for a bite to eat."

His conciliatory manner soothed my anger somewhat. "Honestly, Mike, let's do it another time." I waved my arm in a sweeping gesture. "I have a lot of clean-up work here."

"But I was looking forward to tonight."

The guy couldn't take a hint. "Another time maybe. Now if you don't mind, I need to walk the dog."

I headed down the street, hoping Mike wouldn't follow. Maya pointed her nose forward and trotted by my side. A few minutes later I threw a backward glance, catching a glimpse of Mike's back as he turned the corner.

All around the neighborhood there were signs of damage wrought by the storm. A massive oak lay across the end of my street, a gaping hole where its roots were ripped from the ground. Roof tiles littered lawns. More than one pool cage in the neighborhood had collapsed under the weight of fallen trees. I nodded to a man who was hard at work dragging felled branches to the side of the road.

A few blocks down my ears picked up the roar of the sea. As if reading my mind, Maya led the way to the beach. The sight that greeted me was one of the strangest I've ever seen. Mud flats stretched out for hundreds of yards. Several people tiptoed through the muck that was normally submerged under the Gulf. I turned to a man standing next to me, taking photos of the exposed pilings of the Venice Fishing Pier.

"What's going on?" I asked.

"Weird, isn't it? The water was pulled out by the hurricane. Someone said it's the reverse of a storm surge. I heard there are dolphins stranded up in Sarasota Bay." He nodded toward the people on the mud flats. "Hopefully those fools get back to dry land before the Gulf rushes back."

Casting my gaze to the horizon I wondered where Lalo was. For the hundredth time I thought of him, hoping he was safe.

Bree was still asleep when I returned to the house. Picking up the phone, I called Annie. When I asked if she could recommend an arborist, she gave me a name and number. The guy she recommended said he was swamped with calls to remove felled trees. Perhaps he could come the following week but no promises. No, he didn't know of anyone who could get to me sooner. Frustrated, I went to the garage where I kept the boxes containing my husband's tools stacked against the wall. In the third box I found the chain saw I was looking for. I had no idea how to operate the thing but I had to try and figure it out. Setting the saw to one side, I repacked the box, vowing to get started after breakfast.

Two days later the tree still blocked my front door. Despite my best intentions, I found the chain saw too difficult to handle. In the end I called the arborist and resigned myself to waiting until he could fit me into his schedule. Bree and I put those few days after the storm to good use, clearing all the debris from my yard. Fallen branches were stacked in front of all the houses on my street waiting for the town's trucks to clear everything away. Life was slowly getting back to normal. The grocery store's shelves were fully stocked, the gas stations were back in business and the sun smiled down on Florida like the storm never happened. Even the screen on my pool cage had been repaired. The only inconvenience I suffered was coming and going through the lanai instead of using the front door.

Bree received notice that the college would remain closed until the start of the following week. Our main concern continued to be the lack of communication from Lalo but given the devastation in Cuba, we weren't surprised. We reassured each other that as soon as the seas were calm enough for them to set out, he and Leroy would come home.

Time seemed to drag while we waited. Two days later I was pouring my first cup of coffee when Maya's head snapped up. Her jowls vibrating, she made little huffing noises. I looked up to see a figure cut across the back yard. My heart leaped to my throat when I realized it was Lalo, coming in through the lanai. Maya raced out ahead of me, jumping up to lick his face. I don't remember closing the distance between us to push Maya aside. I pressed my face against Lalo's chest, breathing deeply, drawing the smell of sweat and dead fish into my lungs. Standing there, I took a moment to relish the press of his strong arms against my back before easing us apart. He reached down, wiping away a tear from my cheek with his thumb.

"Why are you crying?"

"I'm not crying . . . Bree and I . . ." My emotions got the better of me. Slapping him lightly on his arm I said, "We were worried sick about you. Why didn't you call when you got closer to home?"

He grinned. "I noticed there's a tree blocking your front door."

"I couldn't figure out how to work the chain saw. Come in. I just made a fresh pot of coffee."

Some of the weariness fell away from Lalo's face when his mouth twisted into a wry smile. "After I take care of that tree."

"I've already called for someone to do that." I scrunched up my nose. "Maybe you'd like to take a hot shower while I fix you some breakfast? We don't have much, but I can whip up some—"

He put a finger to my lips. "First the tree."

I stood back to take a closer look at him. Despite his broad smile, Lalo looked exhausted. Dark shadows circled his sunken eyes, his black whiskers shot with gray, his sunburnt skin stretched tightly over his cheekbones. I reached up and brushed a lock of hair out of his eyes.

"You look like hell."

"Yeah? Well, you look pretty good to me. Where's the chain saw? That tree isn't going to move itself."

We worked side-by-side, Lalo cutting up the tree while I stacked the pieces by the curb. When the job was done, Lalo set the saw down and wiped his brow.

"I guess I'll take that shower now."

Glancing around, I realized he had arrived at my house empty-handed. "Where's your bag?"

"A rogue wave swept it overboard. Everything I had

with me—including my phone—is at the bottom of the sea somewhere between Cuba and Key West."

"I'll throw what you're wearing in the wash so everything will be clean when you get out of the shower."

Thirty minutes later Lalo entered the kitchen looking ridiculous in my fuzzy pink bathrobe. The sleeves reached halfway down his arms, the hem hitting below his knees to expose his hairy legs. Since his clothes were not quite dry, I suggested he lie down to rest until they were ready. An hour later I found him sprawled across my bed, snoring softly.

Bree woke him around noon for lunch. The three of us spent the next few hours catching up on all that had happened since last we saw each other.

Lalo grunted in disgust when I described my meeting with Geri and Special Agent Prane. He listened carefully while I told him of the most recent kidnapping.

"The ransom note said Gator wants the satchel with the money tied to the red channel marker at the South Jetty," I said.

"When?"

"Tonight. Prane thinks Gator will wait until high tide when the bag is submerged. There will be FBI divers in the water this time."

Bree peppered Lalo with questions about his trip. He explained that after arriving in Cuba he and Leroy had gone from marina to marina, asking about the whereabouts of anyone meeting Gator's description. Their search led to an out-of-the-way spot where Gator had been living on his boat with a Cuban girlfriend. Unfortunately, Gator left a few days before Lalo got there. The manager of the marina had no idea where he went.

At that point, knowing the storm was heading their way, Lalo and Leroy had no choice but to tie up and wait for

Irma to pass before heading home. When Bree asked if Leroy's boat suffered any damage all he would say was that they managed to patch her up well enough to get home. They departed Cuba at first light that morning. Although the wind was calm the sea was still rough. Making their way across the choppy waters to Key West, they rested for a few hours before refueling and setting out on the relatively easy run to Fort Myers. Once there, Leroy returned to his family and Lalo drove back to Venice.

When he finished speaking, Bree teared up. "I couldn't find you on my phone."

I saw the humor in his eyes when Lalo and I exchanged glances. "Yeah well, the Cuban cell towers were knocked out by the storm. Then, on the way home I lost my phone. Have you check on the *Chilanga*?"

"We've been a little busy here," I replied. "Let's go to the marina now to see."

Lalo bent down to plant a kiss on Bree's forehead. "You stay here with Maya. We'll be right back."

The *Chilanga* came through the storm without a scratch. Other boats in the marina didn't fare so well. The sailboat next to us had a big gash in the hull where it crashed against the pier. On the flybridge of a fishing boat, a ripped canvas awning fluttered in the breeze. Near the end of the marina a small skiff listed in her slip, half submerged in water. Lalo shook his head as he followed my gaze.

"Sump pump probably gave out," he said. "We'll see what we can do for her after we're done here."

He jumped on board the *Chilanga*. From my place on the dock I watched Lalo test his boat's electronic controls. Green and red lights blinked as he flipped switches. He bent down to pick some charts off the floor before disappearing into the cabin below.

When he reemerged, he stood on the deck and looked around. "You and Bree did a good job making her secure."

His attention shifted to a cabin cruiser in the slip on the far side of the skiff. I raised my hand to block the glare of the sun to read the name painted on her stern. *Abeja del Mar*.

At the sight of the boat Lalo's demeanor switched from laid-back to high gear. He jumped off the *Chilanga* and jogged toward the office. I hurried to catch up.

A scrawny woman wearing a Hawaiian shirt sat perched on a high stool behind the counter. She looked up from the local paper, a smile spread across her face in greeting.

"Well, look what the wind blew in. Where you been, Lalo?"

"Out fishing."

"Picked a helluva a time. You missed all the excitement, what with the storm and all."

Lalo pushed his sunglasses to the top of his head and nodded in the direction of the half sunken boat. "That skiff out there could use some attention."

"Same thing happens ever' time we get a good rain. Damn that Brownie, he's too cheap to buy a new sump pump. Don't you worry about that old boat, Lalo. Eventually Brownie will come along and bail her out. Everything okay with the *Chilanga*?"

"No problems as far as I can tell. When did the *Abeja del Mar* come in?"

She scratched her arm. "You noticed her, did you? Somethin' odd about that one. The guy showed up Saturday like everyone else, lookin' for a place to wait out the storm. Paid me cash through the end of today." The woman shook her head. "I ain't seen the wife but once. Soon after they come in she poked her head out and he set to cussin' something awful. Chased her right back inside. Mexican I'm guessin' from the looks of her. I reckon she's got a baby in there too."

"What makes you say that?"

"Heard it cryin' yesterday mornin'."

The woman squinted at Lalo and cocked her head. "Why you so interested in those folks anyway?"

Lalo slid his sunglasses back over his eyes. "Just being neighborly, that's all. Think I'll pop in to say hello."

"The guy's not there," the lady said. "Borrowed one of the marina bikes a while ago. Said he wanted to pick up a few things from downtown before they head out. Left the wife and baby behind so I reckon they're still on board."

I followed Lalo as he left the office and headed for his truck. Sliding into the passenger seat, he rummaged through the glove compartment. Much to my surprise he pulled out a gun.

"What's going on?" I asked.

"That's Gator's boat."

"How could you know that?"

"The marina manager in Cuba told me the boat's name. *Abeja del Mar.*"

"The ransom pick up is scheduled for tonight. Prane needs to know he's here."

I reached into my purse and pulled out my phone. Lalo stepped out of the truck and covered my hand with his.

"We're going to get that kid out of there first."

Slipping the gun into his belt, Lalo tugged his shirttail over the weapon. From a tool box in the back of the truck he grabbed a handful of zip ties. Stuffing them into his pocket, he scrounged around the box until he found what he was looking for. He shoved the black baseball cap with three white letters on his head.

I frowned in disapproval. "Isn't there some law against impersonating a federal agent? Chances are, if Gator's lady friend sees you wearing that FBI cap, she'll bolt the cabin door and wait inside until he gets back. On the other hand, if I were to approach her . . ."

"What are you thinking?"

"I'll tell her I want to borrow a bucket so I can bail out that little boat."

I waited, unsure what Lalo thought about my idea. After a few moments he nodded.

"Yeah, that might work. I'll be right behind you. If there's any trouble, you run to the office like your life depends on it and call Prane. I'll get the baby off the boat one way or another."

I felt the effect of adrenalin pumping in my blood, my heartbeat quickening as we approached the *Abeja del Mar*. With Lalo standing next to me, I studied the boat. All appeared to be quiet. The cockpit and open seating area were enclosed with plastic walls, the windows and door zipped shut. I drew in a deep breath and called out. When nobody answered, I shouted louder.

"Hello! Is anybody here?"

I counted to ten before stepping on board, calling out as I went. "Do you have a bucket I can borrow? The boat next to yours needs to be bailed out."

I entered the cockpit only to see it was empty. Once inside my eyes were drawn to a full mug of coffee sitting on a table next to a magazine titled *Siempre Mujer*. The cover featured a Hispanic model in a bathing suit, her silken black hair swept over one shoulder as she smiled seductively at the camera. The boat rocked as Lalo followed me on board. Placing my hand on the side of the mug I discovered it was warm to the touch.

The door to the cabin below was closed. I tried calling out once again.

"I hate to bother you, but I could really use some help here." Nothing.

Lalo bent down to whisper in my ear. "That's enough. Step aside."

He placed a hand on my shoulder and eased me out of the way. Taking a few steps back, he raised his gun. The cabin door slid open a few inches and a round faced girl, half my age peered out. Before she could slam the door, I rushed forward and shoved my foot in the gap. A bolt of pain shot up my leg.

Lalo reached over to push the door open. The girl stumbled, falling backward down the steps to the cabin floor. She looked up with large, black eyes as Lalo pounced, pinning her down. Ripping off his sunglasses he looked around. I followed him down.

"The baby must be in there," I said, pointing to a closed door at the far end of the cabin.

Stepping around Lalo and the girl, I turned the handle. Inside I found the child laying on a bare mattress wearing nothing but a diaper. He lay so still I feared he was dead. Stifling a sob with my hand, I froze.

Lalo's voice stirred me to action. "Well? Did you find him?"

"He's here," I called over my shoulder. Gathering the baby in my arms, I held my ear to his chest, relieved to hear a faint heartbeat.

"Something's wrong," I said. "He's barely breathing."

Lalo kept his gun trained on the girl, shouting questions in Spanish. She bit her lip, her eyes moving rapidly between Lalo and me. The girl let out a yelp when he slammed the wall with his fist. As he listened to her reply his face clouded over.

"Check the shelf, over the sink."

I found the bottle and held it up for Lalo to see. "Why would she give him Benadryl?"

"To keep him quiet."

"We need to get him to a doctor and quick."

Lalo stared at the quaking girl. Reaching into his pocket he pulled out his truck keys and tossed them to me. "There's an Emergency Clinic less than a mile away. Before you go, call Prane and tell him what's going on. I'll wait here for Gator to get back."

With the baby hanging limply in my arms I fumbled for my phone. It took me a moment to figure out why Prane's name didn't appear on my contact list.

"This isn't my phone. I must have grabbed Bree's by mistake. Do you know the number for the FBI office?"

"No idea." He looked down at the girl on the floor. "Don't waste time trying to find it. I'll call him from the marina office after I finish here. You go. Now."

With a backward glance I saw Lalo reach into his pocket to pull out plastic zip ties. Kneeling down, he roughly grabbed the girl's arms behind her back. Not wanting to wait another minute longer, I jumped off the boat with the baby clutched to my chest and raced across the gravel lot to where the truck was parked. A shadow emerged from the side of the marina's office. From the corner of my eye I saw a figure running toward me. Feeling the press of cold metal in my side I froze.

Gator leaned in close, his sour breath in my ear. "The kid will ride in back with me. You're driving."

Chapter 48

Cate, 2017

The phone began to ring as Gator directed me to turn right on Harbor Boulevard. He leaned over the seat and ripped my purse out of my grasp. Reaching in, he extracted Bree's phone and stuffed it into his backpack. A moment later, I heard the ping. Whoever tried to call had left a message.

I gripped the steering wheel with both hands as the truck bucked on the broken asphalt lane leading to the deserted Coast Guard Training Center. Gator told me to park Lalo's truck behind the building. He waved the gun in my face, a silent threat. I picked the baby up from the back seat, checking to make sure he was still breathing. His chest rose and fell but the poor, limp child was obviously in desperate need of medical attention. I nodded understanding as Gator gestured with his gun for me to lead the way into the woods. Emerging in the clearing, I sank to the ground.

Gator settled down across from me, arms propped on his knees, the gun held loosely in his right hand. I stared at him, noting how the years had worn him down. He tied what little hair he had in a greasy rat's tail. An angry scar ran across his cheek. That, combined with a bulbous, crooked nose, gave him the appearance of someone straight out of a gangster movie.

The child stirred, whimpering in his sleep. With my free hand I squashed a mosquito against the side of my neck.

Another buzzed in my ear. Gator brushed something from his arm and checked his watch.

I broke the silence. "How long do you plan to hold us here?"

"I told you, no talking."

The child trembled in the deepening shadows.

"At least give me your jacket to keep the baby warm."

Gator made a move to slip his arm out of one sleeve but changed his mind. "It won't be long now. There will be something on the boat to wrap him in."

"What boat?"

His upper lip curled in a sneer. A dirty chuckle rose in his throat as he patted the backpack sitting on the ground next to him. "Any boat will do. I got my rebreather and goggles right here. All I need to do is head out a few miles and wait for the tide to rise before I collect the money."

"The FBI will have divers in the water this time."

A flicker of doubt crossed his face. He stole a nervous glance at the watch strapped to his wrist. "You better pray they don't."

The last rays of light vanished with the setting sun. Crickets sang out in the dark. I did my best to keep the child's face free of the insects swarming around us. The silence drove me mad.

"You made a big mistake coming here."

Gator's fingers tightened around the grip of the gun. "Shut up."

"Maggie told a priest that you killed Savannah."

Eyes half-closed, he studied me in silence.

"I read the autopsy report," I said. "The coroner said the cause of death was suffocation."

"Because of the chloroform?"

"It would appear so."

"Didn't mean for that to happen."

Despite the cold, beads of sweat broke out on Gator's forehead. He took another look at his watch and rose to his feet. "Time to go."

He grabbed the baby from my arms and jabbed me in the side with his gun. "Move it!"

As before, Gator sat in the back with the baby while I climbed in behind the wheel. I followed his directions to a nearby marina, coming to a stop in the deserted parking lot.

I now realized what Gator had been waiting for. The place was closed for the day, the lights in the office turned off. Dozens of large yachts and cabin cruisers floated in the boat basin. Behind the fuel dock a warehouse for smaller boats rose several stories high. When I made a move to get out of the truck, Gator waved the gun.

"Hold it right there."

He kept an eye on me as he went to the back of the truck and grabbed the remaining zip ties from Lalo's tool box. Returning to the cab, he tied my hands to the steering wheel and pressed a strip of silver tape across my mouth. I smelled his rotten breath as he reached across, yanking the keys from the ignition. Slinging his backpack over one shoulder, he slammed the door. I checked the rear-view mirror to see the child was still on the back seat, his little hands curled in fists as he rubbed his eyes.

I watched Gator walk along the dock, peering inside each boat before moving on to the next. He briefly disappeared from sight, re-emerging from a mid-sized cruiser without his backpack. Coming back to the truck he yanked my door open. From the water below, I could hear the purr of an engine.

"Stupid fool left his keys under the seat."

For a moment, when I saw the utility knife in his hand

I thought this was the end. My heart pounding in my chest, I let out a muffled scream. Roughly pushing my head to one side, Gator reached in and cut me free. Looking down I saw a bead of blood where the knife nicked my wrist.

He flashed a nasty grin. "Thought I was going to cut your throat, didn't you? Well, that wouldn't be too smart, would it? I need you to stay on the boat to watch the baby while I fetch the money. Don't worry. I'll drop you and the kid somewhere south of here when this is all over. Now get moving."

I gathered the baby in my arms. He squirmed, making faces in his half-sleep. Gator poked me in the back with his gun, urging me on. When we reached the boat, he gestured for me to climb aboard. I hesitated, knowing escape would be impossible once I stepped inside.

He slammed my shoulder with the butt of his gun. "Move it!"

A yelp escaped my mouth from behind the tape. I managed to stagger onto the boat without dropping the baby. Gator shoved me down the steps into the cabin below and locked me in. I felt the boat rock as he untied the lines holding it to the dock. Moments later, the engines roared and we sped out of the marina. Risking his anger if he came back to check on me, I ripped the tape from my mouth.

We bumped and rocked for a while at high speed. All at once the boat swerved, crashing to a halt. I fell, holding on tight to the child as we skid across the floor. The pop of gun fire filled the air. A window above me shattered, raining bits of glass all around. I screamed, pressing the baby against my racing heart. Seeking shelter from the falling glass I crawled under the table. Blue lights flashed through the broken window. As the guns fell silent, I heard a click. Peering out from under the table I watched as the door open a crack. Shaking uncontrollably, I waited for Gator to barge in. I closed my eyes, expecting to feel the press of his gun against my temple as he held me hostage. It took me a moment to realize it was Steve Prane yelling at me from the other side of the door.

"FBI. Drop your weapons and come out with your hands up."

Chapter 49

The receptionist at the Defender Project looked up to see Lalo leading the way through the front door with an unleashed Maya by his side. The nameplate on the desk identified her as Patricia Redding.

I stepped forward. "Cate Stokes and Lalo Sanchez here to see Ben Shepherd."

"I believe he's expecting you, Ms. Stokes." Her eyes darted to Maya. "I'm sorry but we only allow working dogs on a leash in the building."

Before Lalo could protest, Ben appeared in the lobby. "I think we can make an exception for Maya, Trish." Ben flashed me a grin before escorting us into his office. As soon as we settled around his conference table I introduced him to Bree.

"I've heard a lot about you." Ben said. "Aunt Cate tells me you're going to Levin in the fall."

Bree scanned the diplomas on the wall, admiration dawning on her face as she saw the evidence of Ben's blue-ribbon education. An MBA from Harvard, The Doctor of Law from NYU. She blushed.

"UF is not exactly NYU."

Ben smiled broadly. "The University of Florida's law school is number one in the state. You'll do well at Levin, I'm sure."

He splayed his fingers on the table. "I've got some good

news. My boss, Greg called the Assistant State Attorney this morning to talk about Randy's case. During that conversation he learned Gator's lawyer suggested his client will agree to plead guilty to all four kidnappings in exchange for dropping the murder charge. That opened the door for us to negotiate terms for Randy's release."

"Why do you have to negotiate?" I asked. "Randy is fully exonerated."

"It's not so simple as that," Ben replied. "ASA Hall is digging in his heels."

Lalo grumbled. "All that man cares about is his political career."

Ben nodded agreement. "That's obvious."

"How can the State Attorney stand in the way of Randy's exoneration?" Bree chimed in. "Legally, that is."

Ben arched one eyebrow. "Kidnapping—the charge for which Gator is willing to plead—is a federal offense. Murder falls under the State's jurisdiction. So if Gator admits to abducting Savannah but not murdering her, then the State is not obliged to reverse Randy's conviction."

"They've got Randy over a barrel, don't they?"

"Don't worry, Aunt Cate. We're working on it. If we can get Carrie Ann to admit she made a mistake in identifying Randy as the man who took her sister, we have a good shot at getting a judge to declare a wrongful conviction."

I'd almost forgotten about Carrie Ann. It had been weeks since last we spoke and so much had happened since. "Let me call her."

Ben placed a hand on my arm. "Leave Carrie Ann to us. Marc, our specialist in eyewitness misidentification reached out to her yesterday. As a matter of fact, he's meeting with her this afternoon to start the process. You might be surprised to hear

Steve Prane will be joining them. He's on our side now." Ben
paused, a slow smile crossing his face. "I understand he's not
happy with you, Lalo."

Lalo shrugged. "Yeah, well I made the call as I saw it
at the time. Seemed to me getting that kid off the boat before
Gator returned was better than waiting for Prane to show up."

"He claims your decision put the lives of both the child
and Cate in danger."

I jumped to Lalo's defense. "We both knew the risk we
were taking. It doesn't matter what Prane thinks. Lalo made
the right decision."

Lalo sighed. "I only wish I had waited until you got
into the truck with the kid before I went back to that boat. If I
had, then Gator wouldn't have—"

Dark memories of those hours when Gator held me
at gunpoint flashed in my mind. I interrupted Lalo before he
could finish his thought. "I'm just glad Steve Prane showed up
when he did."

"How did Prane know where to find you?" Ben asked.

I threw Bree a grateful look. "I had Bree's phone with
me. She tracked the location on her iPad."

Lalo explained that after reaching Prane to tell him
about finding Gator's boat, he placed a call to Geri, asking her
to meet me at the emergency clinic. He gave her the number of
Bree's phone and told her to let me know she was on the way.
I realized that was the call that prompted Gator to grab my
phone and stuff it into his backpack.

Bree picked up the thread of our discussion. "Geri got
worried when Cate didn't answer so she called your land line
and asked me if I could track my phone from my iPad. Pretty
basic, really. No big deal."

"It was a big deal to me." I glanced at my watch,

surprised to see how late it was. "We need to go, Ben. Your mother is expecting us at the rehab center."

Lalo stood up and put his hand on his granddaughter's shoulder. "And I need to bring Bree to school. Take your time with your sister. I'll meet you back here when you're finished."

———————

Nancy's appearance gave me cause for concern. She had dropped a lot of weight since last I saw her, her cheeks were sunken, the dark circles under her eyes hinted at sleepless nights. But her face lit with joy at the sight of Ben and me as we walked through the door. She spread her arms wide, gathering both of us in a hug. That was the moment I knew she was going to be all right. Tears ran down my cheeks.

"What's wrong?" she asked. "I don't remember ever seeing you cry before. Not even at Arnie's funeral."

I sniffed, wiping away my tears with both hands. "Maybe I'm getting sentimental in my old age. After the last time I was here I was afraid you—"

"I was horrible to you. Can you forgive me for the things I said?"

I brushed her concern away with a wave of my hand. "No . . . that is, there's nothing to forgive. The important thing is, you're getting better."

"Slowly. The doctors say I might be ready to go home a few weeks from now."

"I'm proud of you, Nancy."

She cast her eyes to the floor. "How can you say that? I'm an addict. Every minute of the day I remember how wonderful the drugs made me feel."

Her words sent alarm bells ringing in my head. Ben and I exchanged glances.

"This is something you're going to fight every day of your life, Mom. Have you spoken to Dad lately?"

Nancy nodded. "This morning. My counselor wants him to come down next week so we can talk about what happens after I leave here."

"What did he say?"

"Oh, you know your father. He started complaining about how much money it was costing to keep me here and wanted to know if it was really necessary for him to waste more money on airfare when he's going to come down in a few weeks anyway to bring me home. I don't think he understands things can't be the way they always were with us."

Nancy gave Ben a crooked smile. "Benny, would you mind running across campus to get me a coffee from the cafeteria vending machine?"

"Sure, Mom. How about you, Aunt Cate? Can I get you anything?"

"No thanks, Ben."

After he left I gave my sister a hard look. "What was that all about?"

"Being here has helped me step back and take stock of my life. I've been unhappy for a long time. With Ben out of the house, I feel totally alone. When Tim is not at work, he's out drinking with his buddies or sitting in front of the television watching sports programs, yelling at me like Archie Bunker to bring him another beer. He doesn't see me as a partner. I'm more like a live-in servant to him. I don't want to grow old like that."

"Have you spoken with him about this?"

"That's what we're going to talk about on Monday when we meet with my counselor. If Tim can't handle the fact that I want a partner in life and not another child, then I'm prepared to go it alone."

"Being alone is no fun either."

"I'd rather start over than spend the rest of my days with things the way they are." Nancy reached over and took my hand. "I don't expect you to understand. Arnie was special. One in a million."

I shifted in my seat, drawing a deep breath through my nose. What I was about to tell Nancy was something I'd held inside for too long. Closing my eyes, I slowly exhaled.

"Arnie wasn't perfect," I told her.

"What do you mean?"

"After he died, while clearing out his desk I came across a photo of him with another woman. I think Arnie might have been having an affair with her."

"Who was she?"

"Ben's biology teacher."

"Candy Stevens? I remember her. She used to come to all of Ben's baseball games." Nancy's eyes opened wide. "Arnie drove her home afterwards. At the time I thought he was just being nice. Oh, Cate, I'm so sorry. I should have said something but I never suspected Arnie would . . ."

I felt a stab of pain. Until that moment I tried to convince myself that the photo of Arnie with his arm around the pretty blond was innocent. That I was only imagining the hungry look in his eyes as he gazed down at her. That the heart drawn in red ink on the back meant nothing. The mystery of who took that other photo of Arnie and Ben at the game was now answered. A wave of anger and hurt washed over me as I struggled with my husband's treachery.

I patted Nancy on the arm. "You couldn't have known. At least now I can let him go and move on with my life."

Ben stepped through the door with Nancy's coffee. "Here you go, Mom. They only had decaf."

Nancy gave him a weak smile. "I know. First thing I'm going to do when I get home is make myself a strong cup of high-test."

Ben glanced at the clock on the wall. "I hate to say it but they're going to throw us out of here soon. Visiting hours are over."

"Oh shoot," Nancy said. "I'm due to attend a group session in ten minutes."

I stood and pulled her into an embrace. "Good luck with your meeting on Monday."

"I'll let you know." Turning to her son she gave him a kiss on the cheek. "Thanks for bringing Aunt Cate. Will I see you again next week?"

"Wild horses couldn't keep me away."

We found Lalo waiting for me in the Defender Project's lobby, chatting with the receptionist. Ben waved goodbye to both of us and dashed off to a meeting. As we made our way across the steaming parking lot Lalo asked how my sister was doing.

"Better, much better. We had a good talk. How did things go with you? Is Bree settled into her dorm room?"

"On the way she chatted about your nephew. She thinks he's 'quiche.'"

"What does that mean?"

"Hotter than hot. Sexy."

I had to laugh. "Bree and Ben? I can't see that ever happening. But Ben did say he's going to recommend taking her on as an L One intern."

"L One?"

"First year in law school. He thinks she'll fit in well at the Project."

I climbed into the cab of Lalo's truck and buckled my seatbelt. Lalo started the engine and cranked the AC to maximum. I closed my eyes and let the cold air blow across my face. As he put the truck in gear, my thoughts drifted back to my conversation with Nancy. When Lalo spoke again it took me a minute to catch up to what he was saying.

"Sorry, my mind was somewhere else. What did you say?"

"I asked if you'd consider working for the Project too."

I laughed. "I'm too old to even think about that."

"Apparently the Project's director doesn't agree. He offered me my old job as freelance investigator. He wants you to be part of the deal.

When I didn't answer right away, Lalo fell quiet. I gazed out the truck window, watching the mile markers tick by.

After a long lapse in the conversation I broke the silence. "Are you serious?"

"Yeah, I'm serious. We can be business partners. Sanchez and Stokes, Private Investigators."

"Fifty-fifty?"

"Fifty-fifty."

"Stokes and Sanchez has a better ring to it."

"Sanchez and Stokes."

I smiled. A short while ago I told Nancy I was now free to move on with my life and leave Arnie in the past. Staring straight ahead I said, "Maybe. But the name needs work."

Chapter 50

Lalo and I found Helen Blue as before, propped up on a hospital bed in her living room, sucking oxygen from a tube. When Poppy led us into the room, Helen woke from a light sleep. Lalo took one of her boney hands and planted a kiss on her palm.

"It's good to see you and your pretty girlfriend again, Lalo."

Poppy spoke loudly enough for the neighbors to hear. "She's not his girlfriend, Grandma. They work together. They've come to tell you they found Gator."

Helen's lips tightened. "Good for nothing white trash, that one."

"He's confessed to kidnapping Savannah Troy," Lalo told her.

"You don't have to yell." Helen shook her head. "My hearing is about the only thing that works like it ought to. So tell me, where did you find the rascal?"

"In Cuba," Lalo said.

"How in the world did you track him all that way?"

"He left a trail of breadcrumbs," Lalo kept a straight face but his eyes were smiling.

"And what about the fella who was arrested for killing the child?"

"His lawyers are negotiating the terms of his release.

With luck he'll be free in a few months."

Helen nodded slowly. "I'm glad to hear Maggie did the right thing in the end. She wasn't a bad girl you know. Just troubled."

Poppy muttered under her breath. "She tried to kill me."

Helen shook her head. "I've told you a hundred times, child. That was her illness. Your mother loved you. Do you know she used to sit in the park across from the school, just waiting to catch a look at you during recess? Your teacher asked if she should call the police but I told her to leave Maggie be. Looking back, I regret keeping you away from her. She should have been part of your life."

Helen's eyes fluttered shut. I counted the seconds, listening to the tick of the grandfather's clock standing in the corner. Placing my hand on her wrist I felt for a pulse. Helen woke immediately.

"Thought I was gone, didn't you?" She gave me a weak smile. "I was just thinking about my Maggie. Tell me Lalo, when was the last time you saw her?"

"About a year ago."

"Where was she?"

"On a park bench in Sarasota."

"How was she?"

Lalo rubbed his face with his hands. "She was in pretty bad shape, Helen."

"My poor baby."

Poppy pointed to the sketchbook I had tucked under my arm. "That was Maggie's. What are you doing with it?"

I placed the book on the bed next to Helen. "Maggie's portraits are wonderful."

Helen stroked the cover of the book. "What about the ones that worried me? The drawings that looked like Savannah?"

Lalo and I exchanged glances.

"They weren't her," Lalo lied. "Maggie probably caught sight of another little girl that reminded her of Poppy and decided to draw her."

Helen's eyes closed, a small smile playing at the corners of her mouth. Her breathing grew shallow. Poppy pulled the covers up to her grandmother's chin and nodded for us to follow her out to the lanai.

As soon as we stepped outside she spun around. "I have the feeling you weren't being completely honest in there. What happened to the lock of hair I found in Maggie's backpack?"

"We checked for DNA," Lalo replied. "It came from Savannah."

Poppy didn't look surprised.

"I see."

"Something else you should know. We showed the sketchbook to Carrie Ann Troy. Helen was right. Those drawings were Savannah."

"Why did you lie about that just now?"

Lalo cleared his throat. "What good would it do to tell Helen the truth? Gator claims it was Maggie's idea to kidnap Savannah. She wanted to keep her but Gator knew that wasn't possible. When he told Maggie they had to return Savannah after he collected the ransom, Maggie left. He never saw her again."

To her credit, Poppy took the news in stride. "If Gator intended to return Savannah, then why did he end up killing her?"

"He used chloroform to keep her sedated and accidentally gave her too much. With his next victims he switched to an over-the-counter cold medicine to keep the kids quiet."

"I hope they lock him up and throw away the key. Listen, it was kind of you to spare Helen the ugly truth. But I needed to know."

When I drew Poppy into a hug, her shoulders shook slightly. I whispered in her ear that everything was going to be okay. She pulled away, wiping a single tear from her eye. Smiling bravely, she nodded.

Chapter 51

Cate, 2017

Two months went by without a single word from Nancy. I left her alone, figuring she needed time to work on her marriage. Ben kept me updated on her progress saying Nancy was back home in New Hampshire and doing well. I knew she would call as soon as she felt ready to talk.

For my part, the discovery of my own husband's infidelity left me feeling raw but one of the many things I learned from my Grief Group was that time would heal. Another thing I learned was that I didn't need those meetings any longer. When I told Annie I was dropping out, I expected she would attempt to talk me into staying with the group. Instead she gave me a broad, chipped-tooth smile and said it was about time.

Meanwhile, I kept busy with an online course which, for fifty dollars a month, promised to prepare me for my Class A private investigator's license. There were a few other details to work out before my partnership with Lalo was finalized. For one thing, we still couldn't agree on whose name came first on the letterhead.

I knew better than to pester Ben for news about Randy Cousins. His lawyer-client confidentiality agreement prohibited him from discussing the case until everything was settled. When I picked up the phone and heard the excitement in Ben's voice, I knew that day had arrived.

"Hey, Aunt Cate. Good news! Randy's release papers came through."

"Congratulations," I said. "That's wonderful."

"Carrie Ann testified to the judicial review board last week. She admitted making a mistake in identifying Randy as the man who kidnapped Savannah. Her statement, combined with Gator's guilty plea did the trick. I'm driving to the prison to pick up Randy this afternoon."

"So they ruled this a wrongful conviction?"

"Not exactly. The State Attorney wanted to press the murder issue even though he knew they didn't have enough evidence to make it stick. In the end, the judge told us to work out a deal. We spent these last few weeks negotiating release terms. They absolutely refused to pay the $1.1 million they owed him for the twenty-two years he spent in prison."

"Seriously? Will Randy get any restitution at all?"

"Some. Enough for him to start up his own ministry when he's ready. He's happy with the settlement."

It occurred to me that during the twenty-two years Randy spent in prison, technology had transformed the world. He never surfed the internet, used a cell phone, or streamed videos on a television. I asked Ben if there was anything I could do to help with the adjustment Randy now faced. Ben assured me that the Project would provide temporary housing and counseling services until Randy got back on his feet and was ready to strike out on his own.

"I'm proud of you, Ben." I let a beat of time pass before I added the words I thought he wanted to hear "I wish Uncle Arnie could be here to see you now."

"I still miss him, Aunt Cate."

I couldn't bring myself to say the same.

When it came time to make the arrangements for Randy's release party, Ben turned to me. My house was too small to fit all those he wanted to invite so I decided to hold the event on the beach near the pier. It seemed a fitting location to celebrate Randy's freedom.

Ben welcomed the guests as they drifted in while I kept busy setting out the food everyone brought to share. After checking to make sure the cooler was well stocked with beer and soft drinks, I set out to find Carrie Ann Troy.

The previous day I called to make sure she received the invitation. I feared she would stay away given the circumstances surrounding her role in sending Randy to prison but she sounded cheerful and promised she would come. I found her in the crowd balancing her son, Jason on her hip. Her face lit up when I approached.

"I'm glad to see you, Cate. I was just saying to Randy that he should mingle a bit more."

Randy Cousins extracted a finger from Jason's sticky grip, wiping his hand on his shirt before extending it to me. "I don't know how to thank you, Ms. Stokes. If it weren't for you, I'd still be locked up in that prison cell. I praise God for sending you to me."

"No one is happier for you than I am, Randy. But the truth is, everyone here worked hard to get you released."

The one and only other time I'd met Randy he was dressed in prison blues, his hair greasy and unkempt, his skin pale from lack of sunshine. The man standing before me had changed. He stood tall, his new cloths clean and pressed. With color in his cheeks and a sparkle in his eye, the transformation from a surly inmate to a man reborn seemed complete.

I took Randy's hands in mine and squeezed. "Is there anything you need? Ben told me the Project was providing you with some assistance. If there anything more I can . . ."

"Thank you kindly, Ms. Stokes but I'm doing fine."

"I wanted Randy to stay with me until he found something more permanent," Carrie Ann said. "But the Project rented him a nice apartment near the prison. That's where he plans to establish his new ministry."

Little Jason grabbed hold of Randy's ear and let out a squeal. A broad smile broke out on Carrie Ann's face as she watched them. It seemed to me that Randy wasn't the only one who had been transformed in the past few months.

"Come on, Randy, I want to introduce you to my mother," Carrie Ann said.

After they walked away I felt someone tap me on the shoulder. Turning around, I stood face to face with Ben. Looming behind him was a young man I'd never seen before.

"Hey, Aunt Cate. There's someone here who wants to meet you. This is my colleague, Marc."

The young man stepped up to shake my hand. "You and Lalo did a nice job with this case, Cate. We used a lot of your research to convince the board of Randy's innocence."

"I'm amazed that he isn't more bitter. Based on what I can see, he has completely forgiven Carrie Ann for sending him away."

"I've seen that sort of thing before. His faith has a lot to do with it."

I took the opportunity to ask a question that had been at the forefront of my mind for months.

"I'm curious, Marc. How did you get Carrie Ann to admit she misidentified Randy as the man who snatched her sister?"

"Gator's guilty plea was the key. But before changing her testimony she insisted on meeting Gator face to face. As soon as Carrie Ann looked him in the eye, she knew he was the man who took Savannah."

Ben spoke up. "We've got several other cases that could use your help, Aunt Cate. Are you and Lalo ready to get to work?"

"We haven't even agreed on the name of our new firm," I replied.

Lalo, a beer in one hand and a slice of cake in the other appeared by my side. "Sanchez and Stokes Investigations. We'll be good to go as soon as Cate gets her license."

I looked around, seeing several people from the Project that I didn't know, most of whom I believed were interns from the University of Florida's Levin College of Law. Ben assured me they worked tirelessly to help prepare the motion for Randy's release. I was pleased they drove all this way to help us celebrate. Among the guests a familiar face caught my attention. Geri Garibaldi tucked her blond bangs behind one ear, raised her can of beer and nodded back at me. Steve Prane stood by her side with an arm around her shoulder. Geri gave me a wave before turning her attention back to Prane.

One person was missing. A few weeks earlier, after reading Helen's obituary in the local paper I sent Poppy a sympathy card. Following up with a telephone call, I assured her she would be welcome at this gathering. She made no promises.

Lalo caught me looking for her.

"I guess Poppy decided not to come," he said.

"She said she felt awkward."

Lalo shrugged. "I get that."

"The important thing is, she finally found it in her heart to forgive Maggie."

"What made her change her mind?"

"Not what . . . who. After Maggie died, Sylvia called to see if Poppy would meet her for lunch. Sylvia felt it was important for Poppy to know how much Maggie loved her."

Lalo shook his head. "Too bad Poppy didn't come to realize that before Maggie was gone."

Shielding his eyes from the sun, Ben searched the crowd.

"Who are you looking for?" I asked.

"Randy. I want to introduce him to Marc."

Lalo pointed to Randy and Carrie Ann who stood together at the far end of the fishing pier.

"I'll get him," I offered.

As I drew near, I saw Carrie Ann take Randy's hand in hers. Her voice cracked with emotion.

"I still miss Savannah, Randy. I wish you could have known her."

"Me too."

"I want to tell you again how sorry I am. All those years you lost . . ."

"Part of God's plan."

It was clear to me that Randy had found his true calling.

Chapter 52

Maggie, 2017

A cacophony of harsh whispers raged in Maggie's head. She pleaded with them to leave her alone, her protest so faint she wondered if she even spoke out loud. From the din of voices, one emerged above the others. She tried to concentrate on his soothing words.

"Be at peace, my child."

She opened her eyes to see a clean-shaven man clad in a black shirt sitting by her side. As he came into focus she saw his white cleric's collar.

He placed a cool hand on her forehead. "There you are. I was afraid we lost you. Can you hear me?"

"Where . . ."

The priest bent down, putting his ear to her cracked lips. "What's that?"

"Where am I?"

"In the hospital. You were found lying unconscious on Caspersen Beach. You are safe now. Rest easy."

Maggie glanced down at the needle in her arm and traced the tube up to a bag hanging by her bed. She made a move to rip the needle out but the priest gently brushed her hand away. Though she sobbed in frustration, no tears seeped from the corners of her eyes.

The priest fumbled with his stole. Slipping it over his head he asked, "Would you like me to hear your confession?"

Gripping the purple stole she pulled him close. Her words came out in a rush. "It all went wrong."

"What? What went wrong?"

"Gator lied. He said I could keep Savannah but then he—"

The priest took both her hands in his. "Slow down, Margaret. God can hear you but my ears aren't as good as they used to be. Now tell me, who is this Gator and what did he do exactly?"

She closed her eyes. "Gator Pope. He took Savannah and he . . ."

As she said his name out loud, she recalled the flare of anger on Gator's face when she begged him for the child.

They were in the woods behind Caspersen Beach. Maggie sat next to Savannah as Gator passed her a pair of scissors. He wanted a lock of hair to put in the envelope with the ransom note. She snipped a blond curl and handed it to him. While he sealed the envelope, she stole another lock for herself, slipping it into the pocket of her dress.

The priest leaned in closer. The touch of his warm breath on her cheek brought Maggie back to the present. He squeezed her hands.

"Tell me, Maggie. Did Gator kill Savannah?"

It seemed like yesterday. Gator left to mail the ransom note, warning her to keep the child sedated until he got back. Maggie had other plans. After a while she reached out and stroked the little girl's cheek, hoping to wake her. Savannah stirred, blinking once before opening her eyes and fixing her gaze on Maggie. Maggie stared back.

Sam's raspy voice shook her out of the trance.

"Now you've done it."

Savannah whimpered.

"What are you doing here, Sam?"

"You shouldn't have let her see you."

"Maybe now Gator will let me keep her."

"You know that won't happen."

Maggie's eyes flew open. She wrenched her hands away from the priest and clapped them to her ears. She looked up, filled with desperation. "I tried to stop him."

"Listen to me, Margaret. You are not responsible for the sins of others."

"But he kept . . ."

"Be at peace, my child."

The priest spoke in soothing tones. Her eyes fluttered shut. As her mind drifted to the past, Sam's unrelenting voice dominating her thoughts.

"You have to do this."

"Stop it!"

"She knows who you are."

"I can't!"

"If she lives to tell them what you did, they'll never let you see Poppy again."

Maggie's breath caught in her chest. Sam was right. He was always right. Dropping to Savannah's side, she stroked her face tenderly before covering the child's nose and mouth. It seemed to take forever for Savannah to stop struggling. At last Maggie bent over the lifeless form, dry sobs wracking her body. When she was finally able to stand she looked around to see Sam was gone. The steady hum of voices in her head were silenced. All she heard was the slap of waves on the beach.

After taking one last look at Savannah, Maggie ran.

"Margaret? Can you hear me?"

Maggie looked up at the priest. "Did you say something?"

"I said you are not responsible for the sins of others.

Do you have any sins of your own to confess?"

A figure stood at the foot of her bed. She blinked a few times, not trusting her own eyes. Sam smiled at her.

"You're back."

"I came to say goodbye, Mags."

Her words came out in a faint whisper. "Not yet. You have to tell him, Sam. Tell him why."

He wagged his head, his eyes full of sorrow. "You know I can't."

As she watched, Sam faded. His image shimmered for a moment and then he was gone.

The priest's lips were moving. He reached out, sliding his thumb across her forehead. Maggie closed her eyes, a peaceful feeling coming over her as she whispered one last word.

"Poppy."

The End.

Author's Note

This book is a work of fiction. Names, characters, organizations and events are the product of the author's imagination. Any resemblance to actual persons, living or dead, is entirely coincidental.

The places depicted in the story are real. Caspersen Beach, the Venice Fishing Pier and Sharkey's on the Pier are all delightful sites to visit and yes, prehistoric shark's teeth can be found on the beach if one has the patience to sift through the sand. To the best of my knowledge, no kidnappings or murders ever happened there.

The legal firm called the Defender Project does not exist, however there are several worthy nonprofit organizations in Florida and around the rest of the country that work diligently to assist innocent people who have been wrongfully convicted. They depend largely on the heroic efforts of attorneys, law students and other volunteers who offer their services for free. Unfortunately, the need for their work shows no sign of stopping. I wish to extend my personal gratitude to Ms. Harriet Hendel, former board member of the Innocence Project of Florida for her undying work in this field and her generous sharing of information from which I derive inspiration.

I also want to thank several people without whom this book would never have seen the light of day. To Roger Hooverman and Sheila Reed, both dear friends and talented writers in their own right whose help and input have been invaluable to me over the years. Also, to my beta readers, Nancy Merel and Jo Weiner who are a constant source of encouragement. And to Dale Wolfson who showed me the true meaning of strength and perseverance in the face of great loss.

Most of all to Pieter Heijens, my husband, my trusted advisor and my guiding light. Thank you, Peet for making my life complete.

More By This Author

Another one of Heijen's *Wrongful Conviction Mystery Series*

SNOOK WALLOW

"Snook Wallow: A Wrongful Conviction Mystery weaves together the stories of two illegal immigrants and the men convicted of killing them.

During a night out with friends, Logan Murphy stumbles upon the scene of a crime. What started as good intentions, trying to help the victim, entangles him in the investigation and ultimately leads to a murder conviction of Jane Doe. A decade later Logan Murphy is nearing the end of the line on Florida's death row. His last hope rests with Cate Stokes, a retired lawyer who reluctantly agrees to take his case. Cate joins forces with retired detective Eduardo "Lalo" Sanchez.

As Cate and Lalo carry out an investigation the truth begins to unravel. The urgency to establish Murphy's innocence and find the real murderer is heightened when the duo discovers a human trafficking ring in South Florida and the chilling realization that Jane Doe was not the only victim. "

Janet Heijens

Janet Heijens is the author of the Wrongful Conviction Mystery series. *Caspersen Beach* once again brings together protagonist Cate Stokes and Detective Lalo Sanchez to challenge a flawed justice system. Heijens proves she can keep readers guessing until the last page.

"Cate peels back layer after layer until she uncovers a violent crime with a shocking motive. Heijens, whose earlier foray into the topic presents a heroine who's smart, resourceful, and empathetic—and more than worthy of an encore appearance." – Starred Kirkus Review of Snook Wallow.

In *Caspersen Beach*, while Stokes and Sanchez squabble like lovers, they set out to prove the innocence of a man who was convicted of a murder he did not commit. Motivated by the deathbed confession of a homeless woman who witnessed the crime, the duo re-open the decades old case. Their challenge is to figure out what is real and what is illusion coming from the mind of an unreliable witness.

A founding member of the Sarasota Literary Guild, Heijens is an active member of the Florida Gulf Coast Sisters in Crime. She lives with her husband, Pieter in Sarasota, Florida.

You can find her on Facebook or contact her at www.janetheijens.com.